A
MATTER
OF BLOOD

A CHIARA CORELLI MYSTERY

CATHERINE MAIORISI

BELLA
BOOKS

2018

Copyright © 2018 by Catherine Maiorisi

Bella Books, Inc.
P.O. Box 10543
Tallahassee, FL 32302

All rights reserved. No part of this book may be reproduced or transmitted in any form or by any means, electronic or mechanical, including photocopying, without permission in writing from the publisher.

This is a work of fiction. Names, characters, businesses, places, events and incidents are either the products of the author's imagination or used in a fictitious manner. Any resemblance to actual persons, living or dead, or actual events is purely coincidental. The publisher does not have any control over and does not assume any responsibility for author or third-party websites or their content.

Printed in the United States of America on acid-free paper.

First Bella Books Edition 2018

Editor: Ann Roberts
Cover Designer: Judith Fellows

ISBN: 978-1-59493-571-8

PUBLISHER'S NOTE
The scanning, uploading, and distribution of this book via the Internet or via any other means without the permission of the publisher is illegal and punishable by law. Please purchase only authorized electronic editions, and do not participate in or encourage electronic piracy of copyrighted materials. Your support of the author's rights is appreciated.

Other Bella Books by Catherine Maiorisi

Matters of the Heart
No One But You

Acknowledgement

A Matter of Blood is near and dear to my heart. Though it was the very first fiction I wrote, the version you hold in your hands today has been rewritten many times and is far from where it started both in the quality of the writing and the story. I loved the characters when I created them and I love them now. I hope you do too.

Since this book was thirteen years in the making, I have many people to thank. My wife Sherry treated me as if I was a writer long before I felt like one. She read it first and often, patiently pointing to my paragraph-long sentences and my tendency to repeat things three times. I'm grateful for Sherry's continued support and for getting that when I disappear into my head I'm writing, not ignoring her.

Next, I have to acknowledge the bravery of my friend Judy Levitz who knowing this was my first fiction, still agreed to read the second draft and give me feedback. And, though my friend Lee Crespi was afraid she might hate it, she snuck a look at Judy's copy and immediately called to tell me how much she liked it. Their feedback was invaluable.

And speaking of brave friends, despite fearing it might destroy our friendship, author Persia Walker gave me a brutal but honest critique that led to major changes in the characters. Thank you, Persia. I hope I made it better

And thanks to my writing buddy, Deb Pines, for always asking what's next?

My sister-in-law Joan Maiorisi, a huge reader, loved it. Of course she's my sister-in-law. But she's not an actress and although I knew it still needed work, her praise encouraged me to persist. Thank you Joan, sister-in-law Barbara Felsinger and cousin Sandra Maiorisi Lappen for your support.

Very early in the life of *A Matter of Blood* I was ecstatic to receive positive feedback from two established mystery writing professionals. The late publisher and mystery writer Howard Kaminsky read it and sent it to his agent. And, mystery writer Peter Lovesey and his wife Jax Lovesey read it, critiqued it and suggested I send it to Peter's agent. Neither of these recommendations resulted in publication but it was this kind of encouragement that kept me plugging away for thirteen years.

Sisters in Crime and Mystery Writers of America have provided opportunities to expand my knowledge of the craft and the business of writing at conferences like New England Crime Bake and SleuthFest. The Mentor Program of MWA New York gave me my first non-family/friend critique and encouraged me to continue to work on the manuscript. The monthly meetings of the New York City chapters of both organizations have given me access to speakers with expertise in various crime-related topics and a warm and supportive environment to connect with other writers, published and unpublished.

Thirteen years is a long time so I'm sure I missed someone. Even though you don't see your name here, please know I'll be eternally grateful.

I was lucky to have Ann Roberts, an accomplished romance and mystery author, assigned as my editor. She skillfully guided this somewhat prickly author (You really expect me to change *my* words?) to "kill my darlings" and strengthen the manuscript. Thanks, my friend.

Thank you Linda Hill for publishing *A Matter of Blood*. Linda, Jessica and the other dedicated women behind the scenes at Bella Books deserve a huge round of applause for doing the hard work required to publish a book. I appreciate all you do, your good humor, and especially the patience you show when answering this anxious writer's questions.

And to my readers: *A Matter of Blood* is set in New York City because it is *my* city and I love it. It features NYPD detectives and, therefore, the New York City Police Department. But if you're looking for a primer on NYPD procedures, this is not the book for you. The police department portrayed is *my* fictional NYPD and any resemblance to the real NYPD is purely coincidental.

I love hearing from readers so please contact me through www.catherinemaiorisi.com. I hope you enjoy *A Matter of Blood*. And if you do, I encourage you to recommend it to friends and on social media and to review it if you can. I'm truly grateful for your support.

Dedication

A Matter of Blood was always the goal.

I dedicate it to all who believed I could do it. And to all who supported me in the doing.

Thank you.

About the Author

Catherine Maiorisi lives in New York City and often writes under the watchful eye of Edgar Allan Poe, in Edgar's Café near the apartment she shares with Sherry her partner, now wife, of forty years.

In the seventies and eighties while working in corporate technology then running her own technology consulting company, Catherine moaned to her artistic friends that she was the only lesbian in New York City who wasn't creative, the only one without the imagination or the talent to write poetry or novels, play the guitar, act, or sing.

Years later, Catherine's imagination came alive and she challenged herself to write a mystery. After staring at a blank screen for a couple of days, she realized she didn't have the foggiest idea how to write a novel. So she spent the next nine months reading every book she could find about writing and tried again. Four months later she had a draft of a detective/mystery novel. Over the thirteen years since then, Catherine never stopped working on the manuscript of *A Matter of Blood*, featuring NYPD Detective Chiara Corelli. She is thrilled to see it in print.

In addition to *A Matter of Blood*, Catherine has published three mystery short stories in the *Murder New York Style* anthologies, two full-length romances—*Matters of the Heart* and *No One But You*—a standalone eStory, *Come as You Want to Be*, and three romance short stories in anthologies. The second Chiara Corelli mystery, *The Blood Runs Cold*, is waiting in the wings.

Writing is like meditating for Catherine and it is what she most loves to do. But she also reads voraciously, loves to cook, especially Italian, and enjoys hanging out with her wife and friends.

Catherine is a member of Sisters in Crime, Mystery Writers of America, Romance Writers of America, Rainbow Romance Writers, the Authors Guild, and the Guppies, an online chapter of Sisters in Crime.

CHAPTER ONE

NYPD Detective Chiara Corelli wasn't surprised to see the men and women in blue waiting in front of the station to welcome her back. She'd expected them. Just not so many. And not the media. Even a block away, the excitement of the crowd was palpable. She took a deep breath, which at seven thirty on this oppressive August morning, was like inhaling steam. Then, as before any battle, she took a minute to psych herself, straightened her already military-straight back and marched toward the maelstrom.

A shout. "Corelli." Her name passed through the crowd, becoming a chant. Her heart sped up, her hand found her Glock, but she ignored the impulse to draw it. She'd fractured the blue line and doing that had consequences. But knowing intellectually there would be anger and hatred and danger was one thing, seeing and feeling it was…unnerving. And disheartening. She steeled herself. She'd never let them see her hurt and her anger at their betrayal. Or her fear.

Head held high, Corelli fought the urge to favor the leg injured in last night's attack and maintained the steady pace she'd set for herself. At the opening she ignored the bright lights and shouted questions of the press and plunged into the funnel formed by hundreds of police officers with their backs to her, hissing her name. The heat, sweat and cloying sweetness of the colognes and perfumes from so many bodies crammed together nauseated her. Her gut clenched but she didn't miss a step. Nor did she miss the calls of traitor, whore and bitch that underscored the hissing that followed her, or the elbows and kicks that connected. And, though she didn't turn to look, she felt the heat of the TV lights and heard the shouted commentary of the TV reporters describing the reception provided by her brethren in blue.

After what seemed like an hour, she reached the door and stepped into the familiar bustle of police business. The air was fresher and she had space to breathe but she was not immune here. "Shame on you," said the first officer she encountered face-to-face, a man she'd known for years. Shocked by the hatred on his face, she braced for an attack, but instead of spitting in her face as she expected, he pivoted and stood with his back to her.

Still ignoring the pain in her leg, she continued on. She'd been told the squad was up a staircase toward the back of the station house. By the time she hit the first step, the only sounds were the ringing phones, the rat-a-tat-tat of her heels, and the shuffle of feet as her colleagues swiveled to show her their backs. Funny, it felt as if their eyes were piercing *her* back as she climbed the stairs.

She braced for more of the same in the squad room, but the few detectives present studiously ignored her and carried on their conversations. She scanned the room, not knowing which, if any, desk was hers.

"Corelli."

She turned toward the voice. Detective Ray Dietz. She hadn't known he was at the oh-eight.

A smiling face. "Over here." Dietz pointed to a desk in the corner.

"Dietz, I thought you'd retired."

"Couldn't see myself farting around the house." He frowned. "What's with the limp and the fucked-up face?"

Corelli tucked her swollen hand into her left armpit. Her other hand brushed the abrasion on her face.

"A pickup truck charged me last night. My red cape was at home so I couldn't wave it in front of the truck to distract it. I tripped, scrambling to get out of its way." She didn't mention the foot that had smacked her already injured knee as she made her way through the morning's gauntlet.

He wrinkled his nose. "There's lots of bullheaded pricks around here. Better keep that cape handy."

She lowered her voice. "How come you're talking to me?"

"Showin' my respect." He tipped an imaginary hat. "Because you got a lotta balls takin' on such a risky job."

"Safer to stay away from me, Dietz."

He cracked his knuckles. "Let the bastards try something."

She sat behind the desk and Dietz dropped into the side chair. While they chatted, she scanned the room, found a few familiar faces, but none were welcoming. One figure, silent and watchful, caught her eye.

She lifted her chin in the direction of the slender, chestnut brown woman standing near the coffeepot. "Who's the fashion plate by the window?" The sophisticated haircut, the tan designer pantsuit, the red silk shirt, and the fancy leather bag slung over her shoulder were more appropriate for a high-priced law firm than the rough-and-tumble life of a detective. But her eyes, the almost imperceptible bulge at her waist, and the sensible black shoes said cop.

Dietz spoke softly. "Detective Penelope Jasmine Parker. Rich girl and former assistant district attorney turned cop, saved a Harlem family of five from a crazed shooter and made detective a couple weeks ago."

"Jeez, I hope she didn't break a nail." *Parker. Shit.* Chief of Detectives Harry Broderick had set the terms for her being back on the job. Either be glued to the hip with a new detective, P.J. Parker, or be chained to a desk. No contest there. Parker won hands down.

He snorted. "Give the kid a break. She's got enough to deal with. Her father is Aloysius T. Parker."

"*The* Aloysius T. Parker? US Senator Aloysius T. Parker?"

"Yup."

"Man, I thought I had baggage." Senator Parker was the most vocal and vicious critic of the NYPD, constantly demonstrating and holding press conferences accusing the department of racism, some real, some imagined.

"Kid's a loner, never connected at the two-nine in Harlem and probably wouldn't have made detective if she hadn't saved that family. Parker is waiting for Captain Winfry too."

What the hell was Broderick up to, saddling her with a fashionista whose father was NYPD's number one critic? Though, if she really was an unconnected loner, it might mean she could trust Parker. But could she trust Broderick?

Corelli studied Parker, trying to get a sense of the tightly coiled woman. Parker stiffened, scowled at Corelli and quickly looked away. Should she talk to Parker now? No, better wait to talk to Winfry. Maybe Senator Daddy got her assignment changed.

Dietz tapped the folders piled in the center of her desk. "The captain wanted you to review these cold cases and see what you can pick up. I gotta follow up on some stuff. See ya later."

"I'm on it." Easier said than done, though. She could only sit still for fifteen or twenty minutes. She was up and down so often that the detectives in the squad and the uniforms downstairs began to grumble at having to stand and turn their backs every time she dashed outside to pace and breathe and then again when she reentered. Some pretended they didn't see her. And after a while most of the detectives in the squad ignored her, except Parker. And, while Parker didn't turn her back, she watched her every move. It was irritating.

After three hours, Corelli was in a rage. Fucking civilians snug in their comfy offices, not worried about shelling or IEDs or suicide bombers, had no sense of urgency. Either Winfry was giving her the cold shoulder or he had forgotten she was waiting. Neither was acceptable. Fucking Winfry. Fucking bureaucratic bullshit. Fifteen more minutes and she was out of there, job or no job. She'd been contemplating signing on for another tour in Afghanistan and going back was looking better and better.

She grabbed the next cold case folder and read the first page. Someone had left a love letter for *her*. In an instant the agitation was replaced by the familiar calm focus and alertness she always felt in the face of danger. She read it again.

TRAITOR—a person who betrays another, a cause, or any trust.

JUDAS—one who betrays another under the guise of friendship.

RAT—a despicable person, especially one who betrays or informs upon associates.

RATTED—to betray one's associates by giving information.

RATFINK—A person regarded as contemptible, obnoxious, or otherwise undesirable.

PUNISHMENT—One dead + Many ruined = Death

She scanned the room. Nobody was watching her. She studied the computer-generated page, thought about fingerprints but knew there wouldn't be any. She'd known investigating other police would have serious consequences, known there was a good chance she might not survive, known if she survived she would be ostracized. But, just back from Afghanistan, she hadn't cared much about living. Now, home four months and no longer undercover, she was thinking that living was better than dying and her death no longer figured as a positive in her equation of consequences. They, whoever *they* were, would have to work hard to get her.

She accepted responsibility for the results of her undercover investigation. One officer she'd exposed ate his gun and a number of others were facing serious jail time, but they were the bad guys, not her. It wasn't easy but she would live with the guilt just as she was living with the killing she'd done in Afghanistan and Iraq. She put the paper in her pocket and checked again to see if anyone was watching. Parker quickly averted her eyes. Could Ms. Fancy-Pants Parker be the writer?

"Corelli." Dietz's voice broke into her musing. "Captain's ready."

"About fucking time."

The room went silent. *Fuck.* She hadn't meant to say that aloud.

"Whoa." Dietz put a hand on her shoulder. "Better take a deep breath before you go down." He looked into her eyes. "The brass dropped in. He had no choice."

She eyed his hand. He stepped back, taking his hand with him. *Shit.* Threatening her only friend. "Sorry, Dietz. It's been a long morning."

She flipped a half salute and moved toward the steps accompanied by a symphony of scraping chairs as the detectives stood and gave her their backs. It hurt. But damn if she'd give them the satisfaction of knowing that. She strode, as much as her achy leg allowed, through the squad, down the stairs past the blue backs and muttering that followed her as she made her way to the captain's office. She took the deep breath Dietz had recommended and knocked.

Without looking up, Captain Winfry waved her to the chair facing him. "Sit. I'll be with you in a minute."

She stared at the top of his shiny head. She still didn't get why he wanted her under his command when no one else would have her.

He looked up. His eyes widened. "What the hell happened to your face, Corelli?"

She fingered the scrape that covered the right side of her face. "A car tried to run me down last night when I was walking home from One Police Plaza. The incident was reported by Officer Marta Ryan, sir."

Winfry's eyes narrowed. His face darkened. Was that a flash of anger?

"Damn it, Corelli. That's exactly why the chief ordered a bodyguard for you."

"Yes sir, I'm supposed to meet with Detective Parker this morning." *But you kept me waiting so it hasn't happened.*

"Other than cars gunning for you and running the blue gauntlet this morning, how are things going?"

"Fine, sir." *If you don't count the kicks, punches, threatening calls or slashing of my Harley's tires while I was at my nephew's baptism yesterday.* "Ready to be back on the job. Am I going to be working with Detective Parker?"

"Yes. But here's the thing. Parker doesn't know she's supposed to work with you."

"Chief Broderick said he'd set it up."

Winfry looked pained. "Well, he selected Parker and told her he had a special assignment for her, but he didn't tell her it involved you."

Lily-livered bastard. "Are you going to tell her?"

"Broderick thinks you're the best person to convince Parker. So, after we're done you'll meet with her."

"Convince her? You mean she can say no?"

"Yes, she can say no."

Fucking Broderick. "Is the special treatment...I mean the fact that she can say no, because of who her father is?"

Winfry looked amused. "Actually, Corelli, it's because of who you are. Broderick feels, and I agree, it's really not a good idea to have someone who doesn't want anything to do with you watching your back."

"And if I can't convince her?"

"If she turns down the assignment, you're on desk duty until we find someone we feel can be trusted."

"Jeez." She bit her lip. It wouldn't do to badmouth the chief to her new boss.

"It's unorthodox, but the chief happens to be right. You're a target right now and you need someone you can trust. She's smart. Yale undergrad, Harvard Law, and a stint as an assistant DA before joining the department. She's proven she's able to keep her head under fire. And she's safe because she's unconnected. But the chief didn't want to order her to do it."

"He could've at least told her she would be working with me."

"Coulda, shoulda. As I said, Broderick was confident you could make the case."

"If I might ask, Captain, I'm *persona non grata*. Why do *you* want to work with me?"

He straightened the folders on his desk. She waited, knowing if she broke the silence he might feel he didn't have to answer.

"A number of reasons, some personal that I won't discuss. Reason one, the blue wall serves a purpose but it's not right to ostracize an honest cop for blowing the whistle on dirty cops. Reason two, I respect you for doing what you did for the department despite the personal risk while undercover and knowing you'd be ostracized after. And reason three, I get a top-notch detective."

"Thank you, sir."

"Dealing with the ostracism is your problem, but anything else—threats, failure by your colleagues to do their jobs or respond as you would expect—I want to know."

He glanced at his watch. "I have a meeting now so you can use my office to sell yourself to Parker. You have forty-five minutes." He punched a number into the phone. "Send Parker to my office." He retrieved the stack of folders and the leather bound notebook from his desk and headed for the door. "Good luck."

Great. When did her old friend Chief Harry Broderick become a coward? He wants me to be safe, but he doesn't have the balls to tell Parker I'm the assignment?

Parker must have run down the stairs because Winfry had just left when she walked through the open door. Seeing Corelli, not Winfry, she frowned and started to back out. "Oh, I thought—"

Corelli stood. "Detective Parker?"

Parker took a step back, as if she might be infected if she got too close.

"Don't worry, it's not contagious."

"What?" Parker looked puzzled.

"I'm Detective Chiara Corelli."

Parker's face darkened. "I know who you are."

Oh, oh. Daddy's little girl is not happy. "We're supposed to meet this morning to talk about working together."

"Really? No one told me."

I'm telling you now, bitch. "Yeah, well, Chief Broderick sorta forgot to mention my name." Corelli put her hands in her back pockets and rocked back on her heels. "I'm your special assignment. The deal is, we work homicides, you watch my back, and I train you."

"Work with the most hated detective in the department?" Parker laughed. "You must be kidding." Her voice was harsh. "The chief did say there wouldn't be any repercussions if I don't want the assignment." She glared at Corelli. "And I don't." She moved toward the door.

"Detective Parker." Corelli's voice was a command.

Parker stopped, her back to Corelli.

"A few minutes, please."

Parker faced Corelli. "Read my lips. I will not work with you."

"At least hear me out."

Parker's jaw tightened. "How about you hear *me*? I do not want to be associated with you. What about that sentence don't you understand?"

What was Broderick thinking? She couldn't work with someone who hated her. She opened her mouth to tell Parker to go fuck herself, but instead she clamped her lips. *Duh.* Every cop hated her. But Broderick seemed to think Parker was safe. She needed Parker, so she'd make nice. "A lot of police feel that way about me, but since the chief stressed that you think for yourself, I expected you'd want to hear the facts before you made a decision."

"I know the facts."

"Hey, if you're comfortable passing judgment without hearing from the accused, you don't have what it takes to be a good homicide detective anyway. So we're done here." Corelli waved her hand toward the door. "Go." *Fuck you. I won't beg.*

Parker frowned. Her hands curled into fists but she didn't move. She seemed to be fighting an internal battle. Corelli held her breath. Even Parker was better than desk duty.

"You're wrong. I would be an excellent homicide detective. But you're right that I'm prejudging you based on gossip, innuendo and the media." Parker's voice was icy. "But why me? There are plenty of experienced detectives, more likely bodyguards, on the force."

"I don't like this any more than you, Parker." Corelli's smile was pained. "But as you said, I'm the most hated detective in the department. Chief Broderick feels I'll have an accident if I don't have someone who can be trusted to watch my back. And given the circumstances, it's hard to know who to trust. Broderick chose you. He says you're an honest, trustworthy cop, who's proven you know how to handle your gun."

"And if I say no?"

"I'm tied to a desk."

Parker nodded. "I see." She looked out the window and back at Corelli. "Not my problem."

Corelli felt a prickle of anxiety. She needed this to work. "It is your problem. Unless you're on the side of the cops in jail waiting for trial and don't care about an honest department."

"Don't be stupid. Of course, I..." Parker chewed her lip. "So talk."

Corelli shifted the two chairs in front of the desk so they faced each other. "Let's sit."

Parker ran her hand over the seat of the dilapidated wooden chair, then sat.

Wonderful. I'm fighting for my life here and Miss Prissy is worried about snags in her fancy suit.

"I know you were promoted because you saved that family, but tell me a little about yourself, where you live, what precincts you've worked in, about your experience with the department."

"This isn't about me," Parker said, her voice a challenge.

Corelli leaned in and locked eyes with Parker. "Whatever you might think of me, Parker, I don't work with strangers. So, either you want homicide badly enough to do this my way or you don't. Better desk duty than not knowing who's standing behind me."

Parker sighed. "I presume you know Senator Parker is my father?"

"Yes, but I don't hold it against you." *Well, maybe I do.*

Parker smirked. "You'd be the first."

"I'm sure being the senator's daughter has its good points, too."

"Of course. I've had a privileged life. We lived in a penthouse apartment in Harlem. I went to Brereton Academy, an expensive private school for girls on the Upper East Side, Yale, then Harvard Law. I–"

"I'm impressed. With an education like that, why become a cop?"

"I spent close to two years as an ADA in Manhattan and a lot of the time I was angry at losing cases that I thought could have been won. I blamed the police for not making solid cases." She raised her chin defiantly. "Now I know how difficult it is to make a case, but then...Anyway, my godfather, Captain Jessie Isaacs, pushed me to stop complaining and do something to change the situation. After graduating from the police academy, I requested the two-nine in Harlem and worked the streets until my promotion two weeks ago. That's it."

"Isaacs is a good man."

Showing the first sign of relaxing, Parker nodded. "The best."

"Why do you want homicide?"

"People get murdered. Their families lose a mother or father or child. They suffer. Society suffers." Parker looked down at her hands folded in her lap. "And I'll be damn good at finding their murderers."

"Confident, aren't we?"

Eyes narrowed, Parker studied her. "You need me, yet you're you trying to alienate me. Why?"

Corelli shrugged. "What do you know about me?"

"As I said, scuttlebutt and what I read in the newspapers."

Lost in thought for a moment, Corelli reached for her braid and gently tugged it. "Some of this is confidential."

"I'm trustworthy."

"I'm betting on it. Right after I got back from Afghanistan, I was recruited by the FBI and the Chief of Detectives to go undercover to investigate an alleged ring of dirty cops in my old precinct."

"The FBI?" Parker looked skeptical. "Everything I've heard and read said you were dirty, a member of the ring who got cold feet and blew the whistle on your friends to save yourself."

"You're the daughter of a politician. Is everything written about your daddy true?"

Parker's eyebrows shot up.

"Right. Anyway, I was undercover for three months. Like Afghanistan and Iraq, I was surrounded by the enemy. Unlike those war zones, I was on my own and my friends and acquaintances were the enemy. Their greed and self-righteousness, their violence astounded me. Yet, I had to act like them or be murdered." She searched Parker's eyes looking for understanding. "I vomited a couple of times every day, partly from fear, partly from repressed anger and partly from disgust. I was throwing up in the bathroom so often that a couple of female detectives asked if I was pregnant. It was grueling." Her leg began to vibrate and she stood to quiet it.

She resented having to justify herself to this dilettante, but Parker was her ticket to working homicides. She sat again and looked Parker in the eye. "I've never killed anybody on the job. I killed in Iraq and Afghanistan because I had to. But anyone earmarked to move up in Righteous Partners, the group of renegade officers I was trying to take down, had to kill to prove their loyalty. In fact, it was when they ordered me to murder a drug dealer and his wife and three kids, that I aborted the operation. I had a lot of names, but not all of them, and none of the top echelon. So it was all for nothing. I failed to get all of them. I failed to get any of the leaders.

"When I told the FBI I was walking, they said they had to protect the investigation and would deny any involvement. That didn't surprise me. But I was shocked by the department's pathetic denial of a story about me being one of the bad guys, a story, I might add, leaked by an unnamed source, presumably Righteous Partners. She studied Parker, hoping she hadn't lost her, and was happy to see her listening, but the look of disdain on her face was not encouraging.

"It doesn't make sense. You were just back from Afghanistan, so why would you accept such a risky assignment? You must have known how dangerous investigating other police would be. Didn't you worry about them killing you, about being ostracized?"

"I went undercover for all the honest cops like me—and you. I knew I might be killed. I knew I would be ostracized, that it would be hard, but I knew I was doing the right thing." *Besides, at that point I didn't care if they killed me.*

Parker snorted. "Very noble. You sound like you're running for office."

"Remind you of your daddy, do I?" Corelli flashed a Mona Lisa smile. "As smarmy as it sounds, it's the truth. I believe in God, country, family, and doing the right thing."

The intensity of Parker's gaze transfixed her. It felt as if Parker was trying to peer into her soul, to pierce her mind and suck the truth from her bones. Corelli tore her eyes away. "And speaking of doing the right thing, I'd better warn you that working with me won't be easy. Not just because I'm a pain in the ass but because of the baggage I carry. Word on the street is that they want me dead. I get telephone threats every day, and they've already come after me twice. This love note was in one of the cold case folders I was given this morning. Take a look." She handed it to Parker. "You need to think long and hard about whether you want to be enemy number two on the Righteous Partners' hit list and whether you can deal with being ostracized along with me."

Parker scanned the note. She looked at Corelli. "Is this your way of making the job attractive?"

She reached for the note. "Just tellin' it like it is."

"Are the damaged face, swollen hand, and limp, by way of Righteous Partners?"

"They tried to run me down last night."

Parker nodded slowly, as if considering the implications. "Not an accident?"

"No doubt in my mind or the witnesses or the chief's, which is why he insists I need somebody to watch my back."

"Why would they try to kill—"

"We're talking scumbag police, Parker," Corelli said, impatient at having to explain. "Police who crossed the line, who think ripping off drug dealers isn't stealing and working for the drug king Salazar and killing dealers who compete with him, is acceptable behavior. And worst of all, police who will kill other police to protect their scam."

"But you've already turned them in."

Corelli fought to keep her voice even. "Duh. Are you paying attention, Parker? I didn't get them all and the ones I missed seem to think I know something that will send them to jail."

"Don't condescend to me. I may be a new detective but I'm not stupid. You dump this thing on me and now you're grading me? I've listened but *I* don't need *you* or this *special* assignment."

Shit I thought I had her, but now she's pissed again. "What about homicide?"

Parker stood. "I'll think about it and get back to you tomorrow."

"Captain Winfry wants this resolved by the time he gets back." She glanced at her phone. "In ten or fifteen minutes."

"In that case, the answer is no. Excuse me, I need the ladies' room." Parker walked out.

Corelli stared after Parker. She'd sure done a whiz-bang job convincing her. *Damn.* She hated being dependent. But desk duty was deadly. Maybe she should follow Parker and grovel. She stood, then thought better of it. If she was any judge of character, Parker would be back. And if not, she would grovel later.

Parker dashed into the ladies' room, glad to find that it was private. She locked the door and leaned against it, her breath coming in quick bursts, the sweat tickling her shoulder blades. She splashed cold water on her face and pressed a wet paper towel to the back of her neck. Damn. Why risk her career and her life dealing with Corelli's shit? So she'd be on desk duty, big deal. God, country, family and doing the right thing were important to her too, but she didn't go around sticking her nose in hornets' nests. She leaned toward the mirror and looked herself in the eye. Except isn't that what she'd been doing at the precinct? Preaching to cops about building better cases, cops who'd been on the job since she was in elementary school.

Coward. She believed Corelli and it offended her sense of right and wrong that the department hadn't protected her reputation, hadn't vigorously defended her. So why was she hesitating to say yes? Not getting cooperation? Nothing new there. The assholes at the two-nine never gave her the time of day. The danger? Being a cop is dangerous. Being an outcast along with Corelli? She was already an outsider. The ostracism? It wouldn't be fun, but if Corelli could walk the gauntlet and endure the abuse, so could she. No, it was Corelli's attitude. Instead of groveling so she could make the grand gesture, Corelli had acted like she didn't need her.

Parker straightened. *Put your pride aside. Trust your gut. Corelli's a good cop and exposing those dirty police was a good thing. You became a cop to nail the bad guys, and bad cops are very bad guys.* She took a deep breath. *Even people who trash her say Corelli is a crack detective. This is your opportunity to get into homicide and learn from the best. If it means putting up with her attitude and being ignored and shot at, so be it.*

Decision made, she went to face the dragon. Detective Corelli was sitting in the same position, straight as a soldier, but with a fuck you sneer on her face. She wavered. As she sat and faced Corelli, she considered telling the bitch to shove it, but then she reminded herself that her goal was homicide. And she always met her goals. She cleared her throat. "I'm in."

The smile that Corelli flashed belied the antagonism that Parker had observed. "You surprised me, Detective Parker. Are you sure you have the balls to walk the gauntlet with me?"

"Damn you. Are you always like this? I'm already regretting it."

Corelli grinned. "You're doing the right thing. Time will tell whether you'll regret it."

CHAPTER TWO

Corelli slammed the door of the unmarked car and quickly scanned Wall Street. Eight-ten in the morning and the place had the feel of an anthill with zombie-like financial worker ants marching from every direction to their jobs. Happy she wasn't one of them, she silently thanked Winfry for pushing them to the top of the catching order. Solving murders was what she did best.

Corelli turned to look for Parker and nearly knocked her over. "Jeez, why the hell are you standing so close?"

"Not much space on the sidewalk."

"Yeah, but—"

"Captain's orders, remember?"

"I doubt he meant for you to get up my ass. Just stay near."

"Sorry, didn't mean to irritate you."

"Apologizing irritates me. Breathing down my neck irritates me. Quoting the freakin' captain irritates me. Suck it up, Detective. Just use your head. Let's go."

Corelli glanced over her shoulder and caught Parker mouthing "fuck you" to her back. She pretended she hadn't seen it but smiled as she pushed through the revolving doors. Inside, she stepped to the wall. Parker followed. Corelli surveyed the lobby: one guard behind a high marble counter and one beyond the turnstiles leading to two banks of elevators. Four security cameras mounted high on the walls, one facing the entry, one facing the counter, and one facing each of the banks of elevators.

Parker followed her gaze. "Should I get the tapes from the cameras?"

"You're with me. We'll get someone else to do it."

They elbowed their way through the crowd waiting to talk to the guard standing behind the marble counter. The grumbles quieted when Corelli flashed her shield. "What floor?"

"Thirty-five," he said, pointing to the left bank of elevators. "The nearest one, the executive elevator for Winter Brokerage. What's going on?"

"An investigation." She narrowed her eyes. "If you or your partner, there," she pointed to the guard standing at the turnstile watching people swipe their ID cards, "mention our presence to anyone, you'll answer to me? Got it?"

"Yeah, I got it but you don't have to get so nasty."

"I need to be sure you understand."

He buzzed them through the turnstile and they stepped into the elevator. Corelli pressed thirty-five. As the elevator started to move, she glanced at Parker and caught the flicker of a smile. "What's so funny, Parker?"

"Sounds like you had a bad night."

"Every night is a bad night, Detective," Corelli said, her voice low and husky.

Parker's smile disappeared.

Damn, that sounded pathetic. Corelli cleared her throat. "Homicide 101. First lesson. One, I want your thoughts and ideas and your questions, especially the ones you think are stupid. Two, unlike TV, we don't play good cop, bad cop. I ask the questions. You take the notes. Three, if you see something, tell me, but be discreet."

"Please don't condescend to me. I've been an ADA and a cop. I know my way around a murder scene."

"But this is *my* murder scene, Parker. Homicide 101 says the lead is in charge. Got it?"

"That's no reason to treat me like an idiot."

"Don't be so thin-skinned. I'm just laying out the rules. Just one more point and the first lesson is over. If you feel sick when we examine the victim, leave the room for a few minutes."

Parker blew the air out her mouth between closed lips. "I don't know if I can do this."

"Do what?"

"Deal with your attitude. I don't ask stupid questions. And, I've seen my share of dead bodies."

"Just sayin'." Corelli glanced sideways at Parker. "So what do we know about the vic?"

Parker sighed and opened her notebook. "Connie Winter, President of Winter Brokerage Services—"

The elevator stopped and the door slid open. They stepped into a frigid room, wood paneled, filled with Persian rugs, graceful furniture, and gold. Gold sparkled in the molded plaster octagons on the ceiling, in the threads running through the green and brown brocade fabric covering the chairs and sofas, and in the elaborate frames surrounding the lush paintings on the wall facing the elevator. A screen decorated in a gold and green floral pattern covered the opening of the marble fireplace. Even the lamp on the wooden reception desk glowed golden. The room reeked of perfume. And money.

The gold-framed mirror hanging over the fireplace reflected a woman crumpled in the chair farthest from the elevators. She leaned forward, a blanket around her shoulders, head drooping, arms clutching her body and appeared dangerously close to tumbling off the chair. A steaming cup of something sat on the table next to her. She didn't register their arrival. The police officer hovering near her glanced at the woman to see if there was any recognition before joining them. He resembled a walrus: soft brown eyes, black curly hair, a drooping mustache, and a heavily muscled upper body. Officer Enrique Hernandez introduced himself then examined their IDs and shields. His gaze lingered on Corelli's face for a few seconds, but he handed her the log without comment and watched her enter the required information.

"What time did you get here, Hernandez?"

"About seven thirty a.m. We happened to be on Broad Street in front of the Stock Exchange when the 911 came in."

"Who called it in?"

He nodded in the direction of the woman. "Sandra Edwards, the victim's assistant."

"And what did you do when you got here?"

He turned his back to Edwards and lowered his voice. "Ms. Edwards was pacing out here in the reception area, nearly hysterical. After we calmed her down, she directed us to the dead, er, victim's office down at the end of that hall, in the corner. It was obvious she was dead, so we didn't touch anything. We checked the entire floor then called it in as a probable homicide. Officer Shaunton went to secure the office with the victim and I stayed here to maintain the log. When the bus arrived, the EMTs confirmed she was dead."

"It's freezing. Did you turn up the air-conditioning?"

"It was like this when we got here." He glanced behind him. "Ms. Edwards seemed to be going into shock so the EMTs left a blanket and my partner got her a cup of coffee. I've tried to keep her talking but she hasn't responded."

"Good work, Hernandez. We'll interview her in an office or conference room nearby. Keep arriving employees in the reception area. If they ask, tell them there's a problem under investigation. I'll send your partner out to help you. You ever catch a homicide before?"

Hernandez nodded.

"Then you know the drill." She handed him her card. "Call my cell if any brass or politicians, including the mayor or the governor or the president of the United States, show up."

Corelli knelt in front of Sandra Edwards, but she remained hunched forward, seeming not to notice. The flowery sweetness of the woman's perfume was sickening. Corelli coughed, swallowed, and took a minute to focus her attention, pushing the fragrance to the background. She placed her left hand on the woman's shoulder and spoke in a low voice, trying to bring her back from wherever she had retreated. After a few minutes Edwards lifted her head. She stared at the bruises on Corelli's face but didn't comment.

"Ready?"

"Yes," Edwards whispered.

Corelli lifted her to an upright position. She flinched when Edwards grabbed her swollen right hand. The blanket slid onto the chair. They remained locked together for a minute as if they might dance then Edwards took Corelli's arm, leaning on her like an ancient arthritic, and they limped down the hall.

Corelli tilted her head at Parker, indicating she should come too, and caught a silent exchange between Hernandez and Parker: his raised eyebrows and her shrug as she picked up the coffee and the blanket.

Edwards led them to a conference room with a view of water towers and rooftops, the East River and the Brooklyn and Manhattan bridges. Sunlight streamed through the large windows, brightening the mauve and gray color scheme, warming the room somewhat. Edwards settled in a chair close to the window. Parker handed her the blanket, placed the hot coffee in front of her on the wooden conference table, wrinkled her nose and turned away, apparently hit with the perfume for the first time. Despite the blanket, Edwards shivered. Corelli removed her jacket and draped it over Edwards's shoulders.

"You'll freeze without your jacket. I'll get my sweater in the closet in the hall and the jacket from Phil Rieger's office."

"Detective Parker will get them."

"Mr. Rieger's office is the fourth on the left."

They were silent, waiting for Parker. Edwards stared at the gun strapped to Corelli's side and tears trickled down her face. She made no effort to dry them.

"Sorry, to be so long," Parker said. "The jacket was in a different office, the one at the far corner. The sign said Human Resources."

"That's strange." Edwards exchanged Corelli's jacket for the sweater.

Corelli slipped back into her jacket, happy for the warmth. "Which way to Ms. Winter's office?"

They left Edwards in the conference room and headed in the direction she'd indicated. The uniform outside the corner office watched them approach, her eyes on Corelli's bruised face.

"Officer Shaunton, I'm Detective Corelli and this is Detective Parker. All quiet here?"

"Yes."

"Go up front and help your partner manage the employees as they arrive."

Shaunton nodded and strode toward the reception area.

Corelli touched Parker's shoulder to keep her from entering the room. Parker tensed and shifted slightly, as if trying to get away from Corelli's hand. *Ah, she doesn't like contact either.* "We'll gather first impressions of the scene from inside the door. You do a rough but detailed sketch, including the position of the body and the furniture. It doesn't need to be a work of art, but it needs to be accurate and complete."

Corelli readied her digital camera. "I'll take pictures."

"With that." Parker laughed. "It's so old it must have about three pixels. Let me." She took out her phone.

"What the fuck are you doing, Parker?"

"My smartphone has a much higher resolution, so we'll get better quality pictures and we won't need a sketch."

Corelli glared at her. "Didn't you hear what I said, Parker? I'm the lead. That means I decide how we proceed. Shove your freakin' phone and all its pixels in your pocket."

Parker backed away. "No need to yell, I'm not deaf. I just thought—"

"I'll do the thinking. You draw the freaking sketch. Got it?"

A shadow passed over Parker's face, but she pocketed the phone.

"Now that we've got that straight, see if you can manage to put on protective gear so we can get to work. Unless, of course, you have some better idea about what we should do?"

"Damn it, Corelli, I was just trying to help. Why do you have to be so nasty?"

"More to the point, Parker, why can't you follow orders?"

They donned protective gear in tense silence.

"Let's go," Corelli said. As they stepped into the unlit office, they were assaulted by a flash of light. Corelli dropped to the floor, pulling Parker with her. They lay there a few seconds, not moving, Corelli's ragged breathing the only sound. The light went off.

"What the hell was that?" Parker said, pulling herself out from under Corelli and onto her knees. The light went on again.

Corelli rolled to her knees. "Sorry." She holstered her Glock. "The lights must be activated by movement."

"That's obvious. What's not obvious is why you dragged me down and drew your weapon. Were you demonstrating a lesson from Homicide 101?"

"Gee, I hope I didn't damage your fancy suit." *Not a wrinkle in my baggy jeans and jacket.*

"My suit is fine." Parker scrutinized Corelli's face. "I'm just glad you didn't shoot me or yourself. Are you all right?"

The concern on Parker's face and in her voice was embarrassing. Corelli liked her anger better. "If I wanted to shoot you, you'd be dead. Same for me. Get over it."

"Are you going to tell me what that was about?"

Corelli took a deep breath and met Parker's gaze. "A couple of tours in Iraq and Afghanistan, followed by three months undercover makes a person…sensitive." *It also makes it hard to sleep, leading to anxiety and anger. And it kills your appetite, leading to clothes that hang on you like a scarecrow.*

"I'm sure you're sensitive," Parker said, retrieving her pen and notebook from the floor. "But you also seem edgy and angry."

"You know Parker, I hope the chief is right and you have what it takes to watch my back, but I damn well know for sure you're not qualified to analyze my mental state. Let's just get to work."

"You're the lead."

"Ah, you remember."

They edged into the room. The stench of decomposing flesh combined with the metallic smell of blood and the stink of excrement engulfed them. The pervasive reek of stale cigarette smoke vied with the fetid odors for dominance. Corelli felt the bile rise and forced it back. Despite the many murders she'd investigated and what she'd seen in Iraq and Afghanistan, death still bothered her. She hoped she never got used to it.

She glanced at Parker, who wore a hint of green around her mouth. Corelli pulled a handkerchief out of her pocket. "Put a handkerchief over your nose and don't breathe too deeply."

Parker frowned but pulled out a handful of tissues. "Most of the bodies I've seen have been outside. The smells seem stronger inside a place like this."

Corelli coughed. "Not to mention it appears she's been dead a while."

From where they stood they could see the back of a high leather chair and the right shoulder and arm of someone sitting in it. Except for the smell, the buzzing of the flies, the blood pooled on the white carpet around the chair, and the bloody footprints leading toward the door, Winter might have been working.

"Unusual," Parker said, eyeing the spectacular view of lower Manhattan sweeping north toward midtown out the two walls of floor-to-ceiling windows. "Most people sit with their back to the view."

"Safer that way," Corelli said. "Nobody can sneak up on you."

"Clearly Ms. Winter wasn't worried about that," Parker said. "Or maybe she thought the view of the Hudson River, Statue of Liberty, Battery Park City, the World Financial Center, rooftops, water towers, and New Jersey, was worth the risk."

"Yeah. It sure worked out good for her."

Corelli's eyes were drawn to the hole in the skyline where the twin towers used to stand. Suddenly she was there. Her eyes and nose burning from the acrid smoke of the burning fuel, her throat raw from the choking black cloud of dust, her ears assaulted by the roar of the huge building collapsing and the screams of people near her. The helplessness. She staggered.

"Corelli." Parker touched her arm. "Corelli, are you sure you're feeling well today?"

She opened her eyes. Old cigarette smoke, the coppery tang of blood, the stink of putrefaction She blinked. She was in her murder scene with Parker looking sympathetic. She wasn't in the middle of… She scrubbed her face. "Sorry, I was thinking about the…twin towers."

Parker turned toward the windows where they should have been. "You were there?" Her voice was gentle.

"Damn it, Parker, swooning over the view is wasting our time. You may have forgotten but we have a murder to solve."

Parker opened her mouth but immediately closed it. "Sorry."

Struggling to subdue the pain of the memories, Corelli welcomed the anger Parker conveyed in that single word. "Let's get to work." *Jeez, two flashbacks in fifteen minutes. I need to relax and focus on the murder, on the victim.*

They stepped around the edge of the blood-soaked carpet to the front of the desk and faced the woman slumped in the chair. Her eyes were open, her body was bloated and distorted, and dried blood covered her face and her hair. The flies were having a good day. Hernandez was right; no question she was dead.

Blood had spurted around the room, speckling the ceiling and walls and coating her clothing and everything nearby including the overflowing ashtray, the glass, the wallet, and the pad on her desk. The reddish-brown of the dried blood contrasted sharply with the plush white rug and the stark white walls and ceiling. Flies were buzzing and maggots had started to do their job. The good news was that the room was freezing and decomposition wasn't as bad as might be expected in the August heat. The bad news was it still smelled like they were knee deep in an overflowing port-o-potty surrounded by rotting flesh. Drops of sweat glistened on Parker's brow and the pen in her hand was shaking. Corelli hoped Parker would leave, if necessary.

She turned her attention to Winter and the bits of brain visible despite the blood. "Do you see anything that could cause that head wound?"

Parker scanned the room. "I don't see anything heavy enough to be a weapon. The handset for the desk phone is missing but a handset is pretty light. I doubt it could have killed her. Maybe the killer made a call and took it so we can't get prints or DNA."

"Make a note to check the phone records."

Treading with care to avoid the blood, Corelli moved to the woman's right side, closer to the body, but still not touching anything. Parker followed.

"Looks like multiple blows."

Parker studied the woman again and considered Corelli's theory. "It doesn't look like she struggled. Why do you say multiple blows?"

"You tell me."

Parker chewed her lip. "She got hit on the right side of her head, but almost all the blood spatter is on the right. There wouldn't be so much blood if that blow or blows had killed her. The bruise on her forehead resembles the shape of the telephone handset, so that would have been before she died too." She stood on her toes. "She was hit on the top of the head, toward the left, pretty nasty. You can see her brain and not much spatter on the left."

"Right. It's likely that blow killed her. The autopsy should confirm that and tell us whether there are any defensive wounds."

Corelli moved around the chair to the left side of the desk. "Did you notice that her chair is on a platform?"

"Yes. She was short, or at least she looks short in that picture on the credenza."

Corelli followed Parker's gaze to the picture in an elaborate gold filigree frame. Winter with a younger, taller woman. "That platform put her above everybody. It says, 'I'm powerful.'"

Parker wrinkled her nose in distaste. "Yet the white and pink chintz furniture gives the office a girly feel."

"What else, Parker? What does the room tell you about her?"

Parker narrowed her eyes. "She flaunts her money. She's wearing an expensive designer dress and jewelry that appears to be real gold and diamonds."

"Well, Ms. Fancy Pants ADA comes in handy. I wouldn't recognize designer clothes even if I saw the label."

Parker glared at Corelli. "Well, if you wore something other than baggy jeans and a too large jacket like some would-be gangsta, maybe you'd do better."

"Touché."

Parker turned her attention to the desk. "Her open wallet on the desk makes you think robbery, but a robber wouldn't leave all that jewelry. And if it was robbery I think she would have fought."

"Good observation," Corelli said.

Parker studied the victim but avoided touching her. "I don't see any obvious defensive wounds. If you saw someone coming at you with something heavy raised up to hit you, wouldn't your natural instinct be to turn away or at least put an arm up to stop them?"

Corelli nodded. "Good question. Could be she was stunned by the smack on the forehead. But we can deduce from the glass on her desk that she was drinking something, so it's possible she was drugged and couldn't react."

"Even with the smell of, er, the blood and stuff, it stinks of cigarettes in here. And under all that blood, the ashtray is overflowing with butts. Ms. Winter clearly felt that the law against smoking in office buildings didn't apply to her. And the way she situated her desk tells me she wanted people to look at her instead of the view."

Corelli crossed her arms and faced Parker. "What's your hypothesis?"

"No sign of a struggle makes me think she knew the killer and was comfortable with him or her being in her office at night.

Perhaps that's why she didn't try to defend herself. Since she was hit repeatedly, it looks like the killer was angry and had an ax to grind."

"My take as well. Either she didn't hear the killer come in, or she trusted that he or she wouldn't harm her. But it sure looks personal."

CHAPTER THREE

While Corelli supervised the photographer and talked to the Medical Examiner, Parker began the detailed sketch of the scene Corelli had commanded her to do, grumbling at the waste of time. But as she worked, she noted that drawing exactly what she saw forced her to closely examine what was in front of her. And she understood why Corelli was adamant about her doing the sketch rather than taking pictures. Ever observant, Corelli noticed Parker closing her notebook and signaled her to join the conversation with the ME. He estimated the time of death between nine p.m. Friday and three a.m. Saturday, promised to get to the autopsy later that day or tomorrow, and reminded Corelli that it would be days before the forensics reports were available. After he left with Winter's body, they watched the Crime Scene Unit until Corelli felt comfortable leaving them to finish while she and Parker interviewed Winter's employees.

Walking back to the conference room where they'd left Sandra Edwards, the senator's voice reverberated in Parker's head. "Bad enough to be a cop, but aligning yourself with the ultimate outsider, someone hated by other police, is just plain stupid." She massaged her temples. The senator had criticized and denigrated her all her life. And his critical voice popped into her head in less than a nanosecond whenever she felt the least bit of doubt. Of course she knew the voice was his and the fears were hers, but still it made her anxious. Yes, she *was* afraid she'd made the wrong decision. But, she reminded herself, she wasn't looking for votes. She wanted to be the best homicide detective she could be. And nothing is for nothing. She'd already learned from Corelli in the few hours they'd worked together. Facing the ostracism and handling the arrogant, somewhat crazy, condescending outsider was the price.

Parker shook her head and focused on the morning so far. At first she'd felt like running away. The stench turned her stomach. She thought she might throw up or even pass out. Lord knows she'd seen enough dead people, but more often than not, the body was outside, fresh, or embalmed. The violence and putrefaction seemed out of place in Winter's luxurious office. She didn't want to think about how bad it would have been if the room hadn't been so cold. When Corelli stepped closer to examine the wound, Parker had held back, afraid she'd be sick. But Corelli's questions helped her focus and detach. How would Corelli grade her so far? She risked a quick glance, but there was no sign.

Maybe she should give Corelli a grade. She'd really freaked when the automatic lights flashed on. Undercover could probably do that to a person who was playing a role, needing to be alert to every nuance. Then, she seemed to flashback to the collapse of the twin towers in the World Trade Center attack. She was probably there and many of the first responders suffered PTSD. Add Iraq and Afghanistan to the equation and the likelihood of PTSD increased exponentially. But whatever was wrong with Corelli, she wasn't making it easy to work with her. The constant ridicule and condescension were offensive and the see-sawing between nasty and nice was unsettling. She was trying not to respond to Corelli's attacks, hoping if she ignored them, Corelli would stop.

As they entered the conference room, Parker inhaled. Edwards's flowery perfume was a welcome relief after the smells in Winter's office.

Edwards raised her head and attempted to smile when she saw them. "Can I go home?"

"I know this is hard." Corelli touched Edwards's shoulder. "Just a little longer and I'll have someone drive you home."

For all she's damaged, there's still caring and gentleness in Corelli. Parker perched at the edge of her chair and placed her notebook on the table.

"What time do the employees usually arrive?" Corelli asked.

"On Mondays in the summer, all the officers including Ms. Winter, arrive around ten o'clock. The rest of the week Ms. Winter is in by eight and she expects them to be here when she needs them. Her husband, Gus, and Gertrude, his sister, get in about ten every day."

"Are she and her husband partners?"

"No. It's her business, but he and his sister work here."

"What does he do?"

"His title is Executive Vice President. I'm not sure what he does." There was no sarcasm but the comment got Parker's attention.

"And his sister?"

"She's assigned to the accounting department, but I hear she doesn't do much."

"How long have Mr. and Mrs. Winter been married?"

"His name is Gianopolus, not Winter. And their twins are fourteen now, so it's about sixteen years."

"How did they get along?"

Edwards looked away. "Like a married couple."

"Could you explain what that means?"

Edwards looked uncomfortable. "Lots of bickering, some arguments."

Corelli sensed Edwards was not being forthcoming but she'd come back to that later. "Who works on this floor besides you and Ms. Winter?"

"The senior officers." Edwards ticked off a finger for each: Gus Gianopolus; Jenny Hornsby, Vice President of Human Resources; Karl Silver, Senior Vice President of Marketing and Sales; Lewis Brooks, Senior Vice President of Information Systems; Phil Rieger, Senior Vice President of Finance; Terry O'Reilly, Senior Vice President of Operations."

She stared blankly at the seventh finger. "Someone is missing. Let me think. Gus, Phil, Jen, Karl, Terry, Lew, and, oh, Brett, Brett Cummings, the Senior Vice President of Investments has only been with us a few months."

When Parker finished writing, Corelli continued. "Please step us through what happened this morning, Ms. Edwards."

Tears filled Edwards's eyes. She blew her nose and blotted the tears. "I arrived about seven fifteen. I turned on the lights, dropped my newspaper and bag on my desk, and put up a pot of coffee. While the coffee was brewing, I signed onto my computer and scanned Ms. Winter's schedule for the day to determine whether anything needed preparation. I went to the ladies' room and then to Ms. Winter's office to see if she'd left anything for me Friday night."

"Did you take any papers from her office? We found only a yellow pad on her desk."

"Anything Ms. Winter works on is confidential, so she never leaves anything on her desk or mine. She has a safe in her office and only the two of us know the combination."

"Did you check the safe this morning?"

"No. When I saw her arm on the chair, I thought she'd come in early to work and dozed off. I didn't want to disturb her so I headed straight for the credenza to open the safe. The light flashed on. I had just sprayed perfume, and at first I didn't smell the...I don't know if I saw the blood first or smelled...smelled the stink, but all of a sudden it hit me. Then I saw her." She started to cry.

"Did you touch anything?" Corelli asked.

Edwards shuddered. "Are you kidding? All that blood. It was horrible. I couldn't help myself. I screamed and ran for the elevators. When I got to the reception area, I thought to call 911. I kept spraying myself with perfume trying to get rid of the smell, but it didn't help. I don't think I'll ever get the smell out of my nose."

"Did she keep anything personal in the safe?"

"Only things she was working on at the moment. Like now, she is...she was...working on an application for military school for her son, Gussie."

Edwards clasped her hands and seemed to fight an internal battle. Corelli waited for her to go on, but it seemed she'd said all she was ready to say.

"Why were you in so early?"

Edwards pulled the blanket tighter around her. "Ms. Winter wants everything at her fingertips when she needs it. When I started working for her, she wanted me to wait until she'd left for the day to finish her work, no matter how late she stayed. I needed to be home with my kids at night, so we compromised. I come in early in the morning so everything from the previous night is ready when she gets in."

"Was there anything unusual about this morning?"

"Only that the office was freezing. Usually Monday mornings are hot and stuffy."

"Was anyone here when you arrived?"

"I didn't see anyone."

"Who would have been the last person to leave Friday night?"

"I'm not sure. I didn't leave until a little before seven o'clock which is late for me but Ms. Winter made an unusual request for me to stay and finish something important for her. The assistants have to sign out at my desk, so I know they were all gone by six. Gus and Jenny left before I did, but I didn't see the other officers. Many of them stay late."

"What did you do after you left?"

"I caught the seven-forty bus to Harleysville, Pennsylvania, where my daughter lives. My son-in-law Gary picked me up at the station about ten thirty."

"We'll need to confirm the timing."

"The schedule and the ticket stubs are at home."

As Parker wrote down Edwards's daughter's name and telephone number, Edwards started crying again. "It wasn't easy working for Ms. Winter because she put her own needs before everybody else's, but she could be kind and generous if she felt she could depend on you."

"Can you think of anyone who might want to harm her?"

"Well, there are a couple of–"

They turned simultaneously toward the shouting coming from the direction of the reception area.

Corelli and Parker jumped up and ran toward the fracas.

CHAPTER FOUR

Under different circumstances it might have been funny: two police officers restraining a flailing man, while a woman beat them with her pocketbook. Both the man and the woman were yelling. Several women sitting in the reception room watched with wide eyes and gaping mouths.

Corelli's arm shot out to prevent Parker from jumping in. "Stop." Corelli commanded. Like a choreographed dance troupe the four of them swiveled to face her and froze. "Pull yourselves together unless you want to be arrested."

Edwards, out of breath from the dash, spoke from behind them. "Oh my, it's Gus and Gertrude."

The officers stepped back but were poised for action should the struggle continue.

Purple-faced, Gus Gianopolus pointed his finger at Corelli. "How dare—"

"What?" Corelli moved closer. Her height forced him to look up to see her face. He stepped back, covering his retreat by smoothing his gray-streaked pompadour and tracing the thin line of hair emanating from his sideburn until it merged with the tuft on his chin.

Mr. Gianopolus was one of those impotent bullies who attempted to rule by tantrum. He'd rolled over so fast that Corelli almost expected him to unbutton his shirt and flash his belly. Instead he continued grooming himself, running a hand down his tie and brushing his well-tailored, immaculate suit.

Four or five inches shorter than her brother's five-feet-six inches, Gertrude's coloring was the same, but her olive skin was oily and her shoulder-length hair could have used an introduction to a comb. Whereas he was trim and fit, she was thick around the middle, carried her shoulders close to her ears, and showed no sign of exercise. Her shoes gave the impression that she had trudged through fields of clay to get to work. Her clothing—a skirt, close-fitting T-shirt, and boxy jacket in an unbecoming fuchsia—sported the name of some unfortunate designer, but it did nothing to enhance her appearance. All in all, it was clear she didn't give a damn about how she looked.

Corelli broke the silence. "I'm Detective Corelli and this is Detective Parker. We're conducting a police investigation. I would like all of you, including you, Ms. Gianopolus, to wait here until we're ready to speak to you. Please come with me, Mr. Gianopolus. Detective Parker, escort Ms. Edwards back to the conference room and then join me and Mr. Gianopolus in his office."

Gianopolus recovered his voice. "What's going on here? What kind of investigation? This is my firm. I have a right to know what's happening."

"In a minute, sir," Corelli said, walking away from the reception area. He followed but continued his harangue. When they neared his wife's office, he saw and heard the activity of the forensic team and started in that direction.

She grabbed his arm. "Your office, please."

He pivoted and led her down the hall. He stopped abruptly as he entered the room, and she had to side-step in order to avoid knocking him over. His cologne was familiar, but unlike Edwards's perfume, it was light, with a tinge of citrus.

"What the hell is going on? I want to speak to my wife."

Now that he spoke with controlled anger rather than shouting, she could hear a slight lisp and traces of a regional accent she couldn't identify. He glared at her, fists curled at his side, obviously used to throwing his weight around. He scrutinized her bruised face, and when she didn't flinch or respond, he shifted his gaze to the left of her shoulder, loosened his fists, and stepped away, defused. He went to his desk, straightened the blotter and leaned against the credenza behind him, nearly knocking over the three pictures lined up there.

The first picture showed a boy and girl dressed in bicycle gear, each with a leg over their bicycle. In the second, the boy leaned against a golf cart watching the long-limbed girl swing a golf club. The third appeared to be a family picture: Gianopolus, the boy, the girl and Winter.

Parker entered, sat at the small conference table and opened her notebook.

Corelli moved to face Gianopolus across his desk. "What time did you leave the office Friday night?"

He gazed over Corelli's shoulder. "My wife and I have no tolerance for games, Detective. Tell me what's going on or get the hell out."

"I need your help, sir. A few questions and I'll give you a full explanation."

He puffed his cheeks and pushed air through his lips. "Our chauffeur picked me and my sister Gertrude up around five thirty."

"What about your wife?"

"What about her?"

"When did you last see her?"

He tugged on the tuft of chin hair. "Right before I left on Friday. What does that have to do with anything?"

"So, the last time you saw your wife was Friday night at five thirty?"

"Didn't I just say that? Are you deaf or is it that you don't listen?" He reached for a wooden box on the credenza, brought out a cigar, and giving it his full attention, clipped and lit it. He puffed a few times, removed the cigar from his mouth, and raised defiant eyes to Corelli's face as he blew a stream of smoke in her direction, like a seventh grader waiting for her to challenge his smoking in the building. She maintained eye contact and silence. He exhibited great interest in the cigar again, coughed and sighed. "Why are you asking about my wife?"

"Did you see her over the weekend?"

He glanced at the door. "Enough. Either you explain or I'm out of here."

She wouldn't get anything from him. "Please, have a seat. I have bad news."

He moved forward but remained standing. She didn't like him, but it was never easy to announce the death of a loved one, or what one assumed was a loved one. She cleared her throat. "Mr. Gianopolus, I'm sorry, your wife is dead."

The cigar stopped en route to his mouth. "Connie dead? How?"

"She was murdered in her office sometime over the weekend."

He sagged into his desk chair. It rolled back with the force of his weight, and slammed into the credenza. No tears, no angst, but shock could do that.

"Can you think of anyone who would want to harm your wife?"

"Right now I can't think." He pressed his temples. "Maybe later. I wonder…"

"You wonder what?"

"Never mind. I need some time alone."

She posted Shaunton outside his office with instructions to keep him there and to call for help if needed. She glanced back and noticed he'd swiveled his chair so he was facing the windows, making it difficult to observe his emotional state. Was that intentional?

CHAPTER FIVE

Gertrude lumbered into the conference room, breathing as if she'd run a marathon. She was smaller than Corelli remembered from the squabble earlier, but not any more attractive. The reek of cigarette smoke and the nicotine-yellowed teeth and fingers signaled a heavy smoker.

Parker, right behind her, benefited from the contrast: slim, fit, neat hair, eyes like glittering coals, dressed in her expensive tailored black suit and an ice-blue silk shirt. A striking professional package behind a bag of rags.

Gertrude dropped into the chair, as if suddenly her legs would no longer bear the weight of her ample body. She kicked off her shoes, stretched and seemed to relax, but when neither detective spoke, the constant flitting of her eyes between them revealed her apprehension. After a brief silence, she couldn't contain herself. "Well, is somebody going to tell me what's going on?"

"When was the last time you saw your sister-in-law?"

Gertrude shifted and pulled herself up in her seat. She lit a cigarette and inhaled deeply. Her left hand fiddled with the straps on her purse.

"What's she saying about me?"

Gertrude had the same accent as her brother but the similarity ended there. His voice was soft and raspy, and even with the lisp, pleasant, while her voice was harsh and ragged.

"Please answer the question."

"Friday morning, in the limo on the way to work. Since she didn't allow me on this floor, I didn't see her before we left Friday night."

When neither of them asked why she wasn't allowed, she went on the offensive. "Hey, what have you done with my brother?" She swiveled in her chair and scanned the room, as if she thought they'd hidden him.

"If you're not allowed on this floor, why did you come here this morning?"

Gertrude swiveled back. "Um, curiosity. I asked the guard about all the police cars and vans on the street. He told me there was a police investigation on the thirty-fifth floor."

Corelli nodded. "What time did you leave Friday night?"

"We always leave at five thirty on Fridays because Connie has to eat dinner before they drive to Southampton." A simple statement, but Gertrude managed to sound aggrieved. "But Connie decided to work late Friday, so we left without her."

"What time did you get home?"

"Must have been about six fifteen when our chauffeur dropped me off."

"Where?"

She puffed on her cigarette and flicked the ashes to the floor. "Park Avenue and 80th Street."

"And what did you do after that?"

"Do I have to answer all these questions?"

Like brother, like sister. "A few more. What did you do Friday night and the weekend?"

"Friday night I called out for Chinese food and watched movies until I went to bed about midnight. The rest of the weekend was kind of the same."

"Did you see anyone or talk to anyone after the chauffeur left you at your apartment?"

"My niece Aphrodite dropped in about eight, but she only stayed fifteen or twenty minutes. About eight thirty the doorman buzzed to let me know the Chinese food was on the way up, and I spoke to the delivery boy. Aphrodite stopped in again Saturday afternoon. That was it."

She took another drag, waved her cigarette, and mimed putting it out. Parker lifted the wastebasket and held it while Gertrude squashed the cigarette against the side. "No more questions until you tell me what's going on."

"Your sister-in-law is dead. She was found in her office early this morning."

Gertrude flushed. "I...That can't be." She crisscrossed her arms, lowered her head and leaned forward, seeming to deflate.

"I'm sorry, but it is," Corelli said. "Do you need some water?"

Gertrude raised her head. "What happened? I know it wasn't suicide."

"Why do you say that?"

She rummaged in her bag, extracted a semi-shredded tissue and dabbed at the sheen of sweat on her upper lip.

"Um, she was too..." Gertrude appeared to be struggling to find the answer. She dabbed her lip again, leaving bits of tissue behind.

"Too what?"

She stared out the window, her hands rolling the damp tissue into particles. The words tumbled out in a rush of anger. "Too sure she was right about everything. Too sure she could do whatever she wanted no matter who it hurt. Too sure..." She turned her gaze to Corelli. "Was it an accident?"

"She was murdered."

She flushed and looked away again. Her breathing seemed to quicken. "Who did it?"

Neither Corelli nor Parker responded.

"I couldn't stand her, but I wouldn't ever intentionally...I couldn't...and neither could Gussie."

"If it wasn't you or your brother, who do you think did it?"

She sat up, and as if someone was standing behind her with a pump, she inflated. "She was nasty." She leaned in close. "Lots of people hated her."

"Who?" Corelli asked again.

She thought for a minute. "Maybe Joel Feldman. She fired him a couple of months ago and spread rumors so he couldn't get a job with any other Wall Street firm."

"Why?"

"Who knows? She didn't need a reason. If she decided it was so, that was it."

"Who else?"

She scratched her head and rubbed her chin. "Maybe Jenny Hornsby. I told her Connie was thinking of firing her, and she knew Connie would do to her what she'd done to Joel."

"Anyone else?"

"Yes. Henry Bearsdon. Henry and his wife Marcia were Connie and Gus's closest friends, but she dumped his law firm Tuesday night with no warning because..." She took a breath and said scornfully, "He wasn't loyal. Can you imagine?" She looked from Parker to Corelli, gauging the impact of her revelation. "So it could've been Henry, but Connie was such a bitch it could've been anybody. Maybe, a stranger, someone she was screwing or, more likely, screwed."

"Can you be more specific, Ms. Gianopolous? Do you have information about a stranger she was screwing? Or screwed?"

"No. I just meant it could be anybody." She wrapped her arms around herself.

"What was so awful about Ms. Winter?"

Gertrude's hand shot up to her face, the fingers splayed over her mouth, broadcasting a confidence coming. "She was mean and vengeful. She treated everybody, and I mean everybody, except her daughter Aphrodite, like dirt, unless they could be useful to her. Then she would be sweet and generous. She used people and tossed them away like dirty tissues, without a thought for their feelings." She shivered as if the memory chilled her. "Connie ruined Aphrodite. She's totally out of control, won't listen to anybody, not even her father. Whoever heard of a fourteen-year-old going to school when she feels like it? She's been thrown out of almost every private school in the city." Her speech was fast and choppy, sometimes muffled by her hand, and Parker seemed to struggle to keep up.

"And poor Gussie, Aphrodite's twin. Connie never gave him the time of day, called him pussycat in a nasty voice. He's sensitive and artistic, very talented, but she was going to send him to military school to toughen him up. Poor kid was traumatized."

Corelli stood. "That's all for now, Ms. Gianopolus. I'll have someone drive you and your brother home. I'm sure we'll have more questions later."

As they walked to their next appointment, Corelli turned to Parker. "Tell me, Parker, who the hell names their daughter Aphrodite?"

CHAPTER SIX

Corelli examined the photos on the credenza behind the desk in Brett Cummings's office. Assuming he was the very tall guy in both pictures, he appeared to be in his early thirties with shoulder-length blond hair, a tanned, muscled body and a killer smile. He was gorgeous. Definitely not what she'd expected.

In one picture, he and a group of people lounged on a boat, everyone turned toward him with glasses raised. In another picture he leaned against the mast of the boat with a lovely blond woman in his arms. Both faced the camera, glowing with health and energy, radiating joy. Corelli felt a surge of longing followed by an overwhelming sadness. *Marnie.* She squeezed her eyes shut to block out the photograph, but she couldn't block the kaleidoscope of images of Marnie that flashed on her eyelids like a movie.

"Detective Corelli."

Parker's voice startled her. Her eyes flew open. "What?" Her voice was too loud.

"Brett Cummings is here."

Corelli composed herself and turned—to face the woman from the photo. Their eyes locked and something passed between them like a jolt of electricity, creating an immediate intimacy that shut out everything and everybody else. The intensity of the connection shocked and terrified Corelli. She wanted it to go on forever, but she also wanted to turn and run. She was having trouble getting enough air. *It's too soon.* She forced herself to look away.

Brett Cummings seemed to be in a similar state. Her shallow breathing seemed loud in the silence. She recovered first. "Expecting a man, Detective?" Her smoky voice contained a tinge of amusement.

Glad for the distraction, Corelli pointed to the picture. "The tall, blond guy holding you."

Cummings laughed. "My brother, the priest, celebrating his ordination on my boat." She sailed across the room and offered her hand. Caught off guard, Corelli hesitated before she waved her battered right hand and offered her left. Without losing a beat, Cummings dropped her bag on the floor and clasped the proffered hand. She repeated her name, "Brett Cummings," in the warm throaty voice that felt like a caress. "That hand looks painful. And your face." Cummings gently brushed the battered side of Corelli's face with the fingers of her free hand. Corelli recoiled but Cummings held onto her hand.

"Sorry," Cummings said.

She didn't look at all sorry. In fact, Cummings seemed to glow. Or maybe it was the sunlight shimmering off her silk outfit, a long-sleeved turquoise shirt and matching turquoise pants, with a gold chain draped around her waist. Her golden hair hung in a long shag, framing her tanned face and accenting her eyes, which reflected the turquoise of her clothing. She radiated vitality and sensuality. And heat.

Parker cleared her throat. Corelli extracted her hand and eased herself into the chair behind the desk. "Please sit."

Cummings hesitated a moment before turning to sit next to Parker in one of the chairs facing the desk. She adjusted her clothes, slid back in the chair and clasped her hands in her lap.

Cummings watched Parker open her notebook and uncap her pen while Corelli admired the eyes that had mesmerized her and the fingers that had caressed her face. Cummings wore an emerald ring, its intense green stone the color of life, beauty, and constant love. *No. No. Get a hold of yourself, Chiara. It's too soon.* She raised her eyes and found Cummings smiling at her. A burst of heat pulsed through her body. She glanced at Parker, who dropped her gaze to her notebook, but couldn't hide the smile flickering on her lips.

Corelli felt-lightheaded, as if someone was brushing her body with feathers. Never in her life had she had such an immediate and visceral reaction to anyone. *Not even Marnie.* She cleared her throat and straightened the already neatly aligned folders on Cummings's desk. "What time did you leave the office Friday night Ms. Cummings?"

"Friday? I didn't check the time but it was probably about nine. Why?"

"And did you see Ms. Winter before you left?"

"Yes. I was heading for the elevator at seven thirty and she grabbed me, ostensibly to get my input on her plan to bring in more business, but what she really wanted was for me to admire her plan. We worked together until about eight thirty."

"And then?"

"I went down to the operations center on the thirty-third floor and checked on a few things. Then I came back up here to pick up some work I needed to do over the weekend and left."

"Do you know why we're here, Ms. Cummings?"

"Please call me Brett. She offered a smile to each of them. "The officer said an investigation was in progress but I'm not sure what that means."

"Ms. Winter was found dead in her office this morning."

A quick intake of breath before she asked, "My lord, how did she die? Does Gus know?"

"She was murdered. Sometime over the weekend."

"Murdered?" She stared at Corelli, horrified, not flirting now. "Why in the world would someone kill the poor little ugly duckling from West Virginia? She had a lot of enemies, but in the financial world we normally don't literally kill the competition."

"Is that how you saw her? Ugly duckling?"

"Well, she wasn't very attractive, physically, or as a person, not to me anyway."

Interesting. The electricity between them suggested Cummings was a lesbian. Was that confirmation? "You've been here a short time. How did you meet Ms. Winter?"

"She recruited me from Sanford Philips & Associates, one of the largest Wall Street firms. She pursued me for months, inviting me out to dinner, the theater, her beach house. Each time raising the offer. Connie always got what Connie wanted. But it wasn't the money that attracted me. I have more than I need. It was the challenge. And, I was curious. So about four months ago I accepted her offer." She paused. "She wasn't well-liked, but it's hard to believe someone would murder her."

"What did you do after you left here Friday night?"

"Our discussion upset me and I needed to think. So I went home—I live in Battery Park City—changed into running clothes and jogged up the Greenway to the 79th Street Boat Basin."

"In the rain?"

"Cooled me off. I had a sandwich and a beer at the café and walked back. It was close to one when I got in."

"Did you see anyone you know at the café?"

"I waved to the manager but Friday nights are busy there. I'm not sure she'd remember."

"What did you need to think about?"

"I learned that Connie's plan for growth was stealing clients from small brokerage houses, essentially putting them out of business. I pointed out she could accomplish the same growth by wooing clients from larger firms without bankrupting them. She laughed and said why waste her time. The smaller firms were the low-lying fruit." Cummings frowned. "I shouldn't have been shocked but I was. I realized I'd made a mistake coming here, but I wanted to think things through before taking any action. A run always helps me think. Sanford Philips said they would match her offer if I came back within six months, so I'm not locked in like some of the others."

"Who do you see as locked in?"

Cummings sat up straighter. She looked like a kid asked to tattle on her friends. She opened her mouth as if to speak, and then closed it. She thought for a moment. "Gertrude, Gus's sister for one. She's totally dependent on Connie. She gets paid a lot of money, but I gather she doesn't do much of anything except cause trouble. She seems angry all the time, makes nasty cracks about Connie and gossips about Connie's personal life."

Cummings tucked her hair behind her ears. "There's also Joel Feldman, the man who had my position before me. She fired him and was making it impossible for him to get another job. Phil Rieger, the VP of Finance clashed with her a few times but nothing serious.

And I heard she and Jenny Hornsby, the head of HR, were having some difficulty. Oh, and, I hate to say it, Gus. Their relationship appeared troubled in the few months I've known them. He seems to fluctuate between obsequiousness and screaming rages."

"One more question, Ms. Cummings. What did you decide Friday night?"

Her generous mouth widened to a killer smile much like her brother's and her eyes sparkled. "I didn't. Around six on Saturday morning I drove out to Sag Harbor and spent the weekend on my boat with friends. That crowd," she said, pointing to the pictures on the credenza. "But there's nothing like sailing to clear your mind. I came in this morning to give Connie my resignation." She stared into Corelli's eyes. "You should try sailing. I'd love for you…er, you both…to come out on the boat sometime, if you're interested."

CHAPTER SEVEN

The intensity of her reaction to Brett Cummings astonished Corelli. After Marnie died she'd felt nothing but grief, loss, and guilt. Being undercover had drained her of even those feelings, left her numb and cut off from life, alone in the empty space left by Marnie.

Her connection with Cummings was intense and instantaneous. And it seemed that encounter had jump-started her libido. And her feelings. Grief, loss, and guilt were edging back. Yet, suddenly she felt lighter, filled with hope and anticipation.

In the few minutes it took her to walk from Cummings's office to the office of the Senior Vice President of Human Resources, Corelli meditated, trying to center herself and refocus on the investigation. She sat behind the desk.

Parker arrived with Jennifer Hornsby, a bird of a woman, small with thin legs and a large rump. The short feathery style of her brown hair suited her beaked nose, close-set eyes and tiny pinched mouth. Head bobbing, hands tucked into the armpits of her brown plaid dress, she leaned forward as if to balance herself as she carefully picked her way into the room. Corelli almost expected to hear her chirp, so bird-like were her movements.

Parker guided Hornsby to a chair and introduced Corelli.

"Sorry to keep you waiting. We'd like to ask you a few questions."

Hornsby said nothing. She appeared fascinated by her right hand, which was fiddling with her gold wedding band.

"Ms. Hornsby—"

She started at her name. "It's Mrs."

"Mrs. Hornsby. What time did you leave the office on Friday?"

"Where's Connie? What's wrong?" Her voice was far from chirpy. It sounded weighed down by the heaviness of each word.

"What makes you think something is wrong with Ms. Winter?"

"I don't know…It's…" She removed her glasses and rubbed her eyes. "The hubbub outside her office, the police. Who else?"

Corelli waited but Hornsby didn't add anything.

"I'm sorry. Ms. Winter was found dead in her office this morning."

The hand motion stopped. "Dead? Who killed her?"

"What makes you think someone killed her?"

"I don't know. Was it natural then?"

"No, she was murdered. Sometime over the weekend."

"I see." The ring action started again. "Do you know who did it?"

"Tell me about Friday night."

"Is that when it happened?"

"What time did you leave the office?"

"About a quarter to six. I visited my husband in Beth Israel Hospital."

"What time did you leave there?"

"I got home about nine."

"Did you see or speak to anyone after you got home?"

"No, I was exhausted. I ate, read for a while, and went to bed."

"Was Friday a particularly stressful day?"

A sad smile flickered at her lips. "Every day is stressful recently."

"Why?"

"My husband is dying. Both my boys are in college and without my husband's income, I…" She took several quick shallow breaths. "And Connie was angry that I didn't go watch her receive a prestigious award from the governor Tuesday night."

"Why didn't you go? It sounds like a big honor."

"I didn't feel well and I knew all the other officers were going. She bought twelve tables at five thousand dollars each, so she had more than a hundred guests—employees, clients, police officials, fire officials, politicians. To be honest, I didn't think it would matter to her if I missed it."

"But it did?"

"Yes. She felt my not being there was a betrayal. And that coupled with…Well, she's been pressuring me to do things I'm not comfortable doing."

Hornsby put her hands in her lap, and for the first time, she seemed calm, almost as if the thing she was trying to avoid saying had come out and she could relax. "When she decided to fire Joel Feldman, I told her he would have good cause to sue. His performance was excellent, investment income was up, and customers seemed happy. But when one of the financial papers ranked investment people and he wasn't the top-rated, she fired him. She didn't want him, but she didn't want any other Wall Street firm to have him, so she spread lies."

Corelli glanced at Parker to make sure she was writing this down.

"What were you unwilling to do?"

"Initially, Connie wanted me to create false work records to show he'd been warned about poor performance. I was reluctant but I probably would have done it. But when he filed a lawsuit, she insisted I testify instead of her and perjure myself, saying he didn't show up or came in drunk, and screwed up deals. All lies. I told her on Friday that I didn't want to do it."

"How did she respond?"

"She admonished me to think it through before I refused. She had me over the proverbial barrel. I didn't want to commit perjury, but my husband hasn't worked for a long time and I need the income and the health insurance. Also, we both knew getting another position would be difficult because she'd make it difficult. Just like she did for Joel."

"Did Ms. Gianopolus tell you that Ms. Winter was thinking of firing you?"

She flushed and began to work the ring again. "I didn't believe her. Gertrude acts like Connie confides in her, but everyone knows Connie despises her."

"Can you think of anyone who might have killed Ms. Winter?"

She laughed, a funny quiet laugh. "You don't have enough time or people to investigate everyone."

"I gather you didn't like her very much."

"She was a seducer and a user. She pursued people and lured them into her web with attention, gifts, and flattery. She made you feel special, and she could be sweet and generous and kind, but the minute you gave yourself up to her, she owned you, and she lost interest. She trapped me like she trapped everyone." A tear rolled down her cheek. "She paid much more than you could earn anywhere else and provided more benefits, so it was difficult to leave voluntarily. If you sucked up to her and followed orders, you'd have a lucrative and prestigious job. Otherwise, she'd fire you. Then, of course, there was the unspoken threat: a ruined reputation making it impossible to find a job in the same field."

"So she replaced Feldman with, er, Cummings?"

"Brett is ranked top in the field and Connie always wanted the best, be it food, people, decorations, children, whatever. It had to be the best. Also, Brett wasn't interested in the job or the company and that always attracted Connie. People who didn't grovel were especially appealing to her, a challenge, and she would go all out to seduce them."

"You mean sexually?" Parker blurted.

Hornsby's laugh, if that's what it was, was harsh, dry. "Not sex. I can only equate it to things I've read about serial killers who are turned on by the kill. When Connie was after someone, nothing and no one else mattered. She almost glowed during the chase."

CHAPTER EIGHT

Sandra Edwards stared out the window. Her face was puffy and raw, her eyes slits. Corelli took a chair across the table from her. "We're almost done, Ms. Edwards."

Edwards sniffed and nodded.

"So far, besides you, we've spoken to Mr. Gianopolus, Ms. Gianopolus, Mrs. Hornsby, and Ms. Cummings. Someone will interview the assistants later. What about the other officers?"

"Oh, I'm so sorry. In the excitement I forgot that some of the officers are on vacation and some take long weekends during the summer. Let me check my schedule."

They followed her to her desk. Officer Shaunton was back at the door of Winter's office. Edwards unlocked her desk and removed the schedule.

"Terry O'Reilly is hiking in Nepal until next Monday. Karl Silver is in Hawaii and should be in next week. Lewis Brooks has been in Japan on business for a week and is scheduled to be there for the rest of the month. Phil Rieger was scheduled to be in today. Let me check my voice mail."

Edwards shook her head. Rieger hadn't called. "By the way, before she went downstairs, Brett Cummings asked me to tell you that we're obligated to conduct some business, executing orders, running the computers, things like that. The people who have to come in will be working on the lower floors. Those not needed will be sent home."

"Thanks. Please give Detective Parker the addresses and phone numbers for Mr. Rieger, Ms. Winter, Ms. Gianopolus, and the chauffer. And if you have contact numbers for the three officers who are out of the country, we'd like them as well. Then we'll have a car drive you home. I need you here tomorrow to help us with any questions that come up, so I'm going to have someone pick you up about seven thirty in the morning."

"That would be fine."

They stopped in the lobby to talk to Gerry Gordon, the guard behind the marble desk.

"How do you guys work?" Corelli asked.

"There are three of us, two during the week and one over the weekend. Monday through Friday one of us is on six to six and the other seven to seven. People with IDs pass through the turnstiles, but visitors have to go to the desk. Anybody on the guest list gets a pass and goes up. Otherwise, the person they want to see has to approve letting them up." He hesitated.

Corelli nodded. "I'm with you."

"There's a porter who works Monday through Friday, four to midnight, cleaning, getting rid of garbage, stuff like that. When the seven to seven guard leaves, the porter locks the door. People can get out anytime without a key, but the only way to get in after seven is to ring the outside bell. The porter answers the door but only lets in people who have a building ID or who are on a list the guard gives him when he leaves."

"Was there a list Friday night?"

Gordon paged through a binder on the counter. "Not this Friday. So only people with IDs could have come in."

"Would the porter have noted anyone he let in?"

Gordon made a face. "He's supposed to but I wouldn't count on it."

"What about this weekend?"

"The weekend guy is on vacation so I worked this Saturday. I got here a little before eight Saturday morning and locked up at six. The building is only open on Sunday if special arrangements are made, and there were no special arrangements this weekend, so it was closed from Saturday six p.m. until six this morning."

"Was the front door locked when you got here Saturday?" Corelli asked.

"Yeah."

"Did you adjust the temperature on the thirty-fifth floor?"

"No. Mihailo, the night porter, locks the elevator and turns the air-conditioner off when he leaves. Nobody from Winter Brokerage came in this Saturday, so I didn't touch either. Why?"

"So nobody went up to the thirty-fifth floor?"

"No. Only the regular weekend people from Winter Brokerage came in on Saturday and they use a different elevator." He reached into a drawer and placed a black three-ring binder on the counter. "See for yourself."

She turned to the entries for Saturday and noted that the only people who came in on Winter's side of the building all went to the thirty-first or thirty-third floor. She closed the book.

"Who turned on the thirty-fifth floor air-conditioning this morning?"

He pointed to the other guard. "Louie, did you turn on CWB's air this morning?"

"Nah, you forgot to turn it off Saturday so I didn't touch it. And you left the elevator open too. You could have at least unloaded the garbage to make it easier for me this morning. Better be nice to me today or I'll report you."

He shook his head. "Damn. Mihailo did it again. I had no reason to touch the thermostat or check the elevator Saturday. Bad enough I had to move the ladder out of the lobby when I came in."

"Speaking of the ladder, we need copies of the security discs. Who's responsible?"

"It's tapes. I'll pass the request on to the building manager when he comes in."

She nodded. "Do tenants have the key to the building?"

"Only us guards, Mihailo, and the building manager have keys. No tenants."

He smirked. "So I hear Ms. Winter was murdered?"

"Who told you that?" Corelli said, her face telegraphing her anger.

He lifted his chin in the direction of the front doors. "Them."

CHAPTER NINE

Corelli and Parker stood just inside the lobby checking out the activity in front of the building. The vans of every TV station were visible, as were the reporters and photographers hanging over the barricades, watching the doors. Corelli rubbed her forehead. What a pain in the ass. She was going to kill whoever tipped the media. "Let's find the freight entrance."

Parker jingled the car keys. "We left the car in front, remember?"

"Right."

"Should I get the car and pick you up at the back of the building?"

"The Wall Street area is like a maze with little alleys and one-way streets. You'd never find me again." She smirked. "And while you might like that, we have a murder to solve. Let's go."

As they stepped out of the building, flashbulbs popped, TV lights blasted, and the crowd surged toward them, screaming Corelli's name and waving microphones and cameras in her direction. She staggered back, her hands covering her head, and started to go down. Parker grabbed her from behind and pulled her back into the building. Parker whispered in her ear. "I've got you. You're safe in New York City."

She opened her eyes. The lobby was quiet and cool. She glanced over her shoulder. The guards and a few people were staring. Parker looked concerned. She brushed Parker's hands off and turned to face her. "Why the hell are you using me as a shield, Parker? Can't you handle a few cameras?"

Parker stepped back but didn't respond.

Corelli wiped the sweat off her face with her handkerchief then pressed her hands against her temples and took several deep breaths to steady herself. When the police had pushed the crowd to the other side of the street behind the barriers, she turned to Parker. "Let's try this again."

They slipped out the door and stood under the building overhang between the pillars. The press was still screaming, flashbulbs were popping and TV cameras were rolling, but this time Corelli was prepared. Taking a minute to assess the situation, she noticed the officers were doing their job, keeping the crowd behind the barriers, but since they considered her a traitor they turned their backs, showing her the blue wall. Could she trust them to cover her back when the chips were down? And what about Parker? She'd done a save just now, but what if the bullets were flying? She took a deep breath. If she let the ostracism immobilize her, she might as well leave the job now. She leaned in close to Parker. "Smile for the cameras, act professional and confident, or you'll look like a scared rabbit on TV tonight and in the newspapers tomorrow."

Parker visibly relaxed her body and plastered a smile on her face.

Corelli did the same. "Let's run for it."

As Corelli ran around to the passenger side, the crowd surged through the barriers and she realized the questions they were throwing out weren't about the victim or suspects. They were asking whether it was true that the brass wanted her removed from the case. She jumped into the car and locked the door. Parker did the same.

"Vultures," Parker muttered.

"They were asking if I was being thrown off the case." Would they, whoever *they* were, try to keep her from working any case, or was there something special about the Winter case?

"Do you think it's true?"

Corelli stared at the uniforms herding the crowd back behind the barricades, at the gaping mouths, popping eyes and wild gestures of the media. She felt like the star in her own private horror movie. "Anything is possible."

She sensed Parker's gaze on her. "Thanks for covering for me. It takes time to adjust." She said it quickly, to the windshield. She didn't want Parker's sympathy, or any of that shit. She turned to Parker. "But don't get excited. You're not getting a reprieve from me. And how about you do your job, keep your eyes on the freaking street and get us out of here?"

Parker glared at her, then put the car in gear. The crowd surged forward but the uniforms held them back long enough for the car to pass.

"Are you a good enough driver to lose them?"

Parker narrowed her eyes. "I won't even deign to answer that."

"Deign? Well, in that case, turn left at Water Street as if you're headed for the house. When we're out of sight, go straight for the FDR north."

"Yessuh, boss lady."

Atta girl. Corelli looked out the side window. And smiled.

CHAPTER TEN

Winter lived in the affluent Sutton Place neighborhood on the east side of Manhattan, an elite enclave for old and not so old money. Sutton Plaza, a short street with two large town houses on each side, intersected Sutton Place. A high fence enclosed the four houses and a small guardhouse inside the fence controlled entering traffic. Gates topped with barbed wire protected the only other entrances to the compound, the walkways behind the houses on each side of the street. Security cameras attached to the houses monitored the three gates.

As Parker pulled up to the gate, Corelli shook her head. "Looks like Winter thought she lived in Iraq."

"Ironic. She spends tons of money on home security and gets knocked off in her office."

"Maybe you should write a poem about it."

"You are one sarcastic bi—"

"I'm more interested in how she got approval to block a public street." Corelli leaned forward, tapping her fingers on the dash as she scanned the compound.

"Money talks."

"You should know."

Before Parker could respond, the guard, wearing a green cap, green uniform, and white gloves, leaned into the car window. He studied them with narrowed eyes and pursed lips, as if evaluating their worth. He parted his disapproving lips to speak, but Corelli flashed her shield, and announced Detectives Corelli and Parker were on their way to see Mr. Gianopolus. Hearing her name, he backed out of the car so fast his head hit the top of the window. He swore, rubbed his head, and started back to his little house, tossing angry instructions over his shoulder.

"When the gate opens, pull in and park in front of the last house on the right, number seventeen."

Only a low brick wall and bushes separated the houses from the sharp drop to the East River Drive and the East River shimmering in the sunlight. Apparently the guard had called ahead, because a middle-aged black woman wearing a maid's uniform opened the heavy wooden door before they could knock. They identified themselves and the maid ushered them through a large foyer to a small, wood-paneled elevator that contained a purple velvet cushioned bench, on which two could sit. She pressed four and the elevator moved up.

No one had mentioned Winter being handicapped, so Corelli wondered whether one of her children had a problem. "Is someone in the family unable to use the stairs?"

The maid, who had identified herself as Cora Andrews, laughed. "No, they all can walk, but no one does, especially Ms. Winter. She never walks if she can ride. The others just follow the leader."

She spoke of Winter as if she was alive. Had Gianopolus not told her?

Andrews tut-tutted. "These kids lose their heads if they're not attached. I cleaned this morning and they already leaving their junk in here." She picked a comb off the seat and bent down to retrieve a drawing charcoal, a large eraser, two lipsticks, a blue pencil, a bicycle glove, and a package of tissues. She stuffed everything into the pockets of her uniform.

The elevator opened onto a dark, cool room that smelled of stale cigarettes and fresh cigars. It appeared this family didn't worry about the effect of second-hand smoke on the children. They waited as Andrews turned on a lamp near the door and announced them. The room resembled the lobby of a luxury hotel. Definitely not a room designed for comfort. The far wall consisted of floor-to-ceiling windows, but now the tightly drawn drapes kept the sunlight at bay. Paintings marched in neat rows and columns on the two side walls. The French provincial furniture was arranged in conversational groupings on top of the plush, Oriental carpets. The sofas, chairs, tables, lamps and ruffled lampshades were all white and pink, as were the elaborate drapes and swags that covered the windows. No doubt about Winter's favorite colors.

Gus Gianopolus sat alone, dwarfed in one of the chairs facing a white marble fireplace; cigar butts and ashes spilled out of a huge ashtray to his right. His head hung as if he were asleep, and he didn't react when the light went on or when Andrews said their names. Her pursed lips and shaking head left no doubt about her opinion of his behavior.

No sign of the kids or his sister. If this was her family, Corelli thought, the house would be filled with relatives and friends and neighbors. There would be food, coffee, and drinks, and the women who were not immediate family would have already decided amongst themselves who would be cooking and serving which meals for the extended family during the wake. A long way from this isolated vigil.

They trailed Andrews as she picked her way through the room to where Gianopolus was sitting. She turned on the lamp next to him and touched his hand. "These detectives come to talk about Miss Connie."

He lifted his head, blinking from the light, and seemed confused until he noticed them. "You again," he said, his voice hoarse. "Can't you leave me alone?"

He no longer resembled the dandy they'd seen earlier. Now his shoes were splayed in front of him, his pants wrinkled, and his white shirt spotted with ash.

"Sorry, but we've got to move quickly," Corelli explained.

Andrews crinkled her nose in distaste as she lifted the dirty ashtray and replaced it with a clean one from a nearby table. She caught Corelli's eye, tilted her head toward the elevator, and getting a nod, left them with Gianopolus.

Parker sat in a chair that shared the light of the lamp, near Gianopolus but out of his line of vision. She opened her notebook as Corelli began. "I'd like to confirm the last time you saw your wife."

His lips tightened. "Friday." His tone implied he thought Corelli a moron. "Every Friday we leave the office at five thirty, have dinner, and drive out to our house in Southampton. Last Friday, I went to her office about five fifteen to remind her to get ready, and she told me to go without her because she had things to do in the city. I said goodbye. She asked me to send the chauffeur back to wait for her. I said I would and left."

"Did you usually spend weekends apart?"

"Is this any of your business?"

She leaned toward him, her voice hard. "Everything is my business in a murder investigation. Sir." Out of the corner of her eye Corelli noted Parker lift her pen and stare. Was she shocked? Too bad. Parker needed to learn this lesson. You can't always be nice. Sometimes you need to be tough.

He studied his drink. "Sometimes, if she had something she wanted to do in the city. Quite often lately."

"You left the office. Then what?"

"Rino, the chauffeur, drove me here."

"What did you do then?"

"Are you insinuating that I killed my wife?"

"Routine, sir. We need to confirm everyone's whereabouts."

He pushed himself out of the overstuffed chair and went to the liquor cart, poured himself another glass of scotch, downed half of it, and refilled the glass. He stumbled over his shoes as he made his way back to the chair. Was he stalling to concoct a story?

"I changed my clothes and walked over to Un Bon Repas, a French restaurant a few blocks down, near the UN. After dinner I came home to pick up some things. I got my car and left for Southhampton about nine."

"Anybody see you?"

"The waiters at the restaurant. And our guard. No one else that I noticed." He sipped his drink. "I didn't think I would need an alibi."

"Where were your children?"

"I didn't see them. It's possible they were here but I didn't notice."

Parker's head jerked up, her pen hung in midair. If he heard her intake of breath, he didn't bother to turn. Gus Gianopolus was the kind of man who ignored people he considered unimportant, so he didn't see the disapproval on Parker's face.

"Who cares for the children?"

"They take care of themselves. They have credit cards, so they can get cash or charge anything they need."

"What about the maid. Does she keep tabs on them?"

"She goes home at six unless Connie needs her. And she doesn't work weekends."

Now Corelli was incredulous. Winter protected her papers and secrets at the office, had guards, gates, and barbed wire to protect her house, but she left her fourteen-year-old kids in New York City without supervision?

"Do the children usually come to Southampton on weekends?"

"If they want to."

"So if you both go to Southampton, they're allowed to stay in the city alone?"

"They're very responsible. When I was fourteen, I was working to help support my mother and sisters."

"Is there anyone who can verify the time you arrived in Southampton?"

He took a swig of his drink, shifted in his seat, and began to tap his fingers on the glass. His ears turned bright red.

"How many times do I have to say this? I was alone. That's A-L-O-N-E. Should I write it down for you?"

She decided she'd pushed enough for now. "I have a few questions about your wife."

He relaxed. "I'm not sure I can answer them."

"Well let's see. How old was she?"

"Almost fifty, I think."

"Where was she born?"

"Somewhere in the Midwest."

"Can you be more specific?"

"No. She was an orphan, raised by her Aunt Clara who died when she was sixteen. Sometimes she said Indiana, sometimes Wisconsin, sometimes Ohio. It was hard to pin her down."

"Does she have a will?"

"She did, but she hinted that she was changing it so I'm not sure where it stands." He squirmed. "I called her new attorney, Paul Donaldson, but he hasn't gotten back to me. I'd like to know if she…I'd like to know where I stand."

"If the children are home, I'd like a minute with them."

His face darkened again. "What could they possibly tell you?"

"It's routine to talk to the whole family."

"Absolutely not."

"Are you hiding something?"

He narrowed his eyes and considered her. Whether he got that she wouldn't relent or he realized that he had nothing to hide, he caved.

"Wait here."

He left the room and Parker let her breath out in a whoosh. "Kind of spineless."

Corelli threw Parker a two-finger salute. "Very perceptive, Parker."

"You think?"

Gianopolus returned with a willowy, brown-eyed, blond girl wearing a light green tank top and skimpy green shorts that exposed most of her tanned body. She was stone-faced, and looked more like thirty than fourteen. A shorter, brown-eyed boy with auburn hair trailed behind in baggy brown shorts and a very large T-shirt that proclaimed he was a Computer Geek. He was a sodden lump, with swollen eyes and traces of dried tears on his cheeks. He seemed younger than fourteen. Huddled together on the end of the sofa farthest from their father, they appeared connected despite the different feelings evoked by their mother's death. He introduced them as Gus Jr. and Aphrodite.

"We're sorry for your loss," Corelli said. "We're investigating your mom's death and we need to know everyone's whereabouts Friday night."

"We didn't kill her, if that's what you're thinking," the girl said. "We just fantasized about it."

The boy tucked his arms into his armpits. He stuttered, "D-D-Don't say that, Aphrie."

"Answer the question, Aphrodite," Gianopolus said. "We don't need your histrionics today."

"Feeling in charge are we?"

He flushed but swallowed the rage that flashed on his face. "Answer the question so the detectives can work on finding your mother's killer instead of wasting their time talking to us."

Gussie elbowed her. "Ouch." She rubbed her side and made a face at her brother. "I came home about six and didn't go out again until Saturday when I went to visit Aunt Gertie."

"Your aunt said you dropped in Friday about eight o'clock."

"Oh, I forgot." She shifted uncomfortably…tugged her shorts down and pulled her hair back. "I hung out with her about a half hour or so. Then I came home."

"Did you expect to see your mother this weekend?"

"I assumed she went out to the beach with Dad."

She turned to the boy. "And you?"

He looked down. "Got home about four on Friday and stayed in my room playing computer games and drawing. I felt sick so I stayed in all weekend." His voice was as soft as his sister's was hard.

"Thank you. I'm so sorry. We're done for now. I know this is difficult but we'll probably need to speak to you both again." The boy began to sob, a lonely, muffled sound. Aphrodite pulled him closer and whispered. Their father acted as if it wasn't happening.

Corelli turned to Gianopolus. "Before we leave, Mr. Gianopolus, we'd like to examine Ms. Winter's bedroom and her office, if she had one at home."

He started to object but caught himself and pressed a button on the table next to his chair.

Aphrodite cleared her throat. "I need some cash."

Gianopolus frowned, reached into his pocket and placed five one hundred dollar bills in her outstretched hand. Without a word she left, pulling her brother after her.

After they left the room, Corelli again addressed Gianopolus. "When can you go to the morgue to view the body?"

"How does she look?"

"Not bad." *At least she won't after they clean her up.*

He twisted the glass in his hands. "I…Can I do it tomorrow?"

"Somebody will contact you to make arrangements."

He extracted another cigar from the box on the table and performed the ritual with the concentration of a priest consecrating communion: sniffing it, clipping it, lighting it, exhaling and studying the swirls of smoke he seemed to find fascinating.

Corelli and Parker watched the performance in silence.

Ms. Andrews bustled in. "You want me?"

He seemed surprised to see her standing there and hesitated before removing the cigar from his mouth. "Show the detectives Mrs. Gianopolus's room and her office. Stay with them and let them out when they finish."

He puffed his cigar and picked up his drink, dismissing them. Corelli had not missed the "Mrs. Gianopolus" as an assertion of ownership.

"Did they share this room?" Corelli asked.

Andrews glanced at the door. "No, they have...No, his bedroom is down the hall."

"How did they get along?"

She glanced toward the door again. "All right I suppose. Didn't seem very close. Always argued some, but it seemed like more in the last few months."

"Argued about what?"

"Mostly over the kids. He didn't like the way she treated Gussie and he felt Aphrodite was running wild. Recently I heard him say something about divorce. She never raised her voice, so it was only him I heard."

"How long have you worked for them?"

"Since they was married, fifteen or sixteen years, but I worked for Ms. Winter for about five years before she married him."

"Do you have anything to do with the children?"

"You mean like take care of them or watch them?"

"Anything."

"When I'm here I'll make them something to eat if they want. But when they were real little, up to round four years old, I watched them during the day and a nurse come in at night. But then it got so I couldn't handle Aphrodite. She wouldn't listen at all. Whenever I complained to Ms. Winter, she took the girl's part, even if she was doing something foolish or dangerous. So I told her I didn't want the responsibility."

"Did she accept that?"

"Ha. I was sure she was gonna fire me, but she knows I'm loyal, so she said must be that they need a real nanny who knows about children. I had a good laugh because I raised four children by myself while I was working for her, and I never had such problems, and she knew it. None of my four, even the boys, ever had any real trouble and now all four have college educations and good jobs."

Her pride was apparent in the wide smile, but then she became serious again. "That girl is strong-minded and stubborn. You say no, she gets crazy. They went through about seven or eight nannies after me. All of them had the same problems. If they tried to punish her or make her do something, Ms. Winter fired them. So the twins been staying alone from the time they was about eleven or so."

"How did she get along with the children?"

"Didn't show no interest in the boy but thought Aphrodite was the sun and the moon. Always trying to please her, giving her things. Aphrodite was nasty to her, nasty to everybody, except me and Gussie and that aunt of hers. They always been like two peas in a pod, always played together. He's easygoing, so she pushes him around, but every once in a while she pushes too hard and he fights back, but she never admitted he gave her the bruises, scratches, or black eye. She'd say she fell or something to protect him from Ms. Winter, like a little mother." She smiled.

They found nothing of interest in the bedroom. The décor was in line with what they had seen of her taste so far—very frilly, very expensive. A picture of her with Aphrodite was the only personal touch. It could have been a room in an expensive hotel, except there was no Bible.

They moved into the office. It was impressive, all leather and wood which gave it a warm feeling missing from the parts of the house they'd seen. The walls were lined with bookcases of cherry wood and stocked with books bound in leather that, for the most part, looked like they had never been opened. A cart similar to the one in the living room was stocked with bottles of liquor and soda, but no ice.

The desk drawers were unlocked and contained only a letter from the East Side Girls Academy, a private school, informing Winter that Aphrodite would be asked to leave unless she made up all missed tests by October 31.

Corelli replaced the letter. "Is there a safe in the house?"

"Never seen one."

It appeared that anything of significance would be in Winter's office.

"We've heard Ms. Winter was difficult. How did you manage to hang on for so long?"

"We did all right. She paid me a lot of money, let me run the house, and mostly she was nice to me. She could be unreasonable, but we worked it out."

"Is there anything you think we should know?"

She hesitated. "I don't know if it's important, but they all was in a tizzy last week. Her wanting to send Gussie to military school upset the kids and they kept nagging her about it. Then Friday morning I was cooking breakfast and Ms. Winter and Aphrodite had words at the table, something about money. That never happened before. And, Friday, Gus came in all steamed up after work, slamming doors and cursing anything that got in his way, like rugs and furniture." She thought for a moment. "And you should talk to Gertrude. There was no love lost between those two. Gertrude was always going on about Ms. Winter to Gus, even in front of the kids, even if Ms. Winter was in the next room. She's a mean-spirited woman and can be nasty. Maybe she did it."

CHAPTER ELEVEN

The bright sunshine and even the high humidity were a welcome relief after that cold, dark, smoke-filled house. Parker got in the car but Corelli strode to the guard house and banged on the window. The dozing guard jerked to consciousness, arms and legs thrashing, momentarily disoriented. After he figured out he was not home in bed, he noticed Corelli, and unfazed at being caught sleeping on the job, stretched and yawned. His behavior didn't fit with what she knew of Winter. Wouldn't someone obsessed with security, someone who always wanted the best and insisted on professionalism and attention to the job want real security?

The guard slid the window open and mumbled something.

Did that lazy ass just call me Mata Hari? Corelli leaned in the window. "What did you say?"

He paled and backed away. "Nothing. What do you need?"

"How much coverage do they have?"

"Twenty-four by seven."

"Who was on duty Friday night?"

"Me."

"Did anyone go in or out?"

He opened a notebook and turned a couple of pages. "Gus Jr. in at four, Aphrodite in at six. Mr. Gianopolus in at six ten, the maid out at six twenty, Mr. Gianopolus out at six thirty, in at eight twenty-five and out nine-oh-five. That's it."

"You watch the side entrances too?"

"Yeah, we have cameras," he said, pointing to the two screens in the corner.

"Aphrodite visited her aunt about eight p.m. You didn't see her come or go?"

He shrugged. "I'm not paid to babysit. Brat musta sneaked in and out when I was busy."

Corelli shook her head. Whatever she was paying, Winter wasn't getting her money's worth. Parker had pulled up next to her. She slid into the car. The guard raised the gate and they pulled onto Sutton Place. At the same time, Aphrodite in red bicycle regalia and Gus Jr. in blue, rolled their bicycles through the side gate behind their house. At least Ms. Sophisticate wasn't driving yet.

Corelli stared out the window as Parker followed her directions to Sheepshead Bay, Brooklyn, where Rino Martucci, the chauffeur, lived. That exchange with the guard bothered her. Not only his expression when he recognized her, but she was sure he had called her Mata Hari. Her friend Jimmy McGivens had called her Mata Hari when she arrested him.

She put her head back and closed her eyes. Immediately images of Cummings—smiling confidently, touching her face, holding her hand—burst into her consciousness. And with the images came the heat and the memory of her sultry voice shimmering through her. Feeling betrayed by her body, feeling she was betraying Marnie, she sat up and fiddled with the air-conditioner. She pretended not to notice Parker's gaze flicking back and forth between her and the road. Where were these feelings coming from? Her body, no, her whole being, was out of kilter. It was making her cranky. Even the sun glinting off the river annoyed her. She reached for her sunglasses and found them and a bag of mixed nuts and raisins that she didn't remember she'd put in her pocket. She offered the nuts and raisins to Parker and for a few minutes they munched in silence.

"What do you think?"

Parker looked self-conscious. "The house is cold, like a hotel, or a demonstration apartment. Nothing personal, everything is for show. If it wasn't for the smell of cigar and cigarette smoke, you wouldn't know anybody lived there."

CHAPTER TWELVE

Parker followed the instructions to Emmons Avenue, but somehow they ended up in a quaint fishing village. She eyed the scene, the line of fishing boats bobbing in the water on the right and the line of restaurants on the left. "Are we still in New York City?"

"This is Sheepshead Bay," Corelli said. "Haven't you ever been in Brooklyn?"

"What are we supposed to do now? Jump in and knock on boats?"

"Very funny," Corelli said, checking the instructions. "Turn around. We needed to make a left back there."

Parker looked around. "Would you prefer I fly over the cars in front of us or those behind us?"

"Stop whining. Use the fucking siren and turn around."

"You are one nasty son of a—"

"Just do it."

Parker stiffened. *I'm done. You can cover your own ass after today.*

It was after five when they found Rino Martucci's house in a row of semi-detached brick homes a few blocks from the Bay. The sleek, black limousine parked in the driveway seemed out of place in this middle-class neighborhood.

"You interview him. Let's see how the former ADA does it. Maybe I'll learn to build a better case," Corelli said as they walked up the path.

Parker stopped on the first step. "Fuck you. I didn't sign on to be a nursemaid or a punching bag. You interview him." One way or another she would get out of this nightmare assignment tomorrow and then savor the thought of Corelli shriveling up behind a desk.

Corelli glared at her. "Afraid?"

"No," Parker said, her mouth tight. "I may be new to homicide but I'm not an imbecile and I won't allow you to treat me like one."

"You gonna report me to Senator Daddy, make an example of me?"

"I hadn't thought of it, but that's a great idea." Parker started down the steps. "I'll wait in the car."

"Ah, the little lady does have a backbone." Corelli reached out to stop her. "C'mon, interview him. Do I have to say pretty please?"

"Go—"

The front door opened and a wiry man in his sixties wearing a western shirt, jeans, and cowboy boots gaped at them. "You the detectives? I wasn't expecting two girls, but, uh, come in." Brushing his long, dyed-black hair from his ruddy face, the urban cowboy turned and strutted down the hall, the heels of his boots hammering the wooden floor.

Corelli swept an arm in front of her, bidding Parker to enter before her. Parker hesitated. No time for an argument but she wouldn't say a word. She brushed by Corelli and followed Martucci into the living room, which seemed designed for lovers of salmon—the color salmon. The upholstered sofa, chairs, lampshades and drapes were all the same putrid salmon color. Maybe he got the set cheap. And speaking of cheap, now that she was close to Martucci, an overdose of cheap cologne combined with the stench of smoke and alcohol made her stomach turn. She definitely should have waited in the car. She stepped back to get a little distance and landed on Corelli's foot.

"Too close." Corelli breathed into her ear. "Get your own space."

Parker slid to the side.

"Make yourselves comfortable," Martucci said, pointing to the sofa. Then, like a hero in a romance novel, he tucked his hair behind his ears and offered what he probably thought was a sexy smile. Parker recognized the type, the kind of guy whose mind hasn't caught up with his body and believes women find him sexy and desirable. Not women his own age, of course, the younger ones. He was anything but sexy and by the looks of the place, there was no woman in his life.

The pop and crackle of the yellowed plastic covering as they sat was loud in the tense quiet. He took the recliner facing them but remained upright rather than pushing back into the comfortable position. Hands shaking, he picked up his drink and the cigarette burning in the well used ashtray. He took a drag, added the butt to the pile, then cleared his throat.

"Listen, I didn't steal the limo. I thought I could make arrangements to bring the car back after Connie, er, Ms. Winter, called to fire me. She didn't have to call the police. After all this time she should know I'm honest." Neither Parker nor Corelli responded. He squirmed and looked from one to the other. "Really."

While he fiddled with lighting another cigarette, Corelli elbowed Parker.

"Hey." Parker gave Corelli a dirty look.

Martucci looked up. "What?"

"Detective Parker has some questions for you." Corelli smiled and sat back.

Parker glared at Corelli. *Damn her.* "What makes you think Ms. Winter wants to fire you?"

"C'mon. She musta whined about how I was drunk when she was ready to leave Friday night and how, horror of all horrors, she had to call a taxi. That's a no-no. Connie don't go nowhere without her limo…and her chauffeur. I guess she's pissed I didn't pick her up this morning, but to tell ya the truth, I hate her nastiness. Better to get fired over the phone."

"What happened on Friday?"

"Does it matter? The truth is, I was passed out in the car when she was ready to leave."

"We want to hear it from you. Start from when you first arrived."

He sipped his drink, ran his fingers through his hair, and wiggled forward in the recliner, struggling to sit up straighter.

"Okay. I got to Wall Street about five twenty. Her highness gets pissy if she has to wait, so I always try to get there a little early. I sat fifteen, maybe twenty minutes before Gus and his big-assed sister Gertrude showed up. Gus said Connie was working late so I should drive him and Gertrude home and then go back and wait for her."

"How were Gus and Gertrude on the way home?"

"Same as usual when they're alone in the car. Gertrude sticking it to him. Called him a pussy and said he should fight back when Connie makes fun of him in front of everybody." Martucci put his drink down. "He mumbled something about a pre, uh, you know, the thing you sign before you get married? Then he says, 'I can't live on that kind of money. And who else is going to provide limousine service and pay you to do nothing except cause trouble?' I figure he hit her where it hurts because she dropped it. Usually she don't stop needling."

"Doesn't the limo have glass between you and the passengers?"

"Yeah, I put it up if they tell me, but I'm like the furniture. They don't see me. Usually I hear Connie and Gus, and then after I drop them off, pain in the butt Gertrude explains it to me."

"Like what?"

"Like Connie dumped her big shot lawyer after that dinner Tuesday night, you know, where she got that big-deal award? I was wondering, 'cause when he tried to get in the limo, she told him to hit the road and left him and his snooty wife standing there, looking like somebody let the air out of them. Made me happy 'cause I didn't have to drive them out to the Island. Anyway, Gertrude said Connie fired him on the spot."

"What happened after you drove Gus and Gertrude home Friday?"

He took a last drag, put the cigarette out, then raising his glass as if asking for permission, he got up to get a refill. He returned with a bottle of Johnny Walker Black and a full glass and placed them both on the small table next to his recliner before lighting another cigarette.

"I got back to Wall Street around seven. It started to pour and I musta dozed because the next time I checked it was nine o'clock. I was pissed. I hadda call my friend Gilly to tell him the bitch was doing it again. The last couple of months she worked lotsa Friday nights and I hadda miss my card game. She could get a taxi or car service home, but she's such a big shot she has to have her limo. It's more important to her than her kids. And it don't matter to her that I have to wait all night."

"Did you argue over it?"

He laughed, drank some scotch, inhaled deeply, and exhaled a long trail of smoke. "Nah. The one time I mentioned it to her she told me in her little girlie voice, 'That's uh, why I uh, pay you the uh, big bucks, Rino. Quit if you uh, don't like it.' She knows she has me by the balls because nobody else pays like her. So, I shut up and never brought it up again."

"What did you do after you called your friend?"

"Like I said, it was nine, and I had knots in my stomach. She treats me like a fucking slave, like I don't have a life. I think the bitch enjoys knowing she owns me."

He sipped his drink. "Do you want this much detail?" He swiped his crotch.

"Great, keep going."

"Anyways, I was starving and I needed a drink. I'm not supposed to leave the limo or drink on the job, but sometimes she don't come out until two or three o'clock in the morning. I knew when she was ready to leave she'd call my cell so I could move the car right to the door. So I sprinted through the rain to the bar across the street for some peanuts and a few drinks."

"Did you notice anybody hanging around outside the office building?"

"Nah. It was raining."

"And what time did you leave the bar?"

"When they closed. I had a lot to drink, so Chip, the bartender, helped me across the street to the limo. I didn't wake up until about five in the morning. I was hoping she might still be there but she didn't answer her cell. I figured she came down, saw me drunk and got a taxi."

"You didn't go up to her office to see what was wrong?"

"I told ya. I knew I was fucked, so I drove home. I've been waitin' for her to call and fire me. I never thought she would send the cops."

"What's the name of the bar?"

He took a long drag on his cigarette, pushed some of the butts aside in the ashtray and put it out, before answering. "The Wall

Street Oasis. Chip is the night bartender. Why are you so interested in all of this? The limo is outside. I even waxed it."

Parker sensed he was hiding something, but she wasn't sure how to push him. Should she tell him Winter was dead? Her leg started jiggling, a sure sign she was nervous, and nasty mouth Corelli would be sure to call attention to it. She needed to make a decision, any decision. *Damn Corelli*. She'd never felt insecure when she was an ADA.

Martucci concentrated on refilling his glass. The plastic cover on the sofa crackled. Corelli poked her again. Pissed, Parker shifted to face her and Corelli mouthed, "Dead."

Right. Tell him. "Well Mr. Martucci, we're not here for the limousine. Actually, Ms. Winter was murdered Friday night in her office."

He was in the middle of chug-a-lugging and he choked, spraying scotch all over himself. He shivered. His hand shook and he placed his glass on the table with excessive care before using his shirtsleeve to dry his mouth.

"You mean Friday while I…Is that when it happened?"

Parker ignored the question and waited for his reaction.

"Hey, I wouldn't—" He put his hands up, as if they were holding him at gunpoint. "I'm no killer. I was asleep in the car. Ask Chip."

"We will." Parker handed him a card. "Don't leave town. Call if you remember anything you think we should know."

He followed them to the door. The swagger was gone and the stink of fear overpowered the smell of perfume, cigarettes and alcohol.

CHAPTER THIRTEEN

Parker retraced their route, only now it was rush hour and traffic back to Manhattan was bumper to bumper. She concentrated on avoiding the jerks who thought if they could just drive over her, the road ahead would be clear.

The interview played over and over in the back of her mind. Overall it had gone well, but she shouldn't have hesitated. She should have known to tell him Winter was dead. She shouldn't have needed Corelli to poke her. What else had she missed? No matter. Tomorrow she'd tell the captain she'd changed her mind about working with Corelli. She'd lose homicide and go back to being ignored, but it was better than being baited and insulted and treated like an idiot. And Corelli would lose too, relegated to desk duty, because who in their right mind would work with the crazy bitch?

Corelli broke into her reverie. "Good job for your first interview."

Sure. And Connie Winter was a sweet little thing. Corelli is a fantastic liar. How else could she scam other cops, her so-called friends, for more than three months?

Parker kept her eyes on the road. "Not my first."

"Right. Ms. ADA has done thousands of interviews. Anyway, Mr. Rino Martucci didn't seem so cocky when we left, did he?"

"Nope."

Corelli cleared her throat. "I haven't been around so many smokers in ages. If we don't solve this case really fast, we'll both die from exposure to secondary smoke."

"How much faster can we go? We haven't stopped to eat or drink or take a minute to discuss the case, and all you do is attack me." *Won't you be surprised when I dump you first thing tomorrow?*

"Just trying to keep you on your toes. Can't take a little teasing?"

"It's not teasing. You're ridiculing and insulting me. I don't like it."

Corelli yawned. "I'm starving. Go to the South Street Seaport, the Buonasola Grill. We'll eat and figure out where we are. In the case, I mean."

"Now you're ignoring me? This might be my only chance to work homicide and you're making it impossible to work with you. I'm not some uneducated idiot and I won't tolerate your aggressiveness and your anger. You need me more than I need you right now. Maybe that's the problem. Well it's your problem, not mine."

"Hey, I didn't sign on to babysit. You want homicide you gotta work for it."

The senator's voice popped into Parker's head. "See what happens when you get involved in someone else's shit?"

Maybe he was right this time. She bit her lip. She wanted homicide so bad she could taste it.

The maitre d' at Buonasola seemed to know Corelli and ushered them to an isolated table on the deck. Corelli sat with her back to the water. Parker opted for distance and pulled out the chair facing her, but then thought better of sitting with her back to the door and moved to one of the other chairs facing the door.

Corelli ordered. "Iced coffee, linguine with white clam sauce, and an arugula salad, dressing on the side."

"Mushroom ragout with polenta, a mixed green salad, and an unsweetened ice tea."

"Good choice." Corelli sat back and focused on Parker. "So who did it, Ms. ADA?"

Parker glanced away. The rage that had been building percolated through her. "Why don't you tell me who did it, oh, high and mighty homicide detective? After all, I'm just a know-nothing trainee. They all sound guilty to me. She was a nasty bitch and she deserved to be murdered."

"Whoa, don't go all prickly on me. I was joking. It sounds like you're ready for lesson two of Homicide 101: not even nasty people deserve to be murdered. It's our job to figure out who did it but it's still early. Relax, we'll think it through together. Don't get so stressed."

"Stressed? How am I supposed to feel with you badgering me? Even if I could tolerate you, the people you ratted out will make sure we fail."

"Jeez, calm down, Parker. You have nothing to worry about. The failure will be mine, not yours. You're my bodyguard and I guess you lose if they kill me on your watch. For obvious reasons, I hope that won't happen. But you lose more if you don't relax and try to learn as we go through the investigation."

Relax with you breathing down my neck, hectoring and pushing? I'd love to learn but how can I if I'm tense and on edge waiting for your next attack? Your career is screwed already but mine is on the line now. Not that you give a flying fuck. "If you fail, so do I, and that doesn't wash off, no matter what you say. This may be my only chance. I've worked hard to get to homicide. If I hadn't saved that family, I never would have made detective. Why? Not because I'm not a really good cop, but because I'm better educated, smarter, and more ambitious than most—and the senator is the number one critic of the department. So I get promoted and they dump this assignment on me."

Parker took a breath, desperately fighting for control. She repeated her mantra. Keep your feelings to yourself. Project confidence. Stay calm. Be assertive. Never lose control. *I'm losing it. But I can't stop.* "Maybe you're naturally self-destructive and condescending and bitchy, but, you know what? I don't care. Why would I want to work with an isolated, crazy woman who hasn't a friend in the world but takes pleasure in inflicting wounds on the one person who's stepped out on the limb with her? Sounds sick to me."

Red-faced, Corelli stood. "That's enough, Detective Parker. I suggest you go for a walk and cool off before you say something you'll really be sorry for. We'll discuss this when you get back. I expect to see you a lot calmer in ten minutes."

Parker jumped up and shoved her chair back roughly. She reached out to keep the chair upright but pulled her hand back as if it burned when she encountered Corelli's hand attempting to do the same. She dashed from the deck, almost colliding with a slender, light brown skinned man, dressed all in black, who she hadn't noticed standing inside the dining room, near the door to the deck.

Corelli rubbed her forehead. And why would she want to work with a detective whose daddy would attack and try to destroy whatever little reputation she still had at the first sign of a problem? She sipped her coffee. *Parker is smart and perceptive. She has good instincts. But maybe she can't handle the pressure of an investigation, the need to move fast to find the killer, the grueling interviews with witnesses that tell lies, the long hours, the missed meals.* True, almost everybody they'd talked to had a motive, but they'd just started. *We only have the Winter case now, but that won't last long. How will Parker deal with the pressures of juggling multiple cases?*

Or was the problem hers? She'd told herself she was teasing, but was she dumping on Parker, taking her anger out on her? It wasn't like her to ridicule, but if she was honest with herself, that's what she'd been doing, ridiculing another woman, a new detective trying to make it in what was still a good old boys' game. According to Parker Corelli was sick, a crazy woman. Was she right? Did the nightmares, the lack of sleep, and the flashbacks—in Winter's office that morning and on the street this afternoon—mean she was crazy? Or could all that be from the stress of coming out of Afghanistan, of coming out of undercover, of getting back on the job, of being ostracized?

Whether it was stress or hormones or something else, she was way out of control. Her reaction to Brett Cummings had thrown her off-kilter and left her feeling vulnerable. Had she been dealing fairly with Parker? No. Clearly, Parker had her own issues and needed a lot of stroking. But she hadn't signed on to be Parker's babysitter. On the other hand, she needed Parker. So she should try to be more attentive and rein in her anger or at least not take it out on Parker.

She stared at the river, considering the best way to defuse the situation and keep Parker on board. She shifted her gaze to the door, checking for Parker's return. Instead she saw the shadow of a man standing inside the doorway watching her. *Shit.* She went for her gun but the jolt of pain that ran up her arm reminded her that her right hand was useless. Her left crossed her body and tugged her holster open.

He sauntered onto the deck. "Hey, boss. How are you?"

The tension drained away. Her face brightened. "Watkins, I wasn't expecting you so soon." She kissed him on the cheek. "You have medical approval to come back?"

"I've been bugging the doctor for weeks, and this afternoon she gave me the go-ahead. When I showed up at the precinct, they sent me to the chief. So now we're both working out of the oh-eight. Dietz told me where to find you."

"You don't mind working with me?"

"Are you kidding? You're my hero. Thanks for requesting me. I'm on restricted duty, but the chief said you could use a friendly face and the support of an experienced detective."

Bless you, Harry, for sending someone I know I can trust.

"We really could use the help. Parker, my trainee, lost it a few minutes ago, from the stress, I think."

"I heard. It sounds like maybe you're a little stressed too."

She shrugged. "Could be."

The waiter brought their food and took Watkins's order. Parker barreled in as the waiter was walking away from the table. Focused on what she wanted to say and dodging the waiter, she didn't notice the man seated at the table until she joined them.

"Detective P.J. Parker meet Detective Ron Watkins."

He leaned over with his hand outstretched. "Parker. Glad to meet you and happy to be joining the team."

She shook his hand. "Nice to meet you too," she said, swallowing the lump in her throat. *Joining the team? Where did this guy come from and how come he's available all of a sudden?*

Corelli twirled some pasta on her fork. "Let's eat. Watkins can catch up when his food arrives. We'll brief him when we're finished."

Parker sipped her iced tea but didn't touch her polenta or salad.

Corelli swallowed then lifted her chin toward Parker's dinner. "Better chow down. Ya never know when you'll get another chance."

When Watkins's food arrived, Corelli moved her almost full plate aside and turned to Parker. "Surprised to see Watkins?"

Damn right. "Um," Parker said, her mouth full. *I can't even have the dignity of being the one to walk away. Corelli is dumping me first.*

"Watkins came off sick leave today. He caught a bullet in the shoulder in a shootout and was supposed to be out for at least another month, but he convinced his doctor to let him come back on restricted duty."

Restricted duty; not my replacement. I'm still in. If I want to be. Better make up my mind.

She forced herself to listen as Corelli reviewed the case for Watkins. Her presentation was organized, clear and logical. Had she studied the law? Now, with her anger and anxiety under control, Parker got that it was still early and they were doing what needed to be done. She watched Watkins. His soft, hazel eyes focused on Corelli's face as she talked, giving her his full attention, as if they were the only two people in the world. Occasionally he asked a question and made notes in a small, black leather notebook. No wedding ring. She'd felt calluses on the tips of his long, graceful fingers when they shook hands. *Probably plays the guitar.* Good looking. A sharp dresser—black pants, black silk shirt, black jacket, black shoes. Everything expensive. About 6'1" or 6'2" and very laid-back. His voice was mellow and educated. She gathered he'd worked with Corelli before and was happy to work with her again. *Am I doing something to cause Corelli to attack me?* She'd see how things went the rest of the night and then decide about getting out.

Corelli finished the review. "When we're done here, Parker and I are going to interview the Wall Street bartender and the night porter at Winter's building. Do either of you have a problem meeting every morning at seven, starting tomorrow?" Hearing no objection, she continued. "We'll meet at the oh-eight. And to be sure they don't doctor our coffee, I'll bring it and my extra coffeemaker. Bring your own breakfast, and milk if you need it. One other thing," Corelli said, fingering the scabs on the side of her face. "I'm told that my old friend Detective Jimmy McGivens announced that my being dead would make him very happy. Righteous Partners, the group of dirty cops, has tried to kill me twice, so they may come after you. Stay alert."

Watkins touched his shoulder holster as if to confirm it was still there. "I noticed you went for your gun but didn't draw when I surprised you. And I see your hand is pretty swollen. You need someone to ride with you, boss?"

"I have someone. Let's all watch our backs, okay?"

Someone? Me? A replacement?

When they settled the check and rose to leave, Parker saw she was right about Watkins's height, but the gracefulness of his movements surprised her. Detective Smoothie seemed to glide.

Outside, Watkins clicked his remote. "See you tomorrow," he said as he slid into a BMW parked in front of their standard issue.

Parker shivered despite the heat. She got into the car expecting Corelli to tear her to shreds over her tantrum.

CHAPTER FOURTEEN

Corelli tapped on Parker's window and waited for her to lower it. "Wall Street is only a few blocks from here. Let's walk. I'm stiff from my fall and being cooped up all day hasn't helped."

Here it comes. She doesn't want me driving when she lets me have it. *Will she dump me? You were going to dump her, weren't you? Yes, but with good reason.* At least she'd still be a detective. But forget homicide.

"Sure, I could use a stretch myself." She slid out of the car effortlessly. Except for the crushing fear constricting her chest, she felt light and free without the encumbrance of the heavy police paraphernalia she had worn for seven years. She really wanted homicide and would even put up with Corelli's shit to stay.

They walked in silence. The evening was warm but not as humid as the day, with a soft breeze and the smell of the East River unexpectedly pleasant. Even limping, Corelli set a good pace, arms swinging, taking deep breaths. Parker kept up but couldn't find the pleasure in it. The tension was excruciating. She felt as if she couldn't get enough air, as if she had been running for a long time.

Corelli interrupted her thoughts. "Let's start with the bartender. You question him."

"Sure." Wasn't Corelli going to say anything about her meltdown or tell her about the new someone?

And then it was there in front of them, The Wall Street Oasis. Inside it was quiet, only the bartender and four women sitting at a round table with popcorn and drinks in front of them. The women checked them out but weren't interested. The bartender, on the other hand, put his book down and watched as they crossed the room to where he stood behind the bar. He was young, probably about twenty-five, with brown hair that flopped on both sides of his face to his jaw where it ran into a droopy brown mustache.

He glanced at their shields then stared at Corelli. "I know you. You're that cop who got a conscience and turned in her friends, right?"

"Can it." Corelli's voice was hard and she looked ready to punch him.

He put his hands up as if to ward off an attack. "Sorry, I didn't mean anything."

Not wanting this to escalate, Parker took control. "Chip around?"

His head swiveled to her and his hand went to his mustache. "That's me. What's up?"

Parker had expected a bartender to be older. "Do you know Rino Martucci?"

"Martucci? No."

"Chauffeur? Works for Connie Winter. He says he comes in here sometimes."

"Oh, you mean Rino?"

Parker put her hands on the bar and leaned in. "Don't fool with me when I'm talking to you." Her voice sounded harsh even to her. "Or we'll take this conversation to the station."

"Sorry, sorry. Yeah, I know Rino."

"Was he here Friday night?"

"Is this about his boss, Miss Winter?"

Parker slipped onto the barstool. "What do you know about that?"

"Everybody was talking about it when I came in tonight." He pulled on his mustache and chewed his top lip for a minute.

"Fridays are slow in the summer. Most people leave before three to beat the weekend traffic, so I was alone when Rino came in about nine o'clock, all wet and wrinkled. He was in a foul mood, cursing Connie, he called her, for treating him like shit. He ordered a double Johnny Walker Black straight up and sucked it down in one gulp before ordering another. Then Mihailo, the night guy over at 63 Wall, came in for his usual—"

"The night porter was here?" Parker said.

"Yeah. He comes in every night between nine and nine thirty. He sat next to Rino and the two of them began commiserating about Ms. Winter. Mihailo hates her because she's trying to get him fired for drinking on the job, and Rino bitches about the way she treats him. Anyway they were making a racket cursing her, and after one of them said something about wringing her neck, a guy that had just come in stood in the doorway and gaped at them."

"Someone you know?"

"Never saw him before. Kinda short, jowly face. After a minute or two he moved close to those two and at first I thought he knew Rino, but he just stood there listening. I tried to catch his eye but he never ordered anything."

He picked up a rag and wiped the already-clean bar. Sensing he was struggling to decide what to say next, Parker remained silent. And hoped she wasn't screwing up.

"Um, Rino called earlier. He didn't want me to tell you this, but he left around nine thirty."

"And the porter?"

"I hadn't realized he was already loaded when he came in, so after the first round, I refused to serve him and he stumbled out a little after Rino."

"What about the other guy?"

"Um, he left right after Rino too."

"So Rino wasn't here until closing?"

"He showed up again, about eleven, really flying. I served him another double, but then I realized how far gone he was, and I cut him off. He fell asleep at the bar. I couldn't leave him here when I closed, so I found his keys and half carried him to the limo across the street, opened the windows a little, put the key in the ignition, and locked the doors."

"What time?"

"Twelve thirty, quarter-to-one. Then I got on the subway to Brooklyn."

"And—"

"Wait, I haven't finished," Chip said. He paused, clearly enjoying his moment in the spotlight. "When I got home I noticed a stain on my shirt, red, like blood. I think I got it from holding Rino."

Chip thought the shirt was still in the laundry basket in his room, so they arranged for a police cruiser to drive him home and pick it up when he closed. That done, they crossed the street to find Mihailo Jovanovic, the porter at Winter's building.

CHAPTER FIFTEEN

They rang the night bell. A few minutes later, a man Corelli assumed was Mihailo Jovanovic staggered out of the elevator and stumbled toward the glass door. When he opened it, the reek of alcohol confirmed he had already made his nightly visit to the Oasis.

"Whatchu girls want so late?"

Parker pulled the door closed as they moved into the lobby.

Corelli gagged and stepped back to escape his body odor. "Are you Mihailo Jovanovic?" She displayed her shield and Jovanovic recoiled like a vampire confronted with a cross. Parker must have caught a whiff of him, because she found a mop and pail to prop the door open, letting in the fresh night air.

He hitched his drooping pants over his protruding belly and attempted to tuck in his stained shirt, but he only managed to push his pants down again. "What you want? I don't do nothing wrong."

Winter had one thing right. This guy should be fired. "We're here about Connie Winter."

"That bitch? Is dead." He wiped his nose on his sleeve.

Corelli glanced at Parker who had backed up closer to the door. "Yes. And where were you Friday night?"

He didn't say anything.

She had to interview this smelly, drunken asshole, but she didn't have to do it on his schedule. She moved into his space. "Mr. Jovanovic, we can interview you here or at the police station. It's up to you. But decide fast, or we'll bring you in."

"Okay, okay. What?"

Corelli turned toward the door, hoping for some fresh air, and caught Parker grinning. She scowled and turned back to Jovanovic. "Start with Friday when you got to work."

He stared at the ground. Corelli pulled out her handcuffs. He raised his hand to stop her.

"I come at four o'clock and clean offices."

"Which offices?"

"In basement: Manager of building, security, locker room for guards, mailrooms for businesses like Winter Brokerage, messenger delivery office and garbage room." He closed his mouth, thinking he was finished.

"Then?"

"Seven o'clock everybody goes home. I lock front door and go to finish clean in basement. Last I come to lobby. Here, I sweep, polish marble floor and walls, shine glass doors and windows, and," he pointed to the fixtures high on the walls, "dust lights. Then, I carry garbage out of elevators after cleaning woman put there and vacuum elevators."

"What time did you lock up on Friday?"

"Seven, like usual."

"And what time did you go to the Oasis?"

"I never—"

"Don't waste your breath. We know you were there Friday night."

He scratched his stomach. "Well, sometimes, if I go, about nine, but always I lock the door."

"That's not what I heard. Didn't Ms. Winter want you fired because you often left the door unlocked?"

His eyelids fluttered. A sheen of sweat appeared on his upper lip. "The bitch want me fired because I go to Oasis sometimes for a drink. What's it to her? It's late. Nobody comes. Always I lock door so nobody gets in."

Self-pity creeping into his voice, Mihailo said, "Night is not easy. I must do everything. No big deal if sometimes I forget to lock the door when I go take a piss or bring garbage out. Like I tell other cop, I have much to do."

"What cop?"

"Comes to see the bitch, always is late night."

"Do you know his name?"

He shrugged. "He puts gun to my head and pushes badge in my face, but his name, no. He says to arrest me if I leave door open, so I always close."

"Describe him."

"Better I don't see too much, so I keep eyes down. I see Mr. Tough Guy wear high-heel shoes like girl. He's big and mean. Pain in my ass."

"Was he here Friday night?"

"Not Friday."

"How do you know he didn't come in when you weren't here?"

"He not ring bell."

"You're absolutely sure you locked the door Friday night? And don't lie. We'll find out."

Mihailo opened his mouth and then closed it. "Yes. I remember. I use key when I come back from Oasis. I stay only a little time, until maybe nine thirty, because that Rino is yelling about her. He gives me a headache. Talk to him. He hate her."

"Did anyone come in or go out after seven on Friday?"

"Nobody. Everybody goes home early Friday. Only me, I work."

"What did you do when you came back from the Oasis?"

"I go to sleep. Two o'clock I wake up and go home."

"Did you turn off the air-conditioner on Winter's side of the building?"

He jingled the change in his pocket. "Friday I forget garbage in elevator. But air-conditioner I always turn off when I leave to save money."

"Are you sure about Friday night?"

His eyes began to move again, searching for help.

"Yes, I remember, after I wake up."

"That's not what we heard."

He looked over her shoulder. "Who said?"

They were silent.

He hiked his pants. Still not looking at her, he said, "Is possible I forgot."

"And is it possible you forgot to lock the door?"

She could smell his fear. "Not Friday. I remember. Is sure I lock."

"Can anyone confirm the time you got home Friday night?"

"No. For two months now, I live alone. The other bitch, my wife, goes because she says I drink too much. Like she knows anything."

He clasped his hands over his belly, waiting for the next question. When it didn't come, he became uneasy, then alarmed. "I didn't do nothin' to the bitch."

"We'll see about that, Mr. Jovanovic. Don't even think about leaving town."

It was late and Wall Street was empty. The sound of their heels echoed in the silence. Now that they were alone again, Parker's anxiety returned. Her whole body clenched. *Would Corelli dump her now?* She glanced to the side, attempting to read Corelli's expression but then Corelli bumped her shoulder. Intentionally.

"Don't think I didn't notice you grinning while I desperately tried to interview Jovanovic without breathing. If I'd known he was so stinky, I would have had you interview him instead of Chip."

Parker didn't know what to make of Corelli's teasing tone of voice. "Yes, I'm sure you would have." That sounded too serious. "But watching you choke was the highlight of my day." *Oops, she didn't intend to sound hostile?* She bumped Corelli back to let her know she was teasing. This was more like it. Parker glanced at Corelli. Was she was smiling?

"Unfortunately for you, I survived."

Parker didn't know what to say to that so she inhaled deeply taking in the fishy smell of the nearby river and hoped they would go back to the teasing.

Suddenly Corelli put her arm out, stopping them both. "Make a note. We need to find out if anybody else saw this so-called cop."

Parker nodded. "I did."

Corelli tipped an imaginary hat. "You believe he locked the door?"

"No."

"Neither do I. So for now, we'll assume he didn't." Parker nodded but didn't comment.

Corelli resumed walking.

Parker tried to get a reading on Corelli's mood but they were marching to some internal Corelli beat and it was hard to see her face. She cleared her throat, wanting to speak but afraid.

"You okay?"

Damn. Put the slightest feeling out there and Corelli tunes into it. *Own it P.J. It's the only way to get what you want, which, at this moment, is to continue to work with her, despite the difficulty.* "I'm sorry about my tantrum earlier. I was really out of line. I would understand if you replaced me with Watkins or whoever you have that's going to watch your back, but I hope you won't." Parker was glad her voice didn't waver. She wasn't begging, just making a statement.

Corelli stopped walking and studied her face in the shadowy streetlight.

"Where did you get the idea that I was going to replace you with Watkins…or anyone else for that matter?"

"Well, I know I screwed up and now that an experienced detective is available, I thought—"

"That's your first mistake of the day. I'm supposed to do the thinking and you're supposed to do the learning."

"But I—"

Corelli's eyes pierced Parker, and, as if she could see the anxiety gripping her heart, she continued. "It's only been a day but so far you're doing fine. I don't need anyone else. I trust you to watch my back and your own. You don't need to feel threatened by Watkins. I have no plans to replace you. And, if I feel it necessary to replace you, rest assured that I will discuss it with you before I take any action."

Parker felt the tension drain. She'd stay in homicide and try not to let Corelli's condescension and ridicule get to her.

"And by the way, you did very well on both of your solo interviews. Relax."

"You're…You're not mad about what I said?"

"Nah, I'm not mad. I'm tired and you probably are too." She glanced around as if afraid someone would hear her. "I'll deny it if you quote me, but I deserved it. I'm sorry." She started walking.

Parker was flabbergasted. The last thing she expected from Corelli was an apology.

After a few minutes, they reached the car. "Drop me off and go get some sleep."

In a swirl of mixed emotions, Parker started the car but didn't give it gas. "Uh, could I have some, er, directions? I don't know where you live."

"What kind of detective are you?" Corelli snorted. "Do I have to tell you everything?"

Parker smiled. "I guess I have a lot to learn. When do we get to mind reading?"

They laughed together. It felt good, more like what Parker had expected.

Corelli rested her head against the seat. "West Side Highway to Fourteenth Street. I live in the Meat Packing district, at the edge of Greenwich Village, almost in the Hudson River."

Ah, the "in" neighborhood where former meat packing factories had been converted into apartments, and fancy restaurants and stores existed side-by-side with the occasional building that still served butchers. When she was in the DA's office, she'd gone there for breakfast with a group that had worked all night. The neighborhood was in transition then, and they'd strolled between the refrigerated trucks loading and unloading sides of beef. Now the Meat Packing district was a hot area.

"There." Parker stopped near the building Corelli indicated. Corelli got out and stretched, and then leaned back in. "Goodnight. Six thirty tomorrow morning."

Parker sat with the motor running and watched Corelli walk to the door, noticing that her limp was nearly gone. Suddenly the door of a parked car swung open. Parker was on the street with her gun drawn and her mouth open to shout, when Corelli put her hand up to stop her. Corelli turned and embraced the woman who was holding a shopping bag in each hand. They kissed briefly— on the lips. Corelli waved to Parker and led the woman into the building.

Parker holstered her gun. *Well, Detective Parker, your detecting skills need some work. That charged interview with Cummings wasn't anything unusual. Detective Corelli is a lesbian.*

CHAPTER SIXTEEN

"Were you waiting long, Gianna?"

"You arrived just after I parked."

Since Corelli had emerged from undercover, her sisters had been dropping in late at night to check on her. They both had keys to the apartment, so if she wasn't there, they waited or left the food they'd brought for her.

"You didn't come to the christening party yesterday so I saved some of your favorites." She began to unpack the smaller shopping bag. "Lasagna, stuffed artichokes, eggplant, arancini—"

"Why bring me all this?" *So much food, so little appetite.*

"I thought you'd be less likely to starve if you could just heat and eat."

"I *can* take care of myself, you know." She'd been on her own since she was eighteen. Trying to hide her anger, she pulled a bottle of pinot grigio from the refrigerator, poured a glass and drank half.

Gianna flushed. "Of course. That's why you look like a scarecrow. That's why every piece of clothing you own hangs on you. That's why you look like a teenage gangsta wannabe in those jeans."

Gianna, her sweet-tempered sister who never raised her voice, spat out the words. Shocked, Corelli pivoted.

Tears glittered in Gianna's eyes. "Really, Chiara, I'm so worried about you. I'm afraid you're anorexic."

Corelli pulled Gianna close. "I'm sorry. I know you're trying to take care of me, but I'm trying to deal with…everything. I just need time."

"You say you're fine, Chiara, but you won't talk about Iraq or Afghanistan. You won't talk about seeing Marnie killed, about missing her. You won't talk about being undercover, and you won't talk about being ostracized. You're not fine. You need help. I think you have Post Traumatic Stress Disorder."

Corelli dropped her arms. *PTSD?*

"And that motorcycle scares me. I read that California veterans of Iraq and Afghanistan were five and a half times as likely to die in a motorcycle accident as Californians of the same age with no military service."

"Damn it, Gianna, you know I've been riding motorcycles since I was sixteen. Marnie and I used to ride together all the time. Why do you think riding now means I'm suicidal? Just like I could've been killed in combat or on the job, I could be killed on the road. It happens. Why the hell are you wasting your time reading horror stories about vets?"

"Because I love you. Because you and I could always talk about everything, but now you explode any time I try to have a real conversation. Because I see what's happening even if you don't or won't admit it. Promise me you'll talk to a therapist."

"I promise I'll think about it."

Gianna studied her. "I'm serious."

Corelli threw her hands up in frustration. "I said I'd think about it."

"Yell all you want. You don't scare me." Gianna moved the biscotti, *struffoli*, and the bows to the table. "And, I'm not going to stop pushing you."

"Whatever." Chiara moved the rest of the food to the refrigerator. "Did Mama and Papa know you were bringing the food to me?"

"They watched me pack it, and Mama added your favorites— the bows that *Zia* Rosaria made and the biscotti and *struffoli* she made—but they didn't ask. So I stuck to my 'don't ask, don't tell' policy."

She glanced at Corelli to see if she had gotten the military reference.

Corelli smiled. "Espresso?"

The middle of the five Corelli children, Gianna was the peacemaker in the family, wanting everybody to be happy together. Sometimes she reminded Corelli of one of those little border collies frantically shepherding everyone toward home, running after strays and nipping at their ankles to bring them back to the herd.

"Decaf." Gianna pointed at the shopping bag she'd left near the door. "Zia Maria finished taking in three of your suits. The rest will be ready in a few days."

"It will be nice to have something more professional than these baggy jeans to wear."

"You could afford to buy new suits."

"Yes, my dear sister, but then I'd have to go shopping in crowded stores, on crowded streets with lots of noise. And you know I hate to shop."

Gianna watched her move around the kitchen. "You didn't always."

Corelli shrugged. "I do now." She poured the espresso, rubbed lemon peel on the lip of her demitasse cup and bit into a bow. The fried dough with honey was her favorite dessert.

"You should be with the family when we get together." Gianna broke off a piece of biscotti. "We laugh and talk but underneath there's a sadness. I miss you. Everybody does."

"I went to the church for the christening even though Patrizia didn't invite me." Her oldest sister wanted Chiara to be like her—a married woman tending her husband and children. Patrizia had loved Marnie and knew they were lovers, but paradoxically she hated that Chiara was a lesbian, a cop, and an independent woman.

"But you should have gone to the party too."

"Didn't I cause enough trouble at the church? Father Alfredo was ready to excommunicate me, and I thought Patrizia would fly over the pews and bite my head off when she realized it was my phone ringing."

"You know Patrizia. All bark and all bite."

Corelli smiled at Gianna's little joke about their critical sister. She chewed slowly, enjoying the crunch and the sweetness. "You and Marco and the kids are my family, Gianna. I feel accepted and loved by you. And you gave me the gift of Simone, for which I bless you. Our little sister would have grown up without knowing me if it wasn't for you."

Gianna nibbled her biscotti. "Why don't you talk to Mama and Papa? Make up? I'll go with you. Simone too."

Corelli pulled her legs up on the chair and wrapped her arms around them. She stared into the room. "It's up to them. Until they accept me for who I am, accept the work I do and the life I choose to live, there's no making up. He's the one who called me *putane*, whore, and disowned me when I enlisted in the army. He's the one who denigrates my life as a lesbian and a detective."

"He can't help himself, Chiara. His values are old country. We spent so many summers there. You saw it yourself. A daughter only leaves home to get married or to be buried, and even then, only with her father's permission." Gianna snorted. "At least to get married."

"He's lived in America longer than he lived in Sicily. The world has changed. He should have changed. Uncle Gennaro was older than him, yet he accepted me totally. He adored Marnie and was proud that we were both cops and in the military." She was agitated now and got up to pace. "Papa can't accept that I do work that men do, and I'm not dependent on a man. You and I both know we would still be one big happy family if, instead of leaving home after high school, I'd married Ettore from his village, even though he became a Mafioso. Better to have a killer in the family than an independent woman." She walked to the sink for a glass of water. "Okay, that thing about the killer is an exaggeration, but you know what I mean."

"I know you're dealing with a lot right now. I didn't mean to pressure you. But my heart aches for you and I'm selfish. I want you back in the family where you belong. Sometimes I think he wants to make up, but he doesn't know how."

"He'll have to figure it out. Don't worry, Gianna. I just need time to deal with losing Marnie, with the war, with the undercover work. I feel very lucky to have you and Simone and Marco and the kids in my life. And *chi sa?* Who knows? Maybe there'll be a miracle that will change Papa's mind. I can wait."

It was after midnight when Gianna left, but Corelli was wide awake. She lit some candles, shut off the lights, and lay on the sofa thinking about Brett Cummings. She had never felt such an intense attraction to anyone, not even Marnie whom she'd loved and planned to grow old with. Marnie, who laughed and teased about Chiara being the commander-in-chief of the lesbian old age community they would move into when they were eighty. Now Marnie was dead and Chiara's body was betraying her. She felt as if she had swallowed a hallucinatory drug, her feelings surging and swelling unexpectedly right beneath the surface, her senses heightened. But it had been a long time since she'd felt so alive. Maybe Gianna was right about her having PTSD. Maybe that's why she'd reacted so strongly to Cummings and why she was having flashbacks.

Whatever the reason, it was too soon to feel this way about another woman. If she ignored the attraction it would go away—eventually. She stared at the candles. In desperation she clicked on the television, hoping that, as usual, the TV would lull her to sleep, but that was not to be. There on her sixty-inch screen in living color was Senator Aloysius T. Parker. Half expecting him to attack her, she sat up and increased the volume. For the first time ever, she listened instead of tuning him out. He was passionate, talking about the inequities in society, that it wasn't fair, it wasn't the American Way, for people to lose their jobs, lose their homes, and struggle to eat while Wall Street executives and bankers received millions in salaries and bonuses. He attacked with the same passion he brought to his rants about brutality and racism in the police department. She agreed about the economy and sometimes he was right about the department. Maybe he wasn't all bad but growing up with a father like him would've been no bed of roses. *At least my father, as old-fashioned and prejudiced as he is, doesn't go on television to convince the world he knows the right way.*

She looked for his daughter in him, but the buttoned-down P.J. Parker was cool and cerebral. She showed none of her father's passion or his messy in your face aggressiveness, nor his short, chubby, dark looks. She fell asleep musing about fathers and daughters.

CHAPTER SEVENTEEN

With Corelli deposited safely at home with her lesbian lover, Parker drove uptown to Hattie's Harlem Inn on 125ᵗʰ Street. After the emotional see-saw of the day, she needed the comfort and straight thinking of her godfather, Captain Jesse Isaacs. Unlike the senator, who criticized everything she did, Jesse supported her choices and encouraged her to follow her heart. But this time her heart seemed to have led her astray. Maybe Jesse could help her understand what had possessed her to agree to work with the most hated and, as it turned out, the craziest and most difficult detective in the department. Then since she was going to hang in with Corelli, maybe he could help her figure out how best to deal with her.

As usual, Hattie's was dimly lit, crowded and noisy. Parker hesitated in the entryway and shivered as the cold air chilled her sweaty skin. Wrinkling her nose at the familiar smell of beer, cigarettes, and fried foods that permeated the wood-paneled walls and wooden floor, she scanned the crowd for Jesse. Although she couldn't make out his features, she recognized his silhouette standing at the bar, the biggest guy there at six-four. The bartender leaned in and said something and Jesse turned to watch her weave through the crowd toward him. He smiled and pulled her close for a hug, crushing her face against his chest. With him the physical contact was only mildly uncomfortable, and she hugged him back. When she couldn't tolerate it any longer, she pushed away. He ordered her a beer and they grabbed an empty table.

"How are you, Detective Parker?" he asked. "Things working out with Detective Corelli?"

"I think so."

"What's happening?"

She gazed at the musicians, and Jesse being Jesse, sipped his drink and listened to the music, giving her space. When she started, he listened without interrupting.

"Why would the chief pick me to protect her? There are probably lots of big strong guys, more experienced detectives that would be better."

Jesse examined her face. "The chief's no fool, and it's no accident that he picked you. He and Corelli go back a long time. He probably feels responsible for sucking her into that undercover assignment. You know most cops would have turned it down, too dangerous, too much to lose or too afraid how other cops would treat them. She's a courageous, dedicated detective, and she did a great job smoking a lot of the rats out of the nest. But some of the biggest rats are still out there. So who do you trust to protect you if you're surrounded by lots of rats, and you can't distinguish those who would be happy to see you dead from the others?"

"I didn't think of it like that."

"The chief considered a lot of detectives before settling on you. He rightly feels you have the makings of a good detective. Even your problems connecting with the other cops at the precinct and having Aloysius for your father were attractive because they meant you weren't tied in. He particularly liked your bravery and cool head under fire."

She stared at him, wanting to believe it. Then she frowned. "How come you know so much about what he liked?"

"He ran it by me. I almost lied so you wouldn't get the assignment, but I figured it should be your decision. It's dangerous but it's an opportunity to learn from the best and prove yourself in homicide. Just don't get yourself killed."

"Corelli is off the wall. She needs me, yet she's needling and condescending, almost like she wants me to dump her."

He seemed lost in thought, then he nodded. "You should Google her, if you haven't already. She's been through a lot, tours in Iraq and Afghanistan followed by the undercover assignment from hell. She's lost a lot and given up a lot. Now it's her against the whole department. Maybe she needs proof that you're committed and that she can trust you."

"I'm not sure I can trust *her*. She's so erratic. Just when I'm about to tell her to shove it and leave her to deal with her own shit, she says or does something nice."

Jesse chuckled. "Don't let that Parker pride, what some would call arrogance, get in the way of this opportunity. Her behavior may be hard to take because you tend to observe rather than join in and get dirty, but it sounds to me like she's treating you as an equal, or at least as she would any trainee."

"If this is participating, I haven't been missing anything," Parker snorted. "I've decided to force myself to tolerate her harassment, but it'll be difficult to do the job successfully because she doesn't think she needs to be protected."

He grinned. "Just be your usual stubborn, persistent self and she'll have no choice. She's got a lot to teach you, P.J. Working with her might not be easy but it will be good for you. But you be careful. Watch both your backs. Remember these guys are stone-cold killers."

CHAPTER EIGHTEEN

At four thirty in the morning when Corelli hit the street it was still dark. She loved this time of day, before the rest of New York woke up and the early morning air felt cool and fresh and soft. In a little while the few wholesale meat markets still operating in her neighborhood would raise their iron gates, ready for business, and the huge refrigerated trucks would back in to load, but right now it was quiet and safe. After stretching, she jogged at an easy pace to work the stiffness out of her knee, crossed West Street to the Greenway path and turned left toward lower Manhattan and Ms. Liberty. It was quiet except for the sound of an occasional car, the gentle sucking of the Hudson as it smacked and receded from the retaining wall, and her own steady breathing.

Relaxing into the run, she picked up speed. A sudden movement ahead, behind the trees on the right, caught her eye. She tensed but controlled the impulse to turn back. She readied the pepper spray and increased her speed, hoping to sprint past whoever it was or blind them. But she miscalculated and smashed into a full-sized poodle running off leash. The dog yapped and dashed away. Corelli staggered forward but regained her balance, checking for damage to her knee as she continued running downtown toward Battery Park and the statue in the harbor. Happy that she hadn't used the pepper spray on the dog, she focused on her breathing and lost herself in the pleasure of running.

Forty-five minutes later when she approached her street again, it was no longer night but not quite morning. The blood-red claws of dawn slashed the gray-black sky. She slowed her pace, switched into cooldown mode, and greeted the early joggers and dog walkers emerging from the shadowy streets like zombies gliding to their crypts.

She dashed across West Street and walked to her building. Except for the familiar hum of the refrigerated trucks now backed up to the loading docks, the street was empty and quiet. At her door, she wiped the sweat from her forehead with the bottom of her tank top, shifted the pepper spray to her left hand, and knelt to remove the key to her building from the bag attached to her running shoe. She stood and put the key in the lock. A hand grabbed her shoulder and spun her around. As she pivoted, she switched the pepper spray back to her right hand, clenched it, and using the momentum of the spin to increase the force behind her swing, hit a face. Hard. She heard a crack and a scream. Another hand grabbed her from behind, spun her again, and punched her in the stomach. She crumpled to the ground.

Two of them stood over her, wearing ski masks. One clutched his nose, the other pointed a gun at her. She couldn't see the blood, but she smelled it and felt the wet, warm drops splattering her body. The bleeder lifted his leg to kick her. Someone yelled. "Hey. What're you guys doing?" Their heads swiveled toward the voice. She rolled over, jumped to her feet, and squirted the pepper spray, first at the one with the gun and then at the other. With the pepper spray container still in her fist, she hit the one holding the gun in the face and was rewarded with the sound of what she hoped was his nose breaking too and another scream, "Bitch."

The men staggered toward the street. Still gasping for air, she leaned against the building and with her left hand yanked her backup gun from the ankle holster under her pant leg. Four people with dogs in tow having a heated discussion walked in front of her, cutting her off from the street. She heard a motor rev and the screech of tires. When the group had passed, she saw the goons tumbling into a van. She sighted the tires as the car peeled away, but her left hand was not nearly as accurate as the right so she lowered her gun rather than endanger the people on the street.

"You okay, Detective Corelli?"

It was George Lopez, one of the guys from the packing house up the street, someone she had chatted with from time to time.

"Thanks to you."

"It took me a minute to make out what was happening, you know, them wearing masks and all. But when that guy pointed the gun at you, I knew I couldn't get to you in time, so I yelled, hoping to scare them."

"You saved my life, George. I owe you a drink, or two or three. Can I send someone over for your statement later this morning?"

"I'm here until two. Were they trying to rob you?"

"Something like that."

CHAPTER NINETEEN

Parker took Jesse's advice. When she got home, she Googled Corelli. There were lots of articles and though she felt a little like a stalker, Parker realized that knowing about Corelli might help her understand her. So she started reading. And was surprised that the only negative articles were the recent ones about the undercover assignment. Parker made notes as she read.

Corelli had joined the army right out of high school for the training and the educational benefits. She served in the military police. She was a twenty-four-year-old New York City police officer when the World Trade Center attack occurred in September 2001. Although she was off-duty that day, she, along with many other police, firemen, and EMTs, rushed to the aide of the people working in those buildings, and she barely escaped before the first building came down. *Sixteen years later and she's still having flashbacks.*

Soon after 9/11, despite having already completed her four-year commitment to the army, Corelli signed up to go to Iraq. After two combat tours of duty she returned home in 2006, rejoined the police force, and completed her college education at night. She'd received a Silver Star for rescuing members of her unit during an insurgent ambush on their convoy. *Damn. It was hard not to admire the woman.*

Corelli was promoted to detective in 2011, right before she signed up for a tour in Afghanistan during the 2011 surge. In February, 2016 she went back to Afghanistan with a contingent of NYPD officers to train Afghani police. They were there twelve months and they were attacked three times. Two members of the training force were killed in an ambush. The group returned to New York City mid-March 2017 and, at the beginning of April, Corelli went undercover in her old precinct.

Parker put her pen down. *I can't even begin to imagine what she's seen. No wonder she's crazy.* There was a lot of information about her NYPD career, cases she'd solved, killers she'd captured, and people she'd saved. *Impressive. But still not carte blanche to be rude and nasty.*

Resolving not to let Corelli goad her today, Parker drove up to Corelli's building at six thirty. In the early morning light, she could see Corelli lived in a converted industrial building that occupied the entire square block. She searched the listing of tenants and pushed the button next to Corelli's name. Her faraway voice said, "Yes?" Parker's name generated a buzz that unlocked the door to the lobby, and Corelli's disembodied voice said, "Come up to eight. I need your help."

Help with what? Maybe carry the coffeepot? She felt the familiar surge of anger but caught herself. She would smile and carry the damn pot if that's what Corelli needed her to do. She pressed eight, the top floor, and as the elevator moaned and creaked its way up, she wondered whether the lesbian girlfriend would be there.

The elevator opened in the apartment, indicating that Corelli had the entire floor, the size of a city block. Parker gaped. Actually, it was only half the floor, so half a city block, but still enormous. And what a spectacular floor it was. A huge expanse of uninterrupted space drenched in sunlight streaming in through the tall windows on three sides. Comfortable-looking sectional couches and easy chairs were arranged in groupings with areas defined by vividly colored Indian, African, and Middle Eastern rugs. The same colors appeared in the tapestries and paintings hung on the white walls and in the cushions piled on the floor and scattered on the furniture. It was dazzling.

The open kitchen was magazine gorgeous, with copper pots and pans hanging on a ceiling rack, granite counters and oak cabinets surrounding an island. One could easily cook dinner for an army on the stove. Corelli, or maybe her girlfriend, must be a cook.

Corelli stood in the kitchen, her smile competing with the sunlight. "Like it?"

"Wow, it's…I'm…It's so bright. Really alive and…yet peaceful." *Different than the Winter house, that's for sure.* She hadn't given it much thought, but based on her impression of Corelli, Parker would have imagined her in a dank, depressing studio, with broken-down furniture in a rundown building, or something like her own sunless one-bedroom apartment that had seemed so luxurious when she moved in ten years ago. Now she had to rethink her assessment of Corelli. An apartment like this must cost a fortune. How could she afford it on a detective's salary?

Corelli expelled that relaxed throaty sound she made when she laughed and said, "Come in. Help yourself to coffee."

Corelli's hair was loose, swirling around her face and tumbling down her back. Made her look…sexy, softer, like she'd just tumbled out of bed, but she was pale, holding her right arm close to her body.

"You all right? You're kind of…white."

"I'm fine, but I had another encounter with my friends this morning. They got in one solid stomach punch but I bested the two of them. Let me fill you in when we get to the office. I'll be ready in a minute."

Parker controlled her urge to shout but couldn't keep the anger out of her voice. "I thought we agreed that I would watch you. What's the chief—"

Corelli put her hand up, cutting Parker off. "It was stupid, but it won't happen again."

"What happened to your hand?" Parker asked, her voice rising. "It's all—"

"Parker." Corelli was smiling, but her voice warned to let it go. "I'll be ready in a few minutes."

Parker nodded. She urged herself to relax. She found a cup, took coffee, and sipped as she surveyed the loft, checking for signs of the mystery woman. She didn't find any. Corelli had gone into the bathroom, the only enclosed space on the floor. Judging by the bookcases and neat piles of books all around, Detective Corelli was a reader. A wall unit facing a sofa housed a TV and a sound system, with records and CDs neatly slotted into shelves underneath. An iPod was nestled in a unit attached to the system. Speakers hung high around the large open room. Parker itched to check out the music and the books. One could learn a lot about people that way, but she didn't want to be intrusive. Actually, she didn't want to get caught being intrusive.

Corelli came back into the living area with a towel in her hand. "Parker, I want to beat the...um, crowd to the station, so would you mind going downstairs?" She pointed to a staircase that Parker hadn't noticed. "And get my holster from the night table near the window in my bedroom and my gun and jacket from the bed, while I clean up here."

Downstairs? "No problem." *Her bedroom?* Even Corelli wouldn't be crass enough to send her in there if the mystery woman was in bed. Would she? Downstairs was the same size as upstairs, but enclosed rooms lined two of the walls. She started with the room with the open door, hesitated in the doorway and smiled. No mystery woman but lots of mysteries. Shelves filled with books and photos lined the walls, and both night tables had books stacked on them. Parker removed the holster from the night table, picked up the jacket, and moved to the opposite side of the bed. She stared at the gun on the pillow. *Damn, she really is one damaged woman.*

As Parker turned to leave, a photograph caught her eye. She lifted it off the night table. A smiling Corelli stood with her arms around a woman with glowing tawny skin, a mane of dark-hair, flashing dark eyes and a beautiful smile. Even dressed in camouflage they were stunning together. She put the picture back on the night table. Had the war turned the relaxed and happy Corelli in the photo into the tense and angry Corelli she knew? Was the dark-haired woman still in her life?

Looking for clues, Parker scanned the photographs in the bookcases. There was a picture of Corelli with her arm over the shoulder of a short, dark, attractive woman, probably last night's visitor. And another picture of Corelli surrounded by a group of men and women all in full battle gear, and several pictures of her with the lovely dark-haired woman, both laughing, hoisting beers and tossing a ball. *Corelli seems to favor dark-haired women. Maybe*

Cummings is the exception. She stretched to see the picture on a higher shelf and grinned at the very young, very serious, tough-looking Corelli in leather, standing with three equally tough-looking girls next to motorcycles.

She pulled herself away from Corelli's life and returned to the kitchen where Corelli had piled the things for the office and was rinsing the coffeepot. Parker held out the jacket and the holster and gun.

Corelli dried her hands. "I'm afraid I'm going to need your help with the holster. My hand is too swollen." She raised it as proof.

Parker flushed. She placed the jacket and the Glock on the table and stepped behind Corelli. She wrapped her arms and the holster around Corelli's waist and leaned forward to buckle it. Her face sank into Corelli's hair, which felt soft and smelled springy. She started to sweat and felt the familiar clutch in her gut. She closed the catch, picked up the gun, and slid it into the holster. She held the jacket while Corelli slipped it on. Relaxed now, Parker picked up the coffeemaker, coffee, and filters. *At least she's wearing clothing that fits this morning. Nice quality and she looks a thousand time better than she did yesterday in her gangsta outfit.*

"Um, Parker, I know this is an imposition, but I couldn't braid my hair this morning and I can't wear it loose. Would you mind twisting my hair and clipping it in place?" She held out a hair clip.

Parker put the coffee things down on the table. *Chief never said anything about personal slave.*

"Thanks."

"You're welcome." She squinted toward the window. "Doesn't the light bother you?"

"No, I love it. If it's too bright I close the blinds. I don't think I could live without light. I'd feel like a mole or something."

A dark cloud seemed to pass between Parker and the sunlight. *Or a rat, like me, running into my hole at night.*

CHAPTER TWENTY

They were early enough to avoid the gauntlet, but as they passed through the precinct, the uproar of everyday activity slowly wound down until the only sound was the ringing phones. Parker felt foolish carrying the coffeepot, and the anger rumbled in her belly, until she realized no one was looking at her. It was Corelli's name they whispered, and Corelli they showed their backs to. Parker glanced at Corelli who didn't seem to notice. Her face had more color than earlier, but she seemed relaxed and unaware of the stares and the backs as she led the way up the stairs to where Watkins waited. *How can she stand it?*

Watkins had taken the desk next to Corelli's, leaving Parker with the one facing her. While they settled, he got the coffee going, chattering all the while to Corelli and glancing at Parker to include her. He had already spread out some bagels and cream cheese on his desk.

He was easy with her. Clearly, they had worked together before.

"Watkins, I've already told Parker, but you need to know that two guys came after me when I went out to jog this morning."

"In broad daylight?" he asked, surprised.

Corelli looked sheepish. "Well, it was four thirty and still dark. For me it was morning, but I guess for them it was still night." She described the attack. "I think I might have broken both their noses." She removed the ice pack and examined her right hand. It was swollen, raw, and red with tinges of black and blue. "And, um, one guy pulled his gun on me, but some people came along and they got away before I could get them or the plate number."

Watkins and Parker exchanged glances. "Probably stolen anyway," Watkins concluded. "Did they say anything?"

"No."

Parker was incredulous. "Do you think they were going to kill you?"

"Seems likely." She sipped her coffee. "They'll try again for sure."

Damn. How could Corelli be so blasé? And how am I supposed to keep her safe?

"One of us should be with you all the time, even sleep at your place," Parker blurted without thinking. *Big mouth. Next I'll be offering to sleep between Corelli and the mystery woman.*

Corelli smirked. "You wanting to horn in on my sex life, Parker?"

Parker felt the blood rush to her face. "What? I —"

Corelli threw her hands up. "Kidding. Just kidding."

Parker imagined slamming Corelli with a bagel and smearing her with cream cheese to wipe that supercilious grin off her face.

"I'll use the treadmill until this passes. I'll be fine if you pick me up in the morning and watch me until I'm in at night." Corelli refilled her coffee and sat. "Ready?"

Detective Dietz came into the room, out of breath from the steps.

"Ah, Dietz, just in time." Corelli waved him to her side chair. "You'll be working with us so you might as well sit in while Parker brings Watkins to date on our conversations with Chip, the bartender, Rino Martucci, the chauffer, and Mihailo Jovanovic, the porter. Also, Parker share your impressions."

My impressions? Parker opened her notebook and took a minute to organize her thoughts. She felt their eyes on her. She took a breath and started. She presented her thoughts as if she was in front of judge and jury—logical, clear and concise. After discussing the bartender, she moved on to the night porter. As she talked, she noted Dietz nodding his head, Watkins listening attentively and Corelli smiling. She concluded, "Although Winter was trying to get Jovanovic fired, he seems more into self-pity than murder, and unless he killed her before he staggered over to the Oasis, he was probably too drunk to manage it. Besides, bad as he smells, I doubt she would have let him near her without a fight." She checked her notes. "On the other hand, we're still focused on him because we believe he's lying about locking the building door. If it was open, anybody could have walked in and murdered Winter."

She went over the chauffer's story. "He really seemed surprised to hear she was dead, but we still need to talk to him about the missing hour and a half and the blood on his shirt."

"Good work, Parker. Dietz I'd like you to help Watkins organize a team to do a thorough search of the thirty-fifth floor for the murder weapon. The search of the office garbage and the receptacles for the building as well as the baskets on the surrounding streets didn't turn up anything, so it probably wasn't tossed."

She waited while they made notes. "A couple of other things. Watkins, make arrangements for Gianopolus to identify his wife today. Drive him yourself and watch his reaction. And Dietz, send detectives to talk to Gertrude's doormen and Hornsby's neighbors."

Dietz looked up from his notes. "Gertrude is the sister-in-law, but who's Hornsby again?"

Parker responded. "Jennifer Hornsby is one of the senior officers in Winter's company."

Dietz nodded. "Sounds like a cast of thousands. Have you eliminated anybody yet?"

Parker glanced at Corelli and got a nod in answer to her unspoken question. "It's still very early but we have eliminated a few people. Three of the senior officers are out of the country. Terry O'Reilly is in Nepal and Lewis Brooks is in Japan and Karl Silver is in Hawaii, so they're clear. Her assistant, Sandra Edwards, seems unlikely but we should be able to confirm that today. And, as I said earlier, the porter probably couldn't get close enough to hit her without a struggle." Parker glanced at Corelli before continuing. "Right now, Brett Cummings is the only one who admits she was in the building around the time Winter was killed. She doesn't seem to have a motive, but unless we confirm the building door was open she might be our only suspect." Parker thought Corelli's face had colored at her comment but Corelli nodded as if she agreed. Parker was relieved.

Corelli stood. "Parker and I are going to search Winter's office again. Then we'll drive out to Sheepshead Bay to find out what the chauffeur was doing between nine thirty and eleven, a detail he conveniently left out of his story."

"Anything else?" Dietz said.

"Yes. Send a detective to take this guy's statement." She handed Dietz a slip with George Lopez's name and address. "George saved me from being killed this morning." She gave Dietz the short version of the morning attack.

Dietz picked up his folders. "If we're done here, Captain Winfry wants to see the three of you in his office."

He offered a quick two-finger salute and walked away.

Each time she had to face the averted eyes and sudden silence of her fellow officers, she renewed her resolve to show them pride rather than shame, and strength rather than vulnerability. She straightened her shoulders, put a smile on her face and strolled down to Winfry's office.

"Enter." He was seated at his desk. "Ah, Corelli. How are things going?"

"You're aware of the media swarm that attacked us leaving Winter's office yesterday?"

"But you got the support you needed to exit, yes?"

"Yes sir." Corelli said. She briefed him about the attack after her early morning run.

"Do you need more protection?"

"No, sir. Detective Parker is up to the job. We've decided that I'll use the treadmill until this is over."

"You good with that, Parker?"

"Yes sir."

He turned his attention to Watkins. "You're on restricted duty. Do you think this assignment might be too dangerous?"

"No, sir. I'm sure it will be fine."

He cleared his throat. "We've got ourselves a political hot potato here. I've received calls suggesting that I remove you from this case."

"Captain, I don't know if it's related, but the porter at Winter's office said a cop whose name he doesn't know and who he couldn't describe, visited often late at night, displayed his shield and threatened to kill him if he forgot to lock the outer door at night. The porter seems to have a drinking problem so he may not be reliable. Maybe the guy was having an affair with Winter and if he is police he might feel I'll expose him like I did Righteous Partners. That might explain the pressure to get me off the case."

"Get me a name. I'll handle the pressure, but you three stay alert. Especially you, Corelli." He stood. "Keep me posted."

CHAPTER TWENTY-ONE

Hernandez yawned and smiled, happy to see them after a long night alone securing the thirty-fifth floor. Sandra Edwards, Winter's assistant, sat in the same chair as yesterday. She started to smile but then her lips quivered and her eyes filled, as if seeing them reminded her why she was there. She ducked her head and studied her hands.

"How did it go last night?" Corelli asked Hernandez.

"Quiet, except for a woman who showed up about ten o'clock. Her English was pretty bad, but I think she wanted to clean. She got upset when I made her leave."

Edwards's head snapped up. "Oh, my gosh. They clean weeknights. I forgot to cancel."

"They who?"

"A cleaning service, New York something or other."

"Always the same cleaner?"

"Oh, yes. Ms. Winter was very particular about who cleaned her office. In fact, there was a problem recently and she threatened to cancel the contract."

"I want to see the owner and the cleaner today. Where are their offices?"

"Brooklyn, I think. The number is in my rolodex."

"Parker accompany Ms. Edwards to her desk and set up an appointment for us to meet them at their offices this afternoon."

As Edwards and Parker disappeared down the corridor, Corelli turned to speak to Hernandez but lost the words when a luminous Brett Cummings stepped off the elevator in jeans and a lavender silk shirt.

"What an unexpected pleasure," Cummings said, her eyes dancing.

"This floor is closed." Damn, she hadn't meant to lash out.

"Having a bad day already, Detective?" Cummings sounded amused. "Sorry. We have obligations to clients. Business must be transacted, with or without Connie Winter. I'll work downstairs, but I need some files from my office."

"Should I take her?" Hernandez asked.

"Stay with the elevator. I'll escort Ms. Cummings."

Corelli marched ahead, stopped at the door to allow Cummings to pass, and then lounged against the wall, watching. Cummings's hair veiled her face as she leaned over pulling folders from her desk and the credenza, but every once in a while she looked up, pushed her hair behind her ears and smiled at Corelli. She was lovely.

"That's it for now." She stacked the folders neatly, but instead of picking them up, she walked to the sofa and sat on the middle cushion. "Please join me, Detective. There's something I need to say. I promise I won't bite."

Corelli hesitated before sitting next to Cummings. "This had better be important."

Cummings shifted slightly so she was facing Corelli. "I want to apologize. My behavior yesterday was inappropriate given the circumstances."

"You're right. It's distracting." *What is that fragrance?*

"There is something else." She cleared her throat. "It's no secret that I'm a lesbian. But I want you to know that I'm thirty-seven and only once before have I felt such an instantaneous, intense attraction to someone. I'd like to spend time with you. Get to know you." She put her hand on Corelli's thigh. "I was flirting yesterday, but I'm serious. I believe a relationship is for life."

Corelli felt as if Cummings was branding her thigh. *A relationship? For life?* She needed to cut this off right now. She lifted Cummings's hand off her thigh, intending to deposit it between them on the sofa, but Cummings held on. *Now what? A wrestling match?*

"You don't have the foggiest idea of who I am. It's the job you find attractive."

"I did say I wanted to get to know you, but I Googled you, so I have some idea of who you are. I know you come from Brooklyn. I know you're forty years old. I know you went to John Jay College of Criminal Justice at night to earn a degree. I know you recently exposed a ring of dirty cops and that your colleagues have ostracized you because of it. I know you served two rotations in Iraq, one in Afghanistan and then went back to train Afghani police. I know you received a Silver Star. I see that you're beautiful, gentle, tough and smart. And that's just for starters."

She took a deep breath and looked into Corelli's eyes. "I've also asked around the lesbian community and I know that you and your partner, Marnie, were together for five years, that you met in the NYPD, that you were there with her in Afghanistan, when she was killed in an ambush last year. I'm sorry for your loss."

Corelli extracted her hand and got to her feet. "Who told you about Marnie?"

The anger in her voice startled Cummings. "One of your friends, but I don't remember who."

"Well, I know who. I only told one friend." She cleared her throat. "I won't lie. I find you attractive and I'm flattered by your attention. But I'm not interested. I suggest you forget everything Catherine Stonecifer told you. Forget me and get on with your life. Now if you don't mind, I have a job to do." She moved to the door.

Cummings opened her mouth to say something but changed her mind. She stood, grabbed the folders off the desk and headed for the door. She stopped in front of Corelli so they were eye to eye. "Blame me, not Catherine. She was trying to explain why I shouldn't pursue you. I'm sorry I upset you. I'm sure you're still mourning Marnie. I know it takes time. But, this is not a game for me. Now that I've found you, I can wait."

Corelli maintained her usual calm, controlled facade as they silently walked to the elevator, but her mind and her heart were running rampant. Feelings of joy and anticipation collided with panic and anxiety. Maybe, she shouldn't be on this case.

In the reception area, she waited until Cummings pressed the down button, nodded to Hernandez and turned into the hall heading toward Winter's office.

"Thank you, Detective Corelli," Cummings said, as Corelli walked away.

Corelli pretended she hadn't heard and casually fled before Cummings could say something embarrassing. Out of sight, she closed her eyes and leaned against the wall trying to regain her equilibrium. She breathed deeply.

"Excuse me," Parker said. "We were wondering what happened. Are you okay?"

Sympathy is not allowed. "I'm terrific, Ms. Good Manners. No need to worry your pretty head." Parker turned away, but not before Corelli saw the flash of anger.

Corelli smiled. She'd irritated Parker and changed the subject. She straightened and followed.

Edwards watched them approach. "There you are. We thought you'd forgotten us. Oh, and there's Gus."

They turned. Gus, unshaven, bleary-eyed, and dressed in jeans and a sweatshirt staggered toward Winter's office, Hernandez close behind. Gus peered through his alcoholic haze and seemed surprised to see them. He was even more surprised when Hernandez blocked his way into the office.

He turned to Corelli. "How dare you…I need to go through my wife's papers…I'll call the mayor, no the governor…I have a business to run. I, I have a…You have no right—"

"Beg your pardon, sir. I do have the right. Your wife's office is a crime scene and no one enters until I'm finished with it. And I'm not finished."

He continued to rant, as if he hadn't heard. "You can't come in here and take over. This is my business now and I'm going in there whether you like it or not." He tried to step around Hernandez, but stumbled. Hernandez steadied him.

"The investigation has priority, Mr. Gianopolus. You can't go into that office right now. Ms. Cummings is downstairs. Maybe she can help you with the status of the business." She felt Parker's gaze on her at the mention of Cummings. "But if you'd rather, we can call a taxi for you. Or if you persist, I can have Officer Hernandez arrest you and drive you to the station. It's up to you."

"You won't get away with this."

"Yes, sir. Which will it be?" She kept her voice level.

"I should have listened to that cop."

"Which cop is that?"

He shrugged. "Big guy. Came to pay his respects last night. He told me you would make things difficult and encouraged me to demand you be removed from the case."

"And have you?"

"Not yet."

"What did he look like? What was his name?"

"I didn't catch his name. He was, I don't know, average looking."

She was sure Gus was plastered and had no idea what the guy looked like. "Did you get his card?"

"He didn't offer one. Better behave." With a wave, he turned and stumbled toward the elevator, tossing an order over his shoulder. "I expect to be notified when you're finished. I'll see Cummings. And I'm perfectly capable of getting home on my own. But that reminds me. Are you finished with my chauffeur yet?"

"We'll be finished with Mr. Martucci tonight." She tilted her head, indicating that Hernandez should follow him to the elevator.

Parker watched him stumble away. "I thought we were going to have to wrestle him down."

Corelli shook her head. "A lot of bluster."

Edwards piped up. "You're right, Detective. He gets nasty, but Ms. Winter used to say, 'he's long on posturing and short on action.'" She blushed. "Oh my, I shouldn't have said that."

"Actually, that is definitely something you should have told us. That old cliché is true. A victim of murder loses not only his or her life but also the right to privacy."

"It doesn't sound like she had much respect for him," Parker said.

"She was working on a divorce agreement." Edwards's hand shot up to cover her mouth.

"Is that the only thing you held back yesterday?"

"How did you…?" she flushed. "She was also working on changing her will."

Corelli held Edwards's gaze for a moment. "Speaking of her work, I'd like to have another go at her office."

"Do I have to come?"

"I'm sorry, Ms. Edwards, but we need you to open the safe, and, if you can, help us figure out if anything is missing from her office. We still haven't found the murder weapon."

Edwards grimaced. "I guess I'll need to go in eventually." She retrieved a flask of perfume from her purse, sprayed some under her nose then removed a dainty white handkerchief and snapped the bag shut. "I'm ready."

Corelli led them into Winter's office. The smell of decaying flesh had diminished somewhat, but the room was still pungent with it and the odor of stale cigarette smoke and the metallic smell of blood. Edwards gasped and turned back toward the door, but Corelli put a hand on her arm to keep her there and to reassure her. "Cover your nose with the handkerchief."

Edwards squared her shoulders and moved to the credenza. "Ms. Winter was afraid I would forget the combination, so we used my mother's birth date, ten-two-eighteen." She knelt, opened the door and removed several large books.

Parker prowled the room, examining the photographs placed on various tables and the magazines and newspapers piled on the cocktail table in front of the sofas.

Corelli watched Edwards enter the combination. "From what you've said, she was obsessed with confidentiality."

"She sure was. And not only with Gus. She seemed terrified someone would learn something about the business that she considered secret. She fired people for leaving confidential documents out on their desks, and she used employee passwords to read their email. I think that's why occasionally people were fired without explanation." She removed a sheaf of papers from the safe.

"Is anything missing from the room?"

Edwards hoisted herself up and leaned on the credenza. She turned slowly, scanning the office. "Everything seems to be in place."

"What about her desk?"

"It was always clear except for the ashtray and whatever she was working on."

"Let's go to your desk and see if we can figure out what she was doing when she was killed."

"Wait," Parker said. "She has all these newspapers with articles about the award she got on Tuesday and this picture with the governor shows her holding a glass pyramid. Do you know what she did with it? I don't remember seeing it at her house."

Edwards thought for a second. "You know, you're right. It was so new that it wasn't fixed in my memory, but she put it right here." She half-turned and patted the top of the credenza. "She was very proud of that award."

"When did you last see it?" Parker asked.

"It was here on Friday. I remember because I nearly knocked it over when I kneeled to open the safe. It was heavy glass. And, oh gosh, she jokingly admonished me to be careful because it was so heavy it could kill me if it fell and hit me on the head."

With that she started sobbing. Parker shrugged her shoulders as if to say, "I'm sorry I mentioned it," but Corelli gave Parker a thumbs-up as she guided Edwards toward the door.

Edwards regained control and dried her tears. "It's so strange. She rarely joked, but she seemed happy last week. That award meant so much to her. I feel so bad."

As Edwards walked to her desk, Corelli hung back to grab a private moment with Parker.

"The pyramid is a good bet for the murder weapon. Excellent work."

"Thanks."

"As a reward you get to do a thorough search of Ms. Winter's office while I review the documents with Ms. Edwards."

Parker shook her head. "Wow. Is that the method of motivation they teach in Homicide 301? Anything in particular I'm looking for?"

"You'll know it when you find it."

"It would be nice to have some idea what I'm looking for," Parker grumbled, as she headed back into the office.

Corelli pulled a chair around to sit next to Edwards. "What do we have?"

"The July thirty-first financial statements and her analysis. She allocated a great deal of her time to analyzing the firm's finances.

She got daily, weekly, and monthly summaries and detailed reports, and of course, the quarterlies. She scrutinized all of them and often called staff in for explanations of expenses or investments."

"Was there anything unusual about any of the current reports?"

"Nothing that I'm aware of, but Phil Rieger, the Senior Vice President of Finance, would know more. There's also a draft of a letter to Henry Bearsdon, terminating her arrangement with his law firm, and a draft of the letter to Paul Donaldson, engaging the services of Donaldson, Friedman and Ratner as Winter Brokerage's attorneys, effective this Friday."

"Ms. Gianopolus said she terminated Bearsdon's firm without prior notice or discussion. Any idea why?"

"She asked Henry to prepare divorce papers and he tried to talk her out of the divorce."

"That was the reason?"

"That was it." Edwards thumbed through the papers. "Hmm. She was working with Donaldson on changing her will and drafting the divorce agreement, but neither is here."

"Why did she want a divorce?"

"I'm not sure about the specifics. I haven't worked on the documents myself and I didn't ask. I guess you can get copies from Paul Donaldson."

"Did Mr. Gianopolus know about the divorce?"

"He wasn't supposed to until she decided what the agreement would be, and I heard her warn Henry she would ruin him if he said anything."

"Do you know anything about a prenuptial agreement?"

"I've heard it mentioned but I've never seen it. Henry should have a copy."

"Anything else in the papers?"

"The plan to take over a small brokerage firm. I've been typing the plan for her and doing the charts she needed, but there's a space for the name, so I don't know which one she was targeting. Ms. Cummings could tell you. They were working on it together."

A shot of heat rushed through Corelli at the mention of Cummings's name. Edwards didn't seem to notice. She was frowning as she looked through the papers. "Odd, the application for North Ridge Military Academy isn't here either. She planned to send Gussie there in September, so getting it done was a priority."

"Maybe she mailed the application."

"Possible," she said, "but not very likely. That was my job."

"I'd like to see Ms. Winter's calendar. Is it on the computer?"

"No, she liked it on paper, not that she did much with it. I kept track of everything." Edwards unlocked her desk and removed a large book.

"I'll need to borrow this for a few days. Also, would you make a list of the people Ms. Winter talked to recently, who she called and who called her?"

"Some of that is noted in her calendar. Whenever I put a call through to her, I entered the name and the time, and if she asked me to get someone on the line for her, I did the same. She was a stickler for tracking her time and remembering every contact." Edwards reached into her drawer again and pulled out another book. "We also maintain this log of all incoming calls including those Ms. Winter didn't pick up." She opened the book. "We write the date, time, name of the caller, their phone number, and the message, if any. The original went to Ms. Winter and the carbon copy remained in the book to maintain a continuous record. This book goes back to April. Earlier months are filed."

Corelli pulled the book toward her as Parker came out of the office, looking happier than when she left.

"Find something?"

Parker extended her hand. "This. It was taped in the safe, on the top, in the very back."

Corelli examined it. "A safe deposit box key." She showed it to Edwards. "Any idea where this box might be?"

"I didn't know she had a safe deposit box. Her personal accounts are with the JP Morgan Private Bank, but to be frank, I've never known her to walk into a bank herself, for anything."

"We'll check the banks. Do you recall any unusual calls or visitors? Any problems in the past few weeks?"

"No. And the calls are all in the telephone log."

"We'll take the key, the calendar and the log with us. Parker will give you a receipt for them and we'll call if we have questions. Also, I have a team coming to search for the murder weapon, and I'd appreciate it if you would hang around until they finish, in case something comes up. Then someone will drive you home."

The rumble of voices from the direction of the reception area announced the arrival of the team.

"Speak of the devil," Corelli said as Watkins appeared at the end of the hall, ambling toward them. Corelli introduced Watkins and Edwards. He greeted her then excused himself to go wait for the rest of his team to arrive.

"We'll continue the twenty-four-hour guard at the elevators until we release the office. Detective Watkins will let you know when you can bring in a service to clean it."

She picked up the two books and stood, ready to leave.

"Wait," Edwards said, grabbing Corelli's arm. "We did get some strange calls. Ms. Winter's picture was in the newspapers and on television Tuesday when she received that award. The next day we got a couple of obscene calls, you know heavy breathing and dirty talk, but there was one man, John something, sounded like a hillbilly, who said he was her brother and that he needed to speak to her. When I buzzed her, she reminded me that she was an orphan and had no family except Gus and the kids. When I told him he must be mistaken because Ms. Winter was an orphan and had no brothers or sisters, he got angry and said I would be in trouble when she found out I was keeping him from her. He said, 'Tell her that her niece Stacy is in real trouble. She'll talk to me.' When I told her that, she said, 'get rid of him, he must be crazy.' But he called repeatedly Wednesday and Thursday. Then he showed up downstairs on Friday. They didn't let him up, of course."

"Do you remember his name?"

"No, it was something foreign sounding but…Oh wait. What am I thinking? It must be in the phone log along with his number. I don't know how I forgot about him, but with all the excitement it seems like weeks ago. At first, he sounded like he really believed Ms. Winter was his sister, but I started to feel nervous when he became increasingly angry and abusive with each call."

CHAPTER TWENTY-TWO

Hmm. Just looking at the written messages we would never have picked up the escalating anger or the fact that this caller claimed to be Winter's brother or that he showed up here and was tossed out of the building. Edwards's knowledge of the players will speed things up.

"On second thought, I'd like to go over the calendar and phone log before we leave. You do the phone log, Parker. I'll do the calendar."

"If we sit in the conference room, I'll be able to help you both," Edwards said.

They settled at the table with Edwards between them. Parker opened the phone log to the last page.

Edwards leaned over and pointed to an entry. "That's him, John Broslawski. He's the one who claimed to be her brother."

Parker wrote the name and number into her notebook and started looking back through the log. "Lots of calls from her kids in the last week or two."

"Yes. The two of them launched a campaign to convince Ms. Winter not to send Gussie to military school. She never picked up for them."

"Did you give her the message Aphrodite left Friday, 'If Gussie goes, so do I.'"

Edwards looked at the entry. "Felicia, Brett's assistant, took the message, but we were instructed never to interrupt her for their calls, so I doubt Ms. Winter saw it."

Parker was at the beginning of the May entries when she turned to Edwards. "There are weekly calls from someone named Tess Cantrell going back about three months, but there's no number or message. Her last call was Friday. Do you know what she called about?"

Corelli raised her head.

"No. Ms. Winter told me not to ask for a message or a number. Occasionally a messenger delivered an envelope from her. I signed for it and gave it to Ms. Winter unopened."

Parker copied Tess Cantrell's name into her notes. "Here's another one who never left a message or a number. Cowboy. He called two or three times a month, including Friday afternoon."

Edwards looked at the message book in front of Parker, as if to confirm her finding. "Cowboy. I didn't ask and she didn't explain, but she always returned his calls as soon as I gave her the message."

"Maybe she was having an affair," Corelli said.

Edwards shook her head. "More likely she was recruiting him."

When they completed a first pass through both books Corelli stood. "We'll take the books, but you'll get them back eventually. Oh, one more thing. The porter said a very big policeman in street clothes used to visit Ms. Winter at night. Do you know his name?"

"Doesn't ring a bell. But I understand the porter is usually drunk at night so I'm not sure I'd trust him."

"I gather some of her guests at the award dinner Tuesday night were from the police department," Corelli said. "Maybe Ms. Winter had a business or personal relationship with one of them?"

"It's possible but I've never seen a police officer here in the office until now, and Ms. Winter certainly didn't discuss her love life with me."

Corelli smiled. "And would you tell us if she did?"

Edwards flushed. "Yes, at this point, I would."

"Good. We'll be in touch but give us a call if you think of anything we should know."

When Corelli and Parker arrived in the reception area, Watkins was there with the search team. He introduced them to the group, remarking that the Police Academy had sent over its best trainees to assist. Corelli thanked everyone for coming and showed them the picture of the pyramid, indicating that it was missing and might be the murder weapon.

She took Watkins aside and filled him in on Broslawski. "Get his address and ask the local police to check him out for us. Also, Parker found a safe deposit box key. Start with the JP Morgan Private Bank and move on from there."

"FYI, boss. Dietz got detectives Heiki Kim and Iggy Filetti, assigned to the team. He says they're both happy to work with you. I'll have them follow up on the key and interview the assistants. Also, Dietz will supervise the search while I take Gianopolus to the morgue."

"Great. I'd also like you to meet with the two lawyers involved. And send someone to check on Phil Rieger in Princeton, New Jersey, but be sure they bring backup. Rieger's been missing since Friday, so we need to be cautious. Edwards can give you names and addresses. Have someone drive her home when you're done."

"See you tomorrow, usual time."

As they went down the elevator, Parker said, "You didn't ask Watkins to track down Cantrell. Should I do it?"

"Tess is a private investigator and a friend of mine. Her office is in downtown Brooklyn, not far from the cleaning service."

CHAPTER TWENTY-THREE

The offices of the New York Office Cleaning Service were on Court Street in downtown Brooklyn, on the second floor of a narrow three-story building with an Italian grocery on the ground level and a yoga studio on the third floor. The twelve wooden steps told the story of generations of use, worn down in the middle, splintery, and not a trace of paint.

A middle-aged woman with Raggedy Ann red hair answered the door. The room contained a desk and a row of molded orange plastic chairs squeezed in front of a spotless window overlooking the street. Another woman slumped in one of the chairs, staring into space.

"Please come in," the red-haired woman said in accented English. "How can I help you?"

Corelli displayed her shield. "We have an appointment with Marek Kozinski."

The redhead's penciled eyebrows shot up. "Ah, you are the detectives."

The woman in the chair raised her head.

"I tell Marek," the redhead said. She knocked on one of the two doors in the room, said something in Polish and waved them in. Kozinski stood to greet them. Average height, wide and muscled, he was a vision in gray: with a full head of steel-gray hair brushed straight back, a gray suit, gray shirt, and a gray and black striped tie. Only his eyes were blue.

He glanced at their identification. "You sit, please." He pointed to the chairs facing his desk. Then with a gesture that seemed unconscious he smoothed his tie several times. When they were settled, he sat in the chair behind the desk, his meaty hands clasped in front of him.

"Miss Sandra says Mrs. Winter has died. Why is needed to talk to me and Agnieszka? We know nothing of this."

"Agnieszka cleans Ms. Winter's office?"

"Yes, she cleans all of thirty-four and thirty-five floors. Mrs. Winter's office last."

"When does she work?"

"She start five thirty in afternoon and supposed to finish by ten thirty, every weekdays."

"I understand that Ms. Winter was unhappy with your service recently."

"Is true. Mrs. Winter very, how you say, particular about her office, and she is happy with Agnieszka, thinks she cleans good, but we have problem because of time."

"Time?"

"Agnieszka must finish by ten thirty, but sometime Mrs. Winter stays in office to twelve o'clock in morning, sometimes much, much later. Mrs. Winter says office must not be cleaned while she is there. Agnieszka must wait until she goes home and then clean office. Agnieszka leaves ten-year-old to watch sick daddy and two babies. Is important she finish on time so little girl can sleep for school."

"Did you speak to Ms. Winter?"

"I say I will put somebody who can stay late. She answers in very cold voice that shocks me." He imitated that same hesitant voice they'd heard from the chauffeur. 'Only Agnieszka uh, must clean my office. You pay uh, two hundred dollars more each week to Agnieszka and uh, add three hundred dollars to the bill.' If Agnieszka will not clean, I will not have contract."

"So?"

"Agnieszka is very angry, but she needs money."

"Where were you Friday night?"

"A business dinner, starts at eight and finish about half eleven." He looked at Parker. "I have Lena give you information after."

"I have some questions for Agnieszka. Please ask her to come in."

Surprisingly light on his feet, he went to the outer room, said something in Polish. He returned with a chair. The small, hugely pregnant woman lumbered in and lowered herself into the orange chair with a soft grunt. Her ankles were swollen and she was wearing worn, open-backed slippers instead of shoes. The maternity dress must have been colorful at one time, but now it was washed out, the fabric so thin in spots that it seemed sheer. Her stringy blond hair hung to her shoulders and her tired blue eyes avoided contact. Corelli felt a pang of guilt for dragging her down to the office in the heat of the day. They should have gone to her home.

"Please introduce us. I understand she doesn't speak English, so tell her we have a few questions and you'll interpret for her."

He spoke to the woman in Polish. She nodded but didn't look at them.

Corelli faced the woman. "Mrs. Cizynski, are you aware that Ms. Winter was murdered Friday night?"

He translated.

She spit out a few heated sentences and stared defiantly at Corelli.

He said, "Yes."

Corelli glared at Kozinski. "I'll decide what's important. You give me the whitewashed version, and I'll take her to the station and bring in an official translator. Got it?"

"Yes, yes, sorry. She said, 'yes, and her prayers are answered.'"

"Why is she so angry?"

Agnieszka nodded as she listened to Kozinski. "The queen cares only for herself. First time she there I say, "I clean while you work?" Other peoples in office let me do that. But she points finger at door and say, 'out, get out.' So I go home." She stared at the floor. Corelli was about to ask another question when she started again. "She complains and Marek says I must always wait for her to leave. Many times I think she not there, but when I look, she is in dark sitting by desk or standing at window staring, with drink of something alcohol. I know because I wash her glass. So I wait. She doesn't work but I must wait no matter how long she stands and stares. One night I leave one o'clock without cleaning, thinking to ask Marek to move me to another job. Beata, my daughter, must not stay up so late. She is having trouble in school."

Agnieszka said something to Marek. He excused himself, went into the outer room and came back with a cup of water for her. She drank some and continued.

"Marek tells me he loses contract if I leave. She will pay more but I must stay. In Poland I am doctor. I am smart like her, maybe smarter, but she treats me like a dog. She traps me. Marek is good to me and I need money. I hate her but I stay."

"What time did you get to her office Friday night?"

"Like usual. Maybe ten. I finish other offices and go to her door, but she is sitting in dark. I go to small room near elevator where I see when she leaves. I have English book to study, but I go to sleep. When I wake up it is after twelve o'clock, but I see she is still sitting there in the dark. I am angry that I should wait to clean office, so I go."

"Did you see anyone else on the floor?"

"Little man with mustache who works there finds me to say don't clean corner office near elevator that night. And, later the big man who comes sometime."

"What time did you see the big man?"

She shakes her head. "I wake when he passes, but I sleep again right away."

"What does the big man look like?"

"The secret police. Always he wears black, has short white hair, mean blue eyes, crooked nose, arrogant, like he owns the world. Once he takes leather jacket off and I see a gun. He drinks with her sometimes, so I have two glasses to wash."

They'd found only one glass. So either the man thought to take his glass or he didn't drink with Winter that night. "How often did he come?"

She thought for a few seconds. "Maybe two, three nights in a month."

Corelli handed each of them her card. "Thank you for your help, Mrs. Cizynski. Please have Mr. Kozinski give us a call, if you think of anything else." She turned to Marek. "And Mr. Kozinski, you do the same. Would she like a policeman to drive her home?"

"I drive her."

Out on the street walking toward the car, Parker said, "God, Winter was a bitch. What did she get out of being so mean? Good thing she's dead or I might kill her myself."

"You wouldn't have the balls."

Parker stopped and stared at Corelli. "Not unprovoked, but then I'm civilized."

"Civilized or afraid to lose control? Wouldn't want Senator Daddy to think you've become one of those bad racist cops, would we?"

"You, on the other hand, are so filled with rage I bet you could kill in cold blood without blinking an eye."

"You betcha."

"How did you get cleared to come back?" Parker shook her head. "You are totally out of control."

"Hey, I'm just tryin' to learn about my new…partner."

"I'm beginning to think you prefer backs." Parker pivoted and walked to the car.

Corelli raised her voice. "So we know you didn't do it. But maybe we need to find this big guy." She slid into the car. "Maybe they drank together Friday and he took his glass. Follow up to be sure they checked the bottles for prints."

Parker made a note.

"What do you think about those two?"

Parker gave her an incredulous look. "Damn it. Are you crazy?"

"Probably." Corelli smiled. "What about those two?"

Parker gripped the steering wheel. "Sounds like Kozinski has an alibi. But if the woman felt anything like the anger I feel toward you right now, she could have easily killed Winter."

"Should I feel threatened?"

"Winter clearly enjoyed torturing the cleaning woman. She had her in a vise, and the woman was desperate for a way out. Maybe you need to think about that."

CHAPTER TWENTY-FOUR

They climbed another rickety staircase in another three-story building on Atlantic Avenue, a few blocks away from the cleaning company. This hall was bright, white, and clean, the doors, railings and steps freshly stained. Parker knocked on Tess Cantrell's third-floor office door and came face-to-face with a six-foot, copper-haired woman wearing tan chinos and a light tan T-shirt. The broad face, splattered with freckles, the pug nose surrounded by soft brown eyes, and the generous mouth gave her an air of innocence. But her size and the muscles made it clear that this was a woman who could take care of herself.

Cantrell spotted Corelli and pulled her close, so close that Parker thought she might smother her or crush her hand. "Damn good to see you." Ignoring Parker, she spoke softly. "I haven't seen you since…um, Marnie. How're you doing?"

Corelli gently extracted herself from the embrace. "I—" She met Tess's gaze. "I'm sure you've heard."

Tess understood the change of topic. "You bet. In fact, I caught your welcome home party on TV. The men and women in blue giving you a hard time?"

"Ya think?"

Tess slapped her on the shoulder. "You got balls, lady. You'll live through it."

"That's the plan." She turned and waved to Parker. "Tess Cantrell, P.I., meet Detective P.J. Parker, the one who's supposed to keep me alive."

Cantrell gave Parker the once-over and extended her hand. "Parker. Didn't I read something about you saving a fam—"

"Yes." Parker shook her hand. A lover? Or just a friend?

Tess frowned, then shrugged. "Is this a social visit?"

"We're here about a client of yours."

Tess raised her eyebrows. "C'mon, what client of mine interests you?"

"How about Connie Winter?"

Tess's eyes narrowed. "Ah, yes, I heard she was murdered. Did that asshole husband of hers do it?"

She dropped onto the sofa and pointed to the facing chairs. "Take a load off."

She rubbed her forehead. "I spoke to her Friday afternoon. What happened?"

"Good question. How did you get involved with her?"

"She called a couple of months ago. Said she got my name from a cop but couldn't remember his name. She asked if I had ever done business in the Hamptons. I said no, which I guess was the right answer because she hired me to watch her husband, mostly on weekends. She thought he was having an affair and she wanted proof."

"Did you ever get the name of the cop?"

"Nope. Sometimes guys call when they refer but not this time."

"Do you know any big white-haired, maybe blond, mean-looking cops?"

Tess laughed. "A couple of dozen off the top of my head. Give me a day or two and I could give you a hundred."

"That's how I feel. Is Gus having an affair?"

"You could say that. He has a steady in East Hampton and another woman in Queens he sees occasionally."

"Did you get proof?"

"You bet. Lots of dirty pictures. She asked me to call her every week and messenger pictures whenever I had them. She paid well and in cash. Every time I sent pictures she sent the messenger back with an envelope, never once questioned the cost. She wanted confidentiality and I gave it to her. Best client I've ever had." She paused. "Holy shit, do you think he got wind and killed her?"

"Could be, but we don't know yet. Did you follow him Friday?"

"No, I sent a messenger with a batch Friday morning, and when we spoke in the afternoon, she said she had enough proof and would call when she had something else for me. And you know, today I got a note from her with a $500 bonus, in cash. Can you imagine sending that much cash through the mail?"

She stood up and walked to her desk, pushed a few papers around and pulled a note out of an envelope. She handed the handwritten note to Corelli, who read it aloud.

Dear Ms. Cantrell,

Enclosed you will find a $500 bonus, my way of thanking you for an outstanding job. The pictures should suppress any attempt to prevent me from proceeding with the divorce. I don't think it will be necessary for you to testify in court, but if it is, you will be compensated for your time.

I am considering investigating several people and if I decide to go ahead, I'll give you a call.

Thank you again, Connie Winter

"She was nice to me. Paid me well. I never had to chase her. And she sent a bonus. That's really something in my business. Most clients don't even want to fork over what they agree to pay."

"Do you have copies of the pictures?"

"You bet."

Tess opened her safe and removed a thick manila envelope and dropped it in Corelli's lap. "There goes my retirement. If she kept using me, I could've started a pension plan."

Corelli thumbed through the pictures and passed them to Parker. "Give Tess a receipt. We'll take them."

Parker shuffled through the pictures showing Gus with two different women: holding hands in restaurants, walking arm in arm, kissing in a car, kissing in a doorway. She stopped at a picture of Gus nude, having sex outdoors next to a pool. She stuffed the pictures in the envelope and wrote a receipt.

"Anything about him, or her, for that matter, we should know?" Corelli asked.

"She was really concerned with confidentiality and told me to leave my name when I called, no number, no name of firm, no message. I followed him for almost three months and he never made me. Not too bright I would say."

"Do you think he could have killed her?"

"Maybe. He has a temper and loses it pretty easily. One night, I watched him slap his Southampton steady around, and if I hadn't been undercover, I would've given him a taste of the same. Got some nice pictures of that. Murder might be a stretch for him but if he stands to inherit I'd say yes. Money is a great motivator."

"Do you have the name and address of the East Hampton girlfriend?"

"But of course." Tess wrote the information on a slip of paper and handed it to Corelli.

"Thanks Tess. You know where to find me if you think of something."

"Do you think he killed her to avoid the divorce and get her money?"

"As you said, money is a great motivator."

CHAPTER TWENTY-FIVE

"That makes four people without a motive: Tess, the bartender, you, and me," Parker joked.

"Make that three. I'm not so sure about you."

"God, you are relentless."

"Hey, that's a good quality for a homicide detective."

"Yeah, right." Parker sighed.

"By the way, I'd probably eliminate the two we saw earlier. I don't see a motive for Kozinski and he seems to have an alibi. Agnieszka definitely has a motive but she is so hugely pregnant I doubt she could move fast enough to surprise Winter. Besides, she's a doctor and I don't think she would let her emotions get the best of her."

"I'm not so sure I agree about her. Doctors do kill. But I was wondering about the little guy with the mustache she mentioned. It seems the group in the locked office is expanding. We have the porter, the cleaning woman, Cummings, the cop, and now the little guy."

"Good point. We need to identify the two men so we can question them."

They were back at the car. "Where to?"

Corelli glanced at her watch. "Maybe we can catch Joel Feldman, the ex VP of Investments at home. He lives a few blocks from here on President Street in Carroll Gardens. Go straight on Court Street and I'll tell you when to turn."

President Street was wide and lined on both sides with well-maintained three-or four-story brownstones, each with a small garden area in front of it. There were no parking spaces available, so Parker double-parked in front of Feldman's house.

Corelli examined the bell. "One name. He must have the whole brownstone. Very nice."

Parker glanced at her. *Your apartment isn't too shabby. Not a brownstone, but a nice building in a hot neighborhood.*

"You handle this interview, Parker."

She eyed Corelli suspiciously, wondering if this was the lead-in to another salvo of criticism. She nodded and pressed the bell. Eventually locks turned and chains clinked, and they were face-to-face with a pale, unkempt man, who appeared not to have slept or shaved recently. And, by the smell that wafted toward them, not bathed in quite some time. His kinky black hair framed his face like a halo in the Byzantine style, and his thick mustache was flaked with little pieces of something red. He clutched a colorful but grungy bathrobe around him. His feet were bare and his legs were white with the same black hair sticking out.

They flashed their shields. "We're here to see Joel Feldman."

He stared at them and started laughing. He sounded hysterical. "You think I killed that disgusting excuse for a human being? I'm glad she's dead. I hope she suffered a very long time, like she made others suffer. But I didn't kill her."

Another fan of Winter. Parker hoped Corelli was taking this in, learning what happens when you mistreat people. She cleared her throat. "Well, now that we've got that out of the way, how about you let us in to talk about it? And we wouldn't mind waiting if you wanted to slip on a pair of pants and a shirt before we start."

He looked down and seemed surprised to realize he wasn't dressed. He stepped aside and motioned them through a long, narrow hall into a living room with pale green walls and a moss green suede sectional facing a white marble fireplace. The late afternoon sunlight streamed in through the French doors, illuminating the easy chair and matching hassock positioned in front of the fireplace. The room was neat and the ambience tranquil, a stark contrast to the distraught man who lived there.

He invited them to sit and offered a drink. They refused the drink but sat on the sofa. He stood as if trying to remember something. "Would it be all right if I take a minute to wash my face and brush my teeth?"

"Go to it," Parker said. She moved to the French doors and looked out at a patio with a huge stainless steel barbeque, a table covered by an umbrella, ten comfortable-looking chairs, and a well-tended lawn shaded by several trees.

Feldman returned fifteen minutes later dressed in black slacks, a short-sleeved, white shirt and loafers without socks. He had shaved and must have taken a quick shower because he definitely smelled fresher and his hair and mustache were damp. He seemed more alert.

He perched on the green hassock. "Listen, I'm sorry about my little outburst, but I've been under a lot of pressure lately. I haven't been myself. But I didn't kill her. Really."

Parker sat opposite him. "What happened between the two of you?"

"Where to start? Let's see. About a year and a half ago I was the top broker at a smallish brokerage house. I was happy there and doing well. Then an article about me appeared in the *Wall Street Journal*. Connie read it and called to congratulate me. She invited me to dinner and offered me a job. I turned it down, but she persisted. She wined and dined me, invited me to her place in the Hamptons, you know, the whole schmear."

"Schmear?" Parker asked. She'd only heard that used in reference to cream cheese on a bagel.

"Yeah, you know, all the different things she did to change my mind. Finally, I said yes. She was happy because she got me and I was happy because I got a good deal. Most of my clients followed me and everything went well until about ten months ago. She started questioning everything I did, every decision I made, and we argued about it. Next thing I know, she fires me and hires Brett Cummings in my place."

"That must have hurt," Parker said.

"No question my pride was hurt, but I knew it had more to do with her screwed-up personality than it had to do with me."

"Didn't it make you really mad?"

"Of course I was angry, but I wasn't crazed. Not until I started to talk to people in the business about a job and learned she was spreading lies about me, saying I was drinking and using drugs, that I wasn't honest, didn't show up for work, and that I did a lot of bad deals. It was insane. And it was all done in a way that no one was sure where the stories came from."

"But I'd been warned about Connie so I'm sure she's the source." He rubbed his eyes. "It's been almost five months. No one will hire me. My money's running out. So, am I sorry she's dead? No way. Did I kill her? No way. Did I threaten to kill her? Yes. And you know what? She laughed. She laughed and said I didn't have the balls to do it. And she was right. I wanted to kill her, but I didn't have the balls."

"How did you find out she was dead?"

"I saw it on the news last night. It made me sad because I can't even hate her anymore."

"Where were you Friday night?"

"Here, alone. Most of my family and friends were sick to death of hearing me rant and rave, and once I started feeling sorry for myself they ran for cover. Maybe her final punishment will be for me to go to jail for her murder, one more unfounded accusation from the grave."

"No telephone calls or anything?"

"I don't have an alibi if that's what you're asking. Except I did order pizza." He went into the kitchen and returned with a menu. He handed it to Parker.

"What time?"

"About eight thirty but they lost my order and it didn't get here until almost eleven. I was starving and I screamed at the delivery kid and stiffed him. I'm sure he'll remember that."

"Do you think you'll be able to get on with your life now?" Parker asked.

With that he started to cry. Desolate sobs from deep down ripped through him. Parker looked away, uncomfortable with his pain. She felt a weight on her chest, her heart raced, and she blinked to hold back the tears burning her eyes.

When his sobs subsided, he pulled a handkerchief from his pocket and dried his eyes. "This is embarrassing. I didn't mean... I'm sorry. It's been awful and I haven't known what to do or who to turn to. I've felt so alone. Brett Cummings is the only one in the business who reached out to me. She called a few times to see how I was doing, but I felt too fragile to talk so I let the machine pick up. Last week she called again. Jenny Hornsby had told her what Connie was doing and she asked if it would be all right if she set up some interviews for me. This morning she called to say she'd arranged an appointment with her old boss." Tears streamed down his face again. He wrapped his arms around himself, as if he had a pain in his stomach. Corelli sat next to him and placed her hand on his shoulder.

As Feldman battled with his feelings, Parker bolted into the kitchen and leaned against the counter, trying to control hers. His sobbing, so raw and forlorn, had pulled her back to an old place, to old feelings of being alone and scared in the dark, listening to her own despairing sobs. She shivered and started the counting thing, one hundred, ninety-nine, ninety-eight... When her breathing calmed and her heart slowed, she rinsed a glass and filled it with cold water from the dispenser in the refrigerator door. Feldman thanked her and drank it down like a man running a marathon. Parker felt Corelli's eyes drilling into her.

Corelli stood. "Can we call someone to be with you tonight?"

"No thanks. I'll call my sister or a friend, but thank you."

They left him sitting there staring out the window and let themselves out.

CHAPTER TWENTY-SIX

Parker grasped the steering wheel. She was embarrassed. No way had eagle-eye Corelli missed her dash into the kitchen to hide her feelings. Some homicide detective she was, crying along with the suspect. Now she stared at the windshield and steeled herself for Corelli's assault. After a minute, she made herself look at Corelli. There was no judgment, only sadness.

"Why would someone try to destroy another person?" Parker said.

"I can't imagine. It's hard to believe she was that cold-blooded. It's as if people were disposable items for her. She bought them, used them, and when she was done, destroyed them."

Parker nodded. "Getting close to her would be like snuggling with a rattlesnake." *Sort of like working with you, now that I think about it.*

"How lonely she must have been," Corelli said, suddenly interested in the dark-haired woman walking a beautiful black Lab across the street. "Winter's life appears so…empty, so focused on materialistic gains, and so devoid of love for herself or other people. And clearly no one loved her except the son she despised."

Parker couldn't see Corelli's face but she could feel her sadness. This case was bringing the two of them down. They sat in silence for a few minutes.

Corelli checked her watch. "Are you hungry? We haven't had much time to eat again today and I know this great place in Bensonhurst. What do you say?"

Parker opened her mouth to refuse. Dealing with Corelli's offensiveness was wearing, but they had to eat, and maybe the hostility would distract her from the gnawing sadness that she hadn't known was still inside her. Besides, Corelli's sadness made her almost likeable. "Sounds good." She started the car. "How do I get there?"

They drove to Bensonhurst in silence. Neither was into small talk and tonight they were both pensive. Corelli pointed to a space in front of a brownstone in a residential neighborhood, not a restaurant in sight.

"Come on," she said, when Parker hesitated.

"Where's the restaurant?"

"You'll see."

Corelli rang the bell and walked in. Parker followed, and hearing the clatter of dishes and the cacophony of concurrent conversations, decided this was one of those fancy restaurants with no sign. It smelled wonderful, kind of like a pizza joint, but better. As they moved in the direction of the noise, a petite, dark-haired woman came toward them. The mystery woman. She put her arms around Corelli and stood on her tiptoes to kiss her lightly on the lips. Parker glanced away to give them some privacy and avoid any deep kissing that might follow.

Corelli introduced them. "Gianna, Parker. Parker, Gianna."

Gianna grabbed Parker's hands, leaving Parker no choice but to face her.

"Welcome to my home, Parker." Gianna's smile was warm. *Home? Not a restaurant?* "Glad to be here."

"Is Parker your first name or is that police talk?"

Parker flushed, uncomfortable with the intensity of Gianna's gaze and the warmth in her voice. "Please call me P.J."

Corelli eyed her and Parker tensed, expecting an attack.

"We were in Brooklyn and starving, and we both could use some cheering up. It seemed like a good time to come to the Tuesday open house you're always bugging me about." Corelli put her arm around Gianna. "Anybody here who wouldn't want to see me?"

Parker relaxed. Interesting that Corelli didn't say anyone she wouldn't want to see.

"All safe. Come. We've already started." Gianni grabbed Corelli's right hand.

Corelli winced and pulled back.

"What's wrong?" Gianna asked, alarmed.

"I hit the punching bag too hard this morning, so it's a little swollen. Nothing serious. It'll be fine."

Hmm. Doesn't want to worry the lover.

Reassured, Gianna turned and led them down the hall toward the noise. When they entered, heads turned toward them. As if rehearsed, the group began to chant. "Chiara, Chiara, Chiara." Parker felt she was intruding, yet the waves of affection she could feel shooting toward Corelli warmed her and made her smile. Corelli beamed, and then laughing, put her hands up and shouted, "enough, enough."

When it was quieter, Corelli said, "Everyone, this is P.J. Parker."

"P.J., P.J., P.J.," they chanted. Corelli laughed. "Stop, or she'll run away." One more "P.J.," and the chanters turned back to their food and their conversations.

You said it, Corelli. Who are these people anyway? Not just lesbians as she'd feared when she saw Gianna, but men and children, black and white, and a couple of women wearing head scarves. She sat in the chair offered by one of the teenage boys. Out of the spotlight, she relaxed and started to see individuals rather than the faceless crowd that had greeted her. Her eyes roamed the room like periscopes scanning the horizon for danger, but stopped short at Corelli's twin. The same lean frame, penetrating blue-green eyes, long, honey-brown hair, ivory complexion and killer smile. But... too young to be her twin. Her daughter?

The girl felt her stare and flashed that Corelli spotlight smile. She came around the table, leaned over so Parker could hear. "Hi, I'm Chiara's sister, Simone. That's C-moan-eh."

"Got it. I thought you were her daughter."

She laughed and grabbed Corelli, who was walking by. "I was an afterthought. There's fifteen years between us."

Corelli pulled her close. "Not true. They really wanted you. The rest of us were practice."

"You'd better not let Gianna and Patrizia hear you say that."

"Hear what?" Gianna asked as she passed by with a tray of pasta for the long table on the far side of the large dining room. She set the tray down, checked the table and put her hand on the shoulder of a boy about thirteen who was refilling his plate. "Tell Maria Carmela to bring out more meatballs, cutlets, and salad."

She came back to their little group. "Hear what?"

"Chiara says that Mama and Papa wanted me, and the rest of you were just practice. I thought you and Patrizia would be pissed."

"Patrizia might be angry, but I agree with Chiara." She moved between them and pulled them close.

Parker observed the three women and realized her mistake. Gianna was another sister, but she was dark and short. She looked like the woman who was at Corelli's apartment the night before, but wouldn't a late-night visitor more likely be a lover than a sister? *But what do I know about lovers?* It had been so long she barely remembered.

"Come on, Parker, let's eat. After all, we came for the food, not fine conversation."

They moved along the table together, Parker holding both their plates, Corelli explaining each dish and piling on their selections. Parker took a little of everything—spaghetti, meatballs, veal cutlets, roasted chicken, stuffed peppers, stuffed artichoke, *scungilli and broccoli de rape*. It was all delicious. Corelli, on the other hand, hardly took anything and left most of it.

By the time she finished her coffee and a cannoli the crowd had thinned but there were still people talking in small groups and kids running around. Gianna's husband Marco, a doctor and a professor at Rockefeller University, brought over the black couple and the Middle Eastern couples and introduced them as his colleagues. After chatting for a few minutes, he turned to Corelli.

"The bike will be ready Thursday. If you don't make it Thursday night for Gabriella's birthday, I'll ride it in Friday and leave it in your garage. Okay?"

Corelli hugged him and started to explain to everyone why she needed new tires, but Simone interrupted to introduce some of her friends from college. Maria Carmela, Corelli's cousin, joined the circle as well. After a while Parker gave up on keeping all the names and relationships straight and relaxed into the pleasure of the warm feelings in the house. Corelli was right to bring them here.

They were sitting in a small circle with some of the other guests, talking, or at least Corelli was talking, when Gianna's daughter Gabriella ran by. "Grandma, Grandpa, you came."

Glancing at Corelli, a white-faced Gianna walked over to two old people, hugged them, and escorted them to the table. Now Parker understood: Gianna looked like her mother, small and dark, with an olive complexion, glossy black hair and glowing black eyes, while Corelli and Simone favored their father. Simone and Maria Carmela greeted the parents and stood between them and Corelli as if to shield her. Marco cast a protective glance at Corelli as he hurried to greet his in-laws.

The room crackled with tension. Parker sensed Corelli stiffen next to her, and sneaking a glance, saw she had no color at all. Corelli leaned toward her and whispered, "Let them get settled, and then stand up and say that we need to be going."

Parker watched Gianna make two plates of food for the old people. Then, although she didn't understand why she was doing it, the next time Gianna passed, Parker stopped her. "Time for us to be going, Gianna."

There was a flurry of activity, of friends and family kissing and hugging Corelli goodbye; some hugged Parker as well. Maria Carmela dashed to the kitchen and returned with a bag she shoved into Parker's hand. "Gianna wanted you to have some leftovers for tomorrow."

Finally, with Corelli flanked by Gianna and Simone, they turned to leave and came face-to-face with the old man and woman. The room went silent except for the kids chattering in the background. Corelli smiled. "*Buona notte*, Mama, Papa." The old man put his head down and started to eat, as if he hadn't heard. The old woman didn't speak, but her pleading eyes followed Corelli as the four of them strode out of the room.

At the front door, Gianna hugged Corelli. "Sorry. This is the first time they've ever come on a Tuesday." The two sisters spoke to Corelli in Italian but Parker deduced from the body language and the tone of voice that they were upset. Corelli reassured them in English. "I'm fine. Don't worry. I'm really glad we came. It was exactly what we needed. Right, Parker?"

Although she had been overwhelmed at first, Parker had really enjoyed being there. "It was. The food was wonderful and it was nice meeting you both." *And seeing a different side of Corelli, the beast.* She held her doggie bag close. "I'll think of you fondly tomorrow when I eat my leftovers."

Gianna embraced her. "You're welcome any time."

Outside, Parker said, "Um, what the hell was that all about?"

Corelli was quiet and then said, "Family problems, that's all. Family problems. Even happy families have problems." She smirked. "But then again, I'll bet Senator Daddy doesn't allow any problems in his house and everything is just hunky-dory in your family."

"Well, Papa Daddy sure didn't celebrate your homecoming." *And I was feeling sorry for her.* "No wonder you're so focused on my family. You probably can't bear to think about yours."

"Touché."

CHAPTER TWENTY-SEVEN

Corelli directed Parker to the Belt Parkway through local streets filled with people out walking and enjoying the warm summer night. As Parker turned on to the main drag, Corelli noticed a crowd of people on one side of the street transfixed by something on the other side. She shifted to see what was so interesting and did a double take. A man standing on the corner across from the crowd held a kid in a headlock and a gun to the kid's temple.

"Pull over. Now."

Parker stopped as ordered and followed Corelli out of the car. "What is it?" she asked as they ran toward the crowd.

"Hostage situation." Corelli stopped, scoping out the scene.

The man, with his arm around the boy's neck and a gun to the boy's temple, screamed over and over, "An eye for an eye. You killed my boy. Now I'm gonna kill yours."

Someone yelled, "Let the boy go." The armed man jerked in the direction of the voice but kept the gun to the boy's head. His eyes scurried over the crowd.

"I'll call for backup," Parker said.

"No. We'll end up with a dead boy and a dead man. And maybe some dead spectators."

"But we really should—"

"Damn it, Parker. Forget should. Do as I say." She could see Parker wavering, worried about the rules. "This is my old neighborhood. I know what I'm doing. Trust me." Corelli scanned the crowd, noting the hands inside jackets, ready for action. "Lotsa guns here. Think how angry Senator Daddy would be if I got you killed."

Parker was incredulous. "I don't believe you. You never stop." She threw up her hands. "I bow to your superior knowledge, but God help you if I get into trouble for listening to you."

"We'll call for backup later, if we need it," Corelli said, continuing to evaluate the situation.

"Later will be too late."

"Stop whining and tell me, how good a shot are you?"

"I'm not…Bull's-eye every time."

"Fantastic. Move around to a position where you have a clear view of the guy, but don't shoot until I give the signal. And if he shoots the boy, call for backup immediately, but don't try to protect me. That's an order." Thank god the neighborhood had integrated enough over the years so Parker wouldn't stand out.

"But—"

"Just do it, damn it." Corelli pushed through the crowd and into the empty circle.

The man yelled, "Back off, lady. I'll shoot the kid."

"Get the fuck out of here," someone shouted in Italian. "What do you think you're doing? That's my grandson's life you're playing with." Corelli glanced over her shoulder. Their eyes locked. *Him.* He glared at her from the edge of the crowd in his white suit, white shirt, white shoes, and his beautifully coiffed white hair. She hesitated. His grandson. She turned back to the man with the gun pointed at the boy's head. The boy was sobbing, his hair wet with sweat and his eyes wide with terror. He was eight or nine, Gabriella's age, old enough to understand. He had wet himself. She sympathized. Her knees felt weak, but she filled her lungs, taking deep steady breaths to calm herself and focus. The boy was innocent. He didn't deserve to die, even if his grandfather… She put her hands up and spoke to the man holding the boy.

"I'm a police officer. Let me help you."

The man expelled a sound that might have been an attempt at a laugh but was more of a sob. "You're too late to help me. I'm a dead man. Go away."

As if saying it aloud made the situation real for him, he shuddered. His gaze bounced back and forth between her and the crowd, now silent, trying to hear their conversation.

"What's happening? Maybe I can help."

"Put your gun down and show me your badge." His voice was low and shaky. His body vibrated with tension, and sweat and tears mingled and spattered around him. Even with six feet between them, the astringent smell of sweat laced with a strong dose of fear filled her nostrils.

"I'm going to remove my jacket." She lowered her hands to the lapels of her jacket, slipped it off, and held it in front of her, maintaining eye contact the entire time. "I'm going to reach into the pocket for my shield. Okay?"

He nodded. Pain shot through her arm as she held the jacket with her swollen right hand and slowly withdrew her shield and ID with her left. She dropped the jacket. "Now, I'm going to place my gun on the ground."

She forced herself not to wince as she used her fingertips to remove the gun from the holster and squatted to put it on the ground. Little did he know that the fingers of her right hand were too swollen for her to pull the trigger. She rose with both hands in the air, shield and ID in her left. "Are you okay?"

He nodded, his gaze shifting between her, the boy, the crowd, and the grandfather.

"Good. Now I'm coming closer so we can talk." She inched toward him.

Suddenly, he shrieked. "Philly, don't come any closer. I'll shoot. Stay back."

She turned. A man in a jogging suit was edging to the front of the crowd. She yelled at the grandfather. "Keep your goons under control. Get him the hell out of here." She turned again to face the man with the gun and inched toward him.

"Don't come any closer."

She was two feet away. She stopped and extended her left hand toward him, displaying her shield. He glanced at the shield and then resumed scanning the crowd.

"I'm Detective Corelli. What's your name?"

"Fra." His voice caught and he repeated, "F-F-Frank, Frank Petralia."

She edged closer, both hands still in the air. "What's goin' on, Frank?"

"That fat bastard killed my son and now I'm going to kill his grandson."

"How can you be so sure he did it, Frank?"

"It was one of his stooges. I know it."

"Is that going to bring your son back, Frank? Do you have other kids? A wife?"

"Yeah. Two other sons and a daughter. My wife tried to stop me." He brushed the sweat out of his eyes. "I want that bastard to feel what I feel."

"What about the other kids, Frank? Do you want them to grow up without a father or worse yet, all dead?"

"It doesn't matter. I'm a dead man whatever I do. He'll never let me live after this."

"What if I can make a deal for you, guarantee safety for you and your family?"

"I don't know."

"Would your son want you to kill a little boy?"

"No." The tears ran faster.

"Let me make a deal for you. And for your family."

Choking back sobs, he nodded. She lowered her hands and walked over to the grandfather of the hostage. Parker was standing to her left in front of the crowd, hand in her jacket, ready.

She leaned in close and said, "If he lets your grandson go, will you put the word out to leave Petralia and his family alone?"

"What the fuck you doing here, Corelli? You screw this up—"

She stared at him. "You know me?"

The crowd buzzed, "Corelli, Corelli."

"You've been in the news. But I never forget a face. Especially little girls who threaten to kill me."

A lifetime ago. "If you're willing to deal, then I can save your grandson."

He replied without hesitation. "Yes. But screw it up, and you're dead." His gaze was intense.

She forced herself to maintain the eye contact and braced herself to conceal the shiver of fear passing through her. "I'll die trying, even if he is your grandson." She brushed the sweat from her eyes. "Do you understand that Petralia and his family are not to be touched, ever?"

"You have my word. And anybody knows me, knows that's gold."

"And since you know me, you know that unless Frank Petralia dies in his own bed of natural causes, I'll come after you and your family."

He nodded. "Get the boy."

He wouldn't be carrying, but his henchmen were scattered in the crowd waiting for instructions. "Tell your men to back off. Then put your hands in the air and follow me."

He whispered something to a bald man with a bulbous boxer's nose, wearing dark pants and a white T-shirt. Then he faced her with his hands up. She watched the word being passed, and some of the men in the front moved back. She put her hands up and led the way, keeping herself between the two men.

As they approached, Petralia screamed, "Don't bring him too close."

Corelli left the grandfather and moved closer. Her silk shirt clung to her and the sweat rolled down her face. Her hands were clammy. She spoke in what she hoped was a soothing voice to Petralia, explaining what was going to happen. His gaze ping-ponged between the boy, his grandfather and the crowd, but she focused on Petralia, edging closer until she was positioned to fling herself between him and the boy.

She turned to the grandfather. "We want everyone to hear what you say, so speak up."

He hesitated, but spoke in a voice loud enough for everyone to hear. "Give me my grandson unharmed, and you and your family will be under my protection. Anybody hurts you or your family is accountable to me." The pledge flowed from person to person in the crowd.

She turned to Frank. "Do you understand that his word is good?"

He nodded but raised the hand holding the gun. The crowd gasped and moved back. Corelli's heart stopped, thinking he was going to shoot, but he casually used the back of the hand holding the gun to wipe his dripping nose.

"Okay, Frank, give me your gun."

He scanned the crowd before placing the gun in her outstretched left hand.

"Now, let go of the boy. Put his hand in mine." She stretched her right hand toward him. The boy clutched her hand sending shockwaves through her body as she passed him to his grandfather behind her.

The crowd applauded. Petralia sobbed as the grandfather grabbed the boy and murmured to him in Italian. Parker took Petralia's gun from Corelli, put the clip into her pocket and tucked the gun into her waistband. She picked up Corelli's gun and jacket, slid the gun into Corelli's holster, and helped her into her jacket.

"Thanks," Corelli said. "Call it in. The local precinct will make the arrest."

Corelli turned to the grandfather. "We'll turn him over to the local cops. They'll want to talk to you."

"Philly will go to the station with him and my lawyer will meet them there to take care of it."

Holding his grandson close, he turned to Petralia.

"Frank, I really am sorry about Joey. Believe me, it wasn't me. Your family is under my protection now, so don't worry. The detectives have to arrest you, but my lawyer will meet you at the police station. He'll make sure you're home with your wife and kids tonight or tomorrow at the latest. You should thank your lucky stars that Detective Corelli came along. I thank her for saving my grandson." He moved closer, so he was face-to-face with her. "And I don't forget, ever."

He turned away. The crowd parted, opening a path for grandfather and grandson. His men pushed through and guided them to a black Lincoln Town Car that appeared suddenly. As the sedan pulled away, all eyes swung back to Corelli and Petralia, who were standing in the street, watching like everyone else.

Corelli took Petralia's arm. "How're ya doin', Frank?"

He started to collapse. Parker grabbed his other arm and they struggled to hold him up. A man came out of the crowd and helped them keep Petralia on his feet until the patrol car arrived. After they helped Petralia into the backseat, Corelli thanked the man. He brushed her forehead and murmured something. Corelli said something in Italian, smiled at the man's response and turned to deal with the officers waiting to arrest Petralia.

She'd expected hostility but, after talking to Toricelli's man Philly, the officers were all business. As the police car drove away, she turned to Parker. "Let's go. I feel like a wet dishrag."

Once they were on the Belt Parkway, Parker turned to Corelli. "Who was the grandfather? He seemed important. What was that about guaranteeing protection?"

"That was Luigi Toricelli."

"Toricelli?" Parker's voice rose an octave. "*The* Luigi Toricelli, the Mafia Don? Holy shit."

Yeah, holy shit. Corelli felt as if someone had sucked all her blood. She knew Toricelli wouldn't have hesitated to shoot her if anything had happened to the boy. She had succeeded, but once she let go of the tension, she felt weak, her legs rubbery. All she could think about now was a stiff drink and a bath. But she felt Parker's tension. The repeated sighs to cover gulping air gave her away. As did the continuous movement of her eyes from Corelli to the highway and back. Corelli pretended not to notice, but then she realized Parker needed to talk.

She shifted in the seat. "You all right?"

Parker turned toward her and then quickly back to the highway and the cars speeding past. "Yes. You?"

"Just tired. Drained actually. This has been a rather stressful day, wouldn't you say?"

"I'd say. We have to make a report. Right?"

"We'll fill in Winfry tomorrow morning, but the arresting officers will take care of filing the report. Be prepared. The *World* will probably have the story tomorrow."

"How do you know?"

"The editor of the *World*, Sal Cantrino, is from the neighborhood and I saw one of his cousins in the crowd taking pictures."

"Did you know that was Toricelli?"

"When I saw who Petralia was talking at, I thought it was him. He was always around the neighborhood when I was a kid, and we all knew he was somebody to avoid."

"How come he knew you?"

"I got in his face and threatened to kill him when I was about fifteen, so he remembered me."

"You what?" Parker's voice rose again. "Sweet Jesus. Why?"

She debated how much to reveal, but she figured she owed Parker the truth after putting her in danger. "I thought he murdered my brother."

Parker's head swiveled toward her, shock on her face. "Did he?"

"He denied it. But I've never been able to figure it out."

"Yet you put your life at risk to save his grandson. You *are* crazy."

"Maybe you're right, Parker. Maybe I am crazy, but that boy is an innocent and didn't deserve to die for his grandfather's perceived sins." She grinned. "Besides, didn't I tell you I always try to do the right thing?"

Parker shook her head but she was smiling. "Definitely, crazy. Do you think Toricelli's going to mean trouble?"

"Quite the contrary. Unless they've changed the code, he owes me."

"Were you scared?"

Corelli considered the answer. "You've been there so you know how it is in these situations. At first I was focused on saving the boy, doing what needed to be done, and I didn't think about the danger. But once I saw Toricelli, I knew if the boy was killed, I would be dead too, and I had to remind myself to breathe. On the other hand, because it was Toricelli, I knew if I could get him to promise protection, Petralia would probably give the kid up. Without protection, Petralia knew he was a dead man." She thought for a minute. "I felt more scared after it was over."

They were silent and Corelli asked, "How do you feel, Parker?"

"Shaky. I was scared. I didn't understand why you told me not to shoot if he killed the kid. Now I see you were protecting me. You figured if the kid was killed, Toricelli would blame you and his men would shoot us both if I tried to protect you. Right?"

"Right. I put us both in danger and I'm sorry, but if we'd called for backup, there probably would have been a shootout and the boy, Petralia, some of Toricelli's men, some police, and others in the crowd would've ended up dead. Not to mention that one of the brethren in blue might have *accidentally* shot me."

She watched Parker process that information.

"I see it now, but I didn't get it before."

Corelli put a hand on Parker's shoulder. "You're sure you're okay?"

Progress. Parker didn't flinch when she touched her. Instead she laughed.

"A couple of stiff drinks and I'll be fine. But for future reference, I'd rather take a bullet trying to protect you than stand by helplessly and watch it happen."

"Very altruistic."

Parker reacted as if Corelli had punched her. She regretted the smart-ass retort, but it had popped out before she'd processed what Parker was saying. "Scratch my nasty remark, Parker. I get what you're saying and I'm sorry for putting you in that position."

Parker relaxed. "Thanks. By the way, what did that guy say? You know, the one who helped us with Petralia?"

Corelli laughed. "That was the parish priest. He thanked me for stopping the spilling of innocent blood. He said I was brave, a hero. Then he blessed me." Her lips twitched. "I pissed him off at my nephew's baptism on Sunday so I asked, 'Does this mean you're not going to excommunicate me after all? He said, 'maybe next time.'"

Parker pulled to the curb in front of Corelli's building. The streetlight was out and the area was dark except for the lights on her building. Corelli got out and started toward the door, but spun around suddenly.

"Thanks for your support, and thanks especially for being willing to follow an order you didn't understand. But call me on it if I do it again. Goodnight."

She felt Parker watching her as she moved toward her building. Out of the corner of her eye she saw a sudden movement and whirled to see a man running toward her. Before she could react, Parker was on the street, her gun drawn. "Police! Don't move."

The man skidded to a stop, raised his hands and pivoted toward Parker. The three of them stood frozen for a few seconds before Corelli laughed. "Parker, I don't believe you've had the pleasure of meeting my nephew." Corelli pulled the boy into a hug. "I forgot I asked him to meet me here tonight. Come over. Let me introduce you." *I'm beginning to think you're on my side, Detective Parker, even though I'm being an asshole.*

Parker holstered her gun and walked over. "Sorry, I'm a little jumpy tonight."

Corelli laughed again. "Don't worry, Parker. You were perfectly justified. I'm not as controlled as you. I probably would have shot him. Detective Parker, my nephew Nicky."

Nicky extended his hand. "That was way cool, Detective Parker. I'm thankful you have a steady finger on the trigger."

Parker shook his hand. "Yeah, me too."

Parker was still watching them when the elevator door closed.

Corelli was exhausted and wished she hadn't asked Nicky to come tonight but, of course, she hadn't planned on rescuing Toricelli's grandson. A quick shower and a drink would help.

"Thanks for coming, Nicky. Your mother give you a hard time?"

"Nope." He smiled. "She was doing something at the church so I left a note telling her I was sleeping here tonight. I'm sure I'll hear about it tomorrow."

"Put your stuff in one of the guest rooms. I need a couple of minutes to get comfortable. I can't believe I'm hungry, but I am. And no doubt you are too. While I shower, grab the salad and pasta from the fridge and open a bottle of wine."

Twenty minutes later she emerged in her pajamas, refreshed from the hot shower. She dressed the salad and warmed the pasta. Nicky poured them both wine and they sat down to eat.

"Do you remember the tiny recorder you set up to download to my computer?"

"Sure. Awesome barrette thingy for your hair. How'd it go?"

"Great. Can you figure out how to print what was downloaded?"

"Not a problem, auntie. The software I use is awesome. How much did you record?"

"All day, every day for three months."

"You're going to need a lot of paper."

"I have nine or ten reams. Show me how to do it, and if I don't find what I need in the first batch, I'll get more paper."

"You got it. Hey, you're not still undercover are you?"

"No, but some people are."

CHAPTER TWENTY-EIGHT

Going up in the elevator to Corelli's apartment, Parker pressed her temples, trying to clear her head. After a restless night, she'd finally fallen into an exhausted sleep thinking about the good feelings at Gianna's house and the love between Corelli and her sisters. But a few hours later, after dreaming about protecting Corelli in a shootout with the Mafia, she'd bolted upright covered in sweat. Over and over, she pulled Corelli to safety and, every time, Corelli dashed back into the line of fire. After a shower and a cup of tea, Parker dozed fitfully until finally at four thirty, she gave up the idea of sleeping. She showered, dressed, and sat at the table with a cup of tea. And obsessed about Corelli.

She couldn't figure her out. Was she brave or did she have a death wish? Was she honest or the rogue cop ostracized by her peers? Was she the loving sister or the daughter shunned by her parents? And, she couldn't reconcile the brave, honest cop and loving sister, with the nasty, condescending Corelli, who harassed and insulted one of the few cops in the department willing to stand with her.

When the elevator pinged the seventh floor, Parker pressed her temples again. She needed to focus. At eight, the elevator doors opened and she stepped into Corelli's apartment. Corelli was at the table with the newspaper open, a cup of coffee near her left hand and an ice pack wrapped around her right hand. "Morning. Have you seen today's *Daily World?*"

"No. Why?"

"Help yourself to coffee. Take a look. We made the front page. There's a picture of us holding Petralia up. You look good, Parker. I look like a wet rag."

Coffee in hand, Parker looked over Corelli's shoulder. There they were on the front page, one on each side of Petralia waiting for the locals to come and arrest him. Corelli was right. Her anxiety didn't show. She looked serious, professional.

While Corelli was getting ready, Parker sipped her coffee and read the article, which described how they had happened on the scene and saved the day. The article had some mistakes. It didn't mention that the boy was Toricelli's grandson, and it made it sound as if she and Corelli had saved the boy, but she hadn't done anything. She thought about Corelli's story about her brother. Would any fifteen-year-old girl growing up in that environment be crazy enough to threaten a Mafia don? She didn't think so. But, then again, the grownup Corelli seemed crazy, so maybe it wasn't the wars or the undercover assignment. Maybe she'd always been crazy.

"Parker, I'm sorry. I need your help again."

Parker retrieved the holster and strapped it on with no thought for the closeness and touching involved. She held out the jacket but Corelli shook her head. "Later." She picked up the ice pack and wrapped it around her hand again.

"How'd your hand get so bad? I didn't notice it last night."

"Toricelli's grandson had a steel grip."

A loud ringing filled the apartment. "That's Watkins. We're meeting here today."

Corelli buzzed him in then went for a refill.

Parker helped herself to a bagel and more coffee and wondered why they were meeting here. Her gaze roamed the apartment. She loved the light and the warmth. How could Corelli afford this huge apartment in one of the hottest neighborhoods in the city? Toricelli knew Corelli. Maybe she was connected.

Indignation shot through her. She was an honest cop. She wanted homicide, but she didn't want anything to do with the Mafia. She shivered. Then she caught herself. She had tried and convicted Corelli without any proof. *Damn, why does this have to be so hard?*

Watkins bounded off the elevator waving the *Daily World*. "Hey, are you two giving autographs?"

Corelli laughed. "No autographs. Coffee and bagels. Help yourself." She waved him to the table and sat opposite Parker. "Did I see you shiver, Parker? Should I adjust the A/C?"

"No, I'm fine."

Corelli wrapped the ice pack around her hand. "Why so glum? Good food and fun, followed by big-time action catching up with you? Or is it the sudden fame?" She smiled.

Her parents snub her. Her Mafia connection is exposed. Nobody knows how many cops in the city are trying to kill her, and she's joking. "I must have eaten too much because I didn't get much sleep."

Corelli's gaze lingered for a few seconds before she turned to Watkins. "Let's work while we eat. It's your meeting."

He put his bagel down, licked his fingers and sipped his coffee.

"Unfortunately, the team's search didn't turn up the weapon, but I told Edwards they can have Winter's office back tomorrow. Okay with you?" Corelli nodded. "We tracked down John Broslawski. He lives in Virginia, uh, no West Virginia, a small town called Hope Falls. A Detective Brown there checked him out and called me late last night to say he's legitimate, so I made reservations for you to go to West Virginia this afternoon on the twelve-twenty-five. I also made a reservation at a nearby hotel. Detective Brown suggested you also talk to Clara Lipkin, the librarian, if she's in town. I made your return late enough to give you time to see her tomorrow morning." He filled them in on the details.

"I'll pack before we leave, Parker. Watkins will drive me to the station so I can meet with the captain while you go home and pack. You can catch up with me when you're finished."

"Works for me."

"Good. Anything else, Watkins?"

"One of Jenny Hornsby's neighbors was walking her dog and saw her go into her house about midnight on Friday. So we have a discrepancy between what she told us and what the neighbor saw. Hornsby could've gone back to the office after she left the hospital around nine." He turned a page in his notebook. "The Friday night doorman at Gertrude's apartment building said he tried to ring her about ten o'clock to give her a package the day man missed. She didn't answer, but he didn't see her leave. Want me to talk to Gertrude?"

"No. We should have time to see her and Hornsby this morning."

"No luck so far with the safe deposit box. JP Morgan didn't have it, so we're checking other banks in the Wall Street area. Also, Dietz and I went down to Princeton to check out Rieger. He'd just come home from a camping trip with his wife and two kids. One of the kids was sick during the week, so it wasn't until seven thirty Friday night that they decided to go ahead with the trip. He went to Winter's office about eight fifteen to tell her he wouldn't be in until Tuesday and walked in on Brett Cummings sounding mad as hell." He referred to his notes. "She didn't say anything while he was there, but she paced the entire time, and as soon as he was out the door, she started again, not yelling, but cold, in-your-face aggressive anger. He heard Cummings say something about ruining people, but he couldn't hear Winter's response. He worked in his office until about eleven and got the eleven thirty train home. His wife confirmed his arrival."

"Interesting that he's pointing us to Cummings. Did he have anything to say about Winter?"

Watkins laughed. "He confided that all was not well in Winter land. She and Gus were having problems. Said Gus strutted around, acting like he was in charge when everyone knew she didn't trust him..." He turned a page. "To order the toilet paper."

Corelli smiled. "He does seem like that kind of guy."

"What does Rieger look like?" Parker asked.

"Short, skinny, lots of brown hair, mustache, kind of nerdy, I guess. Why?"

Parker and Corelli exchanged a glance.

"The cleaning woman described him but didn't know his name. We hadn't realized he was in the office Friday night." Corelli tapped the table. "Now he's confirmed he was there when she was killed. How did he react when you told him she was dead?"

"Shocked. Color drained, like he'd been punched. Said he hadn't heard a radio or seen a paper since Saturday morning."

"Could be he killed Winter after Cummings left and is setting her up as the killer. Let's find out what was so important that it kept him in the office until eleven o'clock on a Friday night. See if there was anything unusual about the finances. Maybe he was stealing. And talk to Cummings. See what she has to say about the argument and confirm that he told Winter he'd be out on Monday."

Watkins made notes. "I saw Bearsdon late yesterday. He has a solid alibi. He was at a retreat in a resort in Canada Friday afternoon through Sunday with his partners and their employees. And their wives accompanied them."

"I also talked to Paul Donaldson, the firm's new attorney. Winter was still working on the terms of the divorce and a new will, so the old will is still valid. Also, Winter sent him pictures of Gus with other women to use in negotiating the divorce."

"Tess Cantrell was working for her. Did Donaldson get any pictures on Friday?"

"I'll check." He glanced again at his notes. "Gus has been calling him a couple of times a day asking about the will, but Donaldson hasn't returned his calls. Also, I have copies of the current will, the latest version of the new will, the divorce papers, and the prenuptial agreement. I thought you might want to read them on the plane."

Parker felt the blood drain out of her. "Plane?" She was phobic about flying.

"Yes. It's the fastest," Watkins said. "Why?"

"I guess I pictured a car or the train." She felt Corelli's gaze and forced herself to meet it.

Corelli turned her attention back to Watkins. "Great work."

He smiled. "Thanks, boss."

"Anything else?"

"One interesting thing. SOC found traces of Winter's blood in the sink and on the floor in the men's room."

"Which is closer?" Corelli asked.

"The men's."

"Hmm. Could mean our killer is a man, or it could be a woman trying to throw us off the track. Find out what time the cleaning woman did the bathrooms," Corelli said. "It might help us narrow the time."

"I drove Gianopolus to the morgue. They cleaned Winter up and moved her hair around so she didn't look too bad. He threw up afterward. While I was there, I picked up the autopsy report. And, by the way, the mayor's office requested a copy."

Corelli raised one eyebrow. "Interesting. Go on."

He scanned the report. "Winter had pre-mortem bruises on her forehead consistent with being hit with that missing telephone handset. She was also hit by a heavier, pointy object from two different angles. The first blow was to the side of the head, probably bled like the devil and knocked her out. After that she was hit on the top of the head a couple of times, more direct and more than necessary to kill by a right-handed killer. There was a tiny pre-mortem cut on her left palm that came from a small, hammered-silver cross they found in her clothes, but no defensive wounds or signs that she fought. ME said the pyramid sounds like a good possibility for the weapon."

Parker pictured Winter's body. She was almost certain there was a heavy gold necklace around her neck. "Did they find a chain or a ribbon with the cross?"

Watkins ran his finger down the list of items. "The report doesn't mention either. Why?"

The intensity of Corelli's gaze made Parker uneasy. Was her logic flawed? She braced for an attack but forced herself to continue. "As I recall, Winter was wearing a scooped-necked dress and a gold necklace. It seems unlikely she would also wear a silver cross. So I'm thinking the cross belonged to the killer. Do you have a picture of it?"

Watkins handed her one of the photographs that had accompanied the report. Corelli leaned over. "It looks like something a woman would wear." She sat back. "So you're thinking the killer is a woman?"

Parker shrugged. "That's what the evidence suggests."

Corelli nodded. "Let's find out if any of our suspects lost a silver cross. Go on, Watkins."

"Lots of stuff on the floor under the blood...four rubber bands, a green pencil, a ballpoint pen, a yellow pencil, four binder clips used to hold big reports together, some paper clips, and a few pieces of her American Express card, one with 'Wint' and one with the expiration date. Most of the bits of paper were too soaked to read and what they got didn't make much sense. Her wallet contained another Amex card with the same expiration date, plus Visa, Master Card, and Diner's Club cards, but no cash at all. Her checkbook was in her purse along with a lipstick, a compact, a comb, and a small mirror." He turned the page, glanced at both of them and continued. "The ME found a couple of unusual things. There were a few horse hairs on her legs and her dress, and traces of horse manure and hay on the carpet."

Corelli tapped her pen on the table. "There's lots of bullshit in the financial district, but no horses, so it's unlikely there'd be manure on the streets. Find out if she, or anyone in her family, or anyone who works on the floor, has any connection to horses. You said a couple. What else?"

"Are the kids adopted? The ME says she was never pregnant."

Corelli frowned. "No one mentioned adoption that I remember. Do you, Parker?"

Parker sat up. "No. Think it's important?"

"I don't know. Maybe. We'll ask Gus. I'm not satisfied with his story. And that reminds me Parker. Give Watkins the info on Gus's East Hampton girlfriend so he can have someone check her out. Then, would you guys clean up while I throw a few things in a bag?"

"Should I come and help?" asked Parker.

"Thanks. I think I'm fine with the packing, but I'll need your help with the jacket and my hair when we're ready to leave. And Watkins, interview the cleaning woman at home and ask about the bathrooms and the cross. Check to see whether she's right-or left-handed."

Corelli headed downstairs to the bedroom.

Watkins looked up from loading the dishwasher. "How's it going? Anybody pop yet?"

"We still have more questions than answers but we've taken a few people off the list. Feldman's alibi is solid." Parker laughed. "I guess if you're going to be a murder suspect it pays to piss off the delivery boy so he remembers you. Corelli thinks both cleaning people are cleared. I wasn't sure about Agnieszka but I'm fairly certain she held the cup of water in her right hand during our interview. If you confirm she's right-handed and never owned a silver cross we can cross her off the list. Oh, and Edwards's alibi checked out." She sponged the table. "If the damn building door was locked Cummings, Rieger and the illusive big blond cop have the opportunity. If the door was unlocked I think Gus and Gertrude are the most likely killers."

"I'm ready, Parker. The scarf and my jacket are on the chair near the elevator."

Parker tossed the sponge into the sink and moved toward the elevator. She helped Corelli into her jacket, pulled her hair back and tied the scarf.

The three of them stepped into the elevator. "So how's the brownstone coming, Ron?"

Brownstone? Parker swiveled to face Watkins. "You own a brownstone?"

"Yes, in Harlem. Couple more weeks I'll be able to move in."

Parker looked from one to the other. *Are you both connected to the Mafia?*

CHAPTER TWENTY-NINE

The doorman conveyed Gertrude's regrets, the message being that she had nothing more to say to them. Corelli asked him to convey her regrets to Ms. Gianopolus, the message being if she didn't speak to them now, a squad car would pick her up and they would talk to her whenever it was convenient for them to get downtown. Maybe tomorrow evening.

Of course, Gertrude invited them up. Looking nice in black slacks and a matching T-shirt, she squinted from the smoke of the ever-present cigarette dangling from her mouth and voiced her annoyance. "Gawd, shouldn't you two be interviewing the hordes of people who hated Connie?"

Corelli controlled the urge to confront Gertrude. Dealing with the lies and evasions of people like her wasted police time. "That's exactly what we're doing, Ms. Gianopolus. We have a few more questions for you."

With a look of disgust, she led them down a long hallway lined with abstract paintings, all signed by Gertrude. *Under all that nastiness is the soul of an artist, and a very good one at that.* Sure enough, one of the seven rooms they passed was a studio with huge windows, furnished with several easels, shelves filled with paints, and paintings stacked in frames against the walls. They followed her into a comfortably furnished living room, alive with plants, the inviting warmth of book-filled shelves lining the walls, and a violin concerto blasting in the background. The apartment was neat, and except for the smell of cigarettes, pleasant. Gertrude was full of surprises it seemed.

She lowered the music and plopped down into what appeared to be her chair. "For god's sake, call me Gertrude. Sit. Now what?"

Parker jumped in. "I see you're an artist. Do you sell or is it a hobby?" Corelli shot her a dirty look. *Waste of time. Irrelevant information.*

She knocked the ash off her cigarette and squinted at Parker. "I sell some." She sounded shy. "But not enough to live on. That's why I have to do mind-numbing work for my bitch of a sister-in-law." Her anger bled through. She took a drag on her cigarette. "My nephew Gussie is also an artist, a very good one, and it made me nuts that with all her money Connie wanted to sentence him to the same kind of struggle. His life will be much better without her."

Parker's question was right on the mark.

Gertrude took a breath and switched her attention to Corelli. "But I bet you two busy detectives didn't come here to discuss art."

"Where were you Friday night about ten o'clock?"

She inhaled again and blew the smoke in their direction. "Here. I told you."

"Your doorman says he rang up about that time to let you know that you had a package waiting. He rang a couple of times but you didn't answer."

She ground the cigarette in the ashtray and fingered the pack as if considering whether to light another. "I was here. Maybe I dozed off for a minute. Maybe I was in the shower. Maybe the TV was too loud. Maybe he buzzed the wrong apartment. How would I know why I didn't answer?"

* * *

On the drive to Winter's house Corelli touched Parker's arm. "I owe you an apology. Your question about Gertrude's art exposed her resentment and anger to an extent we haven't seen before. That kind of emotion can drive a person to commit murder."

"Gertrude doesn't fit my image of an artist and I was surprised at how good her paintings are. It's as if she puts most of herself on the canvas and leaves a bitter shell for the world to see. I wished I could take the question back when I saw your face. But I didn't plan to ask it and I was actually curious."

"Don't knock instinct."

Cora Andrews answered the door and led them upstairs. Gus Gianopolus was in the same chair, in the same smoke-filled room, with the same overflowing ashtray, sipping a drink. From his appearance, it wasn't the same drink. He seemed shrunken, like a rooster without his feathers. Gray and black stubble blanketed the once closely shaved, cologne-bathed face. His hair stood on end, and instead of the elegant suit, he wore pajamas. Most telling was the army of empty bottles lined up next to his chair.

It was ten in the morning. The drapes remained drawn, and he sat in the dark, the silence broken by the hum of the air-conditioner, the occasional siren going by, or a helicopter flying overhead. He blinked against the glare but didn't acknowledge them when Andrews turned on the lamp near him. Shaking her head, she dumped the ashtray into the wastebasket nearby, picked up a few empty bottles, and left the room. He refilled his glass from the bottle of scotch on the table next to him and continued to ignore them.

"Mr. Gianopolus, we have a few more questions," Corelli said.

He pinched the bridge of his nose and rested his head in his hand, his elbow on the arm of the chair. "Did you find her killer?" he asked, his raspy voice made rougher by the booze and the cigarettes.

"Did your wife ever wear a small, hammered-silver cross?"

"Are you kidding? Connie wouldn't be caught dead in silver."

He didn't seem aware of the humor in what he'd said. "Are your children adopted?"

"No way. Her daughter had to have her precious genes."

"That's what I thought. But the autopsy showed that your wife was never pregnant."

He took a drag on his cigarette. "What's this got to do with her murder?"

"We don't know if it's important or not but we have to ask."

Aphrodite burst into the room. "Do you…" She skidded to a stop at the sight of the detectives. "…um, have any cash?"

He waved his hand. "My wallet's on my dresser. Amex said it should be here today." She headed for the door.

Corelli stepped into her path. "One minute, Aphrodite."

"What?" All her teenage exasperation conveyed in that one word.

"What happened to your American Express card?"

Gus answered. "She lost it over the weekend. Damn kids are always losing something."

"Were you in your mother's office Friday night?"

Gus sat up, suddenly alert. "Where are you going with this?"

"We found pieces of an Amex card on the floor of the office. The last name and the expiration date were the same as the card in your wife's wallet. I believe Aphrodite didn't lose her card. I believe your wife cut it up." Corelli watched the girl pale. "Aphrodite, were you in your mom's office Friday night?"

"I'm leaving. You can't question a minor."

Parker moved to block the door.

Aphrodite glared at her father. "Be a real dad for once. Stand up for me. I didn't kill her."

Under the anger Corelli detected fear. "Nobody's accusing you, Aphrodite. You may have seen or heard something that could help us find her killer."

Aphrodite sagged. "You're not mad I lied?" Her defiance gone, she looked like the fourteen-year-old she was.

"Just tell the truth now."

"We had a fight that morning and I told her if she sent Gussie to military school, I was leaving home. Later that day I tried to use my card and they said it had been canceled. So I cut it to pieces and went there and threw it in her face."

"What time?"

"Right after I left Aunt Gertie. I had my bike so I got there fast. Nine-ish?"

"And she was okay?"

"She was her usual bitchy, controlling self. She said I could leave home if I wanted, but I'd go without her money. Then she gave me all the cash in her wallet and told me to think about it."

"Did you see anyone while you were there?"

"I heard music from an office near the elevator, but I didn't see anybody."

"How did you get into the building?"

"That creepy, smelly guy opened the door when I rang the bell."

Maybe the door *was* locked. "Thank you," Corelli said. "You can go."

The girl flounced out. Gus sat back and drained his glass.

Before he could drift away again, Corelli said, "About the children?"

He sighed, puffed up his cheeks and expelled his breath showing how put upon he felt. An older version of his daughter.

"It's a long story."

"We'd like to hear it."

"I don't think it's any of your damn…" He caught himself. "Oh, what the hell." He seemed surprised to see they were still standing. "You might as well sit. And what I say is confidential."

Corelli didn't agree or disagree. If it was necessary to her case she would use it, otherwise she had no need to gossip.

His voice rumbled from a distant place, as if he'd fallen into a hole inside himself. "You've seen pictures of Connie. She wasn't very attractive and I admit that initially it was her money that interested me. She actually pursued me at first and I was flattered, but not attracted. But as I got to know her, I was seduced by her… her drive, her self-discipline and her belief she could do and have anything she wanted. All qualities I lack. I admired her. She seemed to think I was wonderful, and our sex life was pretty good. I thought it was love."

He poured another drink and with a sardonic smile, he continued. "About a year after we were married she declared she wasn't interested in sex anymore and suggested we skip it. Up to that time she seemed to enjoy herself, so she caught me off guard. When I protested, she told me to find it somewhere else, which was even more shocking. In desperation, I reminded her she wanted a daughter. Naturally, Connie being Connie, she had an answer for that objection. She had no desire to be pregnant, but surrogate mothers are legal in California. At that point, I still thought I was in love and that we could work it out, so I agreed. We spent time there looking for a suitable surrogate and undergoing the procedures needed to harvest her eggs for the in vitro fertilization. When her eggs, fertilized with my sperm, were transplanted to the surrogate we came back to New York. But we spent a lot of time in

California with the surrogate during the pregnancy. That's how we had children without her being pregnant."

"Your twins are obviously not identical. How did you end up with two children?"

He laughed from that hollow place. "They implanted multiple fertilized eggs and two of them took. I was overjoyed. But she wanted to abort the pregnancy and go through the process again with only a girl. I convinced her to let the pregnancy go to term."

He cracked his knuckles. "Then when the twins were born, she changed her mind and wanted to put the boy up for adoption. That was the only time in our marriage that I stood up to her. I threatened to divorce her and fight for custody of both children if she did that. She wasn't ready for a divorce and she definitely didn't want the bad publicity, so she agreed." He rubbed his eyes. "I never expected her to make Gus Jr.'s life so miserable. I should have stopped her from hurting him, but I was afraid she would divorce me, and with all her money, get custody of the kids. And I would be broke for nothing."

"How did she hurt him? Physically? Sexually?"

"With words. And withholding love. She never let him get close. He wanted her to love him like she loved Aphrodite. But Connie didn't even pretend to love him, or like him for that matter. It got worse as he got older. She pushed him away if he tried to touch her as if, as if…I don't know. Anyway, she criticized and ridiculed him all the time." He coughed and sipped his drink. "She only cared about Aphrodite. She showered her with gifts and adoration and let her do whatever she wanted, right or wrong. But instead of getting love and appreciation from Aphrodite, she got rejection and ridicule. Aphrodite treated Connie exactly the way Connie treated Gus Jr." He shook his head, as if trying to clear it. "But he's the only one who loved her. Ironic, huh? Aphrodite always tried to protect him, always defended and fought for him. But I…I sacrificed him to save myself." He stared into his drink.

"Has the surrogate mother or someone in her family ever tried to blackmail you?"

"No. She and her family died in a car crash when the twins were two."

"Ms. Winter told you she was an orphan. Is that right?"

"Yes."

"We believe she has family in West Virginia."

He sat forward, alert. "Why would she lie? Maybe it's someone after her money."

"The local police have verified his story but we'll be checking it out too."

"Will he be able to make a claim against the estate?"

"That's a question for your attorney."

He nodded and she could almost hear the wheels turning. "Why did you sign the prenuptial agreement?"

"I didn't want to, but I was in love and she seemed to be in love. To be frank it was sign it or no marriage, so I signed. It was a mistake."

Corelli wasn't sure whether he meant the marriage or the agreement—or both. "Did you know she was planning to divorce you?"

"I think I did. Sounds stupid, doesn't it? It's been hanging over my head as a possibility since I stood up to her when the twins were born. You were either for or against Connie and she considered anyone who disagreed with her, even once, disloyal. I've been waiting for her to dispose of me like she did anyone who was no longer useful to her. Then Henry, Henry Bearsdon her attorney, hinted at it a month ago, and I've been walking on egg shells, hoping it would pass." He drained his glass and lifted the bottle to refill it, but it was empty.

"Was your wife having an affair?"

He frowned. "What makes you think that?"

"We have several reports of her meeting and drinking in her office late at night with a tall, blond man. It seems kind of secretive."

He frowned. "I…had no idea. But Connie was secretive about everything so it could be someone she wanted something from…I doubt it was sex. Who is he?"

"We were hoping you could tell us?"

"Sorry. I haven't the foggiest."

"One other thing, Mr. Gianopolus. Have you thought of anyone who could corroborate your arrival in Southampton last Friday night? The fact that Ms. Winter was planning to change her will and file for divorce gives you a compelling motive for killing her."

His head jerked up. "How many times do I have to tell you? I didn't see her after I left the office. Don't try to pin this on me."

"What did you do with the pictures?"

"What pictures?" He went to the cart for another drink. When he returned, he looked Corelli in the eye. "I don't know what you're talking about. Please leave."

She stood. Parker followed suit.

"Wait." He put out a hand to stop them. "You said she was planning to change her will. Does that mean she didn't execute the new will?"

"That's right."

They left him sitting in the chair, more alert than when they'd arrived.

"No parents would be better than parents like those two narcissists." Parker said, half to herself as they descended in the elevator. "At least if you don't have parents you don't expect anything."

"Remind you of Senator Daddy?"

"Leave my family out of this."

"Or what? You gonna report me to Daddy and he'll call a press conference?"

"Fuck you." Parker turned and walked to the car.

"Ah, so you do know some dirty words." Looking at Parker's rigid back Corelli felt a pang of guilt. Parker had been nothing but loyal. *Why am I keeping her at arm's length?*

* * *

Corelli had planned to stop by Jennifer Hornsby's house on the way to the airport but when she called from the car Hornsby didn't answer.

Now driving to the airport, she tried to make amends. "Sorry if I hurt your feelings, Parker."

"No, you're not."

Her feelings are bruised but so be it. "True, but we need to get back to the case. We know Gus and, therefore, Gertrude gain financially from Winter's death and Jenny Hornsby keeps her job, but none of them were in the building after seven when it was locked. We now know the door was locked when Aphrodite got there about nine o'clock, so only Cummings, Rieger, the porter, the mysterious cop, and the cleaning woman were in the building." Corelli stared out the window. "Neither Rieger nor Cummings appears to have a motive. The porter and the cleaning woman both have powerful motives but Winter would probably have fought either of them. Besides, I doubt the cleaning woman would jeopardize her baby. And we don't know about the cop."

"What do you think, Parker? The porter was definite that he didn't let the mysterious cop in but why should we believe him when he didn't mention letting Aphrodite in."

Parker sighed. "I don't trust the porter. You think a cop did her?"

"Working undercover taught me that cops are capable of anything. Maybe they were having an affair and she threatened to call his wife."

"Just her style." Parker snorted. "But how many cops could she meet tooling around in her limo, going to expensive restaurants or sunning herself in the Hamptons?"

"Given what we know about Winter's personality, odds are it wasn't the uniform on the corner. The mysterious cop is most likely a high-ranking officer. Maybe someone she met at a charitable or political event. According to Hornsby, Winter's guests at that awards dinner included police officials. Maybe he was there. Let's get a list of people she invited and any video footage from the evening."

Parker nodded. "I'll take care of it when we get to the airport." She glanced at Corelli. Then, keeping her eyes on the road, she took a deep breath and spoke in a rush. "We keep going over this list but it feels to me like we're stuck. Stuck on the door. Stuck without motives. Stuck without the cop's identity. How do we figure this puzzle out, oh wise one?"

Corelli didn't miss Parker's hesitation to offer her opinion. Attacking Parker was counterproductive. If she didn't exercise self-control, Parker would stop asking questions and offering her observations. That would be a loss for both of them. Alienating Parker could be an even bigger loss for her. "We keep asking questions, collecting information, and fitting the pieces together. Until we get a complete picture, we continue to dig."

CHAPTER THIRTY

It took them a little more than an hour to drive from the Charleston Airport to the Hope Falls police station, where a uniform escorted them to a conference room. A few minutes later, Detective Stephanie Louise Brown, a slender, dusty-blond, strode in wearing a side holster under a baggy blue linen jacket, jeans, a white T-shirt, and western boots. She walked with her arms held out from her sides, like a sheriff about to draw, but she still managed to look graceful. Perhaps she'd been a ballerina in another life, Corelli mused.

They introduced themselves and shook hands. Brown motioned for them to sit. She placed a file on the table and removed a photo and several sheets of paper. She handed the photo to Corelli. "John Broslawski. He has a record. Mostly minor stuff: petty thievery, disorderly conduct, driving while under the influence. Works as a maintenance man at the local supermarket. Been there about ten years. Has a brother, Peter, who lives in town and owns a small construction firm. Also has a sister, Constance, who ran away from home at sixteen. Eighteen years later she showed up in a stretch limo, rebuilt the library and had its name changed to honor her.

She came to town to visit her niece for a couple of years and then disappeared again.

Brown thumbed through her papers. "The mother died giving birth to Constance. The father died of lung disease about five years ago." Brown looked up. "He was a miner, lots of old guys around here die from that. He never remarried." Seeing no reaction, Brown continued. "John lives with his wife Theresa in a trailer they own. She's a hairdresser in a beauty parlor in town. They have a son, Frederick, married with two children. There's also a daughter, Stacy, a drug user. At first John denied he was in New York, but we checked the bus station in Charleston and got an ID. The ticket seller remembered him because he made a scene about the cost of the ticket. He took the bus to New York last Thursday evening. Claims he went to ask for money to put his daughter in a detox program."

She closed the file. "That's all we've got."

"Thank you. You've done a very thorough job in a short time." Corelli stood. "I appreciate the help. Are you coming with us?"

"Might be better without me."

"Why so?"

"I got a little rough with him when I found out he lied to us."

Detective Brown had warned them about the peeling sign, so they had no trouble finding the Hope Falls Trailer Park, even though the sign read, ' PE ALL ARK'. In any case, *park* was something of an exaggeration since there wasn't a tree in sight and the cinder blocks supporting the rust-streaked trailers stood on parched earth dotted with scattered wisps of brownish weeds. Only the occasional old tire or wreck of a car differentiated the yards.

The curtain moved as they parked in front of number 15, a medium-sized, puke-colored trailer as rundown and sad as the others, except for the painting that covered about a third of the side. An artist with a good eye had depicted a crystal-blue lake surrounded by lush green grass and trees, towering mountains and a cloudless deep-blue summer sky. Two sagging lawn chairs faced the painting, as if one could escape from the drabness of the Hope Falls Trailer Park by staring at the picture.

A short, pear-shaped woman with too much makeup and bleached-blond hair teased into an old-fashioned beehive appeared at the screen door. She reminded Corelli of a colorful Humpty-Dumpty, dressed in a huge bright blue, red, and yellow T-shirt that drew one's gaze to her rotund upper body and bright blue leggings that emphasized the thinness of her legs.

"Hi there," she said, reaching up to tuck some loose hair into the mound. "I'm Theresa. Y'all must be those New York detectives." She tittered. "We weren't expecting girls, but y'all come in anyway."

A man popped up off the sofa as they moved past her into the room. The resemblance to Connie Winter was striking. He had the same pasty coloring, red-brown hair, jowls, and small brown eyes.

"Hon, these ladies are Detectives, um, Corell and Parks. Did I get that right, girls? This here is John."

Corelli and Parker handed each of them a card. "Actually, I'm Detective Corelli and this is Detective Parker."

John mumbled a greeting and shoved the cards into his shirt pocket.

"Sit," said Theresa as she poured four glasses of lemonade and placed each glass on a napkin on the coffee table. She sat next to John on the threadbare brown and orange striped sofa, leaving Corelli and Parker the worn orange easy chairs. Neither the light through the two narrow windows nor the glow of the lamps on either side of the sofa did much to brighten the room, but one of the lamps illuminated the pictures in the three jewel-studded frames. In one, slimmer and much younger versions of John and Theresa wearing leather posed next to a motorcycle. Another held several small snapshots of a girl, presumably the daughter, and traced the progression from happy little girl to emaciated drug addict. Cleaned up, the girl would probably look like her cousin Aphrodite. The third frame contained snapshots of a sullen boy who grew into a sullen teenager. On the far table was a studio portrait of the grown up sullen teenager with a woman and two children, presumably his family. Newspapers, including the *New York Post*, the *New York News*, and the *New York World* were on the chipped Formica coffee table that separated the sofa from the two facing chairs. To the right, images flickered on a nineteen-inch television on a rickety metal stand, but the sound was muted. Worn brown carpeting with a legion of old stains stretched wall-to-wall. The smell of a floral air freshener hung heavily in the room, but it didn't quite mask the odor of cat urine. A small table fan pushed the air around but didn't cool.

When Parker pulled out her notebook and pen, John began to tug a lock of his hair. Theresa pulled the hand away and began to rub it, as if trying to soothe him. Just then the outer door squeaked and a taller version of John limped into the room.

"This here's Peter, John's brother," Theresa said. "Sit there Pete, next to John."

He shook their hands. "Detective Brown asked me to come by to save you time."

"Thank you. We appreciate you all making the time to see us. We're sorry for your loss."

The three of them exchanged a glance, clearly not expecting thanks or condolences. Stephanie Brown must have really terrorized them.

"I'm Detective Corelli, and this is Detective Parker." They handed Peter their cards. "We're interested in whatever you can tell us about your sister."

They looked at each other. "You talk Pete. You're the oldest," Theresa said.

Peter shrugged and cleared his throat. "I'm one year older than Johnny and three years older than Con. Our momma was warned not to have any more kids after Johnny, but she was religious and wouldn't use birth control. When she got pregnant again, Daddy wanted her to have an abortion. She wouldn't listen and died birthin' Con. Daddy always blamed Con."

Their West Virginia accents were thick. Corelli had to listen carefully to understand. A glance at Parker confirmed she too was having difficulty.

"Do you think Connie knew he blamed her?"

"Yes, ma'am. As far back as I remember, every time he got drunk, which was most days, he would beat her and say, 'you worthless piece of shit. Your ma shoulda got an abortion.'"

"I understand your father was a miner. Did he work?"

"Yeah, every day. Old gal down the road kept us til we were old enough for school. She was a drinker too, so most days she passed out and didn't get around to feeding us. I was only three so I don't remember how she treated Con but I do remember Con crying all the time. We mostly watched ourselves."

"And your father didn't do anything about it?"

Peter shrugged. "He usually gave us somethin' to eat before he started drinking at night, although sometimes he passed out first and we ate what we could find. If Con cried, I gave her milk when we had it. When we got older, he wanted Con to take care of feeding us all. I remember one night, I was maybe eleven, he beat Con because she didn't know how to cook. Me and John hid so he wouldn't get us, but he kept hitting her and cursing her, saying that she was good for nothing, and girls were supposed to know how to cook. None of us had anything to eat that night."

He ran a handkerchief over his face. "God, I haven't thought about this in years. How could he do that to a little girl? And we joined right in with him, repeating his words, tormenting her, sometimes beating her. No wonder she left." He put his head in his hands, elbows on his knees, seeing the past with adult eyes.

"Well, she didn't help," John said. "She used to stutter and stammer and talk so low he would get really pissed. And she always burned the food."

"How old was she?" Corelli asked.

"Eight? Ten?" Peter said. "I don't know, but he started early and he never stopped until she left. And don't make no excuses, John. We did it too."

"But when she got bigger, she didn't cry when I hit her," John said. "She laughed and told me, 'someday you'll be sorry because I'm gonna be rich and you'll still be scratching dirt.' I guess she did show us. She made all that money and didn't give us none." John's voice was full of hurt and self-pity.

Peter shook his head, seeming disgusted by his brother.

For the first time, Corelli felt a twinge of sympathy for Winter. "Was there some incident that pushed her to leave?"

"Nothin' special that I knew," Peter said. "She was sixteen, so she musta felt she could get by on her own. She stole the week's food money and hopped a bus out of here. Her note said if he came after her, she'd tell the police about him beating her. We never heard from her again."

John piped up. "Not til about eighteen years later when she came back in a stretch limo with a show-fer and gave Mrs. Lipkin a shitload of money to fix up the library. She made them call it the Connie Broslawski Library. We didn't see her until the big bash when the new library was ready. We got special invites for us and the kids. She wouldn't give Freddie, my son, the time of day, but she became thick as thieves with Stacy and started coming around to take her to Disney World and other places."

"And you had no problem with this?"

Theresa spoke for the first time. "At first we felt lucky because she was doin' so much for Stacy, buying her expensive clothes and toys, givin' her money, driving her around in her limo, and taking her traveling. But then it seemed like Stacy didn't like us no more, like we wasn't good enough for her. Con put big ideas in her head and turned her against us. She told her bad things about us, and we had a hard time controlling her. It was always, 'I'll go live with Aunt Con if you don't do what I want,' or 'Aunt Con will get it for me.' And Frederick was mad at us all the time 'cause she didn't give him nothin'." Theresa started crying. "It was like we lost our little girl. Then when Stacy was about fifteen, Connie was supposed to take her to New York for the weekend, but she didn't come. We tried to get in touch, but we couldn't find any Connie Broslawski in New York. We never heard from her again."

Theresa reached for her glass of lemonade and sipped. "About broke Stacy's heart. She kept making excuses for Con, but when she realized Con wasn't coming back, she went nuts and started running with a wild crowd and using drugs."

So much for sympathizing with Winter. How low, getting vengeance by destroying his daughter. "What made you interested in finding Connie after all these years?"

John cleared his throat. "Stacy tried to kill herself about three weeks ago and she needs a rehab program, but we already mortgaged the trailer to the limit trying to help her. When we saw Connie on TV getting that big award, we knew she would help. She had a different name, but I recognized her right away, especially when I heard her talk. I got the New York papers the next day to read about her."

"Were you able to get in touch with her?"

"I kept calling, but the lady who answered the telephone said Con didn't have no family, so I figured she wasn't giving her my messages. We decided I should go to New York to talk to her. I knew when she heard about Stacy, she'd give us the money. She had so much."

"And did you see her?"

"No. Thursday night I got the bus to New York, Port something—"

"Port Authority Bus terminal," Corelli filled in.

"Yeah, that's it. Bus got in about six in the morning. I got some breakfast at one of those delis they have there, then I walked around Times Square. Boy, that is somethin' else. When it got a little later, I got directions to Wall Street and I went to her office. The guard called upstairs but I think that same lady answered, because they wouldn't let me in."

"I understand you had to be escorted out of the building."

He clasped his hands in front of him and seemed to find them fascinating. "I was really mad 'cause nobody would listen. Stacy really needs help, and those stupid people wouldn't let me see Con."

"What did you do when they threw you out?"

He glanced at Theresa. She offered an encouraging smile. "I waited outside all day. Then about five thirty a limo with Winter on the license pulled up, so I figured it was hers. But a man and a fat lady got in and it drove away. I wanted to ask if she was still at the office, but they left before I could catch them."

"What then?"

"I couldn't find out where she lived, so I figured I'd hang around New York and go back early Monday and catch her when she came back to work. I left there about six o'clock and walked around the city seeing the sights until late. I did the same Saturday and Sunday. I even rode one of those double-decker buses you see in them English movies."

"Did you get a hotel room?"

His eyes boomeranged around the room looking everywhere but at Corelli. "Nah, I slept in that Port place."

"When did you find out she was dead?"

"Monday morning. I went down to her office again. The police were there and somebody said Connie Winter was murdered, so I came home."

"Why did you lie to the police?"

"I was afraid they would think I killed her for her money."

Peter seemed cut off, distant. Corelli wondered if he was thinking about the possibility that his brother was a murderer or feeling guilty about the past.

"Did you?"

Theresa choked on her lemonade. Peter stared at John, who jerked to his feet. "No way. They wouldn't let me in. I never even saw her." His breathing was rapid.

"John wouldn't hurt nobody," Theresa said. "He just wanted her to help Stacy."

"Does Stacy know you located her aunt?"

John and Theresa exchanged a glance before he said, "I told her Wednesday. I was tryin' to make her feel better."

"Where is she now?"

"We don't know," Theresa said, dabbing at her tears. "She walked out of the hospital Thursday morning, and nobody's seen her since."

John put his arm around Theresa.

Corelli watched Parker make a note. If this were a Greek tragedy Stacy would have murdered her aunt to get vengeance. "Do you have a recent picture of Stacy that we could borrow?"

"She wouldn't hurt—"

"It's routine. Since she's missing."

Theresa leaned over and removed a picture from the frame on the table next to her. Parker slid the picture into her notebook and handed Theresa a receipt.

Corelli waited until she had their attention. "Is there anything you would like to tell me? Or ask?"

Peter cleared his throat. "Does she have a family?"

"Yes, a husband and fourteen-year-old twins, a boy and a girl."

Peter nodded. "How are they taking it?"

"As well as could be expected."

John leaned forward. "Do you know if she left us something in her will?"

"Oh, John," Theresa said, as if she was embarrassed that he asked, but her eyes glittered and her mouth hung open. Peter's mouth turned down and he shook his head.

Corelli kept the sneer off her face but not out of her voice. "I have no idea whether she remembered you."

CHAPTER THIRTY-ONE

The next morning at nine a.m. sharp, they parked in front of the Connie Broslawski Library, a three-story ultra-modern glass and brick building that stood out in the dusty, depressed town like a shark in a fish tank.

Parker gazed at the showy sign. "Why Broslawski? Why not Winter?"

"Knowing Winter, there was a reason. Maybe Clara Lipkin can enlighten us."

The lobby was dominated by a huge bronze plaque with a raised likeness of Winter and a message: "Thanks in part to the kindness and generosity of librarian Clara Lipkin to a poor little girl, I have become successful beyond my wildest imagination. I hope my gift will enable other girls to achieve their dreams." It was signed, "Connie Broslawski." The walls nearby were covered with photographs of Connie with various women, individually and in small groups. Some of the women looked like they were sucking lemons, others looked shy, as if they were in the presence of a movie star. There was a picture of Winter with her niece Stacy, but none with either of her brothers.

They walked to the desk and asked to see Mrs. Lipkin. The twenty-something librarian said Mrs. Lipkin had retired a few years ago, but when she saw their shields, she offered to call to see if Lipkin was home from her latest trip. After a whispered conversation, she put the phone down and directed them to Lipkin's house a few blocks away.

The lanky, white-haired woman with warm blue eyes who opened the door appeared to be in her early seventies and carried herself like a runway model, elegant and graceful. She invited them to join her for coffee.

Corelli peered into Lipkin's living room as she led them through the house. Her furnishings were simple, comfortable and tasteful. Everything seemed lived-in but nothing was threadbare or worn. Books were stacked on the floor and on a table near a large easy chair placed in front of the stone fireplace that covered most of one wall. Even the hallway was lined with floor-to-ceiling bookcases, shelves overflowing with books.

The kitchen smelled of cinnamon and freshly brewed coffee. It was the kitchen of a cook, with modern appliances, gleaming white wooden cabinets, granite countertops, and cream-colored ceramic tiles on the walls near the stove and the sink. A rectangular oak table, topped by a bouquet of fresh flowers and set for three, occupied the place of honor in front of floor-to-ceiling windows that faced a yard shaped and shadowed with trees and shrubs and sprinkled with beds of red, yellow, and purple flowers. This room, too, had a well-used stone fireplace. The contrast between Lipkin's house and the Broslawski's trailer couldn't have been more stark.

Lipkin poured coffee and offered a plate of donuts and muffins, before helping herself to a donut. She sipped her coffee. "How can I help you?"

Corelli stirred her coffee. "Do you know why we're here?"

"No idea whatsoever. I returned from a month in France last night."

"A woman was murdered in New York. You knew her as Connie Broslawski, but her legal name was Connie Winter."

Lipkin's hand flew to her throat. "How horrible. When? What happened?"

"Over the weekend. We were told you could fill us in on her background."

Lipkin reached for a tissue from the box on the nearby counter. "Poor thing. She had such a sad childhood." She dabbed her eyes and blew her nose.

"Connie's mother, Sonia Wintczak, was a regular at the library when she was in high school. She was bright and dreamed of being a teacher." Her gaze drifted to the birds chattering and diving for seed in the feeders hanging on the tree just outside the window and then flicked back to Corelli. "But like many of the local girls she married right after high school and her dreams fizzled. By all accounts her husband Bartek adored Sonia and was devastated when she died giving birth to their third child, Constance. He started to drink heavily after her death.

"I met Connie when she started elementary school. It was next to the library and her class came in several times a week for story hour. She was a pathetic little thing, always hunched up like she was trying to hide. Bartek dressed her in castoffs he found at the church. No one ever taught her personal hygiene, so she was dirty, her hair a tangled mess, and she smelled. Her speech didn't help. She hesitated between words and filled in with 'uhs' and 'ums.' Then she made it worse by speaking so low that it was difficult to understand her. Of course, she was tormented by her classmates, the neighborhood kids and her brothers. She was always alone."

"You only knew her through the library?"

"Yes. But I probably knew her better than anyone. She dashed to the library right after school every day to escape the taunts of the other children. Did you ever have a child cringe when you came close? It's not pleasant. At first she was anxious around me, but I talked to her about books and helped her pick ones she would like. I brought food to the library for her and occasionally new clothes. Over time she learned to trust me, so I was able to take her to the apartment I lived in at the time, and show her how to wash herself. I gave her a hairbrush and taught her to brush her hair. I think I was the only adult she felt cared about her. Maybe the only human being.

"It's hard to talk about this without feeling guilty, but back then families cared for their children as best they could. People didn't interfere the way they would today. Sometimes she had bruises on her face and arms, but she ignored questions about them and would never admit that her father beat her. In fact, she ignored any question she didn't like."

"It's not unusual for children who are being beaten to try to keep it a secret," Parker said.

"I imagine so. The kids in her class, especially the girls, ganged up on her and teased her mercilessly, calling her white trash and other hurtful names. And, to add to her humiliation, her teacher, Mrs. Schermerhorn, was intent on forcing Connie to speak clearly. She would make her read the same paragraph over and over in class. Of course, Connie was mortified by the attention, and whenever it happened, she was distraught when she came into the library."

She smiled, remembering. "It was one of those days that she stole the book."

"What book was that?" asked Corelli.

"*Think and Grow Rich* by Napoleon Hill. Someone had left a copy on the table where she usually sat. I guess the title intrigued her, so she started reading it. I usually talked to her but that day she was so focused I didn't interrupt. And when I glanced over to see how she was doing later, I saw her slip the book into a coat pocket. I was surprised, but she had so little in her life I let it go. It turned out to be a providential decision for the library."

Corelli frowned. "What do you mean?"

"You know she left home at sixteen?"

"Yes."

"She was ten when she stole the Hill book. She told me it changed her life. It became her bible. She read and reread it, and it convinced her she could do anything she wanted, if she wanted it badly enough. She laid out a plan to leave home when she was sixteen and started putting aside a little of the food money her father gave her every week. She knew exactly what she wanted. She was determined to make everyone envy and respect her."

"You knew of her plan?"

"No. Eighteen years after she left, she came back to Hope Falls in a limousine with a uniformed chauffeur and created quite a stir. Initially I was the only one she talked to. She wanted to expand and renovate the library and set up an endowment to fund it, but there were several conditions. The library had to be named for her. We had to provide a copy of a special edition of the Napoleon Hill book with a forward written by her, free to anyone who wanted one. There had to be a grand reception for the reopening with certain people receiving special invitations. And, I had to administer the endowment as long as I lived or was mentally able."

"Who did she want invited?"

"Her brothers, their wives, and all her classmates, especially all the girls who tormented her. She remembered every one of their names. She wanted to show them that dirty little Connie Broslawski was successful beyond their dreams. And she did. There was a lot of fawning, and excuse my language, sucking up to her at the reception. Then she never spoke to any of them again, including her brothers and sisters-in-law. Whenever she arrived in her limousine to pick up her niece Stacy, people tried to get her attention by knocking on the windows of the car, but she acted as if they were invisible."

"Do you think she enjoyed her revenge?"

"Absolutely. But, unfortunately, Stacy got caught in the aftermath and it ruined her life."

"Did Connie keep in contact with you?"

"After the party she thanked me for everything and left. We never spoke again but I think she waved to me from her limousine whenever she came to get Stacy. I was never sure because of the dark glass."

"That was it?"

"Not quite. Several months after the reception, a man showed up at my door with a message from Connie Broslawski. She had bought this house for me and provided money to decorate it. Plus, she had set up a trust that would pay me five thousand dollars a month as long as I lived."

"Quite a payback."

"Yes. A great deal of money in Hope Falls. Of course, I never expected anything. I tried to refuse the gift because it was too generous, but the man said he didn't know how to get in touch with her, so I would have to take it. He gave me a note from Connie and left."

She caressed the wooden table. "The note said, 'Thank you for caring. This is for me as well as for you.'"

Lipkin laughed. "So I bit the bullet and accepted. And, I must say, my happy life became even happier because of a small kindness toward a needy child."

"Thank you for sharing that, Ms. Lipkin." Corelli was saddened by her story of Connie Broslawski as a pathetic child, but she was relieved to hear about the generous gift the adult Connie Winter gave to the woman who'd been so kind to her. It was nice to know Winter could occasionally be kind and generous. Up to now, they'd only heard about her cruelty and vindictiveness.

CHAPTER THIRTY-TWO

Waiting to board their flight to New York, Parker struggled to keep her anxiety in check. She'd been close to a panic attack on their way to Hope Falls, but instead of taunting her, Corelli had kept her busy talking about the case. Now, her only source of anxiety was her fear of flying.

"Parker, are you—"

Corelli's phone interrupted. "Corelli." Though Parker was close enough to hear the rapid rush of words, she wasn't close enough to understand what was being said. But a glance at Corelli's pale face told her it wasn't good news.

"How bad is he?" Corelli's voice was low and filled with pain. She listened a few minutes then ended the call. She took a deep breath. "That was Watkins. My apartment alarm went off last night and scared off a couple of thugs trying to break in. But instead of waiting for the alarm people or the police as he's supposed to, my super took on the guys when they tried to leave the building. The alarm people found him unconscious in the lobby."

"How bad is he?"

"They did emergency surgery to relieve the pressure on his brain and now he's in an induced coma. Winfry posted round-the-clock uniforms outside his hospital room and in the lobby of my building."

"Were any other apartments burglarized?"

"No. They think it was Righteous Partners, not your run of the mill burglars."

"The department won't keep cops on him or in the lobby for long. The building will need to get somebody fast."

"I'll hire private security for him. Watkins recommended a friend, an ex-cop, and her writer partner who are available immediately to take over as super. I'm sure they'll be fine, but I'll meet them later tonight and decide."

"An ex-cop sounds like a good idea." *You're going to decide? You own the building?*

"Give me a minute, Parker. I need to call Fran, the super's wife."

Parker listened to Corelli's side of the conversation. "I'm so sorry. I told him not to put himself in danger." She paused to listen. "You focus on getting him better. No, don't worry about money. The insurance will cover all the hospital and medical costs and I'll make up the difference between the long-term disability payment and his salary. Definitely, a long recovery. No. Stay in your apartment. The new super can take the empty one." She hung up.

"Righteous Partners is escalating. I wish I could figure out why they think I'm a threat."

"Maybe they're looking for proof that you're dirty?"

"Or trying to plant proof." Corelli held Parker's eyes. "You think I'm dirty, don't you?"

"How—" Parker looked away.

"You just figured out I own the building. Is that it?"

Parker thrust her chin out. "Partly."

"My uncle had a very successful business importing food and furniture from Italy. He also owned high-end retail stores that specialized in all things Italian. By the time he died five years ago, he had sold all the businesses but not the real estate. He never married so my sisters and I each inherited money and property. He left me the building I live in and my sisters each got equally valuable property in Brooklyn. Actually, I live in his apartment."

She held her phone out. "Call Gianna or Simone or Patrizia right now if you don't believe me."

Parker pushed the phone away.

"What's the rest of 'partly'?"

"Forget it."

"How can I trust you to watch my back, if you think I'm dirty and a liar?"

"Toricelli recognized you. Are you on his payroll?"

Corelli laughed. "Toricelli keeps his eye on anyone who threatens him. My brother was shot in the eye, a gangster hit. I adored Luca and his death devastated me. I thought Toricelli ordered it, so I went to the pastry shop he hung out in and threatened to kill him. He swore he didn't do it. Gianna and Patrizia can confirm it." She held the phone out. "Simone wasn't born yet."

Once again, Parker pushed the phone away.

"The first contact I've had with Toricelli since I threatened him was the other night. If you're still not comfortable, it would be best if you tell Winfry you can't work with me."

Parker met Corelli's eyes. *I believe. And Jesse would've told me.* After a few seconds she closed her eyes and broke the connection.

"Are we good?" Corelli asked.

"We're good, I think."

"I'd like a heads-up if you change your mind."

They sat in silence. Parker tried to calm her flying jitters, while Corelli tapped her toe and checked her phone.

"You know, if you get Winfry to reassign you, you won't have to worry about ruining your clothes anymore."

Sure it was Corelli's anxiety talking, Parker ignored the provocation.

"You're no fun." Corelli tapped her cell phone. "Might as well call in for messages." She listened to a couple of messages, made a note, then catapulted out of her chair as if an electric current had passed through her. Looking tense and on edge, Corelli paced with the phone to her ear.

Parker pushed her anxiety about flying aside. She didn't want to intrude, but she could see that something else had happened, so she went with her gut feeling and fell into step with Corelli. "What's wrong? Can I help?"

Corelli didn't answer. She moved to the window, struggling for control. Parker followed, but looked away, giving her space. Without saying anything, Corelli pressed something on her cell, listened for a minute, and handed it to Parker.

The voice was eerie, like the guy in *Star Wars*. But it was the message that touched every nerve in Parker's body, like fingernails scraping on a blackboard. She shivered.

"So, Corelli, you know you didn't get all of us. Did you think you would go unpunished for fucking up so many lives? Since we can't use a firing squad, and, as we should have expected, you continue to outsmart us, we have a better idea. You will call a press conference Monday afternoon to announce you're resigning from the job because you feel guilty for tricking innocent cops and making them appear dirty. You will also forget everything you think you know about Righteous Partners. If you don't obey, we'll take out your family, one by one, starting with the lovely Simone. You've taken our jobs and our families from us so why shouldn't we do the same for you?"

The next message was from Simone. "Chiara, I'm in a car with these two police officers. They wanted me to give you a message." Parker heard a voice in the background, and then Simone said, "the message is, 'so you know we can.' Oh, here is good. Thanks. They dropped me at the subway. Will I see you tonight, Chiara?"

Parker felt her blood drain. Righteous Partners was demonstrating just how easy it would be to get to Simone. She handed the phone to Corelli.

Corelli sank into a nearby seat and stared at her hands. "Those bastards." Her voice broke.

Parker rocked on her feet, unsure what to do. This was the down side of being close to your family. Somebody could hurt you by hurting them. It was painful seeing Corelli, so brave and fearless for herself, devastated by the thought of her sister being hurt. Parker felt a surge of protectiveness and without thinking about it, knelt down in front of Corelli and took her hands.

"We'll protect her. Don't worry. Let's figure out what needs to be done, and when we get back we'll do it. We'll get them."

Corelli offered a weak smile. "Thanks, Parker. The only one in Righteous Partners who would know that taking away the job would be as good as killing me is my old friend Jimmy McGivens.

He also knows how attached I am to Simone and that harming her or anyone in my family is the way to punish me. But he wouldn't chance doing it himself, and I don't know who else is still out there."

"There must be something besides—"

"I could use myself as bait, but even if we get some of them, they'll be the muscle. It won't make a difference. Simone and my whole family will still be in danger. I need time to think it through."

"If there's anything I can do, anything, say the word."

"Thanks."

Their flight started boarding.

"God, I almost forgot. Today is my niece Gabriella's birthday. The last thing I need right now is to see my family, but I can't miss her party. Would you mind dropping me at the party when we get back to New York? I can get someone to drive me home after."

"No problem." *No way are you going anywhere without me, especially now.* "But I'd like to stay. I could run into the bookstore over there and get her something."

Corelli's voice caught. "You sure you're ready for another encounter with the Corelli clan?"

Their eyes met. Parker let go of Corelli's hands. "Definitely."

Corelli cleared her throat. "You're a brave woman. Let's go."

The flight back was less traumatic. Parker was tense taking off and landing, but her concern for Corelli and her family pushed the fear into the background. She focused on distracting Corelli. They even managed to talk about the case for a while. As soon as they exited the plane they retrieved the car and headed to Brooklyn.

CHAPTER THIRTY-THREE

Corelli decided not to tell anyone in the family about the threat. She would take care of it one way or another. But Parker was uneasy as they rang the bell, afraid she would open her big mouth without thinking and tell somebody. She relaxed when Gianna answered the door and greeted them warmly, as if everything was normal.

"Simone is here already," she said, "and I expect Patrizia and her Joseph in about a half an hour. They'll bring Mama and Papa. Until then, come in and relax."

The house was crowded. The kids running and playing games, the adults standing or sitting in small groups, engaged in loud discussions ranging from politics to the kinds of canned tomatoes that were best for sauce. For the most part, these were not the same people who'd been present on Tuesday.

All heads turned toward them. Conversations paused but quickly picked up again. And then there was lots of kissing, men and women came to Corelli, and Corelli went to some older people who remained seated. Parker guessed this was mostly family.

Simone waved and broke away from her conversation to hug Parker. When Corelli joined them, she pulled her young sister close. Simone tried to step back but Corelli held on. "Did you get my message about those two cops?" Simone asked. "It seemed weird but they said they were testing something for you."

Standing behind Simone, Parker watched a series of emotions pass over Corelli's face—sadness, anxiety, and anger. Holding her sister close, Corelli said, "Don't ever do that again. Never, ever, get in a car with men or women you don't know."

"They showed me their badges so I figured it was okay."

"Especially men and woman with badges. Don't let them get close. Ask them for the password. If they don't know it, run to some crowded public place, call 911, and then call me."

"What password?"

"Scopello."

"Papa's village? Sure. But—"

"No buts. Understand?"

Gabriella dashed in from another room and wrapped herself around Corelli's legs. "Auntie Chiara, you're here. I knew you would come."

Corelli laughed but held on to Simone. And tightened her arms. "Understand?"

"All right. Scopello."

Corelli patted her shoulder. "Good girl." With Gabriella clinging to her legs, she shuffled to the nearest chair, pulled the giggling girl onto her lap, and covered her with loud kisses. Digging in her bag with her good hand she said, "Let's see. I think I have something for you. Oh, no, maybe I left it home. I'm so sorry, Gabriella."

Gabriella glared at her aunt, and refusing to accept that she had forgotten, pushed her hand back into the bag to search. Corelli pulled out a hairbrush. Gabriella frowned and pushed her aunt's hand into the bag again.

Corelli rummaged. "Hmm, what could this be?"

Gabriella shrieked in delight as Corelli yanked out a small box. Her eyes shining, Gabriella tore the paper and opened the box.

"Mama, Mama, look." Gabriella pulled the small gold bracelet out of the box, wrapped her arms around her aunt, and covered her face with kisses. Corelli put the bracelet on Gabriella's wrist, buried her head in the child's neck and held her tight. Gianna beamed.

Gabriella noticed the package with birthday wrapping in Parker's hand, slid off her aunt's lap, and sidled over to Parker. "Is that for me, Detective Parker?"

"Gabriella, that's rude," Gianna said.

Parker smiled. "It's okay, Gianna." She handed the present to Gabriella. "Happy birthday."

Gabriella tore the wrapping paper. "How did you know I wanted to read Nancy Drew? I'm going to be a detective like you and Auntie Chiara." She threw her arms around Parker and kissed her cheek.

Parker flushed with pleasure and hugged her back. "Nobody told me. You just seem like a detective kind of girl." Gabriella dashed off to show her presents to her friends.

Parker and Corelli sat with Simone, Maria Carmela, and Marco and talked about West Virginia and whitewater rafting. The group decided to go rafting in September and invited Parker to join them. She promised to think about it, knowing she wouldn't go. She'd never done anything like that. Corelli seemed subdued, but with everyone laughing and talking at once, no one seemed to notice.

The doorbell rang. Corelli glanced at her watch. "The big guns have arrived."

Parker assumed she meant her parents, because she could feel the tension rise around the table. Gianna led them in and introduced Parker. First, her parents, Mr. and Mrs. Corelli, then her sister Patrizia, her husband Joseph and their children, Nicolo, the young man she'd met outside Corelli's building, Antonio, Elena, Joseph Jr., and baby Luca.

Nicky bowed. "Nice to see you again, Detective Parker."

Parker smiled. "Yes, though a little less tense this time."

"Nicky, Anthony, get more chairs so everybody can sit," Gianna said.

Corelli pulled her nephew Joseph Jr. to her. He whooped and giggled as she tickled and hugged and kissed him. The ruckus attracted Gabriella and she skipped over to greet everyone, one eye on the gaily-wrapped presents.

Gabriella opened her gifts with more decorum than she had shown earlier, but she couldn't contain the shouts of joy as she tore the paper off each gift. When she finished her round of thanks, Gianna sent her and her young cousins to join the rest of the gang. Their departure left an awkward silence.

The two teenagers carried in four more chairs for the adults. Nicky put a chair for himself next to Simone. "Hi, auntie," he said, hugging Simone before sitting.

Nicky and Simone could pass for twins. They both looked so much like Corelli, it was eerie. What would it feel like to have someone else with your face, your body, your mannerisms, Parker wondered?

Simone threw her arm over Nicky's shoulder. "Want to go whitewater rafting with us in September?"

Before the boy could respond, Patrizia, his mother, said, "Absolutely not. It's too dangerous. And you shouldn't be going either." The baby in her arms stiffened and began to howl at the harshness in her voice.

This sister was small and dark like Gianna, only older and angrier.

Patrizia bounced the baby and patted his back, continuing to coo in a voice that was softer but still angry. "Nicky has better things to do with his time. And you two," she said, thrusting her chin in the direction of Simone and Maria Carmela, "should be thinking about getting married, not going on some wild trip." She turned her attention to Corelli. "It's bad enough *you're* a cop. Next thing you'll be trying to sign them up."

Patrizia opened her mouth to go on, but Corelli tilted her head toward Parker, and she clamped her mouth closed. Nevertheless, Patrizia managed to communicate anger and disapproval through her facial expressions and body language. An uncomfortable silence followed, and Gianna jumped in to smooth things over, offering food and drinks.

Corelli stood. "We need to get going. We have a murder to solve."

Patrizia pursed her lips, but didn't comment.

Grinning, Corelli whispered in Marco's ear.

They said their goodbyes and once they were outside, Corelli relaxed. "Maybe I should send Patrizia's address to McGivens," she said, and then seeing Parker's shock, "just joking. She's my sister and I love her, though God knows she's not easy."

Parker started toward the car.

"Thanks for being there Parker. You saved my life."

"What do you mean?"

"You probably detected Patrizia hates my being on the job. She takes every opportunity to nag and harass me, but she would never, ever, air the family's dirty laundry in front of a stranger."

"Is that why you were nodding toward me?"

"Reminding her. Unfortunately, if I can't come up with something before Monday afternoon, she'll get her wish."

Parker put her hand on the car door just as Marco wheeled the big black and red Harley out of the garage. She straightened and stared.

"Here you go. Be careful, Chiara," he said, his Italian accent evident in the quiet.

Corelli kissed him on the cheek and said something in Italian.

"What's that?" Parker asked.

"It's a Harley Davidson," Corelli said, removing a helmet, leather jacket, and leather boots from the storage area. She stepped into the boots.

"Don't play dumb, Corelli." Parker moved between the bike and Chiara and stood with her hands on her hips. "No way are you riding that thing."

Marco rocked on his heels. "*Buona Notte.* Come back soon, PJ," he said, and escaped into the house.

"Out of my way." Corelli moved into Parker's space. "There's something I have to do and I don't want you involved."

Parker held her ground. "If it's too dangerous for me, then it's too dangerous for you."

"Go home, Parker. Pick me up in the morning. That's an order."

The front door opened and Gianna came out. "Marco said there was trouble. What's going on?"

Neither responded.

"Chiara? PJ?"

Corelli tied her boots and rose with her jacket, helmet, and shoes in her arms.

Gianna looked from one to the other. "You're acting like children."

Corelli ignored Gianna and stowed her shoes in the cargo area.

Gianna focused on Parker. "What is it, PJ?"

"The chief ordered me to protect Detective Corelli at all times. Now she's ordering me to let her go off somewhere on her motorcycle without me."

"It's not like you to be so unfair, Chiara." Gianna touched her sister's cheek. "She *is* responsible for you."

Corelli threw her hands in the air. "Two against one. That's what's not fair. All right, Parker will follow me in the car." She turned to Parker. "Will that do?"

"As long as you don't try to lose me."

"You have my word."

"Now that we've settled that," Gianna said, "can I ask where you're going that you need to be alone?"

"To visit a sick friend."

Parker followed Corelli to the Belt Parkway where they made a left, heading deeper into Brooklyn. About twenty-five minutes later they left the Belt, drove over a bridge and turned onto local streets. A few minutes later, on a block with neat bungalow houses that looked exactly like the streets they'd just passed, Corelli signaled and Parker pulled over. She rolled down the window. The car filled with a salty breeze and the sound of a giant breathing.

"Is that the ocean?" Parker asked. "Exactly where are we?"

"Belle Harbor, Queens. The ocean is just down that block. McGivens lives on this street and he walks his dog every night before the ten o'clock news. Stay back. I don't want him to see you, in case he calls it in."

"What if he—"

"I'm just going to talk. But use your judgment. Jump in if you feel I'm in danger."

"I don't like it."

"I need to do what I can. Understand?"

Parker nodded. Corelli continued down the block and parked the Harley. She stepped back into the shadow of a large tree and waited. Fifteen minutes later, the beer-bellied six-footer in shorts and flip-flops strolled in their direction with a Chihuahua on a leash.

Corelli stepped of the shadows, gun drawn. "We need to talk."

"Hey, it's Mata Hari, sneaking around as usual. Where's your shadow?" He scanned the area. "Ah, no shadow. Just you and the mighty Harley. How brave."

"Leave my family out of this, Jimmy."

"You wired?"

She opened her shirt. "Pat me down if you want."

"Nah, I tried that once and we know where that got me. Besides, you'll be in as much trouble as me if anybody hears this conversation." He pointed at her gun. "Put that thing away, Chiara. You know you're not going to shoot me."

"You misjudged me once, thinking I would join your dirty game. Maybe you're wrong again."

"Maybe, but you were doing the right thing then," he said. "Killing me isn't. Anyway, it's not me you have to worry about."

She kept the gun pointed at him. "Maybe I'm desperate because you're targeting my family and they have nothing to do with this. Call off your dogs, Jimmy."

"Arlo is the only dog I have and he's sitting nice and quiet."

She moved to his side and raised her gun to his temple. "How many meals have you eaten with my family? How could you threaten Simone and the others? What's happened to your decency?"

"What is it with you Italians and family?" He pushed the gun away. "What do you think will happen to *my* family and my decency if I go to jail?"

"You should have thought about that before you started stealing and killing."

"I did, sweetheart, and you're more likely to rot in jail than me." He faced her. "You should have thought about the danger of fooling around with people who have everything to lose. It's amazing how upset cops get when they think they're going to jail."

"How about I kill your wife and kids if anything happens to Simone or any member of my family?"

"You don't scare me, Chiara. You're too decent to kill innocents. Now excuse me. I don't want to worry my wife."

"You truly are a bastard. I'm warning you. Stay away from my family."

"Or what?" He smiled. No, it was a snarl, lips pulled back, teeth showing. "I can't wait to see you on TV." He laughed and strolled away, his back to her, as if he didn't have a care in the world. She holstered her gun, followed and tapped him on the shoulder. He turned. "Get lost, Chiara."

She put her hands on his shoulders, pulled him toward her and kneed him. He went down with a scream and she kicked him in the balls. "You harm one hair on anyone in my family and I'll show you 'or what.'"

She watched him struggle to catch his breath. After a few minutes, he stood, hands on his knees. "Bitch." He straightened. "You know, Chiara, it's too bad your whore Marnie died in Afghanistan. Otherwise you might have come home and fucked your brains out instead of turning on your friends." He staggered in the direction of his house.

Bastard, bringing Marnie into this. That was the trouble when friends became enemies. They knew how to hurt you. She walked back to the Harley. Parker pulled up next to her, a big grin on her face.

"Did kicking him in the balls change his mind?"

Corelli shook her head. "It was satisfying, but the only way to deal with people like Jimmy is to be as ruthless and unprincipled as they are. I'm not, and he knows it."

She'd always believed the law, good cops, and the judicial system would protect good people, but now, for the first time, she understood in her gut that sometimes the only way to protect someone you love is to kill. And she wanted to kill the bastard. She might, if she knew who was lined up behind him.

"C'mon, I'll follow you home."

"No. I'll be—"

"You promised."

Damn. She was in a rage at Jimmy McGivens, at the department, at Chief of Detectives Harry Broderick, and at all those "good" cops who failed to step up and stand behind her. She needed to be wild and reckless, to open the Harley up to maximum speed, to confront death and choose life. It was her drug of choice to deaden the knowledge that she hadn't protected Marnie, to deaden the fear that she couldn't protect her family, and to deaden the pain of living. But she'd given her word.

Parker sensed Corelli's anger and expected her to zoom away. But true to her word, Corelli kept to the right lane and maintained the speed limit, enabling Parker to follow at a safe distance. Traffic was light, or what passed for light on the Belt Parkway. Parker drove with her window down, enjoying the warm breeze, the briny smell of the New York Bay, and the flickering light of the full moon on the water.

A burst of light alerted Parker to the swift approach of a vehicle. As she checked the rearview mirror for its position, the car zoomed around her into the center lane, restoring the darkness. One after another, faster moving cars zipped by.

As they neared the Verrazano-Narrows Bridge, Parker relaxed into the ride, from time to time checking the rearview mirror. A black pickup came up fast in the middle lane, narrowed the distance but didn't pass. Parker couldn't see through its tinted windows, but it seemed harmless enough. After a few minutes, the pickup sped up until it was parallel with Corelli, and a Mini took its place in the lane next to Parker. Corelli glanced at the pickup and dropped her speed slightly. Parker leaned forward. Did Corelli see something she'd missed? The pickup stayed in place for a minute, but slowed until it was next to the Harley again. Now Corelli sped up and so did the truck. Maybe some macho guy trying to freak her? Except he couldn't know that a woman was riding the Harley.

The pickup was trouble. Corelli had no place to go. Parker was behind her and another car was ahead of her. Parker slowed to allow Corelli to fall back, but she too was boxed in, a car behind her and the Mini to the left of her behind the pickup.

Suddenly, the pickup veered toward Corelli. She steered toward the shoulder. The pickup pulled back into its lane and the Harley regained the road. The pickup slowed until it was parallel with the Harley again. Parker saw Corelli jerk and realized that a hand holding a gun was extended out the window of the pickup. *Sweet Jesus*. Parker checked the right. No shoulder there, just large blocks of stone. Corelli was boxed in, but she slowed the Harley and fell back, closer to Parker. The pickup dropped back too. The arm extended again. Parker blasted her siren and flashed her lights, startling Corelli and apparently the pickup, because the arm with the gun was withdrawn. It also caused the Mini on Parker's left to drop back allowing her to switch into the same lane as the pickup. Parker sped up behind the pickup, siren at full blast, lights flashing, spotlight shining into the truck, and rammed the truck's bumper. Corelli dropped back a little, out of the line of fire for the pickup. Parker stayed close to the pickup, siren going, spotlight focused on the inside of the truck. Her hands gripped the steering wheel as she alternately pushed and rammed the pickup's bumper. Corelli sped up next to the pickup. *What the hell was Corelli up to? She must be suicidal*. The hand with the gun came out. Corelli dropped back.

Parker rammed the truck and the gun was retracted. Corelli sped past Parker and the pickup and slowed just ahead of the pickup. The gun came out again. Cursing the crazy bitch, Parker put her bumper to the pickup's and pushed, then dropped back and rammed, pushed and rammed. As the gun was withdrawn, Corelli dropped back until she was parallel to Parker. Parker heard the sirens and noticed the flashing red and blue lights in her rearview mirror. The pickup must have heard and seen them too because it took off at high speed. Parker turned off the spotlight and the siren as two police cars sped past, lights flashing and sirens screeching. Parker waved Corelli to the shoulder. Several cars followed.

Her ears were ringing, her heart was racing, and she was covered with sweat. Parker rushed to Corelli who was straddling the Harley and waving her helmet. "Damn, Parker, that was exactly what I needed tonight."

"Are you crazy? Were you trying to get yourself killed?"

"Don't be stupid. I just needed a little rush and those assholes provided it."

Parker filled with rage. "A rush? Is that what being run off the road and maybe shot is to you? A rush? They could have killed you. You are a fucking nutcase. What about the other cars you jeopardized by continuing to bait those guys? What about me battering the pickup to protect you? What if they'd shot through my windshield or stopped short forcing me to crash into them at high speed? Not only are you crazy, you're fucking selfish."

Corelli grinned. "But none of that happened. They didn't kill me or anyone else. I'm alive, thanks to your quick thinking."

Two police cars pulled over.

Parker stared at her. *Is she nuts or is it me?* "It didn't feel like quick thinking. When I saw the gun come out of the window, I knew I had to do something and all I had was the siren, the light and the car. The siren startled them and got the other cars near us to pull away. I figured if they were blinded by the light and their truck was being rammed it would be hard to shoot. But what the fuck were you doing? You were taunting them."

"Ooh, Ms. ADA said a bad word. Have I upset you?"

"You bet your sweet ass I'm upset. I'm playing bumper cars at ninety miles an hour, trying to save your life and you're playing Russian roulette. How do you think your family would feel knowing you died because you needed a rush?"

That seemed to hit home. Corelli's grin drifted away. She put her hands up in surrender. "I should have realized that since McGivens thought I was alone he would send them after me."

Was that an apology of sorts? "Yes, but why did you deliberately put yourself in danger? I wondered but now I'm sure. You have all the symptoms of PTSD."

"Me? PTSD?"

"No question."

Two uniforms sauntered over. "Didju make the 911 call?"

Parker displayed her shield. "I'm Detective Parker. This is Detective Corelli. I was following Corelli in the unmarked. A black pickup tried to run her down and when that didn't work, they pulled out a gun. I called dispatch and reported an officer in trouble. Maybe one of the civilians called 911."

"Why would—" The uniform interrupted himself. "Corelli, you're the one—"

Not liking how this was going, Parker moved her jacket aside and rested her hand on her Glock. "Yes. And they were trying to kill her."

Corelli unzipped her leather jacket and placed her hand on her gun.

The uniform's eyes widened. He looked from Parker to Corelli and put his hands out. "Hey, we're on your side."

The other two uniforms approached. "Witnesses say the motorcycle was threatened and the driver of the car prevented the pickup from doing what it appeared to want to do, kill the Harley rider." The female uniform sensed the tension and drew her weapon. "Everybody relax now. What's going on?"

The first uniform laughed. "We have Detective Chiara Corelli on the Harley and Detective Parker from the unmarked."

"Corelli?" The uniform stared at her. "You can stand down, detective." She holstered her gun. "Some of us out in the hinterlands of Brooklyn think you're a hero."

Corelli and Parker exchanged a look. Corelli dismounted and stood with Parker as Parker described the incident, omitting Corelli's erratic behavior.

"Detective Parker saved my life tonight."

"We'll write it up that way," the female uniform said. "C'mon, we'll escort you to the Brooklyn Battery Tunnel, but you're on your own once you hit Manhattan."

As the uniforms returned to their cars, Corelli leaned in to Parker. "You gonna run home and tell Senator Daddy how you were an action hero today and saved my ass?"

"You really are sick. I'd be too embarrassed to admit that I didn't get rid of you when I had the opportunity." Parker opened the door to the unmarked, wondering if that was a smirk she saw on Corelli's face. No doubt the woman was a nut job.

CHAPTER THIRTY-FOUR

Corelli locked the elevator and leaned against the door, relieved to be home. It was a mistake to try to talk to Jimmy. She was no match for someone willing to lie, steal and even kill to protect himself. And while kicking him in the balls felt great, it wasn't such a smart move. Chances are he would have sent his dogs to kill her in any case since he thought she was alone. Lucky for her she wasn't. Parker had saved her life. And, in return, she'd taunted Parker. It was like she was possessed. The words came out of her mouth before she even thought them. Parker and Gianna both thought she had PTSD. Were they right?

Shrugging off her jacket and holster, she went to her home gym, put on gloves, and attacked the punching bag, letting it feel the full force of her suppressed rage. At first the pain from her right hand shot through her with every punch, but then it became almost pleasurable, and after a while she didn't feel it at all. She screamed and punched until she was exhausted. Soaked in sweat and out of breath, she hugged the bag to keep from falling. When her heart rate slowed, she dropped the gloves and trailing the rest of her clothing along the way, staggered to the bathroom. She turned up the temperature on the huge industrial vat that served as a bathtub, and while it heated, she poured herself a glass of brandy. Back in the bathroom she placed the glass on the ledge surrounding the tub, lit the candles, threw in bath salts, climbed the steps and sank into the already steaming tub with a soft moan.

Drying herself an hour later, she realized that the punching had diminished the anger but hadn't helped her pathetic right hand, which was again extremely swollen and sore. She pressed and probed and flexed, checking for broken bones. Not finding any, she wrapped the hand as best she could. She pulled on a robe, tossed her sweaty clothing in the dry cleaning pile, and hung up the boxing gloves. After making herself a cup of mint tea, she settled down to consider the situation. Unless she rooted out the whole rat's nest, her family would always be vulnerable.

Killing Jimmy might make her feel better, but it wouldn't solve the problem, and, as he pointed out, cold-blooded murder wasn't an option for her. Neither was doing nothing. Around-the-clock protection for all sixteen members of her immediate family could work, but there was no expiration date on revenge and it would be impossible to maintain protection indefinitely. She would have to do what they wanted—schedule a press conference, lose the job she loved and probably go to prison herself. A sudden surge of rage forced her to her feet. She paced the loft, thinking about the dirty cops, so many of them her friends. Their lives ruined by her actions.

She had felt guilty the entire time she was undercover, as if she was the dirty one. Once it was over she'd welcomed the attacks and the anger of other cops. Even the ostracism had felt right. Now for the first time, she felt angry, not guilty. They had stolen, maimed and killed for money. They were worse than the worst criminal and they deserved to be in jail. Exposing them was the right thing, a good thing. Jimmy and the others already identified had nothing to gain by killing her—except revenge. But the ones she hadn't identified, the brains behind the operation, had everything to lose. So far none of those arrested were talking, but only a few, like Jimmy, knew the names of the police at the top of the pyramid. Jimmy seemed confident he'd be protected but the leaders seemed to think she could expose them.

What had the chief said? "Someone living in fear, waiting for the doorbell or the telephone to ring, someone afraid that she would remember something that would implicate them."

Was that someone the cop trying to get her off the Winter case? She was the target and they were only threatening her family because she continued to outsmart them. She hadn't thought life worth living just a few months ago, so perhaps the way to keep her family safe was to let them kill her. But before doing that she would try to find the bastards.

She went to her desk and flipped through the computer printouts stacked there. Every night while undercover she'd downloaded the conversations recorded on her barrette to the FBI server and her own computer. Her nephew Nicky had printed as much as would fit on the ten reams of paper she had in the apartment. She sat with a stack on her lap but didn't read.

The beginning, that first day, was still so vivid. She could have been watching a movie. She and Jimmy had stood in Battery Park in that freak April sleet storm watching a man in a red jacket, who turned out to be Jimmy's favorite snitch, slipping and sliding toward them. Redman, as she'd thought of him, handed her a soggy brown paper bag overflowing with thousands of dollars in hundred dollar bills. Aware that Jimmy was taking pictures with his phone, she hesitated to give him a good view before tossing the bag into the slush and punching out Redman. Jimmy's phone was pointed at her until he scrambled to his knees in the slush and retrieved the money. She shivered, remembering the icy shards biting her face, her freezing hands and feet. Then later, in the car, she'd asked Jimmy why he'd set her up. She could hear his voice. "Because you're too smart not to notice what's going on and too honest to trust." She'd asked what would happen if she didn't join the ring of dirty cops. "Maybe the pictures I took will send you to jail, or, maybe, you'll be dead," her friend said.

Of course, Jimmy hadn't known she was the one doing the setting up, or that she was working with the FBI, the NYPD Chief of Police, Chief of Detectives, and Chief of Internal Affairs. He gave her an hour and fifteen minutes to think about it, and as she'd trudged through the sleet to the subway, she turned and saw him slide into a black Mercedes parked behind his car.

He'd been elated when she said yes. He was cautious about giving her too much information, but he needed her to know how important he was, so he introduced her to some of the others, low-level people like her. And a day or so later, when she'd asked about the guy in the black Mercedes in the park, he'd said, "Oh, that was cow…um, the big guy came to make sure I was still alive after you left." He'd laughed. "Actually, he came to congratulate me. Said I was the only one could get you to join up."

She picked up the pages for day two but gave up after less than an hour. Reading the printouts was a long-term effort and she didn't have the long term. She made another cup of tea and moved to the window. Jimmy was vindictive. He knew that losing the job would hurt her but she doubted he really understood. So even if she resigned, he would want her to suffer. He'd make sure she felt his pain by having Simone killed. And maybe others in her family.

So killing Jimmy wouldn't solve the problem, nor would round the clock protection for her family. She had no choice but to do what they wanted, resign and go to jail where they'd probably kill her. She struggled to find a fourth solution, but nothing came to mind.

CHAPTER THIRTY-FIVE

Corelli was cradling her hand the next morning. Parker could see it looked worse than yesterday. Had she gone out and gotten herself ambushed again? How the hell was she supposed to protect this woman? Parker slid Corelli's gun into the holster and held her jacket for her. Corelli eased her arm into the sleeve and gasped as her hand caught. She tried again and her badly bruised hand appeared. "I beat the hell out of my punching bag last night...or maybe it beat me."

Corelli must have read the disbelief on her face. "Trust me, Parker. I haven't been out since you dropped me off last night."

Once again, they'd arrived early enough to avoid the morning gauntlet, but as they stepped into the precinct, Parker steeled herself for the hostile vibes. Instead, the atmosphere seemed friendlier than a few days ago. Backs were still turned but there were a few smiles.

A female voice called out, "Good job with the kid."

Corelli nodded. Parker smiled. Nothing cops liked better than saving kids.

A man yelled. "Just Corelli grandstanding again."

Parker whirled toward the voice, but everyone seemed absorbed in work. She trailed Corelli up to the squad. Watkins was reading the paper. The coffee was ready.

The coffee at Corelli's house had roused her somewhat, but Parker still felt as if she was walking underwater, so she took a cup and listened as Corelli told Watkins about the threat to her family.

By the end of the story Watkins's hands were fisted. "What are we going to do?"

"I'm open to suggestions. The only thing I can think of is putting feelers out on the street and in the department to see if we can figure out who's still out there. Could you do that, Ron?"

"Sure thing. As soon as we finish up."

"Other than that, I don't know. The chief offered protection for my whole family, but that won't last long, with budgets and all."

She glanced down at her swollen hand. "Right now, it seems as if I'm going to have to do what they want."

"You know I—"

"Yes, I know, Ron. I appreciate you both for offering. If I come up with a plan, you two will be the first to know. And speaking of knowing, Ron, you should know that I was bringing the Harley home from Brooklyn last night when a pickup tried to run me off the road. When that didn't work, they started shooting. Luckily, Parker was following me in the unmarked and ran them off."

"You're shitting me."

"Nope, the intrepid Detective Parker saved my life and I am eternally grateful."

Parker flushed. "Just doing my job." *With no help from you, crazy lady.*

"Yeah, that's why you get the big bucks." Corelli flashed her Mona Lisa smile. "I might as well enjoy the work while I have it. Let's get started."

Parker described their trip to West Virginia, laughing about how Detective Stephanie Brown had terrorized John Broslawski. "We learned a lot about Winter, but we still have questions about her brother. He was hiding something."

Corelli nodded. "We'll see how the investigation goes. We may make another visit. You're up Watkins."

"The cleaning woman's ten-year-old daughter translated for me. She cleaned the restrooms a little after nine. The girl said her mother always wears a gold cross, and the woman showed me a small gold cross on a chain around her neck. And by the way, she's a lefty. Since we know the killer was a righty, we can clear her as a suspect.

"Chip Roberts, the bartender, left a message, said a guy wearing a green shirt walked into the bar last night, and he remembered somebody in a bright green shirt running out of Winter's building the night of the murder when he was putting Rino in the limo. Said he totally forgot about it."

"Man or woman?" Corelli asked.

"He didn't remember," Watkins said.

Parker made a note. "Guess we should have asked what everybody was wearing."

"Something to check out. Go on, Watkins."

"I talked to Brett Cummings at her apartment in Battery Park City. She said she leaves the crosses to her brother, the priest. Claimed she didn't mention the argument with Winter because it was a business matter. Winter was planning to steal business from a small brokerage house. Cummings argued for going after the big guys because the loss could put the small firm out of business. She said she was furious because Winter seemed…" He referred to his notes again. "…devoid of compassion." So she jogged up to 79th Street in the rain to cool off. According to her, she was going to resign on Monday and go back to her old company."

"Did you verify her story about a standing offer?" Corelli asked.

"The president of the firm, Fred Barley, said he made the offer himself. He didn't think Cummings would last with Winter because their values were so different."

"Did he see Cummings as a killer?" Corelli said, determined that her intense attraction to Brett wouldn't keep her from seeking the truth.

He shook his head. "According to Barley she's brilliant and aggressive in business, but not cutthroat, not a killer. And, for what it's worth, I don't see her as the killer. You?"

Parker shook her head. "She seemed genuinely shocked when we told her Winter had been murdered. And I don't think being angry over a business plan is a motive for murder."

Corelli didn't comment so he went on. "Rieger, the head of finance, assured me there's no problem with the company's financials and said he would go over the books with anyone we bring in to audit them. I asked whether he saw or heard anyone go in after he left Winter with Cummings, and he said he was concentrating on what he was doing and didn't hear a thing. But he was evasive about what he was doing. Also, his assistant said he's been secretive and jumpy for the last month or so. Like he was worried about something."

He turned to the next page in his notebook. "The guest list for the awards dinner Tuesday night was a bust. Apparently the mayor gave the police chief tickets to fill two tables and the tickets dribbled down the line. There's no record of who got them or who attended. And the videos I was able to get focused mainly on Winter's table and on the stage during the award. Funny thing, she almost dropped the pyramid when the governor handed it to her. I guess he didn't warn her that it was heavy."

"We'll have to find the mystery cop some other way." Corelli looked at her notes. "Anything on the security tapes?"

"Dietz says there were no tapes in the cameras. The security company replaces the tapes twice a year. The last time was three months ago."

"So, either they forgot to put in new tapes or our guy removed them," Corelli said.

"The cameras are mounted high and would require a ladder to get to them. There's one in the basement but would the killer know it was there? Would he take a chance on being caught? My guess is they never replaced the tapes."

"The ladder was in the lobby Friday night," Parker said. "The guard told us he carried it downstairs Saturday morning."

Watkins shook his head. "It's still a stretch for the killer to stop to remove the tapes. But if he did, someone shrewd enough to take the tapes would be unlikely to leave prints. So it's no surprise we had no hits on the full or partial prints we found."

"Now, the good news." Watkins put his briefcase on the table. "We found the safe deposit box. Winter opened it about fifteen years ago and hasn't been back since. There's some interesting stuff."

He reached into his briefcase, enumerating the items as he placed them on the desk. "One very old child's notebook. One dog-eared copy of *Think and Grow Rich* by Napoleon Hill. Some papers about the library in Hope Falls. Papers about a gift to a Clara Lipkin; a contract with the publisher of the Hill book to print a special edition; a birth certificate for Constance Broslawski, born 1954; a high school diploma for same; papers legally changing her name to Winter; and, a faded picture of a woman in a bridal gown, the groom cut out."

"Great work Watkins."

"Not me." He smiled. "Kim and Filleti deserve the credit." He handed Corelli the notebook. "Winter was ten-years-old when she wrote the first entry. I've already read it. Why don't you and Parker take a look."

"Move over Parker." Except for agreeing when to turn the page, they read in silence.

April 13, 1964. Today is the wurst day of my life an everything is bad. I burn his breakfas an he hit me and give me a bloodie nose and a big cut on my top lip and the blood wont stop for a wile He curse like always and call me a worth less pece of shit an says he shoulda made ma get a aborshun. Peet an jon run after me an they scream the same thin, I hate them. Then melisa she sees I ware her old dress and the girls call me whit trash. Mis scermhorn she makes me say sam thin over an over an all the kids laff at me.

I go to library an my fren Mis lebken is nice to me lik always then I find the book about geting rich and I feel better so I tak it. I never stealed but I need it. Mis lebken didn see. It is better then cinderela caus it is real. its hard som places but it says I can be rich if I want.

May 1, 1964 no body can make me cry now. Ever morn an nite I say the magic word that some day I be rich an I wil show them an they wil be sorrie an I feel happy. I mak plan to tak som monie ever week and go a way.

Corelli made eye contact with Parker and Watkins. "We've heard most of this. You can almost understand her becoming so cruel. Your family sets the pattern for your life, and whether you live according to that pattern or in opposition to it, it's the filter through which you see the world." She refilled her cup and began to pace. "Still, we all make choices about our humanity. At some point, you move on from your childhood experiences and forgive or at least forget. It sounds like Connie Winter held that childhood hurt and rage close, like a precious jewel, so she never got past it."

She sat and they continued reading the entries Winter had made sporadically through her childhood. It was clear that as she got older she was obsessed with her needs and getting back at those who hurt her.

"Here it is," Corelli said. "What she did when she left Hope Falls. Listen to this."

June 1, 1970. Arranged a room in Charleston. Told principal I'm moving to Atlanta to be with my aunt and got a copy of my school records. As soon as school is over and I get the week's money, I'll take the bus. What a surprise for him and the boys. I hope they'll be hungry. I need to keep it a secret, so I'll write to Miss Lipkin later to explain.

June 25, 1970. Charleston. Got a job as a waitress in the Charleston Family Diner. I can work days until September and if I'm a good worker they'll let me work nights while I go to school.

July 23, 1970. I flatter the chef and he gives me food so I can save more money for New York. How can a fat old fart like him believe I think he's smart and wonderful? Men. Yuk.

June 30, 1972. NEW YORK FINALLY. Found a job at Grodine Brokerage Services in the secretarial pool. I'm happy about working on Wall Street where the big money is. Hope.

July 30, 1972. Love the job, trying to learn as much as possible. Found out I can take courses to learn about the business. Plan to enroll in September.

September 20, 1972. Staying late to read stuff on everybody's desk so I know what's going on.

July 1, 1973. Promoted. Now I'm Mr. Grodine's assistant. I'm on my way. Everybody is jealous. No one talks to me. They'll be sorry. Someday I'll own a brokerage firm, bigger than this but first I'll learn everything Richard knows.

November 15, 1977. Richard giving me more responsibility, more money. Getting dependent.

February 9th, 1979. Have a plan. Richard is cooperating. Won't he be surprised.

July 1, 1982. Winter Brokerage Services opened today. I did it.

"That's the last entry. What a cold fish." She tossed the book on the desk. "Anything else, Watkins?"

"That's it."

Corelli opened her notebook. "I have some items that need follow-up." She glanced at the list she'd made earlier while waiting for them to arrive. "Rieger and Hornsby should both be in the office today. Ask Dietz to have them picked up about eleven. Maybe an interview at the station will convince them to share."

"Call the lab about the blood on the bartender's shirt." She checked off the first two items. "The fact that the public street in front of Winter's house is blocked off and gated has been bothering me. See if Dietz can find out who approved it. Also, ask Edwards for the name of the security firm that provides the guards for Winter's house and get copies of their invoices for the last year."

Watkins jotted the items down. "What's wrong with her security?"

"I think it's worth checking out for a couple of reasons. First, the firm Winter is using seems sloppy and unprofessional and that doesn't fit with what we know about her. Second, the other day, the guard, a guy I never saw before, called me Mata Hari. Jimmy called me Mata Hari when I arrested him and again last night. Makes me curious about a possible connection."

"Last night? Is that why you were in Brooklyn? You talked to—"

She laughed. "A minor indiscretion of little value. It won't happen again. See what you can dig up on the firm. Let's meet at Buonasola around two so we can figure where to go from here. Oh, and get Kim or Filetti to follow up with Richard Grodine. It sounds like Winter screwed him royally. Maybe he's been waiting for a chance to kill her."

CHAPTER THIRTY-SIX

They drove south on the East River Drive headed for Sheepshead Bay, each lost in her own thoughts. The glint of the sun on the river pulled Corelli's eyes toward the water. Lulled by the warmth of the sun and the whoosh of the air-conditioner, images of magical summer afternoons at the Bay of Palermo flashed into her mind, taking her back to the happy summers spent in Sicily with her extended family. The saga of the Broslawski-Winter-Gianopolus family contrasted with her experience growing up in a large, loving family on both sides of the Atlantic. She was lucky then and lucky now to have so much love surrounding her. She had failed to protect Marnie but she would protect Simone and her family, no matter the cost.

Reading Winter's diary had saddened her, but thinking about Gus Jr. and Aphrodite growing up in that loveless environment made her angry. It also brought to mind Parker's remarks about not being close to her family. She'd assumed that Parker's family like many black families, was similar to an Italian family—loving, warm and welcoming, with lots of food, drink, and good times. Yet Parker bristled whenever Corelli mentioned the senator and she never mentioned her mother or any other family. Corelli sighed.

Parker maneuvered the car around the usual traffic jams on the East River Drive with the expertise of a New York City taxi driver. "What?"

"I was thinking about families, about how children need love, and about how damaged Aphrodite and Gus Jr. must be, having a mother and father who didn't have love to give."

"At least they had Gertrude and Cora Andrews."

"True." Her cell rang. "Corelli."

"Hey, boss," Watkins said. "Thought you'd want to know that the blood on the bartender's shirt wasn't Winter's."

"Blood isn't Winter's," Corelli mouthed to Parker.

"Also, I'm still digging, but the security firm is called RP Security, Inc."

Corelli felt as if someone had punched her in the stomach. "Are you sure?"

"About the blood?"

"The name of the security firm."

"Yup. Do you know it?"

"I'll explain later but I need everything you can find on them. Be careful about asking other police. Ask Rieger or Cummings to pull their invoices and anything else they can find about them. And give Tess Cantrell a call. I'm sure she has some shady PI sources she can use to dig where digging isn't allowed. Talk to you later."

"Here we are," said Parker. "Maybe Rino can tap a better dance this time." She touched Corelli's arm. "What's going on with the security firm?"

"I'll explain later. Let's get this over with."

Rino Martucci was sitting on the front stoop of his trim little house. He started talking as soon as the car doors opened. "The limo's still here. What's happening? Should I call Gus or something?"

He led them through the hallway, his high-heeled cowboy boots clonking on the hardwood floor. He hadn't mastered the art of walking in heels so his gait was unsteady, and he tripped as he tried, apparently unsuccessfully, to pull a wedgie out of his skin-tight jeans. Corelli's nose wrinkled in response to the same unpleasant smells, cologne and cigarettes, in the same unpleasant living room. "Gus will call you when I say you're clear."

"Um, whadoya mean, *clear*?"

Corelli watched him fidget, eyes flicking back and forth between her and Parker, trying to judge who would lead the assault. He wiped his dripping nose on the back of his hand. *Typical cokehead.*

When his eyes darted to the open kitchen door, Corelli shot a question at him in a loud voice. "Where were you between nine thirty and eleven Friday night?" He flinched. His eyes were wild when he turned.

Instead of responding he lurched to his feet. "Mind if I get a drink?" He dashed into the kitchen without waiting for an answer, but he took the time to close the door. They looked at each other. Corelli crept to the door and opened it. As she suspected, Rino was about to inhale a line of cocaine. Her yell startled him and he exhaled instead of inhaling and the coke sprayed over the countertop. His first instinct was aggressive, but he remembered he was dealing with two cops and swallowed it. His face had paled and he was sweating, but he managed a weak smile and an apology.

He grabbed the bottle of scotch and a glass from the counter and sidled back to the living room. He perched on the edge of the recliner. He placed his hands over his crotch and stared into Corelli's eyes. She knew he was setting her up for the first lie.

"I...I was with this woman I see. She's married, so I can't give you her name."

Corelli leaned in. "If you don't answer the questions, we'll go down to headquarters and book you for possession."

"I answered."

"You get no points for lies. Listen Martucci, this is a murder investigation. Right now you are a prime suspect and you have no alibi for the time of the murder. So give us the woman's name or the truth about where you were. Whatever it is, it can't be as bad as a murder charge."

His hand moved to brush back an invisible hair. He sniffed and wiped his nose on his wrist. His eyes filled. "I didn't do nothing. I told you, I felt like killing her, but I didn't."

"Last chance. Where were you between nine thirty and eleven Friday night?"

He sucked down half the glass of scotch, hung his head, and said in the voice of a sulky ten-year-old, "I'm afraid if I tell you, you'll lock me up."

"Maybe, but murder could mean life behind bars." Corelli took out her cuffs.

"Wait, wait."

She stopped. He emptied his glass.

"I never drank or did drugs on the job before because that was her rules and she pays so good. But, I was fed up. The bitch pushed me too far, treating me like a slave, like I don't have a life. I didn't care if she fired me, so I went to make a coke buy on the Upper East Side. I did some there and then some later in the bathroom at the bar. I got a bloody nose. But I got no proof where I was and nobody up there's gonna alibi me." He wiped his nose on his wrist. "You gonna get me on the coke?"

"You're not off the hook for the murder yet, but the narcs will want to have a conversation about the drugs. By the way, I see you wear cowboy boots. Do you ride horses or spend time near horses?"

Rino shifted in his chair and looked away. "It's, just, you know, a style, but I don't like horses and never rode one."

"Stay put. Don't try to do a runner or—"

"I know, I know. I won't do nothing stupid."

"You're already doing something stupid, combining coke and scotch," Corelli said.

"Yeah, I know. I gotta stop." He followed them to the door and watched them get into the car. "Wait." He walked to the car. "I almost forgot to tell you. I remembered a guy standing outside the bar when I ran from the limousine. I think he was watching Connie's building."

"What did he look like?"

"My height but kinda stocky, flabby with big cheeks. He had on one of those Hawaiian shirts, bright green. He looked familiar but I can't place him."

"You believe him?" Corelli asked, as they pulled away.

Parker thought about it. "Yes. The green shirt corroborates Chip's memory and the nosebleed would explain the blood he left on Chip's shirt. We know it wasn't her blood. You?"

"I think he's telling the truth. We'll give him to Narcotics; they'll want his source."

She shifted to face Parker. "The guy he described could be Broslawski. I'll bet that's what he lied about. He was still hanging around at nine and, if Chip is right, he was coming out of the building around a quarter to one, so he could have killed her."

"Should I try to get a warrant to bring him up?"

"It'll be easier to go down again or get Detective Stephanie Brown to talk to him."

PJ laughed. "She could certainly motivate Broslawski to tell the truth."

CHAPTER THIRTY-SEVEN

Jenny Hornsby shifted her attention from the wall as they settled in the chairs opposite her, but her hand never stopped tapping the Styrofoam cup on the table. Her face telegraphed anxiety rather than impatience.

"Morning," Parker said. "Hope it wasn't too embarrassing, the cops escorting the VP of HR out of your office. Did they cuff you?"

Hornsby shook her head.

"As you know, we're here about the murder of Connie Winter," Parker said. "Please tell us where you were between eight thirty and midnight Friday night and we'll let you go back to work. Otherwise…"

"I don't know what you want me to say. I didn't kill her. What I was doing is private. It had nothing to do with her."

"You're wasting our time, Mrs. Hornsby. You're a suspect in a murder investigation and if you won't answer our questions, we'll draw our own conclusions."

"I have nothing else to say."

"Think about it for a while."

They left Hornsby as they found her, staring at the wall, tapping her coffee cup.

"Well, well, Mrs. Hornsby has balls. We need to apply pressure," Parker said.

"Putting her in a cell might do it, but let's talk to Rieger. Maybe he'll confess and we can forget about it."

Parker stared at Corelli, surprised at the weariness in her voice.

"Sorry, I'm tired. We'll go at her all day if we need to, but I hope not."

Philip Rieger sat erect, staring straight ahead, hands clasped in front of him like a schoolboy. His anxiety was perceptible.

"Mr. Rieger, are you aware that after seven p.m. the only way to get in to 63 Wall Street is by ringing the bell to summon the porter?"

"Yes."

"We believe that Ms. Winter was murdered sometime between nine and two in the morning. As far as we know, only you and Ms. Cummings were already in the building on the thirty-fifth floor, during that time. That makes you a prime suspect."

He froze. "It must have been Brett. I heard them arguing."

"What were you doing in the office until eleven o'clock?"

He stared at Parker. "Don't be ridiculous. Why would I kill her? I have nothing to hide. I said I would work with any auditor you bring in."

"Please answer the question."

"I was going over the, um, month-end financials."

Parker bared her teeth. "Was there something wrong with them? Ms. Edwards said you and Ms. Winter had spent a good part of the day in her office reviewing those reports."

"The financials are fine."

"Then why stay until eleven o'clock on a Friday night going over the same reports?"

He pulled out his handkerchief, swiped at his face, and then carefully folded it and put it back in his pocket. He clasped his hands again and looked down. Parker could hear his foot tapping.

"I was checking out a few things, that's all."

"We've heard you've been worried lately, anxious about something. Why don't you tell us what's going on?"

He jerked his head up. "Who said that? There's nothing wrong."

"Was Connie threatening to fire you? Did she laugh at you and make you so angry that you lost control and hit her?"

"No. She was happy with my work. I had no reason to kill her."

Corelli stood. "Let's go. We're wasting our time."

Parker rose. "How about you make all of our lives easier and tell us what you're hiding, Mr. Rieger."

Sweat beaded on his forehead. He chewed his lip. He leaned closer to Parker. "I'm having an affair and the person was there with me. Please, I don't want to hurt my wife."

Parker rolled her eyes, but Rieger was looking down so he didn't notice. *What is it with men? First they fool around then they want to protect the little lady?* "We have no need to tell your wife. Give us her," Parker hesitated, "or *his* name, so we can verify your story." She felt Corelli's gaze on her.

"I promised I would never tell."

Parker stood. "We'll be in and out all day and night, so ask the officer to let us know when you're ready to talk. We'll get back to you when we can." She moved toward the door.

He ran his hands over his face. "No, wait. My wife can't know." They stood, backs to the door; neither said anything. At last he said, "It's Jenny."

Parker couldn't keep the surprise out of her voice. "You mean Jennifer Hornsby, the Vice President of Human Resources? That Jenny?"

He didn't seem to notice. "Yes, you arrested her too."

"What happened that night?"

"Jenny came back after she left the hospital and we had sex in her office." He looked at his watch. "Can we go now? Gus has asked Brett to run the company, at least for a while, and she's called a meeting for two o'clock."

"We'll verify this with Ms. Hornsby and then you can both go, but, for the record, we didn't arrest you, we brought you in for questioning."

As they walked to Hornsby's interview room, Parker shook her head. "I'm amazed. I never would have guessed she had it in her."

Corelli smiled. "A good lesson to learn, Detective. Never judge by appearances."

Hornsby sat, elbows on the table, head cradled in her hands. She looked up at Parker. "Now what?"

"Mrs. Hornsby, are you having an affair with Mr. Rieger?"

Her face reddened and tears filled her eyes. "I know what it seems like, but my husband is dying. I'm lonely and worried.

Connie has been giving me such a hard time, and Philip has been so warm and caring. It just happened."

Parker cleared her throat. "So, would you like to tell us where you were Friday night between eight o'clock and midnight?"

She spoke to her hands which lay on the table, palms up. "After I left the hospital at eight thirty, I went back to the office to meet Phil. We wanted to be sure nobody would know we were meeting, so when I came out of the subway, I called and he came down and opened the lobby door. We were in my office until about eleven." She shuddered. "It's horrible to think we were making love while she was murdered. My office is on the opposite side of the building, farthest from hers. The door was closed, we had the radio on, and we didn't hear anything, anything at all. When we were done, Phil left to catch his train and I left five minutes later."

CHAPTER THIRTY-EIGHT

As they entered the Buonasola Grill, Parker continued the discussion. "Both Aphrodite and Hornsby confirmed the door was locked. Hornsby and Rieger had something other than murder on their minds earlier but one of them could have done it after sex, before leaving the building at eleven. Otherwise, the only suspects are Cummings, and, if the cleaning lady is telling the truth, the mysterious cop."

"Actually, since the porter had to open the door for Aphrodite, we know it was locked about nine, but Hornsby only confirmed that she and Rieger assumed the door was locked," said Corelli as they seated themselves at her favorite waterside table.

"You mean they saw what they expected to see?"

"Maybe. A mistake we need to avoid."

"So, we *still* don't know for sure if the door was locked after nine o'clook." Parker opened her menu.

"Let's order, then go through your notes while we wait for Watkins. Something has been on the tip of my tongue since we got back from Hope Falls. Maybe your notes will trigger it."

Once they'd ordered, Parker took out her notebook. "Where should we start?"

"Day one."

Parker turned to the first page and started reading her notes at a fast but easy to understand tempo. Corelli stared at the water, listening. Occasionally she asked Parker to repeat something. They were up to their meeting with Clara Lipkin when lunch arrived.

"Let's eat and then continue," Corelli said. She took a bite of her grilled chicken and began to replay the interviews in her mind. A few minutes later she pushed her sandwich aside. "Brett Cummings."

"What?"

"She knew Winter was from West Virginia, but not even Gus knew that."

"You think Cummings killed her?"

"I don't see a motive."

Watkins appeared and sat at the table. "Sorry to be late. I waited for Kim to print out some articles on Richard Grodine. Want to hear?"

The waiter took Watkins's order and left.

"Before Grodine," Corelli said, "do you have anything on Winter's security firm?"

"Not much more than the name right now. But, Tess Cantrell, Brett Cummings, and Phil Rieger are pulling together as much information as they can find."

"Okay, we'll settle for the other stuff."

"Richard Grodine committed suicide about twenty-three years ago. His company, Richard Grodine Brokerage, was small and very prosperous until he lost all of his biggest accounts and it failed. He was deep in debt and killed himself, leaving a wife and three children, Eric, five years old, Richard Jr., eight years old, and Laura, twelve years old." He reached into his case and brought out copies of several articles. "I thought you might want to see these. Check out the pictures."

Parker moved closer to Corelli. "Brett Cummings," Parker whispered.

Sure enough, there was a young Brett/Laura, looking up adoringly at a very tall and lean man. Of course, you couldn't see the coloring in the photocopies, but you could see that she was a softer, more feminine version of her handsome father. The same carriage, same features, and the same generous smile.

Corelli leaned back. "Cummings must have met Winter when she worked for her father. Maybe Cummings is her married name."

"I called around and found some old-timers, people quoted in the articles. Winter left Grodine's firm to start her own brokerage house and stole most of his customers. Not too long after Grodine's firm went down the tubes."

Parker pushed her half-eaten sandwich aside. "So Winter stole her inheritance and caused the father she obviously adored to commit suicide. That's awful."

"It sure is," Watkins said. "It's not unusual for a successful broker to leave and take his clients with him, but these were Grodine's clients, not hers. She convinced them to come with her. You know, even though she's dead, some of these guys hesitated to talk about her."

Corelli cleared her throat. "As far as we know, Cummings was the last one to see Winter alive, and she admitted arguing with Winter about her plan to steal business from small firms. The very thing that drove her father to commit suicide."

"She was a kid when it happened. Why wait so long? I think Gus has the strongest motive and we seem to be ignoring him," Parker said.

"Cummings was in the office. Gus wasn't." Corelli knew Parker had taken to Cummings and didn't want her to be the killer.

"Maybe she didn't plan it. Maybe she lost control during that argument," Watkins said.

Corelli stared out at the river, wrestling with the decision she didn't want to make. She could feel their tension as they waited for direction. Cummings had sparked something deep inside her, and the physical attraction was profound. But, she was currently the most likely suspect and she needed to be cleared or charged.

"I don't think we have enough for a warrant to search her apartment. When we're finished here, you two drop me at One Police Plaza, do a little research on Cummings and then pick her up." Seeing Parker's face, she added, "The chief will have somebody drive me to the station."

"Anything in particular we're after?" Watkins asked.

"Where she grew up, how she dealt with her father's death, whatever you can find out."

Parker's face darkened.

"What is it, Parker?"

"What about Gus?"

"We have to follow the evidence, Parker. Remember, unless we can prove the door was open, only Cummings and the cop had access to Winter. Let's rule Cummings out while we try to find him."

"We're wasting our time."

I hope you're right. "It's what we have to do."

CHAPTER THIRTY-NINE

Like Watkins, Chief of Detectives Harry Broderick's attempts to tap into the grapevine were fruitless. The threats of retribution had silenced everyone. And except for the police guard for her family, Harry had no solution. When she got back to the oh-eight, she considered calling FBI Agent Trillums, the guy who had set up the undercover operation, but she decided it would be futile. The FBI was denying the operation existed so it was up to her to figure this out. And for the next hour she obsessed about how to save her job, stay alive, and protect her family, but there didn't seem to be a way to accomplish all three. Then, resigned to holding the press conference, her anxiety about the threat morphed into anxiety about the pending interview. Head in hands, she searched for the strength to control her feelings and deal with Cummings professionally.

She paused at the door to the interview room, took a deep breath and walked in. Cummings turned, her face dark and furious. Corelli smiled, more a physical reaction than an expression of happiness. Parker had gone sullen. Corelli stepped on Cummings's feet as she settled into the empty seat facing her.

"Sorry," Corelli said, blushing.

Cummings retracted her legs and sat up. "It's my fault," she said, polite even in her rage.

"Well, Ms. Cummings—"

"Brett."

"Brett. We've determined that Connie Winter wasn't from the Midwest as she claimed."

"What has that got to do with me?"

"How did you know she was from West Virginia when even her husband didn't know?"

"But I didn't. I barely knew the woman."

"Detective Parker, please read your notes from our first interview with Ms. Cummings."

Parker found the place in her notes and read aloud. "Why in the world would someone kill the poor ugly duckling from West Virginia who came to the Big Apple and built an empire with brains and hard work?"

"I said that?"

"Yes," Corelli said.

"She must have told me sometime or other, maybe one of the nights we had dinner together when she was recruiting me. I don't remember. Why does it matter?"

"Don't you find it odd that she told you the truth and lied to her husband?"

"Connie said whatever served her purpose at the time."

"So you didn't know this when you started working for her?"

"Where she came from? Absolutely not."

"Maybe you could help me out with something else then."

Cummings shifted in her seat and some of the tension left her body, perhaps feeling that she had gotten by the lie and could relax. She brushed her hair back and leaned toward Corelli, smiling. "I'll do whatever I can."

"Good. Please tell me if you recognize anyone in these pictures." Corelli handed Cummings the newspaper clippings that Watkins had collected. Cummings's smile drifted away and her face lost its color. She wrapped her arms around herself.

"How did you…Where did you…I—"

"Was Richard Grodine your father, Ms. Cummings?"

She stared at the articles in her hand.

"Brett?"

Cummings lifted her head and their eyes locked. "Yes."

"Yes, he was your father?"

"Yes, he was my father. But this has nothing to do with her death."

"That's not how it looks, Brett. Do you want to explain?" *I'm so sorry to cause you pain.*

"There's nothing to explain. He trusted someone who didn't deserve to be trusted. He killed himself because he made some stupid mistakes and couldn't fix them." She put her head in her hands. Her fingers massaged her forehead, and she seemed to shrink into herself. Corelli filled with a flood of contradictory feelings, the desire to reassure Brett competed with the cop's need to get to the truth. She didn't know if she could continue.

"You need coffee or tea?" Corelli wasn't sure which of them Parker addressed the question to, but Cummings answered. "Please. Coffee, milk and sugar. And some water. Is there a ladies' room I could use?"

Parker opened the door and asked Shaunton to escort Cummings to the ladies' room.

Corelli stood. "I need the ladies' room myself. Be right back."

Noting the disapproval on Parker's face, Corelli smirked. "Don't worry. I won't go in with her."

Corelli placed wet paper towels on her forehead and on the back of her neck, trying to relax. She had never felt so vulnerable, so out of control. Her attraction to Marnie had never interfered with her ability to function. Of course, Marnie had never been a suspect in a case, so this was different. Maybe she was different. She'd never faced the kind of threat she was facing now. And her attraction to Cummings was much more intense. Whatever the reason, attraction to a suspect was unacceptable. She needed to marshal her self-discipline and be clearheaded, objective. She didn't want to believe Cummings would kill, but she had motive and opportunity. And Corelli understood, as she had never understood before, that anyone could kill in the right situation. But Winter was no threat to Cummings. And Cummings was smart enough to know that beating her in business was the way to hurt Winter. As she left the ladies' room, she wondered if she was losing perspective and making the case against Cummings to compensate for her feelings.

Ten minutes later they settled down again. Cummings seemed revived. Corelli resolved to remain in control. "Brett, this doesn't look good for you, so I would advise you to not hold anything back."

Cummings sipped the hot coffee, brushed her hair behind her ears and cleared her throat, but she didn't speak. Corelli's heart wrenched at the pain in her eyes, but she forced herself to maintain eye contact.

Cummings sighed. "You're right. I knew she was from West Virginia because she worked for my dad, and he always referred to her as the ugly duckling from West Virginia. I remember hearing him say to my mother, 'She's amazing. A poor, ugly duckling from West Virginia and she's smarter and works harder than my Ivy League graduates who are making five and six times as much.' He was very much taken with her, nothing sexual mind you, just admiration."

"Why didn't you tell us this before?"

"It didn't seem relevant at first, and then I knew it would look bad. It does, doesn't it?"

"Do you want to explain?"

She took a deep breath and tucked the wayward lock of hair behind her ear again. "I worshipped him, you know?" Her eyes flickered to each of their faces, seeking understanding. "We did lots of sports together—swimming, tennis, sailing, hunting, things like that. He taught me the brokerage business, and although I have two younger brothers, I was the one he wanted to run the business. In fact, I was supposed to start working with him the summer it happened."

"What happened?" Corelli asked.

"As I said, Connie impressed my father. She started in the typing pool but made herself stand out. He knew what she was doing. She would find ways to get his attention, like timing her comings and goings with his so she could ask him questions. Nevertheless, he was impressed by her hard work, her persistence, and her brains. Eventually, he made her his assistant."

Corelli couldn't hide her surprise. "He was aware of what she was doing and still he promoted her?"

"He knew she was ambitious but he saw that as a good thing. I don't think he ever imagined how ruthless she was. Over the next seven or eight years, he gave her more and more responsibility and eventually he let her deal with his clients. She urged him to take time off, to let her do more of the work, run the business. She was competent and loyal, he thought. She always seemed to be taking care of him. So he was lulled into letting go of more and more."

Cummings paused and took a sip of coffee. "What he didn't realize was that she was undermining him with his clients, pointing out how little time he was spending on the business. And, she was constantly flattering, praising, and seducing the clients—and him—until she was ready to leave. She rented offices, lined up people—his people—to work for her at extravagant salaries. She took most of his clients with her. He was the last to know."

Her voice broke and she struggled for control. "Not only did she steal his business, she also spread rumors that limited his ability to attract new customers. He was forced into bankruptcy. When he asked her why she'd ruined him, she said she had planned it when she first started working for him ten years before, and it couldn't have happened if he hadn't cooperated. Needless to say, he was destroyed by the whole thing."

"How did he react?" asked Corelli.

"Initially, he was in a rage and determined to rebuild the business, but when he talked to his old clients and tried to cultivate new ones, he realized that his reputation was ruined, and he despaired of working successfully in the business he loved. He became despondent, started drinking and became abusive to my mother. She left him. So deep in debt and alone, he put a gun in his mouth and killed himself."

"You blamed Connie Winter?" Corelli asked.

"Damn right, I blamed her. I was devastated by my father's ruin and even more so by his death. I was in a rage at her for what she had done to him and our family. I was a kid. I wanted to hurt her like she'd hurt us."

"Did you fantasize about killing her?"

"Of course. But I mostly turned the rage inward. I started skipping school and doing drugs and hanging out with a wild crowd. Then, when I was eighteen, I was arrested with some marijuana on me, enough so that I could have gone to jail for a very long time under New York's Rockefeller laws. But I was lucky. My father and I had hunted and fished with the police chief, so he knew me, knew my story and offered me a deal. If I went into therapy and stayed until the therapist discharged me, and if I didn't get into any more trouble, he would drop the charges."

"And did you?" Corelli asked.

"Yes. The therapist helped me see that Connie was right. She couldn't have done it without his help, and the anger was replaced by a determination to make my own way in the business, to be a successful broker, and to do it honestly and fairly. And that's what I've done. I even took my mother's maiden name so that I wouldn't be associated with him. Or her."

"Why did you go to work for her?"

"Curiosity? The challenge? To prove something to myself? All of the above? I don't really know. But when I accepted the job, I refused to take my clients, which left me an out. As I told you, I decided over the weekend to take it. I planned to resign on Monday and go back to my former firm. I actually was feeling pretty good that I'd bested her. Very few people did."

"And your fight on Friday?"

"I tried to convince her to go after the large firms rather than the small. But she wasn't interested. She only cared about getting what she wanted, and it didn't matter who she hurt. I was in a rage when I left because I could see that she was going to destroy that firm like—"

"And you picked up the nearest thing," Corelli interrupted. "What was it Brett? You beat her to death with it, didn't you? All your fantasies come true, at last."

Cummings jumped up, knocking over the chair in her haste. Thinking she was getting violent, Parker bolted from her seat and grabbed Cummings around the waist. Cummings extended her hands palms-up toward Corelli, beseeching.

"You can't think that. I planned to leave. Foiling her plans by warning the owner of the company that she was going to pillage was all the revenge I needed. You've got to believe me."

Corelli pushed on. "It's understandable, Brett. She destroyed your family and she was going to hurt others. She deserved to die. What did you do with the pyramid?" Corelli asked, pressing harder.

"I'm not a killer. Neither was my dad, or he would have murdered her instead of committing suicide."

She collapsed into the chair. "I can't believe this. She's going to ruin my life like she ruined my dad's."

Corelli wanted to believe she was innocent. She avoided looking at Cummings and tried to shut out the profound pain in her voice.

"I'm sorry Brett. I'd like to believe you, but the evidence points to you."

She stood. Her beautiful face flushed with anger. Her gaze pulled Corelli to her and held her as if willing her to believe. Heat flashed through Corelli and she found she was holding her breath, until the condescension in Cummings's voice broke the spell.

"Surely even you must see I'd be smart enough to give myself an alibi."

"That's exactly why not having an alibi is the smart thing for you, a good cover."

"You're railroading me. I thought you were different. I sensed your gentleness and your heart. I thought I could see into your soul, but your pretty face must have blinded me. Now I see that you're just a cop. Just another cop. I want my lawyer."

"Should I escort Ms. Cummings to a holding cell after she calls her attorney?" Parker said.

Corelli shifted her gaze to Parker. "Not yet. Let's step outside for a minute." She glanced at Cummings. Her beautiful face was filled with rage and defiance but the real story was in her beautiful eyes, which brimmed with tears and hopelessness.

Watkins had been watching through the two-way mirror and joined them outside the interview room. Corelli stretched her arms over her head and leaned over and touched her fingertips to her toes, attempting to alleviate the tension of the interview and get rid of the heaviness in her chest. She straightened her shoulders and took a couple of deep breaths. "Though Cummings had motive, means and opportunity, it's all circumstantial without a confession or the weapon, I don't think we have enough to hold her. Any objections?"

Hearing none, she opened the door and spoke to Cummings. "You don't need your attorney tonight. We're releasing you but please remain in the city. I'll have someone drive you home."

She stood. "I'm perfectly capable of finding my way home," she said, brushing past Corelli.

Corelli nodded at Shaunton, who ran after Cummings to escort her out. They watched her hurry away then went back into the interview room. She fiddled with her hair and broke the heavy silence. "The press conference is set," Corelli said, not attempting to hide her sadness. "There's nothing to be done."

Watkins cleared his throat. "A doctor from Bellevue Hospital called earlier. Police picked up Stacy Broslawski Friday afternoon in the Port Authority Bus Terminal, freaking out with a bad drug reaction. The doctor said she kept asking for her Aunt Con, but it wasn't until yesterday that she was together enough to say Connie Broslawski and not until this afternoon that a nurse recognized the name from the newspapers. I guess we can eliminate her as the killer."

Shaunton stuck her head in the door. "Detective Corelli, a John Broslawski is asking for you at the front desk."

Corelli turned to Watkins. "Did you—"

"No. I started the paperwork, that's all."

"Parker, did you—"

Parker grimaced. "No."

All three stared at Corelli. "Excellent timing. Maybe John's here to confess, or maybe he saw something or somebody." She turned to Shaunton. "Give us ten minutes and then bring him up. I'm going to wash my face and get a cup of tea."

She stopped at the door. "I suggest you two move around. You'll need lots of energy to keep up with John."

"Jeez Corelli, I'm worried about you. You're going to end your career in a few days and you're making jokes?" Parker said. "If that was me about to give up my job, you bet your sweet patootie I'd be bouncing off the walls."

Parker's remark was like a knife to her heart. She didn't want to think about tomorrow. "Maybe I just bounce quieter than you, Parker."

CHAPTER FORTY

John and Theresa Broslawski responded like children being claimed from lost and found by their mother, smiling and waving as they struggled out of the low-molded chairs to greet Corelli and Parker.

"Hey, you okay?" Theresa said, peering at Corelli. "You look kinda sick."

"I'm fine, thanks. What brings you here?"

"You didn't answer your cell so we figured you was working," John said.

Corelli nodded. She had turned her cell phone off while they were interviewing Cummings. "Anything in particular you wanted?"

"Yeah," Theresa tucked a hair into her beehive hairdo, "Con's address. We come to New York to pay our respects to her family, but we can't find out where they live."

"It's kind of late now. I'll ask their permission tomorrow and call you with the address."

"Thanks, hon. We're staying at the Northend Hotel all the way up on West 89th Street." Theresa looked up and down the hall. "Uh, how do we get outta here?"

"Since you're here, we have a few more questions for John." She turned to Parker. "Have Shaunton settle Theresa somewhere with a cup of coffee or tea."

"That's okay, hon. I'll stay with John."

"Sorry, we need to talk to John alone. We won't be long." Parker cupped Theresa's elbow and steered her toward Shaunton. Theresa stopped and turned. She gnawed the cuticle on her thumb as she watched John slink into the interview room.

John sank into a chair and tugged on a lock of his hair. When Parker came in without Theresa, his eyes widened with fear and skittered around the room like balls in a pinball machine, bouncing from the door, to Corelli, to Parker, and back to the door. He was probably hoping Theresa would barrel in to save him.

Corelli and Parker sat opposite him. Hoping to shake him up a bit more, Corelli waited thirty seconds before speaking. "What a pleasant surprise, John. We were planning on coming to Hope Falls to see you again and here you are in New York. Do you know why we want to talk to you?"

He shook his head.

"I didn't hear your answer, John."

"No."

"You haven't been truthful, have you, John?"

"Dunno. Tried." The words came out as a whisper.

"John, if you're not honest with us this time we'll have to charge you." Corelli spoke slowly so that he could absorb what she was saying. Blinking, he looked at her for the first time.

"What do you want to know?"

"Start from the beginning, when you arrived in New York Friday."

He stared at the space between Corelli and Parker. "Well, uh, I uh, took the bus to the Port, you know. I told ya Port something."

"Port Authority Bus Terminal."

"Yeah, it's hard to remember 'cause it sounds like boats go there. Anyway, I got some breakfast and got directions to Wall Street, where Con's office is. I started to walk but I got lost. So I asked a lady how to go and she told me about the subway, even took me to where I could get on and showed me how to buy a ticket. It came up right by Con's building. I told the guard I wanted to see her, but when he called and told them my name, they said to keep me out. So I knew the lady who answered the phone was still there. I got really mad and tried to go past the guards and they made me leave. But I knew when she saw me it would be okay, so I hung around outside waiting for her."

"How long did you wait?"

"I told you. Until around six, when I saw a limo with a plate that said Winter pull away. I figured it was her so I left." He chanced a quick glance at Corelli's face and seemed almost to hold his breath.

Corelli smiled at him, shaking her head. "John, John," she said, her voice gentle. "Someone saw you there much later. If you're going to lie, we'll have to hold you."

His eyelids fluttered and his head swiveled, looking for an escape. It was a good imitation of the head spinning scene in *The Exorcist*. "No, no, wait. She didn't get into the limo and I figured she was still working." He pulled out a handkerchief and blew his nose. "So I waited some more. Then about seven the same limo or another one with a plate that said Winter, parked near her building. I figured it was waiting for her, so I stood across the street under a little porch thing near that bar and kept my eye on the door of her building."

He stopped, waiting, probably hoping that he had said enough to satisfy them.

"Go on."

"A little while later the guard that threw me out left. At nine, a messenger girl on a bicycle came. She chained her bike outside, pulled on the door and rang the doorbell. A fat guy opened the door for her. Right after that the sho-fer got out of the limo and ran across the street. He almost knocked me over. Didn't even say he was sorry or nothing. He went into the bar, so I figured she was still working."

"How can you be so exact about the time?"

"That church up at the top of Wall Street has a huge watch that plays a tune every fifteen minutes."

"What happened after the chauffeur went in the bar?"

He grabbed his favorite lock of hair and tugged. "Um, the fat guy came outta the building and stumbled across the street into the bar. I thought maybe he had a bad leg, but when he went past me he smelled like he took a bath in cheap booze."

"Okay, it's a little after nine. What happened?"

They stared at him and he shifted, uneasy with the attention. "Um, a pretty lady with long blond hair came out and walked up real fast toward the clock. It was quiet a while and the shofer came out of the bar and drove away, very fast. After that I decided to leave and come back on Monday."

"Then what time was it when you went into the bar?"

"I didn't—"

Seeing her expression, he stopped. She could almost hear his mind working as his eyes started their dance again. Finally, he seemed to realize he was caught. He sighed. "Nine thirty. The limo driver was in the bar with the fat guy. I wanted to ask him about Connie, but he and that fat guy were both cursin' her, talking about wringing her neck. The limo guy said she could stuff her job. He was sick and tired of waiting all night for the bitch to stop work, so I figured she was still there. I followed him out. He left without her and I decided to wait."

"What time did you go up to her office?"

He looked like he might cry, but he sneezed instead and brushed the handkerchief over his nose. "About twelve thirty. Nobody came out or went in for a while so I decided to go up to her office. I walked in and—"

"Wait, the door wasn't locked?"

"Nah, it was open. People walked out all the time while I was waiting."

"What about going in? Anybody walk in?"

He put on his thinking face, scrunched his eyes. "When that stinky guy went back, he kept dropping his keys and couldn't unlock the door. I felt bad fer him and almost went to help, but then he got it open and sorta fell in. After that it didn't look like nobody waited."

"So you walked in?"

"Yeah. There's a sign in the lobby that said which floor she was on. I peeked in the offices looking for where she was. I saw an arm on the chair in one of them big corner offices so I figured she fell asleep. I walked in and the lights…"

He swallowed. "It was horrible. I didn't want to scare her so I started talking to her right away, but then I smelled the, er, shit, and I saw the blood. Blood was all over everything. Her head… her head was, it was like bashed in, and she was covered with blood and…stuff. It was all over her desk and the floor, even the ceiling. The place stunk something bad. I could tell she was dead. I ran out and down the elevator, almost broke my neck on that big ladder standin' right in the middle of the lobby. I kept runnin' until I hadda stop. I was crying and didn't know what to do so I called Theresa. She said I should come home or somebody might think I did it. I walked all night trying to get it out of my mind and got on the first bus home." He scratched his head and seemed to relax now that it was all out on the table. "Howdidja know I was in her office? I didn't touch nothin'."

"Somebody saw you leave. You might be able to help us out, John."

"Does this mean I'm not going to jail?"

"Maybe. Let's see how good your memory is. Describe everybody that came out or went into the building between about seven o'clock when the limo driver came back and when you went up and found her dead?"

"I can't remember."

"Try. You already mentioned the messenger girl on the bicycle, the pretty blond lady and the fat, smelly guy. You kept your eyes on the door, right? Think. Anybody else go in or come out?"

"Yeah, I was afraid I would miss Connie so I stared at that door the whole time. Let me see." His eyes narrowed, his lips tightened, and his thumb began to rub his nose.

"A short lady. She came out of the subway, I think it was after the fat guy went to the bar. She stood by the door for about five minutes, and then went in." He stretched and yawned. "A couple minutes later that messenger girl came out, unchained her bicycle and rode away."

He tapped his fingers on his nose, ticking them off as he remembered, but he hesitated when he passed his thumb the second time. "Right. I went in the bar at nine thirty but I left after five minutes. A few minutes later, the shofer staggered out and drove away before I could catch him. The drunk guy left right after him. It was quiet until this dapper guy pulled up in a fancy silver car when the ten o'clock chimes were ringing. He pounded on the door of the building, but after a few minutes I think he figured out the door wasn't locked, so he opened it and went in. He didn't stay long, maybe twenty minutes. Then he came out and pulled away real fast, squealing tires and all. I never knew people worked so late on Wall Street. No wonder they make so much money."

"Did you see anyone else?"

"Yup. Five or ten minutes after the guy in the silver car left, another messenger, a boy, went inside but he took his bicycle with him. He stayed about twenty minutes too and as he was riding away, a fat lady got out of a taxi and went into the building. Um, a couple minutes later, the chimes were ringing eleven o'clock and a little guy with a mustache came out and ran down into the subway, and right after that the short lady came out and went into the subway. Um, I think that's about when the limo driver came back and went into the bar again."

John chewed his thumbnail and mumbled to himself, going over what he had seen. "Oh, yeah. A little after the eleven fifteen chimes, this here big blond guy all in black with a leather jacket went in. Maybe ten minutes later the fat lady came out. A taxi came by but it didn't stop when she waved. I guess she didn't want to wait, so she walked over toward the river, you know, by all the restaurants. That blond guy wasn't there too long. When he came out I thought he was gonna have a cigarette because he leaned against the building where it was so dark. I could hardly see him, but I never saw no light. After about five minutes, he walked real fast. I could hear his heels clicking on the sidewalk, sounded like ladies' shoes, and got in his car and left."

"Did you see the car and the plate?"

"Mercedes. Black. But I couldn't see no numbers. Can I have some water? Am I doin' okay?"

"Parker, please get John some water. You're doing great. Go on."

"The last one, I think, was a pregnant lady who came out after twelve o'clock. She seemed in a big hurry. She went down the subway real fast." He took the cup from Parker and quickly emptied it.

"That it?"

"Yeah."

He leaned back, relaxed and self-satisfied.

"Now think a little harder, John. Was anyone carrying anything?"

The thumb rose to the nose again. "Don't remember."

"What about the guy in the fancy car or the big blond guy? Did they have anything?"

He closed his eyes. "No, I don't think so." Then he nodded. "Yes. The blond guy had a black gym bag. It musta been heavy cause it kept slippin' off his shoulder."

"Are you sure no one else was carrying anything?"

He stared into space. "Um, the ladies had pocketbooks and I think the messengers had backpacks, but I'm not really sure."

"What about the pretty blond lady?"

"She had a pocketbook." He scratched his head. "No, wait, it was one of those cases you carry papers in."

"Did you see this guy?" She showed him the picture of Gus that had appeared in the newspaper as part of the awards coverage. He studied it. "Yeah, he got in the limo with the fat lady at five thirty."

"Did you see him again later?"

"I think he was the guy with the fancy car. I mostly saw him from the side when he went in and he went real fast when he left but I'm pretty sure. Can I leave now?"

"One more thing. Stacy's in Bellevue Hospital. She had a bad drug reaction Friday."

He stood. "Is she okay? Can we go see her?"

"Don't worry. She's fine. You'll be able to see her tomorrow. Wait outside with Theresa. Somebody will get you the hospital visiting hours and the address and then drive you to the hotel. I'll call tomorrow to let you know about visiting Connie's family. And John, call me if you remember anything else. Anytime."

She opened the door. "Watkins, please see that John and Theresa get the information they need and have them driven to the hotel."

John hurried out of the room and made a beeline for Theresa. Watkins trailed after him.

Corelli was exhausted. She was running out of time. Parker had been moody all afternoon and was probably exhausted too. Corelli stretched. "So, I'm thinking either Winter was alive when Cummings left or all those other people saw her dead and no one called 911. I know you have a soft spot for Cummings but give us an honest opinion. What do you think, Parker?"

Parker stared at her. "I think you're attracted to Cummings and you're bending over backward to make sure you're being objective."

Corelli flinched.

Watkins gasped.

Parker stuck her chin out. "But, I agree Cummings didn't kill her. Any one of the others could have done it. For what it's worth, that's what I think," Parker said, her voice trailing away, her gaze down.

Corelli felt a spark of anger. "Homicide 201, Parker. A good homicide detective is always objective." She kept her eyes on Parker. "As I said, it appears Winter was alive when Cummings left and I agree that any of the multitude who visited after could have killed her."

Parker raised her eyes but spoke to the empty chair facing them. "Gus had the most to gain by her dying and the most to lose if she lived. And it sounds like he lied about going back to the office. Something fancy and silver would be right up his greedy alley, so let's check out his car to see if it matches. Gertrude gains from Winter's death too, and that fat lady sure sounds like her. She said Gus doesn't have any balls. Maybe she took it upon herself to do her brother's dirty work and save the family fortune? We should eliminate the two of them first."

"She's got a point, boss," Watkins said.

Corelli swallowed her anger, touched Parker's shoulder and waited for her to make eye contact. "Your instincts are right on the mark. Knowing that Gus and Gertrude lied about being there elevates them to the top of the list of suspects."

Parker's shoulders relaxed but she looked away.

Corelli studied her. Was Parker angry because of the way she treated Cummings or because she feared retaliation for confronting Corelli about her attraction? She would deal with it tomorrow. She felt too stressed now.

"We'll start with Gertrude tomorrow morning. I'd like you there too, Watkins, so meet us outside her apartment building at nine."

"No problem," he said, and stood to leave.

"Parker, you can stay and follow up on Gus's car. I'll—"

"No way do you travel without me," Parker said, moving between Corelli and the door.

Watkins froze at the defiance in her voice. The room crackled with tension. Corelli opened her mouth, closed it, and reminded herself again that the chief had ordered Parker to protect her. She breathed deeply, and once more responded to the words, not the tone.

"I was about to say, I'll get a ride home with Watkins."

Parker's shoulders dropped. "Make sure she gets in the elevator, Watkins."

He saluted. "Yes ma'am."

She looked at Corelli. "I'll pick you up in the morning."

CHAPTER FORTY-ONE

The humid August morning air felt like a weight on Corelli's shoulders. The air-conditioned car was a welcome relief, but Parker was icy, barely acknowledging her. No doubt Parker was still angry, but Corelli had nothing left to give right now. She'd been asleep less than two hours when she woke up screaming and trembling and drenched in sweat from a nightmare about trying to save Marnie. She'd taken a shower and stared at the bottle of bourbon for a long time before making a pot of tea. Afraid to fall asleep again, she'd run on the treadmill, lifted weights, done yoga and tried to meditate until morning arrived. Now, the worry pooled in her stomach, nauseating her. Her head felt fuzzy. She was on tenterhooks, uncertain about her future and the safety of her family. She needed to wrap up this case and focus on the threat.

Parker pulled into a parking spot a half block from Gertrude's building. They found Watkins sitting in his car, head bobbing, hands drumming on the steering wheel. Corelli tapped the passenger window and when he didn't respond, Parker walked to the front of the car and banged to get his attention. He snapped the music off and lowered the window.

"Sorry. A new CD. I sort of got lost."

"Ready?" Corelli asked.

"She's not home," Watkins said. "Anything new?"

She shook her head. "Do you know where she is?"

"I followed her to the bakery and then to Gus's. Want to go there?"

"Better yet. Two for the price of one. We'll meet you there."

They walked back to their car. Parker unlocked the doors, cleared her throat and faced Corelli over the roof.

"Sorry, I forgot to ask if you heard anything. Just wallowing in my own—"

"Don't worry. I forgot to ask what you found out about the car." Corelli opened the door and got in. At the first stoplight, Parker swiveled to face her. "Winter Brokerage leases a silver Maserati registered to Gus."

"Good work," Corelli said.

Parker nodded and turned her attention to the road, but not before Corelli saw her self-satisfied smile. Corelli bit back the nasty crack that surfaced quickly. *Let her enjoy the fact that she bested me.*

As they drove up to the Winter compound, Watkins was parking in front of the house and the guard was moving back into his air-conditioned hideaway. He sauntered over to the car, glanced at Parker's shield, and made notes in the book he was carrying. "Must be raiding the damn place," he grumbled, but he walked back and opened the gate.

Watkins rang the bell and relaxed against the railing, face to the sun. Parker fidgeted and glared at the door. "Taking their time about answering," Parker said. "Maybe they're locking us out."

Watkins laughed. "You are one impatient lady. It's been less than five minutes."

Cora Andrews opened the door and greeted them like old friends. Corelli introduced Watkins.

"Sorry, I couldn't leave my pancakes. The family's having breakfast in the kitchen."

"I thought you didn't work weekends," Corelli said.

"Gus thought it might help the kids feel better."

Cora ushered them into a dining area in the large kitchen, the only room of those they'd seen that felt lived in and comfortable. Gus, Gertrude, Aphrodite, and Gus Jr. were eating at a large, round table. The kids were in pajamas, but Gus was dressed and shaved. He invited the detectives to join them for coffee and bagels or pancakes. Corelli accepted the coffee and introduced Watkins to Gertrude and the kids.

Gus was dressed casually but looked crisp and relaxed at the same time. Knowing he wasn't going to be broke agreed with him. Gertrude appeared thrown together and jumpy. Aphrodite stared at them, sullen and quiet; Gus Jr. picked at his pancakes while working on a drawing of the multicolored tulips in a vase on the counter facing them. The kid was talented.

Corelli took a sip of coffee and her stomach lurched. She pushed the cup aside.

"What can we do for you this morning?" Gus asked, all charm, like a salesman in a luxury department store. She liked him better distraught.

Corelli cleared her throat. "We'd like to talk to you and Ms. Gianopolus." A small sound from Aphrodite pulled Corelli's eyes to her face. "Gertrude, that is."

"Me?" Gertrude seemed astonished. "Again? Still wasting your time?"

The three detectives were silent. "Gus, tell them I left with you at five thirty. If you don't believe us, call Rino, he'll confirm the time," Gertrude said, her voice rising. Her hands shook as she lit another cigarette. Finally, Gus lisped in that familiar arrogant tone. "All right. What's going on here? Do I have to call the mayor?"

Sure, just what I need right now. "We have some additional questions based on new information. Is there another room we can use?"

He sighed. "The dining room. It's right down the hall."

Gertrude made a face expressing her disgust and put her hands on the table, the first step in hauling herself up out of the chair.

Corelli said, "Not you, Gertrude. First Gus."

Suspended halfway between sitting and standing Gertrude muttered. "Damn you." She glared at Corelli. "I don't understand. Why—"

"Let it go, Gertrude," said Gus, getting impatient. As if taking his command literally, she dropped into her seat. Then, making a show of ignoring them, she picked up her bagel and licked the cream cheese jutting out the sides.

Corelli noted Gertrude's performance. *She's putting on a good show, but she's extremely tense. Her eyes are anxious, and she's breathing heavily. Good. Let her stew while we question Gus.*

They followed Gus into the formal dining room at the end of the hall. The elaborate glass chandelier that dominated the room cast a soft, glittery light over the gleaming wooden table that could probably seat thirty comfortably. The seats of the chairs were covered with silk in soft blue and pink stripes. A pale blue oriental rug sat under the table and chairs, leaving plenty of the wooden floor exposed. The room was beautiful, but like most of the house it felt empty and cold and could have been a display in an expensive furniture store.

Gus sat at the head of the table near the doorway and clasped his hands.

"Mr. Gianopolus, we've gone over your alibi for Friday night several times, but I'm wondering if you left something out," Corelli asked.

"You know, Detective, this is very trying. My wife and I had our problems, but she still was my wife and I'm dealing with her death. I've told you all I know."

"Yes, I understand. Bear with me another few minutes. What car did you take when you drove out to Southampton Friday night?"

"Mine. A silver Maserati."

"So Friday after dinner, you picked up your Maserati and drove directly out to Southampton. Is that right?"

"That's what I've told you over and over. What's the problem?"

"The problem is a witness saw you park your Maserati and go into your wife's building Friday night around ten."

Gus jumped up. "Is this some kind of trick? What witness?"

"We'll produce the witness when it's appropriate, sir. Would you like to explain?"

He started for the door.

"Mr. Gianopolus, need I remind you that this is a murder investigation? It's our job to ask questions and eliminate suspects, not to incriminate them. We can do this at the precinct, if you like, but I thought it would be more pleasant here."

He stopped, still facing the door. They waited. Corelli's mind wandered to Righteous Partner's ultimatum and suddenly her heart seemed too big for her chest. Each beat echoed in her head. *I can't play games with this pompous ass while my life is going...*

He turned. "Who saw me?"

When Corelli didn't answer, Parker jumped in. "No one you know."

Gus walked to the table and sat down. He ran his fingers through his hair. "Over dinner I realized that waiting for the ax to fall was making me a nervous wreck, so I decided to confront Connie. I stopped at the office on my way out of the city. I said, 'We need to talk.' She said, 'I have nothing to say.' I asked if she was filing for divorce. She ignored me and kept working, as if I wasn't there." He got up and started pacing.

"I said, 'Let's try to work things out for the kids' sake.' She said, 'I'll worry about the kids.' Then I got angry. I said I would fight for the kids and make a laughingstock of her. She walked over to her safe, took out a large envelope and threw it at me. She said, 'Who do you think will be the laughingstock?'"

He looked at Corelli. "The envelope was filled with pictures of me with other women. She'd had a private detective following me for months. She'd told me to find sex somewhere else and now she was using it against me. I was stunned. She started working again and wouldn't acknowledge me. I felt invisible. I was enraged. I screamed but she acted like she didn't hear me. I wanted to hurt her but I didn't know how."

They waited for him to complete the story.

After a minute of quiet, Corelli said, "What did you hit her with?"

"What? I didn't hit her. I did what any coward would do. I took the pictures and ran. I thought of how I had prostituted myself to her, of what I'd become, and I felt sick. I was in a rage at her and at myself. I needed to get away. So I drove like a madman out to Southampton. On the way, I called Bearsdon and left a message about filing for divorce. I knew I would probably lose, but I wanted the kids to know that I fought for them." He sat as his story ended.

Corelli leaned in close and spoke softly. "Come on, Gus. Don't tell me you let her get away with treating you like that. You were in a rage and without thinking you picked up the nearest thing and hit her, and hit her, and hit her."

Gus pulled back and stared at Corelli as if she had lost her mind.

"What did you hit her with?"

"I didn't hit her. I told you I ran away."

"Why should we believe you? You lied before."

"I lied because the husband is always the prime suspect. And I was right. You think I did it, don't you?"

No one said anything.

"You're not off the hook yet, but let's hear what Gertrude has to say." Corelli stood. "Let's get Gertrude, Parker."

"Where's Gertrude?" Corelli asked in the kitchen.

Gussie was involved in his drawing, but Aphrodite looked up from the newspaper she was reading. "Gonzo."

"Gone to the bathroom? Gone home?"

Cora turned from the sink. "She walked out after you went with Gus. Said this was a waste of her time. Didn't say where she was going."

"Parker, get Watkins," Corelli said, sitting at the table.

"What's up?" Watkins said, as he entered with Gus right behind.

"Gertrude has run off. Find her and bring her back. Cuff her if necessary."

Watkins left and they sat at the table.

"Gertrude's not a killer. She's scared," Gus said.

"She has a lot of explaining to do."

"Are you going to arrest Auntie Gertie?" Gussie was shaking.

"I don't know, Gussie, but her running away makes me think she's hiding something."

"You can't arrest her. She didn't kill my mother." He started sobbing and rushed from the room. Aphrodite started to follow but changed her mind. The room was silent.

Corelli could feel Parker's gaze on her, but she didn't say anything until she'd thought it through. "Cora, I'd like to talk to Gussie. Please take Detective Parker to his room."

Gus stood up. "Leave my children out of this."

"Sorry, Mr. Gianopolus, but I need to ask him some questions, and I hate to repeat myself, but it's either here or downtown."

Gus cleared his throat. Corelli waited for his pronouncement, but whatever momentous statement he was about to make vanished as Parker entered with a reluctant Gus Jr. shuffling behind. Cora moved past the table and leaned against the sink.

Gussie slipped into the seat next to Aphrodite, pulled his feet up and wrapped his arms around his knees. With his chin on his knees, his face red and puffy, and tears dripping, he snuffled.

Corelli smiled at Gussie and said in a gentle voice, "I think you could help us. I was admiring your drawing but how are you going to draw the yellow tulip?"

"What?" He sounded puzzled by the change of topic.

"Where are your green and yellow pencils?"

Parker sucked air and the others shifted in their chairs. Parker must think she flipped.

"I lost them."

"You went to her office Friday night, didn't you?" She was guessing that he was the boy on the bicycle who left as Gertrude arrived, that the two colored pencils found under her desk were his. He whispered. "Yes, to beg her to not send me to military school."

"How did you know she would be there?"

"Heard my father talk to someone, his girlfriend I think. He said he was going to the island alone because she was going to be working all weekend."

Gus's head jerked up. "You knew I—"

A cold, hard sound issued from Aphrodite. It could have been a laugh or a quick intake of breath or perhaps a growl, but whatever it was, Corelli prayed she would never hear a sound like that from any fourteen-year-old niece or nephew of hers.

"Of course, he knew," Aphrodite spat out. "Connie knew too, but she didn't care." She pointed at her brother. "Gussie did. He was afraid our happy family was going to be split up."

Before Gus could respond, Corelli interjected.

"What did your mother say about the school, Gussie?"

"What she always said," he sobbed.

"Is this necessary?" Gus said. "Don't make him repeat—"

"Mr. Gianopolus, I assure you I have no need to hurt anyone, especially a child."

She turned to the boy. "Gussie, can you tell me what she said?"

He glanced at his father and not hearing any prohibition, recited the litany in a cruel voice. "You worthless piece of shit. I wanted to abort you or give you away when you were born. I made a mistake then. I won't make another one now. Military school will make a man of you, or if the boys like you, maybe they'll make a girly boy of you."

Gianopolus jumped out of his chair in a rage. "I won't allow you to put him through this. Get out of here. He's too upset to talk about it. I won't allow it."

Corelli was astounded. She tried to hold back, but she was too exhausted to rein in her feelings. She spoke in her normal voice, edged with the effort of control, but the anger and contempt came through loud and clear. "Now you want to protect your son? Protect him from us? Where have you been for the last fourteen years while your wife abused him?"

Gianopolus staggered as if she had hit him.

"Your wife's mother died in childbirth and her father used almost those identical words to torment her from the time she was born. There was no one to stop him, no other adult, just two small boys who joined in the torment to protect themselves."

She was aware of Parker's eyebrows just about floating off her face in surprise. She knew she was losing it, but she couldn't keep herself from tearing into Gus. "I assume you and Gertrude heard Connie abuse him. You should be ashamed. You were adults. You could've intervened, but you stood by and watched, too concerned with your financial well-being to take care of a little boy."

"Heard it?" Aphrodite screamed. "Of course, they heard it. She never let up on him. No matter what he did, it was wrong. It's not fair. He was the one who loved her and she was horrible to him. They heard it, but they never tried to stop her."

"Be quiet, Aphrodite," Gus ordered, the anger making his voice hard and cold.

"What's the matter? Don't like to hear it?" Aphrodite challenged. "Don't want strangers to know? Screw you. You never stood up to her like a real father would have. I hated her and I hate you. Always begging for money. Nothing is as important as the money for you." She began to sob.

Corelli moved toward Gus, wanting to throttle him. Parker must have seen the look on her face. She gripped Corelli's shoulder and put herself between Corelli and Gus. Corelli took a deep breath and struggled with the urge to beat Gus the way she beat her punching bag.

Gianopolus leaned forward in his chair, cradling his head in his hands. She hoped he had heard the words and could ignore the attack. She waited; they all waited. At last he sat up. "You're right. I abandoned both my children. I told myself if I tried to get in the middle it would make things worse, but I knew if I objected she would get rid of me. The only way was to leave with them, but I

didn't think I had a chance against her money and her iron will."
He ran his hands over his face. "Go on, finish. The kids and I will
be dealing with this for a long time."

"Gussie." Corelli knelt in front of the boy and touched his
shoulder. "Gussie," she said, her voice gentle but insistent. "Look
at me."

He raised his eyes. "What?"

"What happened after she got angry and said those awful
things?"

His eyes glazed and his voice sounded distant. "I got angry back
at her."

He's so young and earnest. Corelli fought the urge to put her
arms around him. *What the hell is happening to me? I need to keep my
distance. First Brett, now Gussie.*

"I'm really afraid to go to military school," he confided. "I want
to be an artist. So I grabbed the application out of her hand and I
tore it up, and I yelled at her. I never yell. I usually cry. I said I'd
never go to that school. And she said, 'If I say you go, you go. So
shut up and get the hell out of here.' Then she started to laugh.
And she said it again, 'You piece of shit. You'll never be an artist.'
And then, I…I don't remember."

"Did you leave?"

"Yes, that's it. I ran away."

"And did she say anything when you left?"

"No. She was quiet. There was blood all around. Lots of blood
on her face and her head, all over." Gussie didn't seem to hear the
collective gasp. "So I yelled, I'm not going to military school and
I ran out." He paused. "No, first I dropped the glass thing I was
holding. I don't remember where I got it, but it had blood on it. I
dropped it and I ran. My clothes were all bloody too."

There was absolute silence. Not one of them had expected this.
It was hard to take in the full meaning.

"Do you think I killed her?" he whispered.

Finally, Corelli found her voice. "Can you remember how many
times you hit her, Gussie?"

"No. I was really mad." He whimpered, making mournful,
convulsive sounds, and the tears flowed. He seemed pathetic, alone.
Corelli put her hands on his knees. Aphrodite leaned in close, took
his hand, and put an arm over his shoulder, sobbing with him. Cora

moved out from behind the counter and wrapped her arms around the two children. Gus stared off into space. *Some things never change.*

"Did you take the glass thing with you, Gussie?" Corelli asked.

"No. I just ran away."

"What did you do with your bloody clothes?"

"I put them under my bed."

Winter's office must have been like Grand Central Station on Friday, and it sounded like she managed to put every single visitor into a rage. Corelli thought of those old slapstick comedies where people go in and out of doors constantly, just missing running into each other.

"Will I go to prison?" Gussie asked, sobbing. "That would be worse than military school."

Aphrodite jumped in. "No you won't. Don't you worry, Gus. I'll talk to the judge. It'll be all right."

Corelli felt a rush of feeling. Winter was despicable, and while no one deserved to be murdered, it was difficult to mourn her loss. She felt this murderer needed to be comforted, not punished. No doubt she was in the grip of her feelings on this case. "Gussie, I can't guarantee you won't go to prison but I'll do what I can to help. We have to take you down to police headquarters for a while, but we won't leave you. Your dad and sister will come too. I'll try to arrange it so you'll be able to come home soon."

She turned to Gus, who seemed shell-shocked. "Detective Parker and I need some privacy. Can we use the dining room?"

"Of course."

In the dining room Corelli turned to Parker. "What do you think Ms. ADA?"

Parker hesitated. "If he didn't take the pyramid, where is it?"

"Let's look at John's timeline."

Parker flipped to the page in her notebook.

Corelli ran a finger down the list and stopped. She took Parker's grunt as agreement. "So maybe Gertrude saw him riding away on his bike, realized he killed his mother, and took the pyramid to protect him. We'll ask her when Watkins catches up with her. Do we need it?"

"We have a confession. We'll have his bloody clothes."

"True."

"But it's not a solid case," Parker said.

"I agree. There are too many unanswered questions. I believe Gussie hit her, probably on the right side. She bled profusely and was knocked out. But she was killed by the blows to the top of her head and Gussie is too short to have struck her at that angle with the needed force. Also, how do we account for the bruises from the phone handset and the pre-mortem cut from the silver cross? And if Gertrude took the pyramid, who took the handset?"

"What do we do now?"

"We continue to ask questions until we have all the answers."

CHAPTER FORTY-TWO

Aphrodite protested when Corelli asked Parker to go with her and Gussie while they dressed, but a glance at Corelli's face silenced her, and she stomped out of the room.

Corelli sat opposite Gus. "We're convinced that Gussie hit Ms. Winter but not that he killed her. But I need to document his confession, so I'm going to take him down to the station. I suggest you get on the phone and get a good criminal attorney to meet us there. I can't recommend anyone but I'm sure your attorney can."

"I'll call Bearsdon." He left the room.

Corelli drew into herself.

Ten minutes later Gus returned. "Bearsdon will have an attorney there in an hour."

"Good."

"Maybe I *should have* asked for you to be removed from the investigation," Gus said, suddenly. "Then maybe I would have been arrested and Gussie wouldn't be in danger."

"Why do you say that?"

"At first, I was sure I'd be your quick solution, but after that cop pressured me to call the mayor, I asked a few other cops I know and they recommended that I stick with you. They said you weren't the kind of cop who goes for the obvious solution, the husband. You dig and dig until you're sure you have the right person."

True. Unless I'm attracted to you.

"Who are your cop friends?" Corelli asked.

He gave her the names of four uniforms who worked out of a nearby precinct. "Why?"

"Any of them tall, blond, and mean-looking?"

"They're all mean-looking, but no blonds."

Aphrodite held Gussie close as they entered the kitchen, protecting or comforting, or maybe a little of both. Parker had the bloody clothes in a plastic bag.

Gus stood. "I'll get my jacket."

A minute later the doorbell rang and Watkins and Gertrude walked in. Watkins hadn't cuffed her so she must not have fought coming back.

Gertrude sat in her chair and picked up the bagel with cream cheese that she'd left when she walked out. "Ask away." She looked around. "What's going on?"

"Gussie has confessed to killing his mother. We're on our way downtown," Corelli said. "You were there right after him. Did you take the pyramid, the glass award Ms. Winter received?"

Gertrude opened her mouth but Aphrodite interrupted. "I'm glad you're back, auntie. I forgot to give you this before." She walked behind Gertrude. The silver beads tinkled as Aphrodite draped the necklace around Gertrude's neck. "I made a new cross. Please don't lose this one."

Corelli moved closer to examine the necklace. "It's lovely. Where did you get this, Aphrodite?"

"I made it," she said, grinning at the compliment. "I've been taking a silversmith class since the spring. This is the first one I made." She lifted the necklace she was wearing and leaned over so Corelli could examine it. It was similar to Gertrude's, but instead of a hammered-silver cross, it had a pendant with a red stone in the center.

"That's a real garnet. I made this one for my moth…for Connie, but she hated it. We have the same birthstone so I kept it for myself. I finished Auntie Gertie's Friday afternoon. That's why I went over Friday night." She straightened the necklace on her aunt. "And would you believe by Saturday morning she had already lost the cross?"

"That's unfortunate. Where did you lose it, Gertrude?"

"It's probably somewhere in the apartment."

"Did you make a cross for anyone else? Gussie or your dad?"

"Not yet. These necklaces are a lot of work. Besides, I'm only interested in women's jewelry. I'm designing a whole line to sell."

The autopsy report said the cut from the cross was pre-mortem, so Connie was definitely alive when Gussie left.

Gus returned. "What's going on?"

"We're having a jewelry fashion show," said Gertrude.

"So this is the only cross you've made?" Corelli asked, pointing to Gertrude's necklace.

"Yup, that one and the one she lost," Aphrodite said.

"You made that?" Gus asked, incredulous.

Aphrodite smiled, a sweet fourteen-year-old smile. "Yes. Like it?"

"It's beautiful," he said, and started toward her.

"Better have a seat, Mr. Gianopolus. There's been a change of plans," Corelli said.

He sat without comment.

"Aphrodite, did your aunt put the necklace on Friday night?"

"I put it on her."

Corelli sat next to Gertrude. "Detective Parker, please read Ms. Gianopolus her rights."

By the time Parker finished, Gertrude was wide-eyed.

"Now what?" Gertrude asked, panic creeping into her voice.

"When did you notice that the cross was missing from your necklace?" Corelli asked.

Gertrude took a drag on her cigarette, glanced at Aphrodite, who had sat across from her, made a non-verbal appeal to Gus, and exhaled. For once Gus was quiet.

"I didn't. Aphrodite noticed when she came over Saturday morning. What's this about?"

"You said you got home about six o'clock on Friday, ordered Chinese takeout and remained in for the rest of the night. Is that correct?"

"Yes. Why would I lie?"

"That's a good question, Ms. Gianopolus. Why did you lie?"

"I didn't. I did what I said I did."

"A witness places you at Ms. Winter's office around eleven Friday night. Can you explain that?"

Gus sat up, alert.

"I didn't see…" Gertrude reached for her coffee. Her mouth was tight when she looked at Corelli again.

"You didn't see what?"

"You're putting words in my mouth. No one could have seen me because I wasn't there."

"If you're going to stick to that story, we'll have to go downtown to continue this conversation, and maybe put you in a lineup," Corelli said.

Gertrude lit another cigarette. "Well… I, er…Who is this witness?"

"No one you know. The cross was found in Ms. Winter's office. Actually, the cross was in her clothing, and the Medical Examiner determined she was alive when she grabbed it."

"What does that mean?"

"It means that Gussie didn't kill his mother and that she was still alive when you got there." Corelli heard a gasp from someone. Gertrude took another drag and exhaled before nervously smashing the hardly-smoked butt into the already overflowing ashtray.

"Let's try this, Gertrude. Gussie's blow stunned Connie, maybe knocked her out, and caused profuse bleeding, even a superficial scalp wound will cause a tremendous loss of blood. When you arrived shortly after he left, you thought he had killed his mother. You leaned over to make sure she was dead and she came out of it and grabbed the necklace. You were frightened and you pulled back, leaving the cross in her hand. She was dazed, but you had to get rid of her, so you picked up the pyramid and hit her over and over until you were sure she was dead. Sound right?"

"No. That's not what happened. I'm not a murderer," Gertrude said, tears streaming down her face, "I'm not a murderer."

Although focused on Gertrude, Corelli was experiencing the same heightened awareness and sensitivity as she had felt in her first meeting with Brett Cummings, but this wasn't sexual. Every feeling in the room flowed in—Cora's horror, Gus's anxiety, the pain of the sobbing teens, the intensity of Parker's and Watkins's concentration, but most of all, Gertrude's fear.

Gussie went to his aunt and put his arms around her. "Leave her alone. It was me. I killed her. Please don't hurt her," Gussie said, appealing to Corelli.

Gertrude shuddered. She patted Gussie's arm as if to reassure him, but she couldn't suppress the sobs convulsing her body. Gussie was sensitive and soft, but there was a strength there that wasn't readily apparent. That same inner strength had made it possible for his mother to survive a brutal childhood, but, unlike Connie, Gussie had not only survived, he had retained the ability to love and be a generous human being. Gertrude was sensitive too, and her hurt had made her bitter and critical, but she loved Gussie and Aphrodite, and they loved her.

"You know, Gertrude, Gussie may not go to jail, but are you going to let him go through life believing he murdered his mother?"

Gussie pleaded with Corelli. "Please. I confessed. Send me to jail, not her."

Gertrude used her napkin to dry her tears. "No, Gussie. She's right. I killed your mother. It wasn't what I meant to do, but I did it." She took his hand. "Don't worry. I'll be all right."

"What happened, Gertrude," Corelli said.

"When I got there, Connie and her office were covered with blood but she was alive and trying to stand. She wrapped her arms around my neck, pulling on the necklace. She ordered me to get a doctor. I pushed her down in the chair and told her to relax, that I would call for help. But when I picked up the telephone, she started cursing Gussie, calling him all those foul names. She said she would punish him, send him to jail, cut him off without a cent, and make sure his life was miserable. I guess I lost it. I had the phone in my hand and I hit her in her face, two or three times until she was dead. It wasn't about money. After I realized what I'd done, I took the phone. And when I saw the new will and the divorce papers under the blood on her desk, I knew they would incriminate Gus, so I took them."

"My god, Gertrude," Gus interjected. "How could you?" He stared dumbly at his sister.

"Gus, I swear, I went there to try to convince her that it was a mistake to send Gussie to military school. He's an artist. I know what it's like when your art isn't taken seriously and when you're forced to do things you hate. I was trying to protect him. Something snapped." She patted the kids' hands, blew her nose in her napkin and turned to Corelli. "What happens now?"

"Did you hit her with the pyramid after the phone?"

"No."

"What did you do with the pyramid?"

"I left it. I wanted to take it in case it had Gussie's fingerprints on it. But it was disgusting, covered with blood. I almost threw up. I went to the men's room because it was closer, washed the blood off my hands, and got a wad of paper towels, so I could pick it up without getting blood on me."

"What did you do with it?"

"You're not listening. I left it there. When I opened the door of the men's room to go back for it I saw this guy going into her office. I heard him say, 'Shit, what happened here?' and I knew he would call the police so I ran out as fast as I could."

"What did he look like?"

Gertrude shrugged. "I only saw his back for a few seconds. But he was tall, had short blond hair and was dressed all in black. Black leather jacket, black pants, and black shoes with a heel, possibly boots. And he had a black gym bag over his shoulder."

Corelli exchanged a look with Parker and could see from her expression that she got it too. If Gertrude hit Winter with the telephone and not the pyramid, then she didn't kill her either. So they were back to the mysterious man—or cop.

Gertrude cleared her throat. "Um, what happens now?"

All eyes were on Corelli. "You sit tight at home while we search for this mysterious visitor. You can come here to be with your family but don't leave the city. Understand?"

"You're not going to arrest me?"

"Not now." Corelli glared at the four of them. "Is there anything else any of you haven't told us that we should know?"

No one said a word.

CHAPTER FORTY-THREE

Corelli, Parker, and Watkins left the Gianopolus clan huddled together, comforting each other, a start down what would be a long road to healing. Although Gertrude had hit Winter in the face with the handset of the desk phone, bruising her and probably knocking her out for a few minutes, it was the blows to the top of the head from the pyramid that had killed her. Corelli was confident that Gertrude was not the killer. But, how would they find this mysterious man?

They picked up lunch and settled at their desks at the station house. "We need some quality thinking time," Corelli said. "And while Parker and I contemplate the universe, Watkins, I'd like you to get an update on the status of the Righteous Partners research."

"You got it, boss." He finished lunch and took off.

"We're going to think this through, Parker." She placed a clean narrow-lined yellow pad on her desk and Parker placed her notebook on her desk.

"So, who was still in the building when Gertrude left?"

"The cleaning woman, the porter and the mysterious cop?"

Corelli wrote their names on her pad. "I'm going to include John Broslawski's name since, if his sister was still alive at twelve thirty when he entered her office, he could have finished her off. But, unless Gertrude was lying about seeing a tall man in black, which is unlikely because only the cleaning woman and the porter seem to know about the late-night visits, the mysterious cop is probably our killer."

Parker nodded. "John's statement that a tall blond guy in black left after Gertrude corroborates her story. And, if the mysterious cop didn't kill her, wouldn't he have called for help even if he didn't wait for it to arrive?"

"Good observation. So who is he? Let's list everything we know about the mysterious man in black, maybe a cop."

Parker thumbed through her notes. "The porter, Mihailo Jovanovic, mentioned him first." She read his statement. "He always came late at night. Put his gun to my head, showed his shield, and threatened to arrest me if I left the outer door open. He wore high-heeled shoes like a girl."

Corelli made notes while Parker flipped to another page. "Agnieszka, the cleaning woman, also described him. He looked like the secret police, arrogant, like he owned the world. He dressed in black, had white hair, mean blue eyes and wore a gun under a leather jacket. He and Winter drank together when he visited, two or three time a month."

Parker skimmed through the interviews. "John Broslawski gave a similar description—big, blond, leather jacket, heavy gym bag. Suspicious behavior. Stood in the shadows for a few minutes when he left the building, shoes sounded like ladies' shoes as he walked quickly to a black Mercedes."

"And, Gertrude didn't see his face but described a tall man with short light hair, wearing black and carrying a black gym bag. His shoes had high heels."

"So the mysterious cop carries a gun is tall and blond, wears black, and his shoes have high heels." Corelli sat back and stared at the ceiling. "High-heeled shoes? If he was short, high heels would be for height, but they all say tall or big." An image of the chauffeur, Rino, clippity clopping along on his cowboy boots flashed through Corelli's mind.

"Could our mystery man wear cowboy boots? Wait a second. Cowboy. Someone with that name called Winter two or three times a month. The cleaning woman says the big guy came two or three times a month. Is Cowboy the mysterious cop?"

Corelli sat back trying to remember something she'd read the other night while going over the printouts of the conversations she'd recorded. Something Jimmy said. What was it? The black Mercedes. She'd asked who was in it and Jimmy had said, 'cow' and interrupted himself and said, 'the big boss,' or something like that. Could there be a connection? "Holy shit, Parker. I'll explain later but I'm thinking there might be a connection between Cowboy and Righteous Partners. Give me a couple of minutes."

Corelli stared at the pad, tapping her pencil. "Cowboy boots." She dragged her computer keyboard toward her. "Let's see what Google has to say." She typed in "NYPD" and "cowboy" and scanned the results. She paged through lots of articles about cops wild like cowboys.

"Bingo, Parker. Come take a look. Blond, blue-eyed, Chief Aiden Kelly. Came from the Mounted Division, nicknamed Cowboy because of his walk and the fact that he wears western boots on and off the job. Moved up the ranks in Mounted, served in IA a couple of years and shifted to narcotics. Loves horses and owns a couple. That could explain the horse hair and manure found in Winter's office."

She studied the picture included with the article. *Are you our mysterious cop? Why would you kill Connie Winter? Did she have something on you? How do I approach you?* She stood. "With me, Parker."

"What's up? Parker said, as they walked.

"I want to discuss Chief Aiden Kelly with the captain."

Winfry listened carefully as she outlined her reasoning. When she concluded he said, "You need to be extremely careful, Corelli. Accusing a police chief of murder is risky business under any circumstances, and your position is a little shaky right now."

"What do you think Ms. ADA? Do I have enough?"

Corelli and Winfry looked at Parker. "Sorry, but no. We have no prints, a nickname, some manure, and a description that would fit any number of the thirty-five thousand in the department. Plus, no motive."

"Even if I can get the witnesses to ID him, Gertrude can only testify that he was there, not that Winter was dead when he left," Corelli agreed grudgingly. "Sorry to waste your time, Captain." Corelli turned toward the door.

"Corelli." Winfry's voice stopped her. She turned slowly, not wanting to hear what he had to say. "You didn't waste my time. You updated me on your thinking. But hear me now. You may be right but without solid proof, he could cause a lot more trouble for you than you can for him. Under no circumstances are you to go near Chief Kelly's office. Do you understand?"

Damn. The man was a mind reader. "Yes sir."

"Good. Keep digging. You'll come up with something."

She settled at her desk and picked at her lunch. If she approached him, he would know she was onto him. That wouldn't help matters. But how to nail him? Focus on his relationship to Winter. What brought him to her office so late on a Friday night? Winter wasn't into sex, at least according to Gus, so an affair was unlikely, unless there was something in it for her. Why would he kill her? Winter was driven by the need to accumulate power and money. How did she come to hire Righteous Partners as her security firm?

Whenever she had asked Jimmy what happened to the money they were stealing, he said RP was run like a business. Everybody got a little money up front and they invested the rest for later. If Chief Aiden Kelly was Jimmy's "big guy," he would have lots of cash to invest. But these days large amounts of cash were suspect, so the money would have to be laundered, passed through a legitimate business. Maybe Winter was the launderer. But why fool around with something illegal? What would she do with all that cash? And, if she was laundering the money, why would he kill her?

Corelli considered what she had learned about Winter. She was used to having all the power. She was greedy and had no compunction about pushing people around. She was perfectly capable of blackmailing Kelly or demanding a bigger cut of the pie. Maybe when he walked in and saw her already beaten and bloody, he seized the opportunity. That would explain why he didn't call for help. Hopefully, Winter's records would turn up something on Righteous Partners. She picked up the phone. When she hung up, she turned to Parker. "Let's take a ride."

CHAPTER FORTY-FOUR

Parker was adamant. "Uh-uh. I'm not driving to his house."

"Winfry didn't say anything about his house."

Parker snorted. "You know the captain meant no contact at all. If you try to nail Kelly without something more concrete, he'll crucify you."

"Who put you in charge, Ms. Goody Two-shoes? I know what I'm doing. Get going."

"This is your PTSD talking." Parker opened the car door.

"Fuck PTSD, Dr. Parker. Either start the damn car or give me the keys. That's an order. And if you don't I'll leave you here and go home for my Harley."

"What about me? You're screwing around with my job too."

"Ah, now I get it. You're just covering your ass. So why don't you—"

Watkins tapped on the window. Corelli opened the door. "Ron, I need you to drive me somewhere."

"Come inside first. I think you'll want to see this. Brett Cummings and Phil Rieger worked all night pulling the Righteous Partners stuff together. I picked Brett up and drove her home while she explained it to me."

"We'll finish this discussion after we see what Watkins has, Parker."

Walking in, they ran into Dietz. "Corelli, the captain wants to see you."

Corelli looked at Watkins. "You have anything solid?"

Watkins patted the briefcase. "In black and white." He pulled a page out of the case and handed it to Corelli. She scanned it and handed it to Parker. "I want to bring Winfry in on this. Meet you back here."

Captain Winfry waved her in. "I have confirmation that it was Chief Aiden Kelly who wanted you off the Winter investigation. Another nail in the coffin, but not enough to go after him. Yet."

"Watkins has something important, something that nails Kelly. Want to join us in the conference room while we review it?"

Winfry glanced at his watch. "I have a few minutes."

They sat around the table, Winfry and Corelli facing Watkins and Parker. Watkins snapped the briefcase open and placed a stack of papers on the table. "What we have here is Righteous Partners' investments—statements of earnings for each employee and copies of invoices submitted to Winter Brokerage for the past year." He tapped the stack. "According to Rieger and Cummings, Righteous Partners submitted huge invoices for services like guards at the Sutton Plaza house, monthly fees for rental of the street, guards at the Southampton house, round the clock bodyguards for her, Gus, the kids, and Gertrude, investigation services, and many other miscellaneous charges. Those bills went directly to Winter and she approved them for payment. According to Gus, all the services billed, except for guarding the Sutton Plaza house, were bogus. They also found that the total monthly investment in the accounts of Righteous Partners' employees was always equal to the amount Winter Brokerage paid them."

"I knew it." Corelli jumped up and started to pace. "Winter *was* laundering the dirty money."

"She was wealthy. Why would she risk it?" Parker asked.

"Think, Parker. What do we know about Winter? She wanted it all. She had an insatiable greed. My guess is she was taking a cut and stashing the cash. It was brilliant. Nobody would ever connect her with a ring of dirty cops stealing from drug dealers."

"So where's the cash?" Parker asked.

"She paid Tess in cash. I'm taking bets we'll find other cash payments for things she wanted kept secret or things that weren't business deductions. And there's no doubt in my mind we'll find another safe in her office, one packed with cash."

Watkins handed Corelli a computer listing. "You did pretty well in the time you were on the RP payroll, over thirty thousand dollars, not bad for a few month's work."

"Blood money." Corelli sat and shared the list with Winfry. "She ran her finger down the names and stopped. "Drum roll please. Chief Aidan Kelly, highest paid at almost two million dollars."

"Aha," Winfry said. "These two I know. Captain Jeremy Beckles and Inspector Pierre Abril." Winfry cleared his throat. "Beckles is a bastard, out for himself, put his foot on your face to get a rung ahead of you, and thinks his shit don't stink. And Abril is something of a dandy, in love with himself, into flash and clothes and fine dining, women, and, I hear, gambling."

Elated, Corelli grinned. "Kelly is our cowboy. This explains his dealings with Connie Winter. And like most people who dealt with Winter, he probably had a good reason to kill her. Is this everything?"

"It's everything we've got so far," Watkins said. "Cummings had Rieger put a team together to review all the accounts Winter set up and to identify anyone who might be connected. They'll be working on it until they've gone through everything. And Tess is researching the Righteous Partners corporation to confirm who was involved."

Corelli stood. "I think we have enough to arrest him now, Captain. I'd like to do it myself."

"A little patience, Corelli. We have to run this by a few people first."

"Wait? It's my family at risk and the deadline for the press conference is looming."

"Sit," Winfry ordered. "I know you're anxious to wrap this up, but we do it right or not at all. Now listen. The press thing is Monday afternoon so we have some time. I'll set something up with the Chief of Police, the Chief of Detectives, Internal Affairs, and the FBI this afternoon. And I'll get protection on your family starting tonight. While you're waiting, you three can come up with a plan to start the discussion. Are you with me?"

She wanted to rush out and get the bastard, confront him with his worst nightmare. She wanted to see his face when he realized he was caught and that he'd be going to prison. But the professional knew Winfry was right. Get everyone with a stake committed and leave no loopholes. She took a deep breath. "Yes sir."

Winfry looked at Watkins and Parker. They both nodded. "Let's get the ball rolling."

CHAPTER FORTY-FIVE

She swung the Harley into the driveway between the huge red Cadillac Escalade and the black Mercedes, killed the ignition and dismounted. She removed her helmet and snapped it into place, then draped her leather jacket over the seat. After running her hand through her hair to confirm the barrette was in place, she straightened her shoulders and took a second to focus on her surroundings.

At six thirty in the morning the air was still fresh in this expensive Staten Island neighborhood with its trimmed and polished lawns and lavish landscaping. The roar of the Harley had shattered the early morning quiet and roused the neighbors. A few people came out to their porches while others lifted the curtains or blinds. The movement of the curtain in an upstairs window of Chief Kelly's house indicated he knew she was there. One guy had a cell phone to his ear, no doubt calling the local precinct to complain. All eyes were on her. That was good. They wouldn't notice her backup moving slowly through their backyards. When she proposed she be the one to take Kelly down, she'd expected a battle. Instead the FBI and department brass had backed her. She was pumped.

Kelly stepped onto his porch, dressed in khakis, a T-shirt, a jacket and western boots. Too bad. She'd hoped to catch him in his pajamas. She assumed he was armed and guessed he'd called for backup before coming out. But it didn't matter. Anyone headed this way would be stopped at the barricaded entrance to the street. He was on his own.

Corelli started up the path. Kelly watched her approach. She felt as if they were enacting a slow-motion scene out of *High Noon*, with the good guy and the bad facing off.

He waited for her to step on the bottom step then spoke softly as if trying to avoid disturbing the neighbors. Or having them hear. "What the fuck are you doing here, waking the whole fucking neighborhood, Corelli?"

She answered in a loud, clear voice. "I'd like a word, Chief Kelly. We can do it out here or inside. Your call."

He swore under his breath and lifted a hand and waved to his neighbors. "Sorry about the disturbance," he yelled. He turned and walked into the house. She followed but stopped to unlock the door. She left it ajar. The house was dim and quiet. She wondered about his wife. The last thing she wanted was for the woman to be caught in the middle. He led her into a large living room.

"You're in deep shit, Corelli, barging into my house, disturbing my neighbors. You'd better have a really good story."

"Oh, I do. I think it will really interest you."

He motioned for her to wait. They listened to the clop-clop of heels coming down the stairs. The front door closed and then a car started. Corelli caught a glimpse of red through the front window.

He turned back to her. "Nothing you have to say is of interest to me. Get the fuck out of here or I'll make your life more miserable than it already is."

"I don't think so. Let's chat about Righteous Partners."

"Your group? The one that ripped off drug dealers. The one you and your dirty friends ran before you ratted them out. What has that got to do with me?"

"Maybe you'd rather talk about RP Security?"

He glanced at the window. "Listen, Corelli, I know you've been stressed with threats against your family, so if you leave now you can avoid arrest and I'll forget this ever happened."

"C'mon, you can do better than that, Chief. Look, I'm not wired and I'm unarmed."

Her swollen right hand had nearly healed, but she'd bandaged it this morning to protect it. She started to unbutton her shirt with her left hand.

He put up a hand. "Spare me. Whether you're wired or not, doesn't matter. What do you want?"

"Well, if you don't want to talk about Righteous Partners or RP Security, how about Winter Brokerage Services?"

His eyes wandered to the window again, probably wondering where his backup was. "Winter? Isn't she the woman who was murdered?" When Corelli didn't respond, he shrugged. "I read the papers." He drew his gun. "I think it's time you left."

"Pretty smart, your investment scheme. You and Winter made a good team. What happened?"

He stared at her.

"We all did pretty well. She unfolded a copy of the investment list and started to read the names and amounts. "But you, of course, did the best. Let me see. Aiden Kelly, one million, nine hundred sixty-seven dollars and thirty-four cents. Not bad."

"Give me that." He rushed her. She stepped aside and shoved him. He stumbled and the gun went off. Before he could recover, she threw her weight against his back. He waved his arms trying to get purchase but fell flat on his face. She stomped on the hand with the gun and he let go. "You bitch. I'll kill you." She kicked the gun away. He grabbed her ankle, toppled her. Breathing heavily, he scampered to his knees and threw himself at her. She flat-palmed his nose as she rolled away. He went down. "Fuck." He covered his nose and she could see blood seeping between his fingers. She jumped up and retrieved the gun. Using the sofa to leverage himself, he kicked her leg. She went down with a grunt but grabbed his leg and flipped him onto his back. She got to her feet quickly and pointed the gun at him, hoping he didn't know she wasn't left-handed. Hands on his knees, he leaned over, gasping for breath. Suddenly he grabbed the lamp next to him and threw it at her. She dodged the lamp and assessed him. A bloody nose, a limp, and a hand he was clutching to his side. "You're not looking so good, Chief. It's time to finish this."

"McGivens said you don't have the chops to kill," Kelly said. He lunged.

She side-stepped. "He's right," she said, pivoting, and kicking him in the balls. He screamed, fell to the floor, and curled into a ball, gasping. "But," she whispered in his ear, "I'll bet my friend Jimmy failed to tell you how much I love kicking bad guys in the balls." She knelt on his chest and pulled his hands away from his crotch, one at a time. Using her right hand to support her left, she cuffed him. She straightened. "Sorry, Chief Kelly. My foot slipped," she said in a loud clear voice so the recorder hidden in her barrette could pick it up. "You are seriously out of shape. Be sure to use the gym in jail."

As she was Mirandizing him, her backup rushed in. She grinned at Watkins, Parker, Winfry, and FBI Agent Trillums, who gave her a thumbs-up. "Chief Aiden Kelly, you are under arrest for theft, money laundering, racketeering, and the murder of drug dealers Lester Rodriques, Tony Blackwell, and Jaime Nunca and his wife and three children."

"And the murder of Officer Vanessa Forrest." Captain Winfry stared down at Kelly. "You dared offer your condolences at my daughter's funeral after ordering the hit, you bastard."

Corelli's eyes widened. Now she understood why Winfry had taken her under his wing. By the time she'd gotten wind of the order to execute Vanessa it was done and she'd been filled with shame and guilt at her failure to save an honorable officer. After she aborted the operation she fingered the two cops that had assassinated her. But she hadn't known Winfry was Vanessa's father. She signaled the uniforms standing in the doorway. "Take him in."

They pulled Kelly up and started toward the door. He stopped in front of her and locked his arrogant blue eyes on hers. He leaned in close and whispered. "This isn't over, Corelli. Give my regards to your family."

CHAPTER FORTY-SIX

The Harley led the parade of NYPD and FBI cars back to the station. Corelli should have been jubilant. And she was. Sort of. Bringing Righteous Partners down, completing the gig she'd signed on for with the FBI, and mitigating her failure, were all causes for celebration. But she took Kelly's threat seriously. It wasn't over. Guys like Aiden Kelly and Jimmy McGivens thought stealing from and killing drug dealers and their families was acceptable, and they believed they were entitled to the spoils. Anyone who crossed them had to be eliminated. They would find a way to hurt her and the best way was through her family. The only way to keep her family safe was to do what they wanted, hold the press conference tomorrow and hope they kept their word.

As the caravan rolled across the Verrazano-Narrows Bridge, Brooklyn opened up before her, on the left Bay Ridge, on the right Fort Hamilton, Dyker Heights and Bensonhurst. *Bensonhurst.* Maybe there was another way.

Her spirits lifted when they arrived at the station. Someone had alerted the media and reporters and camera people from every TV, radio, and print news organization in the city were milling about.

Her anger at the media notwithstanding, she had the intense pleasure of taking Chief Aiden Kelly on the "perp walk" through the hungry pack. She'd insisted Parker hold his other side, the side closest to the media people. Wearing sunglasses to deal with the flashing cameras she smiled at the screamed questions and the attempts to push mikes in her face. Kelly didn't cover his face or duck. He stood straight and stared at the cameras. As she pulled him along, he screamed, trying to be heard above the roar, that Detective Corelli was up to her dirty tricks. But the press must have been briefed because they didn't give him a break. She booked Kelly, took a few congratulatory calls, and met with Winfry, who suggested she take a couple of hours of quiet time at home. Parker dropped her off and promised to come back in an hour.

It had come to her on the ride back. One call would do it. She only had to ask. But it would go against everything she believed in. How could she ask a bad person for help, especially since this bad person and others like him were the reason she had become a cop? In the old days, she was like her father. She'd known exactly what was right and what was wrong. It was her strength and her weakness, and she always did what she knew was right. Had going undercover, living a lie and dealing with people who had no morals, thrown off *her* moral compass? Was that why she was considering asking a criminal to help her? No. It was the situation. She'd never faced a moral dilemma like this. The right thing, the moral thing, would be to let the system take care of it. But when you were up against ruthless people who played by their own rules, the right thing was often the wrong thing. She now had a very personal understanding that sometimes good people had no alternative but to do something illegal to accomplish a good.

She showered to clear her head, but it didn't relax her. Too wired for coffee, she brewed a cup of peppermint tea, pulled the shades, lit candles and a stick of incense, and stretched out on the sofa in the semi-darkness to focus on the problem. But the rage propelled her to her feet. She began to pace. She was thinking morals, but Jimmy McGivens and Aiden Kelly were criminals of the worst kind, selfish bastards who put themselves above morals. Even if she did as they'd ordered, held a press conference and gave up the job, it wouldn't be enough. She would have to pay for her part in putting them in jail. And her family was her Achilles' heel. She picked up her tea, walked to the window, and stared at the Hudson River toward the bend in the island that blocked her view of the Statue of Liberty. Out of nowhere, it seemed, a huge ocean liner materialized and slowly cruised up the Hudson toward midtown. She watched it sail by. Life is like that. There's always something unexpected—good things, bad things, ambiguous things, things you can't control. It was childish to say this isn't how it's supposed to be, or it's not fair. What is, is, and you deal from there. She had established the rules. She could break them.

She picked up the phone and dialed. "Hey Sal, Chiara. Thanks for leaving Toricelli's name out of the article about the rescue of his grandson." She took a deep breath. "Can you put me in touch with Toricelli?"

Sal said he would call, but it was complicated and would take a while. He would call someone who had to call someone and eventually somewhere along the line Toricelli would get the message and send a lieutenant to bring her to him, probably late that night. Decision made, she felt lighter. She dressed and was waiting when Parker buzzed to say she was downstairs. Watkins would meet them at Winter's office. There was still one more piece to uncover.

She was certain the list provided by Cummings and Rieger was complete, that it included the ones she'd exposed and those she hadn't gotten, including all the ringleaders. She'd wanted Kelly for herself but she'd left the arrest of the others on the list to Winfry, so she could get back to the Winter case. She was positive that Kelly had killed Winter but she needed the proof. He must have a place where he kept the cash and drugs they stole until he could dispose of them, and maybe the pyramid was there. Teams of detectives were searching his house and cars and the farm where he kept his horses. And Winter must have had a place to store the cash until she could dispose of it. They'd determined she'd paid a lot of bills in cash. Rino, of course, hadn't reported any income so he was going to be busy with narcotics and the IRS. Cora Andrews, the housekeeper, on the other hand, had duly reported the correct income and paid taxes on it each year, the same with the office cleaning service. But that was a drop in the bucket compared to the amount of money Righteous Partners had stolen. She guessed Winter had a ton of cash sitting someplace close where she could get at it.

Parker stopped in front of 63 Wall Street. "You really think she was storing the cash here?"

Corelli smiled. "I do." She gave Parker the once-over. "You gonna crawl on the floor like that?"

Parker looked down at her suit. "Why wouldn't I?"

"Your designer suit might get dirty or worse yet, stained, and what would Senator Daddy think?"

"I noticed you changed out of your jeans and motorcycle jacket. Aren't you worried?"

"I'm not prissy, like you."

"I'm ready, if you are," Parker said, exasperation in her voice.

They tore Winter's office apart, looking for a safe under the carpeting, behind the furniture, even removing the ceiling tiles, but they found nothing. Finally, Corelli plopped down on Winter's sofa. Watkins and Parker sat in the chairs facing her. Doubt on their faces. Could she be wrong? No. She was sure Winter was laundering money for Righteous Partners.

She couldn't see Winter lugging a bag full of cash home and hiding it there, and she didn't go to banks, so forget a lock box. It had to be here, somewhere close. She stared out the window and thought about Winter. Greedy. Untrusting. Paranoid about security. Sadistic. Power hungry. She put herself above others, her throne a desk and chair on a platform, her riches on display. She held everything close.

Corelli got up and examined the platform. The carpeting was nailed to the sides, so it couldn't be moved. She pushed the chair aside and got down on her hands and knees. Parker and Watkins moved around to observe her. She wasn't sure what she was looking for, maybe a loose board. Then her finger found a space. She moved closer to see what was there and pressed. A click and part of the platform popped up about an inch. She glanced up, smiling. Parker and Watkins knelt down as she folded the trapdoor back. The three of them stared into the hole.

"A safe," Parker said. "How did you know?"

"I tried to put myself in her head. I knew it couldn't be far. She would want to hold it and count it and enjoy the feeling of being smarter and richer than everybody else."

Corelli didn't think Winter would use the same combination for this safe as she had for the one she shared with her assistant, but she gave it a twirl then had Watkins call Gus and ask for Aphrodite's birth date, but that didn't work either.

She sat back on her heels. "We need the name of the company that installed the other safe."

"I have it." Parker thumbed through her notebook. "Gingrich Security Services." She read off the emergency cell phone number and Watkins punched it into his phone.

"Let's close it up. I'd like to see what he knows about it," Corelli said. They closed the panel and moved the chair back. "I'd also like to get pictures of him opening it."

Forty-five minutes later, Watkins escorted Will Gingrich into the office and introduced them. "As you thought, Mr. Gingrich did install a second safe for Ms. Winter."

"Here or at her home?"

Gingrich grinned. "Under that platform."

Corelli smiled. "Very appropriate for Connie Winter, sitting on her money."

"The carpeting is nailed to the sides so the platform can't be moved," Gingrich said. "She wanted to be sure no one would accidentally stumble on the safe. Shall I show you?"

"Let's get the photographer in here first," Corelli said.

Parker left the room and returned with the forensic photographer, who had been waiting in the reception area.

With the photographer videotaping, Gingrich repeated Corelli's action and popped the panels open, exposing the safe. He opened the safe and stepped back. Corelli knelt. Next to some personal papers, there were rubber-banded stacks of hundred-dollar bills. Millions as far as she could tell, some packages of white powder, probably cocaine, a number of dated hard drives, and a stack of dated discs. Corelli sorted through the discs. Many were labeled, Righteous Partners/Chief Aidan Kelly. She looked at Gingrich. "Is there a camera here?"

Gingrich nodded. "She was one paranoid lady. She swore me to secrecy but I guess it doesn't matter now." He pulled out the center drawer of her desk, removed a false back and pointed to a switch. "The switch turns on a movement-activated video camera. No movement, no recording. When the hard drive is almost full the unit emits a low humming sound. When she got the warning she would call me and we'd meet here late at night. I'd replace the drive and sometimes she asked me to download certain days to discs." He pressed a panel on the wall behind her desk, exposing a narrow space with shelves stacked with blank discs and unused hard drives. When the wall was closed, an embedded camera focused on Winter's desk. "She always paid in cash."

They retrieved the final hard drive and watched him download the last two days to discs. He explained how to view the discs and they packed up everything and carted it back to the precinct.

After stashing the cash in the station safe, Corelli invited Captain Winfry and the detectives who had assisted in the investigation to view some discs with her in the conference room. They started with the disc from her last day. It corroborated the stories told by Cummings, Rieger, Gus, Gussie, Gertrude, Aphrodite, and John. It showed an enraged Gussie striking Winter with the pyramid, and Gertrude hitting her in the forehead with the desk phone and running out of the room.

When they got to Winter's interaction with Chief Aiden Kelly, the excitement in the room was palpable.

"Holy, shit," Kelly said. "What happened here?"

Winter was groggy. "My fucking son and that bitch Gertrude. They'll pay for this. I think I need a doctor. Where the hell is the phone? Never mind. Get my cell phone from my bag."

He ignored her request. "Righteous Partners discussed your demand and we feel the split we've been doing is fair."

"I'm the one who has all this cash piling up and no way to spend it."

"That's your problem. We're taking the risk and we have a big payroll."

"It's not optional, Aiden. One phone call and your little game will be over and you and your friends will be in jail." She rubbed her forehead. "Shit I have a headache. Call me an ambulance."

He stared at her. He bent down, picked up the pyramid and hit her on the top of the head, a couple of times. He checked her carotid artery, and satisfied she was dead, wrapped the pyramid in a newspaper he had in his gym bag and put the pyramid in the bag. He used his handkerchief to wipe prints from the liquor cabinet and the bottles inside. Then he scanned the room and left.

Watkins stopped the tape. The room was silent for a few seconds before Corelli said, "Gotcha, Kelly." Everybody laughed.

After a break, they viewed the first Righteous Partners disc featuring Chief Kelly explaining where the money came from and how it could benefit Winter Brokerage. Then Winter laid out the terms of a mutually beneficial deal, a deal that she would later unilaterally decide to renegotiate. As she watched, Corelli realized that if Winter hadn't been so greedy, she might still be alive.

Corelli and Winfry made the calls that needed to be made. The ADA viewed the discs and agreed that Kelly should be charged with Winter's murder in addition to the other charges. There was still a lot to do, but Corelli needed to be home to wait for Toricelli's call. She was wiped out so she sent everybody home for the evening. Parker drove her to the Gianopolus house so she could let them know they'd found the murderer.

As they were driving downtown so Parker could drop her off at home, Corelli needled Parker. "So Ms. ADA, did we build a solid case? Will Senator Daddy be proud?"

"You know, you are a pain in the ass, Corelli. Yes, we did, or you did. But I'm not sure what Senator Daddy will think because like your Italian daddy, he doesn't want to acknowledge that I'm a cop."

CHAPTER FORTY-SEVEN

She lay down to wait for the call. Thinking about Toricelli brought memories of her adored brother Luca lying in his coffin. She'd been devastated by his death. Toricelli controlled the neighborhood, and the mafia-style murder, shooting out his eyes, convinced her that Toricelli was responsible. She'd been crazed and craved revenge. She'd needed to do something to make the pain go away. Now twenty-five years later, she smiled at the memory of her fifteen-year-old self, staring into the eyes of Luigi Toricelli, the most dangerous man in the city. She'd promised to kill him like he had killed her older brother, with a bullet in each eye, but only after she cut off his balls.

She hadn't considered that Toricelli could easily have had her killed, or worse, he could have laughed at her. But to his credit, he'd treated her with respect, listened, and let her express her rage, first in English and then in Italian. She'd wanted to be sure he understood. He'd denied killing Luca and promised to find out who did and tell her. Of course, he never did and she still wondered if he was responsible.

Many teenage boys in the neighborhood romanticized the money and glamour of the mob and didn't understand what they were getting into, but not Luca. He had hoped to go to college and would have been at school that September if her father hadn't demanded that he stay to work in the restaurant. His death was the pivotal event in her life. It changed her from an obedient daughter to a somewhat wild but serious, determined teenager, committed to living her life her way, focused on being independent and doing what she needed to do to fight the Toricellis of the world.

So much for fighting the Toricellis of the world. Here she was waiting for him to call so she could beg for his help. She smiled at the irony. But as much as she hated the thought, she'd accepted that there are times that evil is the only weapon against evil. The phone startled her. A woman's voice said, "Hi. I'm waiting in front of your building. I'm driving the red Honda Civic tonight."

She changed cars three times for her protection, so no one could connect them.

He was in the fourth car and spoke in Italian when she slid onto the backseat. "*Buona notte*, Detective Corelli." It was dark, but she recognized his voice.

"*Buona notte*, Signor Toricelli."

He continued in Italian. "You wanted to speak to me?"

She responded in Italian. "Yes. Thank you for coming out so late." He was quiet, as if he understood how hard this was for her. "I need your help." She hesitated, wondering if he was smiling at the irony, but pushed on. He was her only hope. "My family is being threatened, and those responsible are standing in the shadows so I can't see them or fight them. They say I can only save my family by dishonoring myself. But, I don't believe they'll honor that agreement."

She took a deep breath suddenly afraid he would laugh.

"Tell me."

Corelli explained everything—the undercover assignment, the Righteous Partners story, the press conference, the attempts to kill her, Jimmy's lust for vengeance, Kelly's threat, and the threat to Simone and the rest of her family.

He was silent. She waited for his response, hardly daring to breathe. She heard him draw on his cigarette, and exhale. Funny, she hadn't noticed the smoke filling the car.

"I know you won a Silver Star in Iraq for bravery. Then you came home and went undercover for three months with a gang of cops who would kill you without a thought. After that, you fought two men with guns, probably cops, broke their noses, and lived to tell the tale." He sounded impressed. "And you risked your life to save my grandson. You are a brave woman, braver than many men."

Uncomfortable with the flush of pleasure she felt at the admiration in his voice, she cleared her throat.

"A dirty cop threatens your family again."

"What do you mean again?"

"Luca was killed by a dirty cop. He was an innocent who happened to see something he shouldn't have, something to implicate the cop in murder. The cop made it look like we did it."

"Who? Why didn't you tell me? You promised."

His voice was soft. "You were a little girl. What could you do? And then you were a cop, sworn to defend and protect. Would you have killed him in cold blood?"

"Probably not. But who was it?"

"Eddie Consuelo. He's dead a long time now. He was careless and things caught up with him."

"Did you? Wait. Don't answer that question. I'd rather not know."

He laughed. "Don't ask, don't tell."

God, does everybody make these stupid jokes?

"We will talk with Chief Kelly, Detective McGivens, and all the others. Perhaps we can convince them that it would not be in their best interest to hurt you or anyone in your family. Give me the list and we will start tonight."

"Please, don't kill…I'm sorry. I'm asking for a favor, I have no right to tell you how to do it."

"We will be as gentle as they allow."

"But can you get to them in jail?"

He smiled and patted her hand. "Don't worry."

Duh. How stupid. She knew the rumors about him controlling the jails. "*Mille grazie, Signor.* A thousand thanks. I can never repay you."

"*Prego.* This is just a small installment on what I owe you. Sleep well. It will be done. Someone will call when there is something to tell you."

CHAPTER FORTY-EIGHT

The next morning Parker called John and Theresa to let them know that a limo would pick them up and take them to meet Gus and the kids. Then she joined Watkins in completing case reports. Corelli was tied up in meetings the entire day. By six o'clock Parker and Watkins were pacing. Boredom had set in.

"Did you hear that all the Righteous Partners members in jail decided to plead guilty so there won't be any trials?" Watkins asked. "They've all been arrested. Corelli thinks the threat to her and Simone is gone but how can she be so sure? I'd think retribution would still be high on their list."

"If she thinks it is," Parker said, "I guess it is."

"You're right. She should know. Do you know how she got them to back off?"

Parker stared out the window, thinking about the Mafia boss. "Maybe, but I'm not sure. Anyway, it's not my place to say." She turned to Watkins. "Do you know why she went undercover?"

"I guess she felt it was the right thing. She's willing to risk everything for what she believes, what she feels is right. Not many of us would take on something so dangerous."

"Right. I didn't know her before, but sometimes she seems a little out of control. Have you noticed?"

Watkins cleared his throat. "Has she ever mentioned Marnie to you?"

"Who's Marnie?"

"Her partner. Not her work partner, her life partner of five years."

"What about her?"

"They were together in Afghanistan. Marnie was blown up in front of Corelli. I think she's still dealing with that."

"Wow. Why didn't anybody tell me that?"

"Not many people know."

"But you do?"

"Yes, Marnie and I are old friends."

He gazed out the window, ran his hands over his face and turned back to her. "I know Corelli's been riding you pretty hard. How are you feeling about her?"

She thought for a while before responding. "She doesn't let up, but I admire her strength. I don't know how she worked under that pressure this week, waiting to hear if she was going to have to quit and if her family was going to be safe. I've learned a lot from her. Call me a masochist but I'd stay with her, if she still wants me now that she has you and other experienced detectives."

"Speaking about wanting you, when are we going out?" He put his hand on her arm. "Let's have dinner and then maybe you'll come hear me play."

She pulled her arm away. "I'm not interested, Watkins. It's not a good idea to get close to co-workers."

"We have a lot in common."

"Like what?"

"We both come from well-to-do families, both educated in private schools and Yale, things like that."

"How come we never ran into each other?"

"I didn't grow up in Harlem. I was adopted by a white family and grew up on the Upper West Side."

"Lucky you."

"What's that supposed to mean?"

"Just what I said. You were lucky to be adopted by a wealthy family."

"But secretly I wanted to be poor and black in Harlem."

"I always felt out of place in Harlem and guilty for being so privileged. And the senator's activism didn't help," Parker said, laughing for the first time. "So how did you end up a cop?"

"I'm conscious of the disparity between where fate dropped me and where I could have been. I want to help change things."

"How did your parents feel about you being a cop?"

"They weren't overjoyed, but they were supportive. They worried about the violence and about my associating with the wrong kind of people." He smiled. "They never did say whether they meant other cops or the criminals. What about yours?"

"Obviously, the senator wasn't too happy. He took it personally."

"You refer to your dad as the senator?"

"Yes."

"Yes what?" Corelli said, striding into the room. When they didn't answer, she went on. "You both can go home and get some rest. Be here at noon tomorrow for a wrap meeting."

"I'll wait to drive you," Parker said.

"Winfry said he would drop me when we're done, so go home. I'll see you tomorrow."

CHAPTER FORTY-NINE

Corelli unlocked the door to her apartment. She hadn't realized how much tension she was carrying until earlier that day when Toricelli's associate called and said in Italian that everything was taken care of and that Jimmy and all the others would be pleading guilty. Now she was exhausted but satisfied with the resolution of the case. Hopefully, her life would return to normal. Being back on the job was a good start. Parker was a good fit for her. And she was feeling more confident she could trust Parker.

The light on her answering machine was flashing. She would take care of it later. Her agenda for tonight was simple. A glass of wine to unwind, maybe a soak in a hot tub followed by a good book. Sometime after the glass of wine, she would listen to messages. She poured a glass of Malbec and switched on the TV out of habit. The news was replaying Kelly's perp walk followed by some clips of her after the undercover operation became public. The anchor used that as the lead-in to U.S. Senator Aloysius T. Parker, better known as Senator Daddy, speaking at a press conference. It took a few seconds to register that he was talking about her.

"Detective Chiara Corelli is as dirty as they come, and now she's slandering Chief Aiden Kelly, a good cop who has worked hard to get drugs off the streets, just to make herself look good." He stared at the camera and it felt as if he was looking into her eyes. "And she's a racist in the bargain. Yesterday, when a rich white boy confessed to murdering his mother, she didn't arrest him because she needed more proof. It turned out it was someone else, but we all know if the perpetrator had been a poor black kid from Harlem who said he murdered his mama, she wouldn't have taken the time to be sure he actually did it. His sorry little black ass would be sitting in jail right now. He would be waiting to go to trial with a lawyer who couldn't care less and would advise him to plead guilty and go to prison."

Corelli felt as if she had been kicked in the gut. When he finished, she realized he hadn't mentioned Parker. Had Parker betrayed her after all?

The phone rang. She hesitated, but picked it up.

"I'm sorry," Parker said.

Corelli's voice was harsh, the rage spilling out unfiltered. "Sorry for what? For whispering in Senator Daddy's ear?" She slammed the phone down.

The phone rang again. Corelli debated with herself but picked it up. "Yes?"

"Despite what you imagine, I haven't spoken to the senator in five years."

Was she telling the truth? The only sound was their ragged breathing. "Does this mean you don't want to work with me?" Parker sounded devastated.

"I don't know what it means." She hung up.

She stared at the phone. She'd begun to trust Parker. Was she so out of touch? She was too worn out to think clearly tonight.

The answering machine was still flashing. She wished she could ignore the messages, but it might be about the case. She took a deep breath. She needed to calm down before she did anything. She sipped her wine, kicked off her shoes, and rotated her shoulders forward and back to ease the tension. When she slipped her jacket off, her cell phone fell out of her pocket. She retrieved it and noticed a voice message from an unidentified number. She removed her holster and gun, then keyed in her password. The voice was soft and tentative.

"Detective Parker called earlier to tell me I'm no longer a suspect and that Connie was murdered by a cop involved in the group you exposed. It's a shame. For all her money, Connie was a bitter, vicious, unhappy person. Oops, is that talking bad about the dead?" She paused, and when she spoke again she sounded pained. "Detective...Chiara, as I said, it's been a long time since I had such an instant and vital connection with someone. I felt as if I could see into you, feel your soul, and I thought...I sensed you had the same experience. So I was hurt and angry that you could think I would kill someone. But this morning Detective Parker helped me realize that in your job you can't take things on faith. You have to go on the facts you have." Now there was a hint of a smile in her voice. "Please don't laugh, but if you care, I want you to know that I forgive you." Another long pause and she added, "I'm sure you're still mourning Marnie. It takes time. But I'd still like to get together sometime just to talk. You know where to find me."

She never said her name but Corelli reacted to her voice as if she were in the room. She saved the message and put down the phone, flushed and warm. She definitely needed time to think this through.

She grabbed the pad and pencil and pressed play on the answering machine.

"Hi sweetie, it's Gianna. All of Bensonhurst is buzzing about you. All of a sudden you're a hero instead of a weirdo. Oh, a little rhyme." Corelli smiled. "Anyway, people who avoided you and would change the subject if your name came up, now are bragging about being related or knowing you. Marco and I have always known how wonderful you are, and now everybody else is catching up with us. The kids are bursting, so proud of their *zia* Chiara. Give me a call when you have a chance. Maybe I can invite everyone over to kiss your ring. Love you."

When she heard Patrizia's voice, she steeled herself. "Chiara, I don't understand why you want to do that job, but I guess you're good at it. The past couple of days everybody in the neighborhood has been talking about you. You're a hero for saving that boy and catching that killer." She paused and cleared her throat. "Joey and the kids are...Well, we're all proud of you."

Watch it Patrizia. You're giving me a swelled head.

She grinned when she heard Simone's voice. "What can I say? You've always been my hero. I'm always astounded by you, big sister. You don't have to risk your life to impress me. Anyway, you're hot in Bensonhurst this week. All my friends are dying to meet you. Call when you have a chance. Love you."

The mechanical voice said, "That was your last message."

Nothing from Papa. A proud and stubborn man. Maybe they would never reconcile, but it was time for her to move on, time to stop living her life in opposition to him.

She sat back and sipped her wine. It was clear to her now that she had been like him, believing everything was black or white. But her experiences in Iraq, Afghanistan, and working undercover forced her to recognize the complexities in people and life, to deal with the moral ambiguities, to confront her deepest fears, and do whatever was needed to survive and to protect her family.

She hoped she was more flexible now, but she'd lost the old clarity about what she believed, what she felt, and what she wanted. Well, maybe that wasn't exactly true. Maybe she wasn't sure she should believe what she believed, feel what she was feeling, or want what she wanted. Maybe, she needed to think about the walls she'd built to protect herself, walls that isolated her.

She smiled. Like it or not, her walls had already started to crumble. It was scary. Her heightened senses, surging feelings, and even her loneliness, made her feel out of control but more alive than ever. She knew she would never forget Marnie. She'd always love her. But it was Marnie who was dead, not her. Marnie would want her to live and love and be happy. She didn't know what would happen with Brett Cummings. But she knew she didn't have to choose between loving the dead and loving the living.

Bella Books, Inc.

Women. Books. Even Better Together.

P.O. Box 10543
Tallahassee, FL 32302

Phone: 800-729-4992
www.bellabooks.com